W9-BMT-659

THE VAULT

By the same author

WOBBLE TO DEATH
THE DETECTIVE WORE SILK DRAWERS
ABRACADAVER
MAD HATTER'S HOLIDAY
INVITATION TO A DYNAMITE PARTY
A CASE OF SPIRITS
SWING, SWING TOGETHER
WAXWORK
THE FALSE INSPECTOR DEW
KEYSTONE
ROUGH CIDER
BERTIE AND THE TINMAN
ON THE EDGE
BERTIE AND THE SEVEN BODIES
BERTIE AND THE CRIME OF PASSION
THE LAST DETECTIVE
DIAMOND SOLITAIRE
THE SUMMONS
BLOODHOUNDS
UPON A DARK NIGHT

Short stories

BUTCHERS AND OTHER STORIES OF CRIME
THE CRIME OF MISS OYSTER BROWN AND OTHER STORIES
DO NOT EXCEED THE STATED DOSE

THE VAULT

Peter Lovesey

First published in the United States in 2000 by Soho Press Inc.
853 Broadway
New York, NY 10003

First published in Great Britain in 1999
by Little, Brown and Company

Copyright © Peter Lovesey 1999

"Annus Mirabilis" from *Collected Poems of Philip Larkin*
reproduced by kind permission of Faber & Faber Ltd.

The moral right of the author has been asserted.

All rights reserved.

Library of Congress Cataloging-in-Publication Data

Lovesey, Peter.
    The vault / Peter Lovesey.
      p. cm.
    ISBN 1-56947-208-4 (alk. paper)
      1. Diamond, Peter (Fictitious character)—Fiction. 2. Police—
England—Bath—Fiction. 3. Bath (England)—Fiction. I. Title.

PR6062.O86 V38 2000
823'.914—dc21   00-041010

              10 9 8 7 6 5 4 3 2 1

one

SOME WEIRD OBJECTS ARE handed in at Bath Police Station.

WPC Enid Kelly, on desk duty this afternoon, sneaked a look at the Asian man who had brought in a pizza box. She was sure of one thing: it didn't contain a pizza. She just hoped it wasn't a snake. She had a dread of snakes.

"How can I help you, sir?"

The man had the black tie and white shirt of a security guard. He lifted the box up to the protective glass partition. No airholes. Officers on duty learn to watch out for any container with holes punched in the top. But there was a bulge. Something bulkier than a pizza had been stuffed inside. Bulkier than two pizzas. "This I am finding at Roman Baths."

"What is it?"

The man glanced at the other people in the waiting area as if they might not wish to hear. Leaning closer to the glass, he said, "Can I pass through?"

"Just a moment."

Enid Kelly turned for support to the sergeant filling in a form at the desk behind her. He came to the glass.

"What have you got here, sir?"

"Some person's hand, I am thinking."

"A *hand?*"

"A hand I said."

"It was in this box?"

"No, no, no. My lunch was in box. Tomato and mushroom pizza. This was best thing I could find to carry hand in."

"Let's see." The sergeant unfastened the security panel and the box was passed through. It felt too heavy to be a hand. But how can you tell how much a hand weighs on its own?

He opened one end. "It looks more like a chunk of concrete to me." He let it slide out onto the desk.

"Ugh!" said Enid Kelly, beside him.

"Get a grip."

The hand was skeletal, enclosed in a thin casing of concrete or cement that had partially collapsed. Some of the small bones had broken off and were lying loose. Shreds of what looked like dry skin tissue were attached. It could have passed for a damaged piece of sculpture.

"Where exactly did you find it, sir?"

"In vault. I am stepping on floor and my foot sinks through."

WPC Kelly winced again.

"Down in the Roman Baths, you said?"

"This was not exhibition area, sir. This was vault."

"So you said. What do you mean by vault? A cellar?"

"Cellar—what is that? Excuse my poor English. I am doing security check this morning. My first week in job. I have strict orders from head man, Mr Peacock. 'You visit all parts of building. All parts. Go through entire building every day.' "

The sergeant picked up the thing and felt its weight again. "So is it Roman?"

"I can't tell you, sir."

The sergeant didn't commit himself either, except to suggest nobody else went down into the vault until the matter had been investigated.

* * *

THE BONY hand, resting on its pizza box, was deposited on Detective Superintendent Peter Diamond's desk.

"What's this—a finger buffet?"

"The thing is, sir, we don't know if it's a matter for us," the sergeant explained. "It was found at the Roman Baths."

"Give it to the museum."

"It wasn't in the Roman bit. This vault is part of a later building, as I understand it."

"Medieval?"

"When's medieval?"

"Later than Roman," said Diamond in a tone suggesting he could have said more, but needed to press on. "Where exactly is the vault?"

"On the Abbey side, below street level."

"But what street?"

"Not a street, in point of fact," the sergeant said. "That square in front of the Abbey."

"The Abbey Churchyard?"

"Yes."

Diamond spread his hands as if no more needed to be said.

The sergeant frowned.

Plainly something did need to be said. "If you're looking for old bones, where do you go?"

The penny dropped. "Funny," said the sergeant. "Being paved over, I never think of it as a churchyard. You can use a word a thousand times and never give a thought to its meaning."

The wisdom of this failed to impress Peter Diamond. "Leave it with me. It'll come in useful as a paperweight." Seeing the shocked look this produced, he added, "And Sergeant . . ."

"Sir?"

"Thanks."

"What for?"

"Giving me a hand."

The sergeant's attempt at a laugh was unconvincing.

Diamond leaned back in his chair. He was ready with a dozen more hand jokes. Twenty, no problem, he thought bleakly. Without a murder to occupy him, he could spend the rest of the afternoon playing word-games. Life at Manvers Street had become a doddle in recent weeks. His murder squad urgently needed some employment. A bony relic from the Roman Baths was unlikely to produce much of that. The most exciting event all summer had been a bomb scare in the Pump Room. An abandoned briefcase had been spotted there one Friday morning. The centre of Bath, the Abbey and the Roman Baths, was cordoned off, causing maximum disruption. The army bomb disposal squad was summoned from Salisbury. The experts decided on a controlled explosion. A robot trundled across to the suspect briefcase. The blast brought down part of a chandelier and showered the Pump Room with cut glass and fragments of Offenbach and Chopin. The briefcase had belonged to one of the Pump Room musicians.

When the desk sergeant had gone, Diamond took another look at the hand. If it was ancient, how had it come to be encased in concrete? Just to be sure, he arranged for the thing to be delivered to the pathologist at the Royal United who generally dealt with unidentified bodies.

t w o

A MAN IN A cream-coloured linen suit and panama hat stood mystified in the flagged open space in front of Bath Abbey. The West Front with Christ in Majesty above the Heavenly Host and the ascending angels was lost on Professor Joe Dougan. For the past ten minutes he had paced the perimeter of the square staring at the shopfronts, oblivious of the people at the cafe tables, the crocodile-files of children waiting to tour the Abbey and the crowds cheering the buskers juggling with flaming torches. Shaking his head, he went over to one of the benches in the centre, where a woman was cooling off with an ice-cream.

"These people, Donna."

"What do you expect in the middle of August?" said his wife, pencil-thin and with a faint blue tinge cast by her great kingfisher-coloured straw hat from Selfridges. "You're going to get tourists any place this time of year."

"Not the tourists." The professor took off his polaroids and gave them a wipe. "I was making a point about the entire British nation."

"So what's the problem?"

"The crazy way they use numbers. You walk into a store and ask for something and they point upstairs and tell you it's on the first floor."

"The first floor is the ground floor in this country," his wife said. "The second floor is the first floor. I don't have any problem with that."

"I know, I know. I'm just remarking on the logic, or absence of it. This place is the Abbey Churchyard, am I right? Am I reading the map right, Donna?"

"It says so on the sign over there, Joe."

"Okay, we agree on that. The Abbey Churchyard. I can overlook the fact that it doesn't look one bit like a churchyard."

"There must have been tombs here one time," said Donna.

"Uhuh?"

"We could be right over someone's grave."

"Maybe."

Now that it had been drawn to Donna's attention she didn't like it. "I'm eating an ice-cream and there could be a dead person under here."

Joe carried on as if he had not heard. "I don't understand the way they number the houses, when they number them at all. That's number six over there." He was pointing to the optician's under the Georgian colonnade at the entrance to the yard. "It has no number that I can see, but the lady inside told me it's definitely six. And the restaurant next door is seven. Terrific—they actually have a number over the entrance. The English Teddy Bear Company must be eight. Abbey Galleries is nine. We have rising numbers, right?"

Donna indulged him with a nod.

Joe came to the crux. "So what did they do with number five, Abbey Churchyard? Do you see it?"

Donna turned her head through the limit of its movement. "Honey, I don't believe number five is here."

Joe said with all the authority of Dodge Professor of English at Columbus University, "It has to be here someplace. They wouldn't start with number six if they don't have one through five, would they?"

Donna gave a shrug. "This is England. Maybe they would."

Joe sighed. "Is it possible they lost some buildings?"

"Lost them? How would they do that?"

"The war."

"That was half a century ago. Don't you think after fifty years they'd change the numbers if some shops were taken out in the war?"

"Want a bet?"

Joe seemed to be accepting defeat. Donna took another look around. Behind her, the eighteenth century Pump Room and the entrance to the Roman Baths extended along the entire south side, a grand design of columns, pediments and balustrades. "All these places look old to me."

Joe slumped onto the seat beside Donna and was silent for some time. The activity around them continued. Appreciative screams rewarded an exceptional feat of juggling. A woman holding aloft a walking-stick with a blue scarf tied to it was addressing a group of tourists, pointing out the features of the Abbey front.

Donna said, "You could ask the guide over there."

"I already did."

"And . . . ?"

"She doesn't know—or doesn't want me to know. This is not information they like to give out. Don't ask me why. They don't list it in the guidebooks. It isn't in any of the histories we bought in the book town."

The book town. Remembering, Donna took a solid bite of ice-cream that made her eyes water. Five days before, Joe had insisted they visit Hay-on-Wye, on the border of England and Wales, where he had heard there are more used books on sale than any place else in the world. While her culture-vulture spouse had gone from shop to shop picking up treasures, Donna had ruined her shoes in the rain looking for a hairdresser who would fit her in without an appointment. No chance in Hay. She had passed the rest of that afternoon drinking lukewarm tea in a succession of dark teashops smelling of damp retriever dogs.

Joe was still fretting. "This is something British I don't understand, like they're ashamed of what happened here. If we had number five, Abbey Churchyard back home in Columbus, you can bet we'd have a board outside and a souvenir shop in the hallway."

Donna said with a slow smile, "And a theme park out the back."

"All I want is the satisfaction of knowing which building it is."

"Like a little round plaque on the front?"

"That would be asking too much."

"I guess so many famous people lived in this city that they don't trouble with plaques."

"That isn't so. They put them up for the names they want to honour. Jane Austen, Lord Nelson."

Donna shrugged. "Seems to me they don't want anyone to know what happened in number five."

three

THE PATHOLOGIST, JIM MIDDLETON, phoned just before Diamond was due to pack up for the day. "About that body part you sent over . . ."

"Hope you didn't mind," Diamond got in quickly. "We didn't know if you were short-handed."

"Leave it out, old boy. I've heard them all before. You wanted to know if it was Roman?"

"Or later. You heard where it was dug up?"

"Later is the operative word. It's not a carbon-dating job. Those bones are relatively modern."

"Meaning what?"

"Now you're asking. Bones are notoriously difficult to date. Too many variables, you see. But any fool—that is, any fool with medical training—can tell that this hand didn't belong to Julius Caesar."

"Modern, you said," Diamond prompted him.

"If you want an accurate opinion, ask a bones man. From my limited experience, I'd say it's no more than twenty years since that hand was opening doors and using a spoon and doing other things we don't mention."

"As recent as that?"

"Depends. Are the nineteen-eighties recent? I estimate not more than twenty years, but it could be as few as ten. Difficult to be exact. I don't have much experience of post mortem specimens set in concrete. About normal size. Mature, but not old. Chip out the rest of the bones and I'll try and tell you some more."

Diamond mumbled some words of thanks and put the phone down.

Instead of going home, he collected Halliwell and they walked through the still-sunny streets to the Roman Baths, situated in the centre, near the Abbey. Ironically, none of the exterior of the famous complex is Roman, however hard the Victorians tried to make it appear so. Even the statues of Roman emperors glimpsed from the street are late Victorian pieces. The genuine stuff is six metres below street level.

The staff inside were ushering the last visitors from the building. The security guard Diamond most needed to see had finished his shift and left.

"We'll go down and take a look." Just to escape from the clammy heat outside would be a bonus.

"We close in five minutes," said the man in charge.

"Go ahead. I'm not stopping you."

"We can't leave if you're still on the premises."

"That's up to you, squire. Is there any lighting down there?"

A torch was produced. The access was off the main entrance hall, down a curving flight of steps and through a couple of rooms used by the staff.

Someone had pinned a notice on the door stating "POLICE DO NOT ENTER."

Diamond turned to Halliwell. "Abandon hope, then."

The hinges gave a sound that set the teeth on edge. He picked out the structure with the torch. Solid stone steps down. Six massive stone pillars along the centre supporting arches across the top. This was emphatically a vault. You couldn't demean it by calling it a cellar. Dungeon-solid walls without even a skylight. A flagstone floor.

Musty, too.

Halliwell said, "Just the place for a *Rocky Horror* party."

The two detectives followed the circle of light down the steps. In truth, Diamond felt uneasy. Whether it was the chill down here after the warmth, or the dark, or just the knowledge that there might be other dismembered parts of a body buried in concrete, ice-cold drops of sweat trickled down his ribs.

He flicked the torch beam across the floor, giving nothing away about his reaction to the place. "Can you see the hole, Keith?"

They spotted it on the far side, a space between flagstones, close to a wall festooned with cobwebs thick as fishing nets. A few chips of cement lay around the edge. A pickaxe was propped against the nearest pillar.

"Don't go any closer," Diamond warned. Halliwell had been on the point of stepping forward.

Halliwell turned in surprise. "It's been here twenty years, sir."

"Yes, and some daft bugger put his foot in it. We don't need another."

Upstairs, it was actually a relief to be enveloped by the afternoon heat again.

"Ever done any concreting?" Diamond asked on the walk back along Pierrepont Street.

"Not my thing."

"Nor mine. I'm told it's satisfying work. You shouldn't skimp the preparation. You want to make sure your hardcore really is hard. Shame when it gives way."

AS HE was an hour late getting home, he suggested a pub meal. Stephanie said it was a lovely idea and he knew right away from the look on her face that she was going to broach a difficult topic with him. He hoped to God it was not a visit from his strange brother-in-law, Reggie.

In the pub, he had to explain why he preferred plaice and

chips to a pizza. Steph heard the story of the hand in the pizza box.

She asked, "So will I see you on TV tomorrow appealing for information?"

He shook his head. "I'm in no hurry. It's not as if there's a killer on the run. Well, if there is, he'd be out of breath by now, wouldn't he?"

"You sound as if you mean to make it last."

"There are worse places to be than the Roman Baths. Everything's laid on there. Phones, refreshments, loos."

"Careful. You'll make me envious."

They were strolling home across Victoria Park in the evening sun, mellow from the drink, when Stephanie finally judged the moment right.

"Something rather intriguing came in the post today. An invitation."

"We get nothing else but invitations," he said. "Furniture sales, wine-tasting, Reader's Digest."

"This is personal. Hand-written. 'At Home', it says. Next Thursday at eight."

"*At Home?* What sort of party is that? Doesn't sound like the kind of bash I enjoy. Who's behind this rave-up?"

"Assistant Chief Constable Georgina Dallymore."

"God help us."

"I didn't know you had a woman boss."

"She's new. She's got to be new to send out a thing like that."

"Give her some credit. She's off to a good start if she's throwing a party for the staff," Stephanie pointed out.

"I'm not sure if you're right about the staff. Nobody mentioned it today." An uncomfortable thought was dawning. "Suppose it's only us."

"There are sure to be other people. Perhaps it's only senior ranks."

"That's worse."

She let him chew on that for a while, and then returned to it. "I know you dread these social occasions, but they always turn out better than we expect. Who knows, we may get champagne."

He rolled his eyes. "At a police do?"

"Nice food. Music. Party games." Now she was pushing it to absurd lengths, softening him up, and they both knew it.

With a reluctant smile, he said, "Hide and seek. They won't see me for dust."

"Hunt the Chief Constable."

"Wouldn't know him if we found him."

"Musical Chairs."

"The top brass are good at that."

They continued on this tack, giggling like a couple of teenagers, until Steph quietly said she would send off an acceptance in the morning. He didn't protest.

They watched the sun setting over the Mendips. "This is how I want to spend my evenings," he confided in a rare outpouring of candour. "With you."

Steph smiled to herself. This new Assistant Chief Constable had started well, putting the wind up Peter Diamond by inviting him to a party.

There were other ways of taming the beast. She put her hand up to his neck and found a strand of his sparse hair and curled it around her finger. "Do you know what I'd like right now?"

His eyebrows lifted.

Steph looked into the distance. "A ride on one of those swings."

"They're for kids."

"Can you see any kids using them?"

He laughed. "You want me to look the other way?"

"No, come over and give me a push."

PROBLEMS NEXT morning. The man in charge at the Roman Baths was the sort of blinkered official who brought out the worst in Diamond. Probably he was low in the hierarchy. It was just bad luck that today he was the most senior in the building. "You can't go through the staffroom. My people won't care for that one bit."

"No, the idea isn't to go *through* the staffroom."

"What do you mean?"

"We need a place to tip the rubble."

"The staffroom?" The boss-man practically choked. "That's out of the question. It's fully in use by the guides and the sales staff."

"So you'll relocate them."

"This simply isn't on."

"It's easier than relocating us," Diamond pointed out, as if his team already occupied the place. "You don't want my people shifting barrowloads of rubble through the entrance hall where the public come in. Even if you put down ground-sheets, the dust is hell."

In tourist attractions, the paying public take precedence over everyone else. Diamond won this round. It was agreed that a temporary staffroom would be found.

"Another thing, sir. How far back do your records go?"

"Which records?"

"Records of building work. At some point in the past twenty years, somebody did some concreting in the vault. I presume they used materials brought in for building projects. Do you follow me?"

"I'm not optimistic." That scarcely needed saying. The wretched man was looking suicidal after giving away the staffroom. And if he didn't put a gun to his head, the union would tear him to bits.

"When did the last major excavation take place?"

"Before my time. About 1982 to 1983, when they opened up the area under the Pump Room."

"Obviously there was rebuilding associated with the work."

"I expect so."

"And it's possible the vaults were used for storage?"

"I suppose so."

"And they must have been used on other occasions since? All the contractors and all the dates, then. And I'll need to see the paperwork myself."

"This is extremely disruptive."

"Disruptive is my second name, sir."

With heavy sarcasm, the boss-man said, "Are you sure there isn't anything else I can do for you?"

It was unwise. The big detective didn't hesitate. "Now that you mention it, there is. You can fix it for me to use the Pump Room for tea breaks."

Reddening, the wretched man said, "I'm afraid that isn't possible. The caterers are independent of the museum."

"So how does it work?" Diamond breezed past that obstruction. "Don't tell me you never eat in there."

"I might occasionally, when it's necessary to look after an important visitor, but it isn't a regular arrangement. I eat outside."

"That's your choice."

"Yes."

"I won't insist that you join me."

Down in the vault, the Scene of Crime team had already installed arc-lighting and were taking photographs. The SOCO in charge confirmed that the place had been used at some time by builders. He showed Diamond some sacks that had contained cement. Tests would establish whether it matched the cement found surrounding the skeleton hand.

"You'll be digging up the rest of the floor, no doubt, looking under the flagstones," he said to Diamond.

"Personally, no."

"You'll keep us fully informed of what you find, won't you, sir?"

"From hour to hour," Diamond promised. "You'll get no rest." He went up to see if the Pump Room was open yet.

To the strains of *Kismet* from the Pump Room Trio, he had coffee in there with the security man who had dug up the hand, a Pakistani immigrant refreshingly pleased to be assisting the police. The concrete was crumbly, he cheerfully assured Diamond. It would be easy enough to dig out other bits of the corpse.

LATE THAT afternoon, sheer bad luck dictated that Diamond and the new Assistant Chief Constable appeared at opposite ends of a corridor in the Police Station. As they approached each other dismay was written in Miss Dallymore's eyes. Oh my God, here is one of my senior officers, and I can't remember his name. I must brazen my way through it. Let him think I recognise him, that I am actually looking for him.

"Ah, just the man."

"Ma'am?" Diamond could not avoid this, embarrassing as it was on both sides. Being subordinate to a woman was not the problem; it could have happened with anyone new.

"You're going to tell me you're terribly busy, I dare say."

"No more than usual."

"That's good, because I had you in mind for something."

"Yes?"

"The PCCG."

Sets of initials were his blind-spot. He wasn't sure if the PCCG was some form of honour, or something to be avoided like the plague. "Me in particular, ma'am?"

"With all your experience . . ." The ACC smiled, as if the rest could be left unsaid. Georgina Dallymore had a disarming smile. Diamond would probably have thought her a good-looking woman if he could have ignored her shoulder-flashes. "With all your experience . . ." did begin to sound like recognition.

"What I've done is nothing exceptional," he said modestly.

"You'll do splendidly. They're lucky to get you. It's at the Meeting Room in the Victoria Gallery, seven on Wednesday evening. Tell Helen you'll be representing us, and she'll let you have the paperwork."

These were hammer blows. *Meeting Room . . . evening . . .* and, most alarming of all, *paperwork.*

Helen, the ACC's personal assistant, enlightened him. The PCCG was the Police and Community Consultative Group, a talking-shop with representatives of local residents' associations, the Council, the City of Bath College, the Racial Equality Council, Victim Support and similar groups.

"You'll want an agenda and the minutes of the last meeting," Helen said, opening a drawer in her desk.

"Does it say what time they finish?"

She turned to the back page of the minutes. "No, it isn't mentioned here."

"Just my luck."

"Why don't you ask Chief Inspector Wigfull? He's a regular on this committee."

"Wigfull? That's all I need."

John Wigfull was the ultimate infliction. A high price to pay for stepping into a corridor at the wrong moment.

four

A PATCH OF SUNSHINE lingered in one corner of the garden of the Royal Crescent Hotel, where Professor Joe Dougan ordered pre-dinner drinks. He and Donna were with their new friends from Zurich. They had met Marcus and Anne-Lise Hacksteiner in the outdoor heated plunge pool the previous morning. Few situations are more likely to get a conversation going than sitting toe to toe in a small round pool.

The Hacksteiners had been to a matinee at the Theatre Royal. "It was a whodunnit," said Anne-Lise, speaking English as if she had lived here for ever. "And rather well done."

"Did you guess the murderer?" Joe asked.

"Anne-Lise doesn't guess," said Marcus. "She likes to analyse the plot and arrive at the logical solution."

"And did you, Anne-Lise?"

"Oh, yes."

"Get away!"

"But my logic was different from the logic of the writer."

Joe Dougan wasn't sure how seriously to take Anne-Lise. She didn't smile much. "You mean you picked someone else as the killer?"

"She insists her solution was superior," said Marcus. "Probably it was. I don't have that kind of brain. I took a wild guess."

"The least likely person in the cast?"

"Exactly."

"Let me guess. You were spot on?"

"No, I was wrong, too."

"You guys break me up." The more Joe saw of the Hacksteiners, the more he liked them. Rich as they obviously were, they didn't flaunt it. Joe had learned only by chance that they had the top suite in the hotel, the Sir Percy Blakeney, at nearly seven hundred pounds a night.

After the drinks were served, Donna said, "Well, I just wish we had chosen the theatre."

A muscle twitched at the edge of Joe's mouth. He said nothing.

Anne-Lise said graciously, "You were much more sensible. It was too nice an afternoon to spend indoors."

Donna shot a triumphant look at her husband. She had said the same thing to him earlier, and more than once.

As if he hadn't noticed, Joe said to Marcus, "I think you'll like this single malt."

"Come on, Joe," said Anne-Lise. "You can't keep us in suspense. How did you spend the afternoon?"

"Indoors, same as you. You did the whodunnit. We did the wheredunnit."

"The what?"

"The wheredunnit. When I go on vacation I like to seek out the places where creative things happened. It gives some focus to a trip. So in Vienna, we looked up the Mozart house. In Paris, the Rodin museum, and so on."

"And in Bath, Jane Austen?"

"Too easy," said Donna in a downbeat tone that the others did not yet understand.

Joe explained, "My modest ambition in this city was to find the *Frankenstein* house."

Marcus turned to face him, eyebrows pricked up, prepared to challenge the assumption.

Joe smiled.

"You did say *Frankenstein?*"

Joe gave a nod. "Where Mary Shelley wrote the book, back in 1816. Simple enough, you might think."

"But you are mistaken," said Anne-Lise in her prim, categorical style of speaking. "It was written in Switzerland. It is well known in our country."

Marcus chimed in, "If you want to see the house it is on the shore of Lake Geneva."

Joe raised his hands, feigning self-defence. "Fine. I'm not going to argue this one with you good folk. I know the story, how Shelley and Mary Godwin, as she was then—she was only eighteen—were entertained at the Villa Diodati by Lord Byron and his physician, Dr Polidori, and how the weather was atrocious and they were housebound, and Byron proposed that they each write a ghost story."

"And of course the woman's was the only good story of the four," said Anne-Lise, with a half-smile at Donna. "It came to her in a dream."

"Not exactly," Joe dared correct her. "It was not the result of a dream. Mary Shelley explained in the introduction that she was lying in bed awake when the images came to her."

"So it was a day-dream," said Donna, rolling her eyes.

"And I have to tell you that *Frankenstein* wasn't written in Geneva," Joe steadily pursued his point. "It had its conception there, yes. Then they returned to England. Shelley stopped off in London, leaving Mary to find rooms in Bath. She picked number five, Abbey Churchyard, and that's where she wrote most of the book. You can read her diaries. You can read letters. She records the progress of the chapters."

"Are you sure?" said Anne-Lise.

"Joe is a professor of literature," Marcus reminded her, and then asked Joe, "What made them choose Bath?"

"Secrecy. Mary's step-sister Claire had been travelling with them. Byron had made her pregnant and they didn't want her parents to find out."

"Oh, no!" said Anne-Lise, as shocked by Byron's behaviour as if it had only just happened.

"They were a wild bunch," said Marcus.

"And how. Mary herself already had two children by Shelley, who was married, with two kids of his own."

Anne-Lise gasped.

Marcus, more calm about nineteenth century morals, said, "So there were children in the party?"

"Only Mary's second baby, William. The first died as an infant."

"You *have* researched this," said Marcus.

"He's like a dog with a bone," said Donna with a sigh.

"So the set-up was this," said Joe in the same steady, authoritative voice. "Shelley and Mary with their little son William, less than a year old, rented rooms in Abbey Churchyard, and Claire, heavily pregnant, was nearby at number twelve, New Bond Street. Mary passed the time reading the classics, writing *Frankenstein* and taking lessons in art."

"With a baby so young, I'm surprised she had any time," said Anne-Lise. "Did they have servants?"

"A Swiss nurse, called Elise."

"That would explain. Swiss nurses are very good."

"And I guess Claire sometimes helped with the baby."

"Maybe Shelley took his turn," said Marcus.

"No chance. He was up to his eyeballs in family troubles. First, Mary's half-sister, Fanny, killed herself in Swansea with an overdose of laudanum. Then Shelley's wife Harriet threw herself into the Serpentine in London and drowned."

"Oh, my God," murmured Anne-Lise. "All in the same year?"

"All in the last three months of 1816."

"Quite some year," said Marcus.

"That wasn't the end of it. Two weeks after Harriet died, Shelley and Mary got married."

Anne-Lise's blue eyes shone at the first good news in some time. "In Bath?"

"In London. Soon after, at the end of February, 1817, they moved to Marlow and she put the finishing touches to *Frankenstein* there. But there's no question that the greater part of it was written in this city. Which is why I was motivated to find the house."

"And did you find it? Is that where you were this afternoon?"

"No," said Donna flatly. "This beautiful afternoon we passed in the public library."

Joe was unfazed. "Checking ancient maps of the Abbey Churchyard. And I can tell you, friends, that I finally got my answer. I know precisely where *Frankenstein* was written."

"How exciting!" said Anne-Lise, genuinely enthralled.

"I found a picture of the house. It was right next to the Pump Room, actually attached. A narrow, three-storey house, one of a group built around 1800. I guess their rooms were upstairs. It functioned as a kind of shop, a lending library, to be precise."

"Do you know, we were there yesterday and I never even noticed it?" said Anne-Lise.

Joe nodded. "Unfortunately—"

"It's gone?"

"Knocked down when the Pump Room was extended."

"Too bad," said Marcus.

"When?" said Anne-Lise.

"In 1893—a time when all kinds of excavations were taking place behind the house. The City fathers decided to promote Bath in a big way as a spa city. So a row of not very distinguished buildings next door was expendable."

"Where exactly was the house? That yard in front of the Abbey?"

"Correct. Numbers two through five originally stood where

you now find the entrance to the Roman Baths. You can see where the Shelley house was sited. It's a lower elevation than the rest, a linking block that houses a corridor leading to the extension."

"Didn't anyone try to save it?"

"The Roman Baths were bigger news than *Frankenstein*."

"Isn't there a plaque on the wall?"

"Stating that this is the site of the house where *Frankenstein* was written?" Joe shook his head.

"Plenty of people would be interested."

"It would increase the tourism significantly," said Anne-Lise.

"Quite possibly."

"So will you be visiting the Mayor of Bath to suggest it?" asked Anne-Lise.

Donna said, "Anne-Lise, my dear, don't put ideas in his head. I don't want my entire trip taken over by *Frankenstein*."

"Let's go in to dinner, shall we?" said Joe.

"The only good suggestion I heard from you all day," said Donna.

five

TWO DAYS ON, AND there were compensations for Peter Diamond. The Pump Room had definite advantages over the police canteen as an eating place. This room with its tall windows and Corinthian columns, its chandelier and musicians' gallery, was surely one of the finest in Europe. Kate, the winsome, long-legged, black-stockinged waitress Diamond had cultivated as an ally from the beginning, saw that he got the pick of the menu. The trio played *I'm a Stranger in Paradise* and Keith Halliwell was too over-awed to step inside and interrupt the idyll.

Down in the vault, the working party was under instructions from Diamond not to rush the job. "We're in no hurry, lads. This poor sod has been lying under the floor for up to twenty years. A week or two more will make no difference."

The complexity of the case was underlined when the list of building contracts was presented to Diamond.

"As many as this?"

"You asked for them all, and that's what you've got," said bossman with a smirk.

"Half of these must have gone out of business by now." His finger moved up the page. "Why so many here?"

"That would have been prior to the opening of the extension. Much of the temple precinct was uncovered then."

"In nineteen-eighty-two to three?"

"And for quite a bit before. What you're looking at now is a record of the construction work, not the excavation. We opened to the public at Easter, 1983. Substantial electrical and building work had to be carried out in the weeks before."

"Making it accessible?"

"Yes. And safe. Proper walkways and so forth."

"You can see the way my mind is working. The vault where the bones were found is on the same side."

He took the lists back to Manvers Street and gave Halliwell the task of calling contractors to extract lists of their work-forces.

"Just as long as you don't expect a miracle, sir," Halliwell said. "At this distance in time . . ."

"I know, Keith, it's a pain and I'm a slave-driver."

"You're assuming that whoever buried the hand in the vault was a builder?"

"I can't think of anyone else with a reason for doing cement work down there."

"So do you think the victim was working on the site as well?"

"We'll see what we uncover."

"Have they found anything else?"

"Not yet."

Halliwell screwed up his face. "Wasn't the hand attached to the rest of the body?"

"Apparently not."

A CALL from the front desk. "Sir, someone wants to speak to you about the Roman Bath inquiry."

"To me personally?"

"Yes."

"Who is he?"

"*She*. She, em, says you may remember her. A Miss Smith."

Amusement in the voice is easy to detect on the phone. "Are you having me on?"

"Ingeborg Smith."

"Ah." An image snapped into place. A crowded room. Microphones heaped in front of him like horse-droppings. The press conference he'd called last autumn at a difficult stage in the Bloodhounds inquiry. And this pale-faced young woman with a stud in her nose—or was it a ring?—hitting him with a volley of penetrating questions.

"I do remember now," he told them downstairs. "She's press. A freelance." His first instinct was to duck this. Then he remembered the tenacious way Ingeborg Smith had questioned him in front of the press corps, just this side of civility. It might not be wise to give her the elbow.

He saw her in an interview room downstairs. "I hope you have something amazing to impart, Miss Smith," he remarked as he walked in. "It's a busy old week."

"I'm glad to hear it," she said. The nose decoration was a silver ring through the right nostril. Since the last time another had been added on the same side and there was also a gleam from under the fine, blond hair over the left ear. "What was the motto of the Pinkerton detectives? *We Never Sleep.*"

Her features are up to fashion model standard, he found himself thinking. Maybe she thinks some minor mutilation makes her more approachable. "*We Never Sleep.* Try telling that to the Police Federation."

"What's their motto, then?"

"I wouldn't know."

She laughed.

"No," he started to explain. "*That's* not their motto, it's . . ." Then he gave up. "What exactly are you doing here?"

"Getting a story, I hope. Is this true about the hand in the cellar?"

"Where did you hear that?" he parried.

"I was tipped off by one of the guides at the Roman Baths. You kicked them out of their staffroom, I was told, and large policemen are in there sieving loads of earth and mortar for human remains."

"So what's your angle on this? *Staff in Revolt over Police Dig?*"

"Come off it, Mr Diamond. That's no story."

"*Police in Revolt over Police Dig?*"

A wide smile. She felt in her handbag and handed across a business card. "I work with the nationals when a story of potential interest comes up."

He was wary. "It's at a very early stage. I can't give you anything you don't already know."

"No information on the victim?"

"What victim?"

"Oh, come on, Superintendent, the owner of the hand. It was buried less than twenty years ago, they're saying."

"That's yet to be established."

"I am the first to approach you, aren't I?"

"The first of the press, yes."

"Don't you think I deserve an exclusive?"

He said, "My dear Miss Smith—"

"Ingeborg will do."

"I doubt if there's much in this for you."

"There's the rest of the body, presumably. Do you think it's in the cellar?"

"I'm keeping an open mind. And it's a vault."

"Your mind is a vault?"

He smiled. "At this stage, yes. Just a large, empty vault."

"No theories, then?"

He lifted a palm to indicate that the point had been made already.

She moved on. "Let's try something else. Where's that female detective inspector you work with?"

"Julie Hargreaves? Transferred to Headquarters."

"Oh? At whose request?"

He felt the blood rise. "That's off limits, Ingeborg. We don't discuss personnel with the press."

She held out her slim hands in appeal. "Fine, I won't press it. I admired her style, the way she did her job."

"We all did."

"You must have chosen her as your deputy. Do you think a woman brings something extra to a crime squad?"

He pushed his chair back, prior to leaving. "I don't have time to chat."

She smiled. "Worth a try. Some time, I'd like to write a profile of you."

"Whatever for? I'm not a story of—what was it?—potential interest."

She ran her eyes over his substantial form. "If I pulled a few strings, I could interest a features editor in you."

"That's really made my day."

"I'll tell you one thing for sure. You're going to be sorry you dropped Julie from your team."

He didn't rise to the bait. The truth of it was that Julie had left at her own request. The strain of working with him, defending him, interpreting his moods, smoothing ruffled feathers, had finally got to Julie. And those who knew him best said that she had made his job too easy. Confrontation was his fix.

But he must have learned something from Julie, because he let Ingeborg Smith leave without a blasting. Even after she reminded him to pick up the business card he had left on the table.

SOME GENIUS from the forensic lab at Chepstow phoned him later. In the process of removing a substantial chunk of concrete adhering to the hand found in the vault, they had discovered the bones of a second thumb and two fingers. It seemed that two hands had been buried together.

"It makes sense," Diamond said. "If you go to the trouble of digging a hole you might as well use it for both."

"Assuming they both came from the same victim," the Chepstow man threw in casually.

"They did, didn't they? This is a left hand and a right?"

"It would appear so."

"Can't you fellows ever say a straight yes or no?"

"If we did, and we made a mistake, you'd be one of the first to complain, Mr Diamond."

"That's for sure, squire. All I want to know is are we talking about a pair of hands?"

"That I couldn't say with certainty."

"They're about the same size? Could you say that with certainty?"

"Oh, yes."

"Thank Christ for that. So there isn't any reason to think they're from different people?"

"Realistically, it's unlikely, but—"

"Don't complicate things. My life is hard enough."

LATE THE same afternoon, twenty minutes before the diggers in the vault were due to down tools, one of them working close to the external wall called for the sergeant who was supervising. At a depth of half a metre his brush had revealed a brownish domed shape that looked awfully like a human skull.

The sergeant ordered an early finish, and put a call through to Diamond.

NEXT MORNING, the vault was transformed into something like a *Star Trek* set: machinery, extra lights and SOCOs padding about in their overshoes and white paper zipper overalls. From the doorway Diamond registered an appearance and then slipped upstairs for a Pump Room breakfast.

Certainly it was a skull, he learned when he returned. They allowed him close enough to see it *in situ*, with most of the surrounding soil brushed away. It lay upwards, resting on the jaw, not quite so sinister as a clean skull may look, because the cavities for eyes and nose were blocked with earth. In this state it would be lifted by a pathologist and taken for examination. Any organic matter preserved inside the cranium could well provide DNA material.

"Any immediate clues?" he asked the senior man.

"Well, she was probably under thirty, by the state of her teeth."

"*She?*"

"See the ridges around the eye sockets? They're not so prominent as they would be in a male. And the nasal junction here is less developed."

"I wasn't expecting a female," Diamond said as if he doubted the opinion. "The hand was quite large."

"Some women's hands are big. You can't tell the sex from hand bones."

"Is Jim Middleton on his way?"

"He's doing post mortems this morning. He promised to be here by two."

Muttering, Diamond returned upstairs. In the staffroom he paused to speak to the two young constables working with a sieve over a wheelbarrow. A huge heap of earth and rubble lay on a tarpaulin. "Is this load sorted?"

"No, sir," said the spokesman. "That's waiting."

"What happens to the stuff you've sieved?"

"We wheel it across the way. There's another room."

"And have you found anything?"

"Some bits that could be finger-bones, or toes, or nothing at all."

"Do you want a break?"

"Sir?"

"I said do you want a break? Take ten, no more. I'll see if I have better luck than you."

Wide-eyed at this eccentric behaviour from the top man, they hesitated. But when he picked up the spade, half-filled the sieve and started shaking it over the barrow, they left him to it.

The gesture was not wholly altruistic. Diamond had a reputation for treating his staff without much consideration. The news that the old slave-driver—or whatever they currently called him—had taken his turn at the digging would spread around Manvers Street like word of a pay rise.

And a mindless task like this was an aid to concentration. He needed to reassess. If the victim was a woman, it seemed unlikely she had died as a result of a brawl among labourers. Women *are* employed on building sites, and were in the early nineteen-eighties, but the female brickie would have been a novelty. Her absence would have been noticed. What other reason would a woman have for being in the vault? he asked himself. Maybe she had been one of the archaeologists.

He preferred that, a scenario in which one of the builders lusts after a student in tight jeans jigging her bottom as she scrapes at the floor of the temple precinct. From most men, she would get looks, or remarks. But there is always the oddball, the psycho who believes she is put there to provoke him.

Either she willingly goes with him. Or she is tricked into going. Or forced. In the vault, he turns violent. Whatever goes on there—an argument, a rape, a fight—it ends with her death. He dismembers the corpse in the belief that it will make detection more difficult. He buries the parts in concrete.

This presupposes that no one interrupts. Well, the vault was used by the builders for storage. Maybe sand and cement had to be collected from time to time, but there would be intervals when no one was about. A body could be covered with a tarpaulin and left in a dark corner until the killer had an opportunity to dispose of it, perhaps at night, when everyone else had left.

The theory also requires that when the girl goes missing, no one raises the alarm. Archaeology is often carried out by student volunteers. And as anyone knows, students are not the most reliable people around. One young woman fails to turn up one morning and nobody thinks much of it. Not everyone likes squatting in a trench scraping at the soil by the hour and finding nothing.

So was there a young student who went missing in the early nineteen-eighties?

Scores, probably.

"No luck, sir?"

He looked up from the sieve. The ten minutes had passed and the constables were back.

"You're the ones who got lucky. I filled another barrow for you."

DEATH AND THE MONSTER.

The thing had started without the passion that came later. It grew in his brain by stealth, fitting into his life as no more than an idle thought here, a possiblity there. He could not trace its origin; the monster is so all-pervading that every child has heard of it. It seeped into his consciousness and was reinforced by the images everyone grows up with and has nightmares about.

"My application was at first fluctuating and uncertain; it gained strength as I proceeded and soon became so ardent and eager that the stars often disappeared in the light of morning whilst I was yet engaged in my laboratory."

Only now did he accept that he was a willing slave to Frankenstein and his monster.

seven

DIAMOND WAS IRRITATED BY Halliwell's talk of brickies, chippies and sparks, as if one morning on the phone had turned him into a master mason. "Let's see these names."

"The brickies?"

"All of them." He ran a glance over the top sheet. "What use is 'Taff' to anybody?"

"Welshman, sir."

"That narrows it down to about a million."

"These are only my rough notes. I jotted everything down. Any scrap of information might jog someone else's memory."

" 'QPR supporter.'?"

"Football."

"I didn't think it was underwear. There's no need to grind your teeth, matey. I'm just as brassed off as you are. We're going to have to do the rounds of the builders' yards asking questions."

"When you say 'we' . . ."

"I know, Keith. You're going to ask me where the manpower is coming from. I'll pull a few strings. It's a job for Uniforms."

"It isn't easy tracing workmen, sir. There's so much sub-contracting. A brickie and a sparks may work side by side and belong to different firms."

"I don't care who employed them. These herberts all know each other."

"Yes, but after twenty years—"

"Don't exaggerate, Keith. It's more like fifteen." He grinned and softened enough to explain his theory about the victim. If she had been a student volunteer helping with the dig, her name might be on some list kept by the people in charge.

Halliwell threw in casually, "The Bath Archaeological Trust."

"Come again."

"The people in charge."

"Go to it, then."

AT TWO, he phoned the Roman Baths and asked if the pathologist, Jim Middleton, had arrived yet. He had not.

"So is all work in the vault suspended?"

The senior SOCO confirmed that it was.

"The skull still waiting to be lifted?"

"Yes, sir."

"Leave it with me," he said with menace. "Just because this skull has been buried since 1983, that idle bastard thinks he can take all day over his lunch."

He called the Royal United Hospital. It turned out that Middleton was having trouble with his car and had taken it into the garage for repairs.

He slammed down the phone. Immediately it rang. He snatched it up, "Jim?"

"No." A woman's voice. "No. This is Ingeborg Smith."

He emitted a sound combining a groan and a growl. "Look, I'm waiting for a call."

"Would that be from the pathologist?"

He was caught off guard. "What do you know about that?"

She said in a calm tone that only added to his stress, "I'm at the Roman Baths. I know Dr Middleton is supposed to be here, and isn't. This skull they uncovered last night is female. Do you have any idea who she might be, Mr Diamond?"

He had to draw in a long breath to control himself. "Did somebody let you into that bloody vault?"

Ingeborg said coolly, "I told you I was interested in this case, and I have an idea on the subject."

"If you know anything at all pertaining to this investigation, Miss Smith," he said with heavy formality, "you'd better tell me now."

"An idea, I said."

"Just a theory, then?"

"You don't have to sound so disparaging. It could save you a lot of time. Can we meet? Are you coming over here?"

"I'm far too busy—"

She butted in with, "I could give you the name of a post-graduate in ancient history who got a job as a guide at the Roman Baths in 1982 and disappeared the following year."

"A woman?"

"Of course."

"How do you know this?"

"Like your people in the vault, I've been digging."

"What's the name?"

"I'd rather not say down the phone."

"Don't piss me about, Ingeborg."

"I mean it. This is sensitive information."

She was going to get her interview now. Tamely, he offered to see her at the Baths in half an hour.

JOE DOUGAN and his long-suffering wife Donna stood just inside the swing doors at the Pump Room entrance having a difference of opinion.

"But I don't need the rest room," Donna repeated.

"We established that a moment ago," Joe ground on in his professorial style. "All I'm asking is that you step inside there and look around. It's not a place I can go myself."

"You can go to the men's room."

"Donna, I don't need the men's room."

A moment's silence underlined the lack of contact between their imaginations.

Donna knew she would cave in. She always did. "It's easy for you to say 'look around'. I'm going to get some strange looks."

"Yes, but would you do this for me?"

She said with deliberate obtuseness, "What am I supposed to look at? I've seen a ladies' rest room before now. There isn't anything to interest me in places like that."

"So you will go in?"

"What makes this ladies' room so special? What do you want to know about the place?"

"Just tell me if everything is on this level, or if you have to go downstairs. If it *is* in the basement, examine the walls."

"Go figure," murmured Donna. "He only wants me to read the walls in a rest room."

"Don't you follow me? It could be part of the original Frankenstein house."

Shaking her head, Donna walked to the door of the Ladies' Room and disappeared from view.

Joe waited, tapping his foot.

Donna came out again after only a couple of seconds. "No basement. It's all on this level and totally modern. Now can we go?"

Frustrated, Joe looked around, orientating himself again. Without answering Donna, he stepped along the corridor.

Her patience snapped. "Stay here if you want. I'm going shopping."

Joe was preoccupied. A short way ahead, he had spotted some stairs down to a door marked "Staff Only".

Without giving him another look, Donna walked out of the building.

Joe was not deterred by the sign on the door. He went down

the curved stone stairs. Inside the staff room, two men in black overalls were sieving earth into a wheelbarrow.

"You don't mind if I go through?" he said, pointing across the room. He was already on his way.

"Who are you?" one of them asked.

"Professor Joe Dougan."

The title made enough of an impression to allay suspicion. "Mind how you go, professor," said the workman. "It's muddy."

Joe pushed open the second door and was astonished. Below, at the foot of some steps, arc-lamps on stands gave a brilliant view of what was clearly a vast ancient cellar, with arched vaulting above solid pillars of stone. His mouth went dry and a pulse beat in his head. He had surely found what he had hardly dared hope would still exist—the basement to number five. The Pump Room extension must have been built over this. They had not demolished the original vault when they cleared the rest of the old house at the end of the last century.

The presence of the lights was odd, and so were the flagstones stacked against the walls, but he was so excited that he thought little of it until someone dressed entirely in a white overall appeared at his side and asked, "Do we know you, sir?"

"I don't believe you do," Joe answered, still euphoric at this discovery. "I'm Joe Dougan. Professor Joe Dougan." He shook the man's hand.

"Andy Mills. You see, we were expecting Dr Middleton at two."

"I don't know about that," said Joe.

"We were told he had some trouble with his car."

"That would explain it, then," said Joe affably.

"You're here in Dr Middleton's place?"

"Suits me," said Joe. "I'm just delighted to see all this."

"I have a spare oversuit if you'd care to use one, Professor."

Joe thanked Andy Mills. His own linen suit was liable to get dirty down here. They had taken up the flagstones and the floor appeared to be under excavation.

He pulled on the oversuit. They even had gloves and over-shoes for him.

"It's there, against the wall," Andy Mills told him. "The access is not marked as well as it should be, so would you follow me?"

Joe followed, not entirely sure what this was about, but happy as a cat in a creamery. His one regret was that Donna had not shared this moment. She would take some convincing when he told her about it.

Mills asked, "Didn't you bring your kit?"

"Just what I'm dressed in," said Joe. "What are you going to show me?"

"Didn't they tell you?" The man stopped and crouched. "It's right here."

Joe did likewise and found himself looking at a human skull at the bottom of a shallow excavation trench. "Well, isn't that something?" he said. "Is it real?"

Andy Mills gave an uneasy laugh.

Joe stood upright again. It was uncomfortable squatting. "Got anything else?"

"That's it," said Mills, increasingly perplexed.

"I'll just take a look around, if you don't mind. This chance is too good to miss." He stepped across the lumpy floor to the opposite wall.

"Don't you want to lift the skull?" said Mills.

"No thanks."

There was an uneasy pause.

Mills eventually said, "You think it should remain here?"

"To give it to you straight," said Joe, "the skull doesn't interest me. The cellar doesn't need dressing up. For me, it has great atmosphere without the extras."

After another interval Mills said, "Excuse me asking, professor. You *are* from the Royal United?"

"No, from the Royal Crescent, if you want to know. Is this important?"

*   *   *

INGEBORG SMITH was hovering near the Pump Room entrance when Diamond approached, looking as usual as if he had escaped from an old black and white film in his trilby and striped suit. He asked her graciously if she would mind waiting a few minutes while he checked with his people inside.

The men sifting the rubble in the staff room were not the pair he had met in the morning. They told him someone had come in earlier and gone into the vault through some misunderstanding. Dr Middleton had still not arrived. And nothing new had been discovered in the sieving.

He returned upstairs.

He and Ingeborg sat in the open at one of the tables outside Monks Coffee House, opposite the Pump Room entrance. From there, Jim Middleton would be seen arriving, if he appeared at all.

The Abbey Churchyard was quite a sun-trap this August afternoon, and they ordered ice-cream rather than tea. Diamond loosened his tie and kept his jacket on. Too many police officers were coming and going. Out here he felt conspicuous looking relaxed with the blonde journalist.

"I may get up at any time," he cautioned her.

"Leaving me to pay?" she said.

He took a five-pound note from his back pocket and pushed it under an ashtray. "This student you mentioned over the phone—who is she?"

Ingeborg was reluctant to come to the point—*that* point, anyway. "What are the chances of someone like me joining the police?"

He almost needed the question repeated. "You mean this seriously? You have a career already."

"People switch jobs. Could I work in CID?"

"Not right off. You'd go through training school first, Probation. Two years on the beat." He was unsure if this was a serious enquiry, or some debating point she was leading up to.

She asked, "Isn't there a fast track?"

"Accelerated promotion? That doesn't apply until you're qualified, and then it's mainly for graduates."

"Two years in that gruesome uniform?"

"We've all been through it."

She smiled. "Skirts and black tights?"

"You know what I mean. After that, you might get transferred to CID if you're promising—and lucky."

"How soon?"

"Depends."

"On who you know, I suppose."

He was careful not to return her faint smile. "That can be a factor. You're not serious about this, Ingeborg? It's not a bit like journalism."

"Do you think I could do it—detective work?"

"You have some of the qualities."

"But . . . ?"

"But could you put up with the discipline? Can you handle routine as well as stress? Stupid colleagues? Coarse remarks? Idiot people doing idiot things? I have problems myself."

"With coarse remarks?"

"I'm trying to see it from your point of view."

"Don't try. If you're on about women being given a hard time, that's not unique to the police. You're not selling it very well, Mr Diamond."

"That isn't my mission, Ingeborg. If you choose to join, don't ever say I talked you into it."

Her eyes glittered amusedly. "No fear of that."

"Now can we talk about this student who disappeared?"

She nodded. "When I heard about the skull being female, I asked around. My ex-landlady is a whiz with anything like that. She's convinced we're all going to be raped and murdered one of these days, and she memorises every case of violence and abuse that supports her thesis. Unsolved cases, missing girls. Her recall is amazing. She reels them off like the football results. I'd back her against your computers."

"She remembered this case?"

"I didn't tell her what it was about. I simply asked her about women who went missing during the nineteen-eighties. She gave me upwards of a dozen names. This one fitted the best."

"So who is she?"

"Violet Turner, known unofficially as Tricks."

"Any reason?"

She turned her large shrewd eyes on him. "Tricks Turner. If you can't work *that* out . . ."

"She was on the game?"

She shook her head.

"Generous with it?"

"After three years reading Ancient History at Durham, wouldn't you be?"

"I thought Ancient History was full of that sort of thing. So when did she come down here?"

"She was a postgrad at Bristol. Topped up her grant by working one day a week as a guide at the Roman Baths. I checked all this in the local press, and my landlady had the details right. In February, 1983, Violet Turner went missing. Never completed her course. Hasn't been heard of since."

"Was it given much space in the papers?"

"Very little. There was never a time when they were certain she was dead. People assumed at first that she'd taken off on a trip with some bloke. When she didn't come back after two or three months, the alarm was raised. Her parents, up in Newcastle, knew nothing and heard nothing from her."

"Was there a man in her life?"

"At least four."

"They would have been questioned," said Diamond. "There should still be statements on file. Did they publish a picture?"

"Yes, in black and white. She was dark, apparently. Large eyes. Reminded me a bit of that girl who played *Tess*."

"Nastassja Kinski? No wonder she was popular." Up to now, he had only the image of the skull in the vault with its earth-filled eye-sockets.

"Is that helpful?" Imogen asked.

Wary of her agenda, he played it down. "One thing you'd learn if you ever joined CID is that the most promising leads aren't always the right ones."

"If it is her, when do you expect to announce it?"

"You want to scoop the others?"

"It's my job."

"There are tests—once I finally get a pathologist to the scene. We're unlikely to get an identification for some days. Dental records may help. I can't see us going public on a named individual until we're sure. You'd be unwise to rush into print yet."

"So what shall I write—that you haven't yet linked this with the disappearance of Violet Turner, who worked in the Roman Baths and disappeared in 1983?"

He almost snarled, "Don't bait me." As he was saying it, he spotted Jim Middleton striding across the yard. "Stay in touch," he heard himself tell her unnecessarily as he got up, but it softened the last remark.

He caught up with Middleton in the corridor. "What happened?"

The pathologist swung around. "Jesus Christ, Peter, you shouldn't creep up on people like that. I nearly dropped my guts-bag."

"We expected you at two."

"Sorry, old friend. The gearbox went on my Ultimate Driving Machine."

"You could have phoned."

"What with? I don't carry one of those ghastly mobiles."

Diamond didn't pursue it. "This way. It's down in the vault."

"Where the hands were found?"

"Yes." He escorted Middleton down to the vault.

"My word," said the pathologist as he shook open the protective overall he was handed, "you've got major earthworks here. Is the skull where you found it?"

"Exactly as it was. We brushed away some of the earth around it, that's all."

"And no doubt brushed away the hairs I'll be hoping to find." He stepped into the overall and zipped it up. "Hair is durable. It often remains after other tissues have decomposed. No, I won't complain. Let me help you with that." He grabbed the back of the garment Diamond was struggling with and hauled it up to shoulder height. "Don't they make an XXL?"

They put on overshoes and walked over to the skull. Diamond said, "The Scene of Crime team say she's female."

"I wouldn't disagree with that." Middleton took a torch from his bag and bent over the skull. "No hair that I can see." He tapped the cranium lightly with his gloved knuckle and stroked its surface with something like affection. Then, against all the rules, he burrowed with his fingers, took a grip and plucked the entire thing from the earth and placed it on the level above. "And where were the hands found?"

"Some distance off. Over there, between two flagstones."

Middleton flicked off some earth, pressed the skull backwards and opened the jaw. "Because, you see, the evidence suggests that the hands and the skull are not related."

He felt himself blush scarlet. "Get away."

"Have you noticed the colour? I know it's difficult under these lights, but I'd call this brownish-yellow. Caramel, shall we say? The hand bones I saw were paler, whitish in colour."

"They were in concrete. They weren't stained by the soil," Diamond pointed out.

"Fair enough. What clinches it for me are the teeth." Middleton worked the jaw again, and for an instant the skull looked animated, seeming to enjoy Diamond's confusion. "Several molars missing, but no dental work. Unusual in a modern adult."

"True."

"Now run your fingers gently over the cranium, like this."

Diamond did as instructed.

Middleton turned to face him, smiling. "I know it's not so obvious through latex, but do you feel the coarseness of the surface texture? I mean you can see the cracks in places. This is deterioration I would expect after many, many years of seasonal changes in temperature. Heat-waves, frosts. And I'm not talking ten or fifteen years, Peter." He bent closer, pressing the torch almost to the bone. "It looks to me as if petrification is well under way, meaning that this little lady is turning into a fossil. She was dead a few centuries before the owner of the hand was born. You don't want me on this job. You want an anthropologist."

A DAY as discouraging as this should have ended with a couple of beers. Instead, he found himself in the Victoria Gallery looking at a carafe of water. He was seated at a long table between the Head of CID Operations, John Wigfull, and a woman with a wheezy chest. It was five to seven and the meeting of the PCCG was shortly to begin.

Diamond casually asked Wigfull, "Have you, em, had an invitation from Georgina?"

"Georgina?"

"Dallymore."

"The new ACC." Wigfull blinked nervously several times. "No. Have you?"

"I expect she's doing it alphabetically," Diamond said. "It's an 'At Home'. Thursday. I suppose I'll turn up."

An extraordinary stillness came over Wigfull.

Diamond said, "I won't have any evenings to myself at this rate."

Eventually Wigfull managed to think of a comeback. "Heard about your skull."

"Oh, yes?"

"Couldn't they estimate the time of death, then?"

"I knew it was old."

"But not prehistoric?"

"Prehistoric, my arse."

"How old is it, then?"

"Medieval, Middleton says."

"Oh—a mere five hundred years or so?"

Diamond turned his back and introduced himself to the wheezing woman. She said she was from Victim Support and he told her she couldn't have chosen a more suitable person to sit beside. She eyed him warily.

The meeting got under way. As the senior policeman present, he was forced to defend the latest crime figures. Violent crime was on the increase, and Councillor Sturr, across the table, wanted an explanation. "I'm a forthright man, Superintendent, and I don't mind telling you these figures are deplorable. We employ you to keep our streets safe, and look at the result. It's getting steadily worse."

Diamond was tempted to give the forthright man a forthright riposte, but this was not the occasion. "If you're worried about the streets, Councillor," he said in as measured a way as he could at the end of a trying day, "you need not be. Most of this increase is domestic violence."

"Is that supposed to be good news?"

"It's my answer to your concern about our streets. They're relatively safe."

"Our homes aren't."

"They never were. Someone in your family is more likely to attack you than a stranger."

"What a world we live in now."

"The figures are rising because people are reporting it more, thanks to the better climate of opinion."

The last phrase was totally misunderstood by one of the delegates, who interrupted to say he was sure Mr Diamond was right about global warming. He had noticed riots always happened on hot summer nights.

The aptly-named Councillor Sturr returned to the attack. The name was familiar; he was a millionaire who had made his money out of stone-cleaning, washing the fronts of old buildings, a profitable business in Bath. He was probably still under forty, slim, in a tailored grey suit, with brown eyes that missed nothing, and dark hair slicked back. He was always in the local press, giving away the prizes at flower shows and school speech days. This combative stuff was another side to the man. "So what are you saying, Mr Diamond? That this increase is down to people attacking each other in the privacy of their own homes?"

"Not entirely, but broadly, it's true."

"Weasel words, Superintendent."

"Yours, sir, or mine?"

Diamond heard Wigfull's sharp intake of breath.

The Councillor bulldozed some more. "Look here, I was brought up in Bath. I know this city as well as anyone sitting around this table, and I tell you it's turned into a dangerous place. What with drugs and beggars and barmy people who ought to be locked up, it's no wonder these figures are so shocking. When I was a boy it was safe for kids to go out to play on a warm evening like this. Now, I think twice about going out myself."

Diamond nodded, as if to confirm the dismal truth. "You're speaking of the nineteen-sixties, I would guess."

"I was born in 1963, the year sexual intercourse began, according to Philip Larkin's silly poem—but my parents didn't think much of Larkin or the so-called sexual freedom and nor did most of the people of Bath. Flower power, hippies, the Beatles and all that nonsense. The revolution came late to Bath. The buildings here were covered in grime in those days, but it was a clean place to live in. Law-abiding and safe."

"Safe?" said Diamond.

He nodded. "I could go out playing on summer evenings and my parents knew I would come to no harm."

"They let you play outside?"

"Yes, indeed. In those days nobody had ever heard of the dreadful things that happen to children now."

"That isn't quite right, Councillor," Diamond said as he marshalled his thoughts. This happened to be a period he knew well from his collection of books on the post-war detectives. "You wouldn't remember a local man called Straffen, who strangled two little girls your own age. Here in Bath in the early fifties, before you were born. And if you weren't aware of him at the time, I'm sure your parents were, and the good people of Bath. He made all the headlines."

Sturr straightened in his chair, as if ready to take issue, but Diamond had more to say.

"Sadly, it's always been a risk sending children out to play." His eyes locked with the Councillor's, slipped away and came back to him. "I get weary of people telling me life was so much safer in the old days."

A silver-haired man lower down the table said, "I remember Straffen. Wasn't he saved from the gallows?"

Diamond nodded. "He was found insane and committed to Broadmoor. Six months later he escaped and killed another child."

The Chairman cleared his throat noisily and asked if anyone else had an observation on the Police Report. Wigfull, ever the ambassador, spoke of the success of Operation Bumblebee, the clampdown on burglary. Another initiative, Operation Vulture, had also helped to reduce crime. Diamond was glad it was Wigfull giving the spiel. Personally, he rued the day when the image-makers had been let in to package police work. They made his job sound like something out of a *Batman* comic.

Others wanted their say now, and the sooner they spoke up and shut up, the better, Diamond thought. He disliked the self-congratulation that lurked around the table. We are sitting down with senior policemen, so we must be upright citizens.

It all reached a merciful end at 9.45 p.m. He got up to go and found Sturr at his side. The man reeked of aftershave.

"You really shot me down in flames with your child-murderer, Superintendent," he said. "I asked for it. I laid it on a bit thick."

Diamond took this as a peace offering. "You only repeated what most people say. I hear it so often that I like to put the contrary view sometimes. Devil's advocate."

"Have you got a minute to spare?" Sturr gestured to Diamond to follow him.

Irksome as it was to follow a beckoning finger, curiosity prevailed. And there was some satisfaction in seeing John Wigfull taking this in with his cow-like stare.

The next room was in darkness, the building having closed to the public some hours before. Sturr felt for the light-switch and Diamond saw that they were in a small annexe that served as an extra gallery. About twenty pictures were displayed there, white-mounted in silver frames.

"Take your time," said the councillor, as if there was something to be done.

It had to be an inspection of the pictures. Dutifully, Diamond made a circuit, pausing briefly at intervals. Picture galleries were rarely on his itinerary. To his eye, the works on display were pretty similar, brownish and indistinct. In some cases, the artists had left patches unpainted. Was a picture finished if the paper showed through? He dredged deep for something positive to say. "Unusual."

"I thought you wouldn't want to miss these," said Sturr. A charged quality had entered his voice, "They belong to me, you know. Early English watercolours. I loaned them to the city for two months. DeWint, Cotman, Girtin—they're all here. The plums of my collection."

"Must be worth a bomb," Diamond was moved to say.

"You'd be surprised at the prices I paid. I study the art market and look out for bargains. I wanted you to see that I'm not the philistine some people take me for. I have a degree in chemistry. I have a respect for the arts as well."

Diamond thought he had better demonstrate some respect of his own. One of the paintings, at least, had something other than a few wretched sheep huddled under trees. "I like that blueish one with the dark figure moving across the icy background."

"The Blake? Yes, I'm particularly pleased to own that. We have to say 'attributed to . . .' because it isn't signed and isn't listed in the catalogues of his work. It doesn't even have a title, but I say it's definitely a Blake, and several experts agree with me. The stylistic features are unmistakable. Are you familiar with Blake's work?"

Occasionally, Diamond's grammar school cramming came to his aid. "*The Tyger?*"

"I was speaking of his art," said Sturr. "The fluidity of his line. The power of the images. His figures, whether mythical or human, are instantly recognizable."

Diamond went closer to the picture. "Who's this then?"

"I meant recognizable as the work of Blake."

"Got you." He would still have liked to know what it was about, the tall, shabby, long-haired figure striding through a desolate landscape of snow-covered rocks.

The councillor explained, "Mythological, I'd say. The figure doesn't look entirely human to me. Blake was haunted by visions, of course. Oh, yes, there's no question that he painted it. Superintendent, you're a connoisseur. You picked out the pearl of this little exhibition. It's the only Blake I possess. He produced an enormous amount, but much of his work was engraving, and I only go in for watercolours. Mine is one of the best private collections in the country and I want to share it with people."

"Great art belongs to the world."

"My sentiments exactly. We could get on well, you and I," said Sturr. "So what's your real opinion. Off the record, aren't our streets more dangerous than they used to be?"

Whatever he privately believed, Diamond was not admitting it to this man, fellow connoisseur or not. "It's swings and roundabouts," he said. "If you're talking about streets, the chance of being killed by a car was higher when we were kids than it is today."

"Don't give me that. There are far more cars on the road."

"Far fewer deaths, though. If you don't believe me, check it out."

"Are you responsible for traffic?"

"No, sir. I investigate murder, when it happens."

"And how often is that?"

"Often enough to keep me in employment."

"Are you working on a case right now?"

Diamond smiled. "No, I'm looking at pictures."

"You can't be all that busy, if they let you have an evening off." Councillor Sturr had not got elected for being tactful.

"I'm working on a case from a long way back," said Diamond, "when the world was supposed to be a safer place." He was not known for his tact either. And this had not been an evening off.

eight

THAT NIGHT, IN THE privacy of their suite at the Royal Crescent Hotel, Joe Dougan came clean with Donna.

"Want to see something special?"

Donna had just showered and changed into her nightdress. Her eyes, usually so expressionless, widened and sparkled. "Why, have you brought a friend?" she teased him, loosening her hair. Then she noticed he was holding out a book, one of many he had carried away in triumph from Hay-on-Wye the previous week.

"Jeez, Joe, it's bedtime."

"You don't have to read it."

She had no desire to handle a book so old that its binding was turning to a reddish powder. "What is it?"

"*The Poetical Works of John Milton.*"

"Terrific."

Ignoring the sarcasm, he said, "Yes, I happen to agree with you. It is terrific."

An argument at bedtime is not conducive to sleep or anything else. In a change of tone, Donna asked, "Is it the first edition?"

"Lord, no. A Milton first edition would be more than our joint savings, and that's if you could find one. No, this little baby dates from 1810. Dr Johnson's edition."

"Uhuh?"

"I got it for twenty pounds."

"Are you sure you didn't get rooked? It's not in very good condition."

"Showing signs of use, I'd say," said Joe, undeterred.

"Don't you have a clean copy of Milton back home?"

"I have three. The point about this one is . . . Well, I guess I should have told you before now. Take a look."

Donna said. "If you don't mind, Joe, I'd rather not. I don't want to wash my hands again."

He sighed. "I'll hold it for you." With an air of ceremony, he held it for Donna to see. The front cover was a greyish board. In the top right-hand corner, someone had inscribed in ink that had faded almost to yellow:

M.W.G.
5, Abbey Churchyard,
Bath.

Donna took a quick look and got into their vast four-poster bed.

Joe asked, "What do you think?"

"What do I think? I think you found a book from five, Abbey Churchyard, the house we were looking for. Didn't you tell me it used to be some kind of library?"

"This is not a library book, Donna. Take a look at these initials." He held it close again.

"M.W.G.?"

"Mary Wollstonecraft Godwin. I believe this is Mary Shelley's personal copy of Milton's poems."

After an interval Donna said, "If it belonged to Mary Shelley, how come she didn't write M.S. on the front?"

"Godwin was her name when she first lived in the house in 1816. She and Shelley didn't marry until the end of the year."

Donna was not convinced yet. "So you think these letters must be her initials?"

"Honey, they are hers. She was Mary Wollstonecraft Godwin and this was her address when she wrote *Frankenstein*. That's not all. At the front of *Frankenstein* is a quote from John Milton's *Paradise Lost*. In her preface she mentions Milton with admiration. So we know she possessed a copy and this is the one, her personal copy of Milton."

Donna still didn't have any inclination to handle the book Mary Shelley had possessed. "You found this at Hay and recognized the address?"

"That's what I'm telling you. The find of a lifetime. The shop people had no idea. But I have the John Hopkins University edition of Mary's letters back home and that address stood out for me."

"Incredible," murmured Donna. "You remember the house where she was living in 1816 and you forget our wedding anniversary."

"Once," Joe pointed out. "Once in twenty-four years."

"You'd better remember next year."

"Will you let me finish? Like I was telling you, when we came to Bath I wanted to see the house for myself."

"Why didn't you tell me about the book until now?"

"You know me, Donna. I like storing up surprises. I was hoping to show you the house first and then let you share my pleasure at finding the book. It was a body blow to discover number five was gone. Well, I thought it was until I found my way down into the cellar today. That made it all real."

"You already told me," said Donna, unable to suppress a yawn.

"It was the cellar to number five, no question."

"Fine. Are you going to wash your hands before you get into bed with me?"

"Okay, okay." He put down the book and padded into the bathroom.

Later, in bed and with the light out, he chuckled and said,

"They thought I was a medical examiner. They were expecting the medical examiner down there to look at a skull they found under the floor."

"Let's change the subject," Donna suggested.

"They ought to know there would be bones down there. It's built on a churchyard."

"Can't you talk about something cheerful if you must talk? You know I'm nervous in this old-fashioned bed. I'm going to get nightmares listening to you."

"Sorry." He pondered a moment, then said, "What do you want to do tomorrow?"

"See some shops."

"Good thinking. Let's do that."

Donna turned over and faced him. "The shoes over here are pretty. And good value."

Joe's mind was not on shoes. "There was a time when booksellers had their own little stickers that they fixed inside the covers of books they stocked. There's one in that copy of Milton, a neat little oval with the name and address: O. Heath, Rare Books, Union Passage, Bath. Just out of interest, I'd like to see if Mr O. Heath is still in trade."

"Joe," said Donna in a flat tone.

"Honey?"

"That isn't shopping."

NEXT MORNING, Diamond was in the Assistant Chief Constable's office explaining to Georgina why he did not expect quick results from the Roman Baths. "We found this skull, as you know, ma'am, but it turns out to be medieval. Probably it was there from the original churchyard and got disturbed when they were digging for foundations."

"For the present buildings?"

"No. For the houses that were there before. They were knocked down in the eighteen-nineties. This vault is part of the original construction."

"I see. But the other remains you found—the hand bones—are modern?"

Diamond was unwilling to say so. "God knows when they were hacked off. Bones are difficult to date. I've been trying to get an estimate from forensic. They're estimating between ten and twenty-five years ago."

"Can't they be more precise?"

"They're still doing tests."

"When you say 'hacked off' . . . ?"

"They mean it was crudely done, ma'am, using an axe or the edge of a spade."

Georgina stood up and stared out of the window. "So what's your theory?"

"Obviously the rest of the body is somewhere else. The hands were removed because the killer thought the victim might be identified from fingerprints."

"Fingerprints?" The word was pitched high in disbelief.

"You and I know the world has moved on, ma'am, but did the killer? This was up to twenty years ago, before DNA testing came in. People thought fingerprints were the only giveaway."

"Fair point," conceded the ACC. "So where is the rest of the body? Not in the cellar, you think?"

"We dug to a depth of four feet," Diamond said heavily, as if he personally had done all the spade-work. "The job is almost done. No, there wouldn't be much point in dismembering the body and then burying the bits in the same place."

"So where's the rest of it?"

"It could be part of the view you're looking out on."

The ACC took a moment to work this out. "You mean absorbed into a building?" She fingered her white collar. "One hears these gruesome stories. It's possible, I suppose. But in Bath?"

"In Bristol, if that upsets you less."

Georgina's back was registering all the tensions between top brass and brassy copper. "If this was the intention, why go to all the trouble of burying the hands in the vault?"

Having started this hare, Diamond had to run with it. "The risk. He's stuck with a body that he has to get into a truckload of hardcore, or whatever, out in the open, on a building site. Anyone might spot something and switch off the machinery."

"So he removes the hands."

"And the head, probably."

"But the skull you found was ancient."

"I'm not saying the real head is buried in the vault. He could have taken it to some other place, carried it out in a holdall. I may be wrong, ma'am, but the picture I have is of two blokes working on the Roman Baths extension. They fall out for some reason. There's violence and one is killed, possibly in the vault where they keep their tools. The survivor has to dispose of the body. He's scared by what he has done, but after a bit he realises he's well-placed to get away with this."

Miss Dallymore turned to face him. "You make it sound plausible, Peter."

"I've had time to think, ma'am."

"What are our chances of catching up with him?"

"Pretty remote, to be honest. If we knew the victim, it would be a start. I doubt if we ever will. Builders' employment records are sketchy, to say the least."

"What's your advice, then?"

"Keep it on file, but scale it down."

"You can't see us progressing much more with this one?"

Diamond nodded.

Reasonable as this appeared, Georgina was having some difficulty with it. Clearly something else was on her mind. She eyed Diamond thoughtfully. "I believe I'm correct in saying that there's some media interest in this one."

Diamond started to say, "I'm not aware of any . . ." Then stopped and started again. "Do you mean a woman called Ingeborg Smith?"

"I was thinking of her, yes."

"She's independent. What do they call it? Freelance."

"So I understand. A bright young woman."

"You've met her, ma'am?"

The ACC coloured noticeably. "I joined the Bath Camerata recently. Ingeborg Smith is a member."

Now Diamond reddened. "A club?"

"A choir, actually. Singing is a pastime of mine. The Camerata are very good. I don't know if my voice will be up to their standard, but that's beside the point. Miss Smith is a very accomplished alto. Over coffee the other evening she surprised me by mentioning this case. To give her credit, she declared her interest right away. She quite properly thought it right to state that she knows all about the police activity in the vault. She seemed to think she had passed you some vital information. Naturally, I made no comment."

Illuminating as this was about the ACC's private recreations, it came to Diamond like a low punch. He knew Ingeborg was a sharp mover. He had not anticipated this. Stiffly he commented, "The information may have seemed useful at the time, ma'am, but events have moved on."

"I see."

"This was before we eliminated that old skull from our inquiry. Miss Smith had a theory about a missing woman."

"She seems anxious to be of use."

And how, thought Diamond. "Did she tell you she wants to join the police?"

"Really? No, she didn't say so."

"I expect she's saving it up. Better not say I tipped you off, ma'am."

"Right you are."

"She'd be an asset by the sound of it."

"Do you think so?"

"To the police choir, anyway." Diamond took a half-step in the direction of the door. "If that's all, ma'am?"

"There is one other thing," said the ACC, as if she had just thought of it. "You made a strong impression last night at the PCCG, I was informed."

"PCC . . . ? Ah, yes."

"You put the crime statistics into perspective very neatly."

"Did I?"

"But if I were you, I should soft-pedal with Councillor Sturr at future meetings. He's a powerful man in the community."

"Did you say 'future meetings'?" Diamond felt a pulse throb in his forehead: the old hypertension. Surely that meeting had been a one-off. The way he'd been dragooned into going, simply because he'd happened to walk up a corridor at the wrong moment, had not suggested it was a permanent arrangement.

"Absolutely. From all I hear, you represented us admirably. I can't think of anyone better equipped to do the job."

He reeled out of that office in no doubt who had lumbered him. John Wigfull. Who else could have taken back tales of the meeting? Between Ingeborg Smith and Wigfull, he would have to watch his back in future.

IN A shop at the lower end of Milsom Street, Donna was trying on pink high-heeled shoes with the dinkiest little bows you ever saw. They were adorable, only they pinched. The assistant went off to look for something similar in a wider fitting and while Donna massaged her toes and wondered if she could put up with the discomfort, Joe suggested meeting later for coffee in a French place they had discovered the morning before. Donna didn't reply. For just such a situation as this, Joe had collected an address card from the cafe. He wrote 11.30 across the top, placed it beside Donna's bag and left unobtrusively.

He found Union Passage without difficulty. It was one of those narrow walkways that add so much interest to the older English towns. Too bad that O. Heath no longer had a bookstore there.

He made enquiries in a couple of shops and they said they had no recollection of a secondhand bookshop in Union Passage, unless he meant a charity shop.

"No, no, this was a regular bookstore dealing in rare antiquarian books," Joe said for the second time.

And now he was in luck, because one of the customers, a tall, white-bearded man, said, "Excuse me, but if you're speaking of Mr Heath, he retired a long time ago. It must be ten years, at least. The business closed down altogether, which was a pity, because it was a smashing little shop, an absolute treasure house for book-lovers."

"Do you know what happened to him?"

"Mr Heath? He's still about. I see him in the library sometimes, elderly now, but very upright still. I can't tell you where he lives."

"Maybe the library can. Where is it?" Persistence was one of Joe's virtues, though some would argue that it was the other thing. He looked at his watch. Donna would still be testing the endurance of the shoeshop staff.

The library assistant he spoke with said they weren't allowed to pass on addresses, but it was quite possible that the information he wanted was on the shelves. Her eyes slid sideways, towards the section where the phone directories were. Why the British never said what they meant in simple words, Joe had never fathomed. But the information was helpful. The only O. Heath listed in Bath lived in Queen Square. He didn't need to ask for directions. He had his pictorial map. It would just be a short walk.

*   *   *

THE VOICE came loud and clear over the answerphone: "Do I know you, Professor?"

"I'm afraid you don't, sir. I'm from Columbus, Ohio, and I recently bought a book that—"

"A book? Come up straight away. First floor, first left," the voice cut in.

A tall, silver-haired gentleman in brown corduroys and a black polo-neck was standing at his open door. He extended a hand. "Oliver Heath. I'd better say at once that I've given up dealing, but I do enjoy meeting another book man."

Joe was shown into an apartment that might easily have passed for a bookshop. A couple of the floor-to-ceiling shelves had ornaments and family photographs, but otherwise only the spines of books were showing. Good books, too, many in fine bindings.

"Do you specialise?" Oliver Heath asked. "As you see, I go in for criminology and the theatre. You'd be surprised how much overlap there is."

Joe had the precious copy of Milton's poems under his arm. He took it from its paper bag. "Then I begin to understand how you were able to part with this one, sir. It falls outside your main interests."

"May I see?" The old man took a pair of half-glasses from his pocket. Handling the book with the care of a specialist, he glanced at the cover, opened it, found his sticker inside, examined the title page and leafed through the rest. "The one-volume Dr Johnson edition. I do remember this one. I suppose I remember most of the books I acquired over the years. I can't tell you what I paid for it, but it was on my shelf for a good long time. Not in the best of condition. I expect I disposed of it when I gave up the business in Union Passage. Where did you find it?"

"At Hay-on-Wye."

This was cause for a smile. "Sooner or later everything of no special distinction seems to end up there." He handed back the book.

Joe felt insulted. He had not intended to point out to Oliver Heath that the find of all finds had slipped through his hands. He had no wish to inflict unnecessary pain. But that condescending phrase "of no special distinction" caught him off guard. He reacted instinctively. "Sir, I wouldn't have thought Mary Shelley's personal copy of Milton was without distinction."

The smile faded. Oliver Heath gave a prim tug at his spectacles. "May I see it again?"

"Certainly."

A longer inspection. He took the book closer to a desk-lamp. "I take it that the hand-writing on the cover leads you to assume it belonged to Mary Shelley?"

Joe nodded. "Those were her initials before she married and that was her address."

"She lived in Bath?"

"She wrote *Frankenstein* in Bath, or most of it."

Oliver Heath became conciliatory. "Strange. I didn't know that. Here I am purporting to be a bookseller and I didn't know that."

"You're in good company," said Joe. "It's a piece of information you have to go looking for. People with a special interest in the Shelleys know about it, but for some reason it's ignored in this city."

"Intellectual snobbery, no doubt."

"I wasn't going to say that."

"But I can. I know my own city. They're happy with stories about silly young women in poke bonnets, but the greatest of all monster novels is about as welcome here as a cowpat on the cobbles. Well, congratulations, Professor. You evidently found a bargain in Hay. Would it be indiscreet to ask how much it cost you?"

"Twenty pounds. I, em, rubbed out the price."

"Sensible, in the circumstances. Twenty is about right, going by the state of it. You can probably add several zeroes if you can prove the ownership beyond all doubt. Intrinsically, it's nothing special." He opened the book at the front. "Do you see where some of the fly-leaves have been cut out? Rather neatly, I have to say—but it matters to a collector."

Joe had not noticed before. "Why would anyone do that?"

"Paper was harder to come by in the old days. Expensive, too. Blank sheets had their uses for notepaper, or whatever." He closed the book carefully and handed it back. "I suggest you get that inscription authenticated. There are scientific tests for ink. Then if you want to make a tidy profit I would offer it to one of the London auction houses."

"I don't know if I'll sell it," said Joe.

The blue eyes glittered in approval. "There speaks a true book man."

"Would you remember who you bought it from?"

"You're hoping to trace the provenance?" said Oliver Heath, his eyebrows peaking in surprise. "I don't think that's very likely with a book as old as this, unless it's been in a private library for many years."

"Any chance of that?"

He spread his hands to gesture that he had no answer. "I'm trying to remember who sold it to me. Not one of my regulars, I'm sure of that. I have the feeling he was not a bookish person at all." He tapped the end of his nose with his forefinger as if that might stimulate thought, and apparently it did. "I believe it was Uncle Evan."

"Your *uncle*?"

"No, no. He's about fifty years my junior. He's the puppeteer."

"Would you mind saying that again?"

"The puppeteer, Uncle Evan. He runs a puppet theatre for

children. He's quite well-known in Bath. Very talented. Built the theatre himself, makes his own puppets, paints the scenery, writes the scripts and works the strings as well."

"Is he interested in poetry?"

"I couldn't say. You can never tell with people. He has depths, but I wouldn't have thought he troubled with things like *Paradise Lost*, unless he was planning to turn it into a puppet show."

Professor Joe Dougan winced at the concept. "But he definitely owned this book before you did?"

"Yes, I'm certain it was Evan, no doubt needing to raise some funds for one of the shows."

"Where do I find this theatre?" Joe asked.

"Lord only knows."

"Doesn't it have an address?"

"It's not a building. It's a mobile thing. Collapsible. He drives it around in a van, doing shows for schools, hospitals, birthday parties and so on. I don't know where you'll catch up with him."

"Do you know his surname?"

"If I did, it's gone. You could ask at the Brains Surgery. He's well known there. I think he gets some of his bookings through them."

There was a long, uneasy pause. "You did say 'Brain Surgery'?" Joe sought to confirm.

"Brains, with an 's'."

"That's where I should go to ask for Uncle Evan?" he queried the advice slowly, spacing the words. He was beginning to have doubts about the competence of Oliver Heath's brain.

"Don't look so shocked. It's a Welsh pub. In Dafford Street, Larkhall."

"A Welsh pub in Bath? You wouldn't be putting me on?"

"My dear chap, Brains Bitter is a beer brewed in Cardiff. The pub's name is a play on words."

"I understand now." Joe grinned. "I had a mental picture that was truly bizarre."

"Dare I suggest, professor, that you read a little less of *Frankenstein?*"

THE ANTIQUES trade is big in Bath. Go window-shopping in any direction and it isn't long before you are looking at Staffordshire dogs and Japanese fans. Two areas have a concentration of the trade: the streets north of George Street at the top of the town, stretching right up to Lansdown; and Walcot, on the main route out to the east. Walcot cheerfully admits to being the dustier end of the market, its shops co-existing with used clothes outlets and takeaways. Here, on Saturdays, the old tram shed becomes a flea market and hundreds of bargain-hunters jostle among the stalls.

At the far end of Walcot Street stood Noble and Nude, a shop unlike any other, three floors and a basement crammed with bygones, without the slightest attempt to classify them. This hoard was presided over by Margaret Redbird, a formidable little woman known in the trade as Peg the Pull, from her genius for "pulling" or buying cheaply from gullible sellers. Why Noble and Nude? For no extra charge, Peg would tell you that she plundered Swinburne as cheerfully as she plundered everyone else:

> "We shift and bedeck and bedrape us,
> Thou art noble and nude and antique."

The shop's name seemed right for Peg. Noble she certainly appeared. She might have been born a duchess, for every syllable she spoke was beautifully articulated. Nude she was not (when in the shop)—but a hint of the erotic was good for business. Her vitality attracted men and she was old enough—close to fifty, if the truth were told—to lavish endearments on males of all ages and get away with it. She was small, energetic and playful, all of which helped her strategies in the antique game.

Peg had been in Bath over twenty years and amassed a collection that was two-thirds junk, but with enough good things among the rubbish to have serious collectors slavering. Finding the treasures was the problem. You went through a confusing series of small rooms connected by stairs that themselves served as display areas, leaving only the narrowest ways up between figurines and candlesticks. Everywhere the display was haphazard. Each surface was crowded with ceramics, glassware and silver, all unclassified. If you opened the drawers in the furniture they spilled out prints, postcards and photographs. From hooks in the ceiling another whole area was put to use. Suspended on strings over the customers' heads were dolls, teddy bears, saucepans, parasols, hats and birdcages. A full-sized waxwork of a woman in a red velvet dress was poised on a swing like a Fragonard beauty, her petticoats wired out to give the impression of movement.

Peg managed her business from a boxed-in position behind the grandfather clocks facing the front door. Hidden, not very cleverly, under her desk was a small safe. In it she kept the cash, and a few precious items such as a silver watch, once allegedly owned by Beau Nash, an eighteenth century pearl necklace and a letter written by Oscar Wilde.

Visitors came through steadily from the time Noble and Nude opened, about ten in the morning. Not all came to look at the stock. Peg kept her finger on Bath's pulse by dispensing gin and tonic to a fair cross-section of local society. Keeping up with the gossip was a professional necessity. When someone died at a decent address, Peg was invariably the first to offer deepest sympathy and expert help in valuing the contents of the house.

Essential to the system, a friend with time to spare was on call to mind the shop when Peg went on a valuing foray. This useful person rejoiced in the name of Ellis Somerset. Ellis knew everything about silver and quite a lot about china, yet his overriding passion was Peg. Her charm enslaved him. Each time she called him Gorgeous or Poppet, he turned pink with pleasure, regardless that she used the same words for the milk-man and the bank manager. This morning Peg had summoned him and he was here soon after lunch in his suede shoes and olive-green corduroy suit with the red bow-tie that gave a help-ful air of authority. Ellis was not much over forty, slight, well-groomed and red-haired. To borrow a phrase that rather suited him, he was a single man in possession of a good fortune. Pity he had a face like a turnip.

"I shouldn't be more than a couple of hours, if that," Peg was saying. "This is one of the Minchendon family, old Simon, who had that tailor's at the top of Milsom Street at one time. He was gathered last Tuesday. Heart. His nephew asked me to run an eye over the furniture."

"You're in for a treat," said Ellis, quite as well-briefed as Peg about Bath's recently departed. "Old Si didn't buy rubbish. When I was up at Bartlett Street one afternoon a couple of years ago, he picked up a set of Queen Anne spoonback chairs, a four and two. They cost him two-fifty apiece, but they'll be worth twice that now."

Peg was giving a crocodile smile. "Not this afternoon, ducky."

Ellis raised an eyebrow. "You'll get us a bad name, Peg."

"Tell me something new." She reached for the black straw hat she wore for funerals and valuations.

"All right. I will. I know you don't bother much with anti-quarian books—"

"Each to his own, blossom. Old farts with elbow-patches trade in books."

"Yes, but listen to this, straight off the grapevine. Remember an old boy by the name of Heath, who owned that antiquarian bookshop in Union Passage?"

"Of course I remember him. He's still alive, I think."

"He certainly is. He was in Shades at lunchtime telling this story to a crowd of us, and now the trade is buzzing with it."

"Buzz it to me, then," Peg said indifferently.

"It seems he had an unexpected visitor this morning, a professor from Ohio, or Oregon, or somewhere in the colonies, wanting an opinion on a book of poetry by John Milton. Nothing special about the edition, except this little American reckons it once belonged to Mary Shelley."

Peg wriggled her little nose in disbelief. "Oh, yes? And how does he know?"

"It carried her initials, I was told, and the address—five, Abbey Churchyard—and that, apparently, was where *Frankenstein* was written. Did you know that?"

"I'll own up. I did not," Peg said without the slightest stirring of enthusiasm. "Now, if anyone is serious about the furniture, ask them to come back later, when I'm here, right? Anything else, you can deal with."

"I haven't told you the interesting bit," said Ellis.

"Snap it up then, sweetie."

"This professor found that number five was knocked down years ago. It was where the entrance to the Roman Baths is now. But he doesn't give up easily. He discovered that the original vaults are still there, and he managed to go down and have a look."

"Is this going to take much longer, Ellis, because I'm expected at Camden Crescent ten minutes from now?"

"Hold on. It's worth it. He reckons the police were down there digging, and they'd just found a human skull—in the vault of the house where Mary Shelley wrote *Frankenstein*. Spooky, isn't it?"

"What do you mean—'the police were down there digging'? What for?"

"I don't know. Looking for something, I suppose. Stolen goods? Your guess is as good as mine."

"And they dug up a skull?"

"It makes your blood run cold, doesn't it?" Ellis breathed some drama into his piece of gossip, frustrated that Peg had missed the point. "In the place where this great gothic horror story was written, the monster put together from bits of old bodies, they actually discover this."

"But what about the book?" she said.

"*Frankenstein?*"

"Milton's poems."

Ellis stared back.

"Did the American part with it?"

"I didn't ask." Ellis gave up. Peg's only interest in the matter was whether a transaction had taken place.

After she had left for Camden Crescent, he picked up the phone. He knew someone in the newspaper business who would appreciate the story.

TRYING TO sound normal, Joe bent his head to a taxi window and asked, "Do you know the Brains Surgery?" Back home, any driver faced with a question like that would push down the door-lock and look the other way. But it made no problem here. He was allowed into the cab and they drove out of the centre to the part of Bath called Larkhall.

And it really did exist, a substantial brick-built public house with the name in bold lettering on each side of a corner of Dafford Street. *Dafford Street.* Joe was glad he had not needed to name the pub and the street together. He paid the driver, went through a Regency-style entrance into the public bar and asked for a half-pint of Brains.

"The bitter, sir?"

Joe was not sure what the bitter was, but he said that would do. While it was being poured, he checked the clientele, wondering if Uncle Evan could be one of the three standing by the pool table, or the man practising at one of the dartboards.

The Brains Bitter appeared on the counter. Joe paid, leaned closer to the barman and said he was looking for Uncle Evan, who ran the puppet shows.

"Evan? He comes in regular." The barman called across to the pool players. "Anyone see Evan today?"

One of the three came over, cue in hand. "Are you wanting to offer him a job, like?"

Joe explained that he wanted to talk about a book.

"What sort of book—an encyclopedia?" The last word was drawn out in a cadenza of disapproval.

"No, sir, don't get me wrong. I'm not selling anything. I happen to own a book that may have belonged to this gentleman once. I'm trying to find out where it came from originally."

"Is that it, under your arm?"

"As a matter of fact it is." Joe was keeping it under his arm for the present.

"Better show it to me, then. I'm Evan."

Joe was suspicious. If this was Evan, why hadn't he spoken up before? But the barman gave a confirming nod. "You picked the right time to come in, mister."

Joe felt at a disadvantage in this setting, among these people talking in their Welsh lilt. He wanted to be sure this was not a try-on. The man claiming to be Uncle Evan was around forty, dressed in jeans and a check shirt, with black hair worn in a pony-tail. His glasses had round metal frames that reminded Joe of John Lennon. Behind them, his deep-set eyes locked with Joe's.

"I can't hold up the game too long."

Joe noticed the hand clasping the cue. The fingers were long, the nails shaped. It was not the hand of a labouring man. He thought he could picture those fingers working puppet strings. It might be safe to let him handle the book. "Mr Heath—who used to have the bookshop in Union Passage—says he believes he bought the book from you."

"Did he now?" Evan—if that was he—rested the cue against the bar-counter.

With some reluctance, Joe handed over the precious Milton.

"What's so special about this?" asked Evan, thumbing through it. He paid no attention to the inscription.

The ultra cautious Joe decided to play the raw American tourist card. "You buy something really old like this, you want to know who owned it before you."

"Seems to me it's just a book."

"Dr Johnson's edition."

"Is that special?"

"It's going to have a place of honour on my shelves."

After a pause, Evan said, "You're telling me it's worth more than I sold it for, is that it?"

"So you did own it?"

"Yes—and you came here to gloat?"

"Not at all, sir. I'm just trying to establish a chain of ownership. Do you happen to remember how it came into your hands?"

Evan vibrated his lips. "It's a bloody long time ago."

"Would another drink help you to remember?"

"Thanks. I'm on SA." While the pint glass was being filled, Evan went on, "Far as I recall, and this was the best part of twenty years back, I got it in Bath, out of an antique shop. Don't ask me why. You go into these places and come out with things you never expected to buy. Milton. My God, I must have been trying to impress someone, mustn't I? A girl, I reckon."

"You wouldn't remember which shop?"

Evan frowned.

"I could line up another beer," Joe offered.

The face lit up. "I do remember. It was in Walcot. It's still there. Noble and Nude."

THE FIRST phone call came around three in the afternoon.

"Superintendent Diamond?"

"Speaking."

"John Delany, *News of the World* crime desk. I understand you're in charge of this case concerning the dismembered bodies."

"What are you on about?" Diamond hedged, wondering what was in this for a national Sunday.

"The bodies in the vault. A couple of hands. A skull. Have you found anything else yet?"

" 'Dismembered bodies' is laying it on thick."

"It's only one body? The same victim?"

" 'Victim' isn't a word I'm using."

"Why not?"

"Look, we found some human bones in a cellar, a skull and a pair of hands, as you said. The cellar happens to be built over a churchyard. We believe the skull is several hundred years old. I wouldn't think this has any news value for a paper like yours."

"Parts of a body under the cellar of the house where *Frankenstein* was written? You're joking, Mr Diamond. It's going to make front pages all over the world."

n i n e

AFTER YEARS OF STEEPING himself in the story, he felt driven, not precisely as Frankenstein had been, nor with the same objective, but just as powerfully. "My *limbs now tremble, and my eyes swim with the remembrance; but then a resistless and almost frantic impulse urged me forward; I seemed to have lost all soul or sensation but for this one pursuit.*"

Driven towards the final killing.

"The road of excess," wrote the poet, "leads to the palace of wisdom."

Shortly he would find out.

t e n

CAMDEN CRESCENT, WHERE PEG Redbird arrived to carry out the valuation, is a flawed masterpiece. In 1788, the architect John Eveleigh sought to emulate John Wood's most famous building with a crescent of his own. The position above Hedgemead was arguably superior to the Royal Crescent, with sensational views to the east across the Avon Valley towards Bathwick Hill. The style was to be classical, the concept more ornate than Wood's. Building got under way at each end and the first houses were in place when problems were revealed at the eastern end. The foundation was unsafe. The exposed strata that had appeared to be sound for building had hidden faults, and slippage occurred. Four of the houses had to be abandoned. Poor Eveleigh was committed to the project and obliged to build the rest of his crescent, leaving an unsightly gap like an old fighter's grin, with the extreme eastern house standing alone for many years, mocking his grandiose ambition.

The rest of the truncated Crescent has survived two centuries of surveyors' reports, and is regarded as tolerably safe and one of the best addresses in Bath. Peg had hopes of some good finds in old Simon Minchendon's home.

The nephew who opened the door professed to know nothing about old furniture, but Peg was wary. The death of a relative often brings out the worst in people. She was pretty sure he would have his own ideas which items were the gems. Anything he talked up would get a high valuation.

His name was Ralph Pennycook, he told her, and he had come up from Brighton for the funeral.

"Some good antique shops there," Peg commented, trying him out.

"In the Lanes, you mean? I don't bother with all that crap," he said of the corner of Brighton everyone in the trade found irresistible. "If I go into town, I head for the computer shops." True, he looked custom-built for staring at a screen, with a slight curvature of the spine and deep-set brown eyes behind thick plastic lenses. A young man who neglected to look after himself, Peg decided. He was definitely under-nourished. Possibly that was why he was dressed in the black pinstripe jacket that looked like the top of a suit and made an odd combination with his blue corduroy trousers; he needed to wrap himself up, even in this hot summer.

"I hope you don't mind me asking. Are you the executor?" Peg enquired. These things need to be established at the outset. Private sellers sometimes offer goods that don't belong to them.

"What gives you that idea?" he said.

"Well, how exactly . . . ?"

"I'm the lucky bugger who inherited this lot, aren't I? Poor old Si ran out of family. Uncle Tod and Aunt Nell were mentioned in the will, but they snuffed it before he did."

"Then what exactly do you want from me, darling? A full valuation? You can't dispose of anything until the probate comes through, and that can take months." She added, "Presumably."

"Yeah."

There was an awkward pause.

He resumed, "The bank are acting as whatchamacallits."

"Executors?" Peg supplied the word. Whatever else he had come into, this young man was not blessed with a silver tongue.

"And they want to make some kind of list."

"An inventory."

"Yeah. An inventory." Except he made it sound like "infantry".

"And a valuation, no doubt?" said Peg.

"Right. I thought I'd get me own one of them done—to protect me interests, like—and I was told you're the best in Bath."

"You want the full monty, piece by piece? That's going to take some time," said Peg, her eyes travelling over the contents of the entrance hall, making a snap valuation of her own.

"That isn't what I said." He cleared his throat. "I'm, er, jumping the gun. You're the first to see the stuff. The geezer from the bank is coming to do the proper job on Monday."

"So where do I fit into this arrangement?" asked Peg, playing the innocent.

"You get first sight of what's here." He looked away. He was sweating, in spite of his brash manner.

There was another uneasy interval.

"It all belongs to me," he insisted once more, reading Peg's thoughts as she watched him with her bright, miss-nothing eyes. "I need some cash in hand for a project I have in mind."

"When you say you want to protect your interests . . ."

"You know what I mean, don't you?" said Pennycook. "I'm offering you a few choice items now, if you want to do business. A few things wouldn't get onto the, em . . ."

"Inventory. And you'd save yourself some tax."

"You got it."

His cards were on the table, then. Peg's were not. "I wish you hadn't told me, ducky. I don't get involved in anything irregular."

"It happens all the time," he informed her superfluously. "Look, see me right on this, and I'll see you right later, when I got probate and I can sell the rest of the stuff legit. Do you do clearances?"

This was not a man who was ignorant of the trade, Peg noted, but she, too, was playing a canny game. "House clearances? I don't bother with them as a rule. It's more trouble than it's worth."

"So you're telling me to piss off?"

"Sweetie, the difficulty with what you're suggesting is that serious buyers of antiques—quality antiques—like to know the provenance of the items they acquire. See the bracket clock behind you on the shelf? That's William and Mary. If I were to offer anything as fine as that for sale, they'd want to know who owned it before me. If I said Si Minchendon, you and I could easily land ourselves in trouble."

He glanced up at the ceiling, as if the plasterwork interested him more than Peg's last remark.

She added without enthusiasm, "I suppose we could look at some less distinguished items."

"Want me to show you over the gaff?"

"Since I'm here, you might as well," she said, "but I can't promise a thing."

They toured the house and Peg's expert eye missed nothing. Old Si's furniture was collectable, no question, and some of the smaller items such as tripod tables and side-chairs could be removed without anyone knowing they had been there. In the drawing room were some bits of china she rather liked, a pair of Coalport plates by William Cook and a Minton pot pourri vase painted for the Great Exhibition of 1851. She priced them fairly, then said she wouldn't be able to go to such a price if he wanted to sell them prior to valuation. This put Pennycook in the position of reducing the figure and seeing if she would take the risk. With a show of reluctance, Peg agreed to buy them for two-thirds the price she had named.

The landing upstairs was lined with watercolours, landscapes that she suspected were by minor painters of the late nineteenth century, serene in concept and unremarkable.

Except two that stood out. Instead of patently English scenes where animals grazed and the only suggestions of humanity were cottages and church towers, these were nightmarish. In one, two figures in a bleak, craggy setting that suggested a theatrical backdrop faced each other like protagonists. The other was an interior, even more melodramatic. A woman lay across a bed in a posture of death, her head hanging down, scarlet marks of strangulation on her neck. A man stood staring at her in horror, while at the open window a fiendlike creature stood grinning and pointing at the corpse.

Peg immediately thought of William Blake. The theatricality of the settings was an indication; so was the peculiar rendering of the figures, their muscularity showing through the folds of garments that flowed with the composition. If these were by Blake, they were by far the most valuable things in the house. She moved past them without betraying undue interest, wondering how long they had been hanging there. The problem with removing pictures is the telltale patch they leave on the wallpaper. But helpfully this paper looked reasonably new.

Little else upstairs was both portable and saleable, as Peg pointed out. Si's real interest had been furniture and you couldn't remove large pieces without leaving gaps. Pennycook was forced to agree. Clearly, he was disappointed. They had done less than nine hundred pounds' worth of business.

"You're looking for cash, no doubt," said Peg.

"Cash, yes. It's got to be cash."

"I don't carry large amounts, ducky. It isn't safe."

"No sweat, lady. I trust you—but you will collect the stuff sharpish, won't you?"

"Later today?"

"That'll do."

"I'll send a man with a van. He's very discreet, is my Mr Somerset. You can call at my shop in Walcot Street if you want the money today. I put some by for this. To be frank, I expected to spend a little more, but you can never tell."

Pennycook's eyes widened. "There's nothing else you noticed, going round?"

Peg took her time, and frowned, as if straining to remember anything at all. "There was a slightly chipped chaise-longue upstairs, mahogany, upholstered in blue velvet. Late Victorian, I'm certain."

"In the back bedroom?"

"Yes. I could probably find a buyer for that, even in the state it's in. Bath is full of rich women with a Madame Recamier fantasy."

"Anything else?"

"The tripod table in the front room. It's been repaired, I noticed, and not very expertly. And you have a couple of watercolours on the landing, rather *grand guignole*. I don't know if you'd call them a pair, but I think they're by the same artist. Throw them in and I could raise the offer to fifteen hundred, on the understanding that I have first choice of the more valuable items when you get probate. Does that sound better?"

Infinitely better, going by Pennycook's reaction. The deal was done. "Will you be there tonight?" he asked. "Can I collect the dosh tonight?"

"Any time, darling. I live over the shop."

Peg hurried back to Noble and Nude to read up on William Blake.

THE ROMAN Baths were under siege by the media. Nobody was being admitted to the vault. Camera crews and photographers, radio people and reporters, were blocking the main entrance. Bewildered tourists stood in Abbey Churchyard not knowing how to get to the ticket booths.

It fell to Peter Diamond to try and defuse the problem with a hastily arranged press conference at Manvers Street. If nothing else, it would relieve the pressure at the Baths. He was ill-prepared. He knew nothing about Mary Shelley and little of *Frankenstein*. All this had blown up just when he was doing his best to tiptoe away from the case.

They filled the room that was used for sessions with the media. He had to force his way in through the crush. Surrounded, not liking this one bit, he stood with Halliwell at his side watching the scuffles between the camera crews.

"This will be brief," he began, and was told to speak up, and did. He fairly bellowed, "Do you want to hear this, or not?"

They listened to his summary, the discovery of the hand in the vault by the security man, the estimate by the pathologist that it had been buried there for up to twenty years, and the decision to look for more remains. He described the unearthing of the skull and stressed that it was much older than the hand bones, and almost certainly from a medieval burial.

As he spoke of the skull he was aware of intense scrutiny to his right. Turning, he locked eyes with Ingeborg Smith. The reproach in that ambitious young woman's gaze was understandable. Her exclusive had been crushed in this stampede. She blamed him.

"Forensic scientists are carrying out more tests on the remains," he continued, shifting his look to another part of the room. "I don't expect any results before next week, and then I don't expect much. We already know the salient facts."

All as downbeat as he could make it. Then the questions hit him like machine-gun fire:

"What about the Frankenstein connection, Superintendent?"

"Did you know you were digging in the Frankenstein vault?"

"Is it just a coincidence, these body parts turning up there?"

"Have you found any nuts and bolts?" This earned a laugh.

He had to raise both arms for a chance to reply. "You're going to have to believe me when I tell you I knew nothing about the history of the vault until this afternoon, when I heard it from one of you. It makes a good story, and good luck to you, but I doubt if there's any connection with the remains down there."

"Isn't it well-known that Mary Shelley lived over the vault and wrote her book there?"

"Not well-known to me. I've been here some years and never heard a word about it. I imagine you lot will remedy that."

"When the hand was discovered, didn't you take an interest in the history of the house?"

"The house you're talking about doesn't exist. It was demolished a century ago, except for the vault. The hand is less than twenty years old."

"So the answer is no?"

"Correct."

"Is this a murder inquiry, Superintendent?"

"I wouldn't call it that."

"Dismembered bits of a corpse buried in cement?"

"There could be an explanation that doesn't include murder."

"What's that?"

"No comment."

"What are you getting at, Mr Diamond? Some kind of hoax? The bones are real, aren't they?"

"Oh, yes, but I'm keeping an open mind about how they got there. To come back to your question, I'm the murder man in Bath, so you can see that we're taking it seriously."

"Do you have a theory who was responsible?"

"Let's be clear. We don't know whose hand bones they are. We don't know how they came to be in the vault. We have no witnesses, no motive, no description of the perpetrator or the victim."

"You're still digging down there?"

"It's almost complete."

"Can we go down there, get pictures? If we can get pictures today, you'll be saved a lot of hassle."

"That sounds suspiciously like blackmail."

"Just the truth, Mr Diamond."

"When we finish the search, you can get your pictures, but it won't be today."

"You said the skull is much older than the hand?"

"Yes."

"Where exactly was it found?"

"Buried under the flagstones, some distance from where the hand was found."

"Probably medieval, you said?"

"I did."

"So it was down there in 1816, when Mary Shelley lived in the house?"

"I can't say for sure. It could have been."

"Would you describe it, Superintendent?"

He was becoming impatient. "Look, I told you it's an old skull."

"Male or female?"

"Female."

"Adult?"

"Yes."

"But not attached to the rest of a skeleton?"

His patience snapped. "For crying out loud, this is the site of a churchyard. If we dug any deeper, we'd probably find many more bones. Hundreds of them." He realised as he spoke that it was unwise. He had just fed them a quote they could splash all over their front pages. It was time he drew the curtains on this pantomime. "Right. I've given you the statement, told you everything I can at this point."

"Not everything."

"Come again." He turned to the speaker and found himself facing Ingeborg.

"You told us the skull is female. What about the hands?"

"Can't say."

"Won't the forensic lab be able to tell you?"

"It's unlikely. If they turn out to be large hands, the supposition is that they belonged to a male, but it's only guesswork."

"So what's the next step, Mr Diamond? If the lab can't tell you much more, where do you go from here?"

"We find out who had access to the vault fifteen to twenty years ago."

"And who went missing?"

She was still on about the postgraduate woman. "Of course. It's under investigation. For your information, about a hundred and fifty thousand people go missing every year. Nationally, I mean."

Someone else said, "You don't sound very confident of a result, Superintendent."

"Would you be?" He turned to Halliwell. "Let's go."

Outside, a messenger from upstairs told him he was wanted immediately by the Assistant Chief Constable.

ALONE IN the carpeted office upstairs. That huge mahogany desk. A group photo taken at Bramshill, the police training college for senior officers. Another of Georgina in uniform shaking the hand of Margaret Thatcher. A shelf of books, mainly reports by the look of them. The saving grace was the corner cupboard used by the previous ACC for his supply of whisky.

He heard her quick footsteps along the corridor. "The Police Authority like to be kept informed of developments," she told him importantly as she swept in.

"Councillor Sturr?"

"How do you know I was with John Sturr?"

"He parked his Mercedes next to my old heap in the staff car park."

"Sit down, then." No offer of a scotch. Not so much as a lemonade. "How did the press behave?"

"They didn't swallow me alive, ma'am," said Diamond. "But it was crowded in there. I had to shout. Makes your throat go dry."

She didn't even glance at the drinks cupboard. "What did they want to know?"

"They're only interested in the Frankenstein stuff. Frankenstein! The things you get thrown at you in this job."

"Did you know of this connection?"

"Not until this afternoon. I know Jane Austen lived here, and Beau Nash and General Wolfe. Frankenstein, no."

"To be accurate," the ACC corrected him, "it was the creator of *Frankenstein*, Mary Shelley."

"You'd think it was the monster himself, the way they were going on about body parts."

"She was here only a few months, but it appears she wrote most of the book at the house in Abbey Churchyard. There's no question that she lived there. In fact, her personal copy of Milton's poems was doing the rounds of the antiquarian book trade this very morning, and it's inscribed with her initials and the Abbey Churchyard address." Georgina threw this in casually, apparently to let him know she had her finger on the Bath pulse. "We're going to be in the spotlight shortly, I'm afraid."

"Going to be?" he said with irony.

"This is why I asked you to see me. You'd better disregard the conversation we had earlier, about scaling down the investigation. We're coming under public scrutiny."

Diamond frowned. "What are you saying, ma'am? That we have to put on a show for the media?"

"I didn't put it quite so crudely, but that's the gist of it, yes."

He felt a rush of blood. He was about to say something insubordinate. If Julie Hargreaves had been here, she would have put a restraining hand on his arm. But she was not. "I'm a copper, not a circus acrobat."

The ACC said in a voice as dry as the scotch she didn't dispense, "What are you implying?"

For the first time in their dealings, Diamond allowed the ACC's gender to influence his conduct; if she had been a man, he would given her a mouthful. "I'm not *implying* anything, ma'am. I speak straight. I work for the police. I obey orders, but I expect them to be based on policing priorities."

The features across the desk tensed and turned paler. "Policing priorities can include public relations, you know."

"So that's it," said Diamond. "This is window-dressing."

Her eyes flashed. "If you ever rise above your present rank, Superintendent, you may come to appreciate that window-dressing, as you call it, is a necessary part of the job. As you know, I'm giving a party tonight—in my own time and at my own expense—and several members of the Police Authority will be there. I don't do it out of anything else than a sense of duty. Some of the people I've invited would not be my choice of guests—I don't mean you—but one does it just the same, to show the flag."

"You're telling me to show the flag?"

"There's more to it than that. What was found in the vault requires investigation. You and your team have no other inquiry under way at the moment. I agree with you that this one presents difficulties, but that's no reason to walk away from it."

"This isn't the only unsolved suspicious death in the past twenty years."

"It's the most recent to come to light. Who do you have working on it at the moment?"

"Apart from the diggers? DI Halliwell and a couple of civilians."

"Step it up, then. Get more people onto it. We ought to establish the identity of the victim."

"Oh, yes?"

"And another thing, Mr Diamond . . ."

"Yes, ma'am?"

"I don't like the way you've conducted yourself in the last few minutes, don't care for it one bit. If you and I are going to continue to work together, I suggest you do some window-dressing of your own. This confrontational style of yours, I won't put up with it. Understood?"

After a pause: "Understood, ma'am."

THE NEXT stage in Joe Dougan's odyssey brought him from The Brains Surgery to Noble and Nude. Peg Redbird, the owner of the most cluttered antique shop Joe had ever seen, was out doing a valuation when he arrived. He asked her assistant, a talkative, red-haired man in a bow-tie, if the shop had been in existence for some time and was told Peg herself had opened it in 1975. Joe said he would wait for her. He was sure he could find plenty to interest him until she returned.

He went upstairs looking for books. Most antique shops have a small stock somewhere, and this was no exception. In a back room he found some stacked along the lid of an upright piano, but they were disappointing. Paperback detective stories of the nineteen-thirties, by the likes of Margery Allingham and Ellery Queen. Joe didn't have time for fictional mysteries. There were mysteries enough in English Literature to keep him occupied.

He looked at his watch. For this, Donna would exact compensation. Champagne with dinner tonight. Or a visit to a stately home tomorrow. Or a new hat. Or all of those. He hoped the owner of this place would not keep him waiting much longer. But there was no question that he would give up the chase. People said there was an obsessive side to his personality ("people" meant Donna more than anyone else; she was obsessive in describing him as obsessive). Well, he had to admit that once started on something he liked to see it through to a conclusion, regardless of the time expended. But "obsessive" was not a word he would have used about himself. He preferred "tenacious".

Another long interval elapsed before he heard voices downstairs. Certainly one was a woman's. Hopeful that the wait was over, he picked his way through an obstacle-course of vases, ancient sewing-machines and wind-up gramophones and started down the stairs.

It is one of those universal truths that people in the antiques trade have loud voices, and these carried up to him.

The female voice was saying, "Darling, I had him on toast. Well, he was ripping off the taxman, and we both knew it, so he couldn't expect top dollar, could he?"

The man asked, "But did he have a sense of what it was worth?"

"There's one born every minute. You'll see when you pick up the goods. The chaise longue is an eyesore, but it will sell, and the rest of the stuff is very collectable indeed. You're going to love the Coalport. And Ellis . . ."

"Yes?"

"There are a couple of pictures, rather lurid watercolours. If you want to remain my bestest friend, handle them with TLC."

"Valuable?

"I don't know, do I, until I get a better look at them?"

"Who's the artist, then?"

"Never you mind, old dear. Just bring the goodies back safely to Peg."

Joe made a sound in his throat to let them know he was approaching. He was glad to have overheard the exchange. He would play a cautious hand with Peg Redbird.

"Oh, I clean forgot," the man said, clutching his red hair in consternation. "This gentleman came in specially to see you. He's been waiting some time."

Joe stepped forward and introduced himself. Peg stood up and shook hands when she heard he was a professor. The prospect of some business with a wealthy academic galvanized her enough to want her colleague to leave. "Ellis, would you be an angel and see about renting a van? I promised you'd collect that stuff from Camden Crescent today."

Left alone with Joe, Peg practically rubbed her hands as she asked if he was a collector.

"Not exactly, ma'am. If I see something I like, I buy it. Books, mostly."

Her disappointment was quick to show. "Books? You're in the wrong shop, precious. I don't go in for books. If I get some in as part of a job-lot, I pass them on to a bookseller."

"That I can appreciate, ma'am. I won't take up much of your time." He took the Milton out of its bag. "I was told you acquired this some years ago and sold it on."

"If you really mean years ago, I did have a book-room when I started," she said, taking the book and opening it. "I stocked anything in those days just to fill up space. There's nothing worse than empty rooms."

"Do you recall this book?"

She turned it over in her hands without opening it. "You're going to tell me I sold it for peanuts, no doubt. Milton isn't exactly a best-seller and it's not in the best of nick."

"I only paid twenty pounds myself, ma'am."

"What's so special about it?"

Joe was determined not to tell her yet. "This is the Dr Johnson edition of Milton. Both of them are on my current Eng. Lit. syllabus. This is a special find for me."

"What I don't understand," said Peg sharply, "is where I come into this. You don't want to sell it back to me?"

"Oh, no. I'm keeping it now."

"Well?" She looked annoyed.

He was in danger of crumbling under the cross-examination. "This is pure sentiment, I guess. This book is going to have an honoured place on my shelf at home. Almost like a friend. I like to know about its past, where it lived, who owned it . . ." His voice trailed away.

Peg tapped her finger on the cover. "Some Bathonian owned it at one time. 'Five, Abbey Churchyard'. That's local."

"Really?"

A clicking sound came from Peg's mouth. "Someone told me something about Abbey Churchyard today."

Joe attempted to close that avenue. "You must have a memory of how you acquired the book."

"Don't bet on it, professor. I wouldn't have bought it on its own, so it must have come in with some other stuff."

"More books, you mean?"

Peg narrowed her eyes, straining to think about several matters, and raked a hand through her dark-tinted hair. "No, it was part of another purchase. It was in some sort of container, with other things." Suddenly she snapped her fingers. "I do remember. Do you know what a writing box is?"

"Something containing writing paper?"

"Well, yes, but this was a specific item of furniture. A rather clever thing, much used two hundred years ago. I've got one somewhere upstairs, but it would take ages to find it. Look, the best way I can describe one is this. Think of an old-fashioned school desk with a sloping lid and a space inside for all the stuff a kid uses in school. You know what I mean?"

"Sure."

"Well, imagine it without legs."

"Okay."

"You could rest it on a table or on your lap, right? Now a writing box looks exactly like that when it's in use, but you can close it up. The part you write on is hinged halfway down, so that you can fold it back on itself and it makes the shape of a box. Do you follow?"

"I know exactly what you mean, ma'am," said Joe. "I've seen them back home. They're nice pieces."

"That's how I acquired this," Peg said, patting the front of the book. "It was inside a writing box, along with a sketchbook of some sort and a cut glass ink bottle."

A tingling sensation crept the length of Joe's spine. With an effort to sound only faintly interested, he said, "Did you keep any of these items? The sketchbook, for instance?"

"No, I got rid of that. It had a few inept pencil sketches as far as I remember. Nothing anyone would wish to frame."

His stomach tightened. "When you say 'got rid of' . . . ?"

"I unloaded it on someone."

"Sold it?"

"I don't give anything away, my love. I'm in business. I'm just trying to think whether the box upstairs is the one the book was in, or another. It hadn't been looked after, I can tell you that much."

"Could I see it?"

She sighed. "Listen darling, you've caught me on a busy day. I ought to know where everything is, but I don't."

"I won't take up much more of your time, ma'am. Do you happen to remember who sold you the writing box?"

"It was years ago," said Peg. "I don't know why I bothered. Sympathy, I reckon. Some poor soul in need of a few shillings for the gas meter."

"An old person?"

"I couldn't say."

Couldn't, or wouldn't? Joe was getting a distinct impression that Peg was stalling now. She may even have made the connection with Mary Shelley.

He shifted his ground. "I might be willing to offer you a good price for that writing box."

Her eyes glinted. "You haven't seen it, sunshine. It could be riddled with woodworm."

"I know you're busy right now. Maybe I could find it if I go looking."

"Be my guest," said Peg.

* * *

"ANYONE WOULD think we'd been sitting on our butts for the past week," Peter Diamond complained to Keith Halliwell.

Halliwell gave him a look long enough for the words to be played back in his mind.

Remarkably, an extra tinge of pink suffused his cheeks and he launched into an elaborate self-justification. "I took my turn with the sieve and shovel. It wasn't all tea and toast in the Pump Room. And you've been slogging away, tracing these bloody builders. I don't like my squad being jumped all over by a pipsqueak straight out of Bramshill. So what have we got, Keith? Are we anywhere nearer to naming Hands?"

"I've got the names of twelve who worked on the site in the early eighties," said Halliwell. "Most of the activity was in the winter of eighty-two to eighty-three. It's a matter of tracing them, to see if they're alive, and what they remember about the others who worked there."

"You want more manpower? It's yours."

"Really?"

"Her Worship has spoken. It gets high priority as long as it stays in the papers, though she didn't put it in quite those terms."

"I'll see to it."

"Good man." In a confiding mood, he propped his elbow on Halliwell's computer monitor and felt it tilt under the weight. "These things move," he said in surprise.

"It's the adjustment. I shouldn't lean too hard on it."

"You know me, Keith. Never leaned too hard. Never will." He got back to the topic he had been about to broach. "There was a question in the press-room that stopped me in my tracks."

"From the Smith woman?"

"No. Some other hack. I couldn't tell you who it was. He asked if we'd considered a hoax as a possibility. I hadn't. Had you?"

"No." Halliwell was clearly puzzled. "What would be the point?"

"Practical joking. We're fair game, Keith. Some con artist gets hold of some bones and buries them in the cellar under the house where *Frankenstein* was written."

"Who would do that?"

"A medical student," said Diamond as if it were screamingly obvious. "They have to buy a skeleton, don't they? They used to, one time. They need them in their studies, anyway. All he has to do is remove the hand, plant it in thin cement and wait for it to be discovered. He'll be laughing his bloody head off tomorrrow morning when he reads the papers."

"You think so?" Halliwell said, unimpressed.

Diamond backed off a little. "It's not impossible."

"It's a bit far-fetched, isn't it? For a start, he'd need to know about the *Frankenstein* link. Not many people did until this afternoon. You didn't, and nor did I."

"Someone made sure the press got onto it, didn't they?" Diamond said with more animation. "If there *is* a hoaxer, he must have tipped off the press. I got it from the *News of the World*, some wiseguy called Delany. John Delany. Who was his source, I wonder? It's got to be followed up."

Halliwell nodded and said almost apologetically, "If he spoke to you personally . . ."

"I know," said Diamond with a martyred air. "It's down to me."

But before he could do anything about it, he was called to the phone. The BBC wanted to know if he was willing to be interviewed on *Newsnight*, on BBC2 at 10.30 p.m. It could be pre-recorded, if necessary.

He said he had nothing to add to the press statement he had already made.

There were two more requests for television interviews in the next half-hour. "You'd think I'd won the bloody lottery, wouldn't you?" he said to the woman on the switchboard. "They only want me to talk about a monster who never existed. Tell them I'm on a flight to the Bahamas, love, or washing my hair tonight. I leave it up to you. Anything to get them off my back."

"Like going to the ACC's party?"

"God, I am, too. It never rains but it pours."

eleven

ONLY A MAN OF Joe's dogged determination would have continued. Hands filthy from shifting furniture, breathing passages coated with dust, he progressed steadily through the rooms of Noble and Nude. He had long since lost a sense of where he was in the building. He ignored the other people browsing through the rooms. Just occasionally he would check his watch. Surely Donna would forgive him being late for dinner if he brought back Mary Shelley's writing box. Unfortunately he had not located it yet. Time had moved on to the point when he could not very well face Donna without some substantial find. So he continued to rummage.

There was another pressure. Peg Redbird's antennae were twitching. That remark about Abbey Churchyard meant she would not be long in making the connection with the Shelleys, if she had not already done so. No question: the writing box had to be found at this visit and carried away tonight.

Where was it, then?

A shock awaited him in the room where the wax woman sat on her swing. He actually nodded and was about to say, "Hi." So who's the dummy here? he thought. You, or me? Shaking his head, he got on with the search. Some time later he glared at the wax woman and moved on.

This was getting desperate. The light was going. He was tired, hungry and dispirited.

Then he struck gold. He might so easily have gone past. Folded up and covered in dust, the wooden box would not have attracted the attention of anyone who was not looking specially. It was in use as a plinth for a monstrous black vase big enough to have contained one of the Forty Thieves. To have supported such weight it must have been stoutly constructed. One glance at the side, where the hinged top section met the bottom in a diagonal, convinced Joe. Opened out, it would make the shape of a desk.

Unfortunately there was a problem. The vase. He couldn't get his arms around the thing. Shifting it even an inch was difficult.

He didn't want assistance. His plan was to examine that box in private. The only way of moving the vase was by tipping it on its edge and turning it. He would have to hope it didn't smash in the process.

Placing the copy of Milton on a window ledge behind him, he collected two large cushions from a settee in the next room and arranged them beside the box.

He grasped the rim of the vase, braced himself and hauled it towards him. There was movement. An ominous creak came from the box as the vase shifted off its base. He managed to stop it tipping too far and applied enough force to get it moving sideways. The task now was to drop the thing onto one of the cushions without either cracking it or crushing his feet.

He was not used to manhandling large objects. At first he managed the weight with ease, having found the point of balance. Then as he was rolling it towards the edge, the vase leaned a shade too far towards him. He was forced backwards. Instinctively he tugged at the rim to stop himself falling over. The inevitable happened. The massive shoulder of the pot thumped against his chest. He was powerless to hold it.

Disaster.

He went down.

The vase crashed on the cushion just to his left, missing him narrowly. The broadest part hit the floorboards and smashed. The sound must have carried through the entire building.

He said, "Jeez," and lay still, shocked and winded.

From somewhere downstairs, Peg's voice called out, "What happened?"

Some other visitor to the shop called back superfluously, "Something fell over, I think."

Somebody looked in and asked if Joe was all right. He answered that he was fine. Probably he was, apart from bruises. His elbows hurt and his backside was numb, but he could feel no sharp pain. He sat up, rubbing his left elbow.

The woman at the door said, "It's a wonder this isn't happening all the time, there's so much crammed in."

Joe murmured agreement.

"Are you all right?"

"Hundred per cent." He struggled to his feet and summoned a smile. "Better off than the vase."

"Let's hope it isn't valuable."

"It isn't any more." Quick footsteps sounded on the stairs and Joe had an impulse to grab the precious writing box off the floor and hide it from Peg. He was sure, however, that when she saw the broken vase she would remember what it had been standing on.

He stood like a schoolkid whose baseball has smashed a window, trying to think of some excuse.

Peg arrived. The first thing she said was, "What was it?" The second thing: "Oh, it was you."

"My fault, ma'am," he admitted. "All my fault. Shouldn't have tried to move it. I'll pay for the damage. Is it insured?"

"You're joking, ducky," Peg told him. "I can't afford to insure this lot." Her eyes took in the whole scene. "You found the box, then. I should have remembered it was here."

"Like an idiot, I tried to remove the vase. Was it a special piece?"

"Egyptian," said Peg.

"Oh, my God." Thousands of years of history were lying in pieces at his feet. "How much was it worth?"

"How much is anything worth?" said Peg indifferently. "Only as much as someone is prepared to pay. This has been here for years. Nobody ever made me an offer."

"If it's from Ancient Egypt, some museum would have been glad to own it."

"*Ancient Egypt?*" said Peg. "Who said Ancient Egypt? This only goes back to 1924. It was made for the British Empire Exhibition at Wembley. The Egyptian Pavilion. It's a cheap imitation, ducky. I can live without it."

Deeply relieved, Joe said it was still his fault and he ought to pay compensation.

But Peg was dismissive. "Forget it. Open up the writing box and I'll tell you if it's the one your book was in."

He needed no more encouragement. His hands were shaking, whether from shock or anticipation he didn't know. He felt for the fastening and found it was a brass plate with a lock. "It won't open. Do you have the key?"

Peg rolled her eyes upwards. "Now you're asking."

"You must have had it when you looked inside."

"I'm sure I did, sweetheart. But putting my hands on it now is another thing. I've got a million keys in my office. Finding the right one will be the problem."

He stood up again.

"Why don't you bring the box downstairs?" Peg suggested. "Is that your book on the window sill? I'll hold that for you."

"No, I can manage," Joe said quickly, snatching it up and thrusting it under his arm. "What about this mess?"

"Leave it. I'll get Ellis to clear it later."

Ignoring the twinges in his back, Joe stooped and lifted the writing box with extreme care. It was not so heavy as he expected. He followed Peg through the labyrinth of rooms and down the stairs.

In her hideaway behind the grandfather clocks, she reached
for an old biscuit-tin, and scooped up a handful of small keys
and dropped them on top of her desk. "You don't have to hold it
to your bosom, dearie. Put it here and take your pick."

He did as instructed and wiped away the dust with his sleeve.
The shape of the vase's base was still imprinted.

"Care for a sherry while you try them out?" Peg offered. She
was into her sales pitch now. He was already under an obligation
after breaking the vase.

"Thanks, but I hope it won't take that long," he said. "My
wife is waiting to go out for dinner."

"You Americans eat so early."

Joe started trying keys. This extra delay was almost too much
to endure. Peg poured herself a large Amontillado, grabbed
some more keys from the tin and sat watching. She seemed to be
enjoying the performance. At one point she remarked that she
still couldn't be certain if it was the correct writing box. "I'll tell
you when I see inside."

Joe's hopes were on a higher plane. Secretly he wished for some
incontestable link with Mary Shelley. Maybe some embossed initials, or a sheet of notepaper with something in her handwriting.
Antique writing desks frequently had secret drawers built into
them. Was it too much to hope that he might discover an unpub-
lished love poem by Shelley?

The lock was resisting all his attempts. He could eliminate
some keys at a glance. He had a rough idea of the size he needed.
Some fitted the hole, but none up to now would turn the lock.

Peg put down her glass and provided another handful from
the biscuit tin.

"How many more are there?"

"I don't want to depress you."

"I'd rather know."

"Two more biscuit tins to go," she said. "The Victorians had a thing about security. They locked everything. Bookcases, wardrobes, writing desks, work baskets, sewing machines, even chests of drawers. Put them out on display and you soon lose the blessed keys. Believe me, darling, they're an infernal nuisance. My solution is to keep them all here in boxes."

"Great—if you label them. Or leave the furniture unlocked."

"Don't sound so glum, professor. We're getting there slowly. I couldn't bear to force a fine old piece like this. It's really elegant, isn't it? The wood hasn't been looked after, but it would come up nicely with some polish. This is walnut. Belonged to a lady if I'm any judge. Men's writing boxes are bigger and more robust, reinforced with brass along the edges. Makes you wonder what they did with them. Threw them at the servants, I expect."

Joe's thoughts were strictly in the present. "Suppose you sold me this without the key. How much would you want?"

She took a long, thoughtful sip. "There's no extra charge for the key."

"That isn't what I meant."

"I think we should go on looking."

"But if I run out of time."

Her eyes were pitiless, opaque. "I'm sorry. I can't quote you a price without seeing the inside myself. The finishing is so important."

"I could make you a substantial offer."

She smiled and shook her head. It was becoming obvious that she knew she had a coveted item here.

Joe tried some more keys unsuccessfully. "Would you mind if I called my wife at the hotel?"

"It's over there, on the milk-churn."

The call to Donna would have been difficult under any conditions. With Peg Redbird sitting a couple of feet away (allowing him some privacy had not crossed her mind) it was a minefield.

Donna must have been sitting next to the phone, because she was on the line before Joe heard the ringing tone. The menace she put into the words, "Who is this?" would have petrified a lesser man. Joe's reaction was to unloose words at the speed of a tobacco auctioneer. He told her he was unavoidably detained by an accident in an antique shop that had been his fault. He was not hurt, but there was some damage to property and he wanted to put matters right before leaving. He guessed he would be back inside the half-hour and if she cared to call a restaurant of her choice and book a table for two he would make it up to her.

He should have put down the phone immediately. The delay allowed Donna to start. Her delivery was no slower than Joe's. It was a marvel her teeth stayed in. She let him know that she had been expecting him back each minute for the past two hours and as for putting matters right, he had better think about putting them right with his own wife. After the stress she'd been under, she expected something a damned sight better than a meal out. And soon.

He promised to leave at once and dropped the phone as if it was red hot.

Peg said, "It sounds serious."

"It's getting that way. Look, would you let me buy the box now and take it back to my hotel? I'll get a locksmith to open it without damaging the lock."

She shook her head. "Sorry, my pet. I'm not selling without seeing inside it."

"You understand my problem. My wife is expecting me."

"Would she let you come back later and try some more keys?"

"Don't you close the store now?"

"I've got to wait for Ellis with the van. He's collecting some furniture I bought today. We'll be here until midnight, I should think, trying to make space." She smiled. "You helped."

"Really? I don't know how."

"The vase."

He said he was sure to be back by ten. He picked up Mary Shelley's book.

Peg said she would carry on trying to unlock the writing box.

A thought struck Joe. "You wouldn't force it while I was away?"

"Ducky, you weren't listening. I wouldn't damage that box for all the tea in China."

Now a worse thought struck him, a sudden strong suspicion that Peg had known all along where to find the key and was only waiting for him to leave.

twelve

THE SMELL OF DAMP, ancient stone and the cool of the
night were marvellously suggestive, transporting him to the
vaults and charnel-houses Frankenstein had visited in pursuit of
the secret of life. "*One secret which I alone possessed was the hope
to which I had dedicated myself; and the moon gazed on my midnight
labours, while, with unrelaxed and breathless eagerness, I pursued
nature to her hiding-places.*"

Unlike Frankenstein, he was untroubled by the horrors. He
embraced them eagerly.

thirteen

WHEN IT BECAME OBVIOUS that the television people would not let up, Diamond agreed to record an interview for BBC *Newsnight* that meant a drive to Bristol for a link-up with London. He got to the studio around six-thirty. They powdered his bald patch in Make-Up—"topped, if not tailed," as they put it—and then he found himself in front of a camera facing a famous talking head on a monitor. Usually he relished watching politicians ducking and diving under fire from Jeremy Paxman. Being on the receiving end was a different experience. Tonight he didn't much like what he saw of this formidable interrogator. If the lush crop of dark hair wasn't provocation enough for a bald man, the smile that came with the questions was.

"You seem to have got yourself an unusual case down there in Bath, Superintendent. What's all this about *Frankenstein*?"

Diamond replied dourly that he didn't have anything to say about *Frankenstein*.

"That's rather odd if I may say so because according to the evening papers, you're digging up bits of human anatomy in the cellar of the house where *Frankenstein* was written."

"That may be so," said Diamond, already wishing he had not agreed to do this.

"There's no 'may be' about it, Superintendent. Either it's the *Frankenstein* cellar, or it isn't. Have you read Mary Shelley's book?"

He admitted that he had not.

"Better get hold of a copy, hadn't you?"

"I've got more important things to do."

Paxman pricked up his eyebrows in a way familiar from years of *Newsnights*. Talking to a TV screen was a new experience for Diamond and concentration was difficult.

"You're familiar with the story, anyway—how Frankenstein put together this creature from spare parts gathered from dissecting-rooms and tombs?"

"I should think everyone has heard of it."

"And you won't deny that you're finding bones down there?"

"The bones have got nothing to do with *Frankenstein*," Diamond insisted.

"So can you reveal exclusively on *Newsnight* that he isn't a suspect?" The lips curved a fraction, in case any viewer had not picked up the irony.

"He's fiction, as far as I know."

"Well, that's good news for nervous viewers. What about the monster?"

Diamond felt he had endured enough of this. "I'm speaking to him, aren't I?"

There was an awkward moment when nothing was said. Then: "*Touché*, Mr Diamond. Bath Police are well on the case, by the sound of things." Paxman glanced at his notes. "You're quoted as saying you could find hundreds more bones in this vault."

He knew that remark would be turned against him. "It's over a churchyard."

"Over a churchyard?" Just one of the eyebrows popped up. "While you're catching up on your reading, you'd better look at *Dracula* as well. He could easily come into this."

"It wouldn't surprise me—if you people have your way."

"If you don't mind me saying, you sound slightly disenchanted by all the attention, Superintendent."

"I'm trying to keep it sensible, that's all."

"That's a pious hope I should think. Is there any way we can help?"

"Am I allowed to be serious for a moment?"

A smile.

"We're keen to interview anyone who worked on the Pump Room extension—which is over this vault—in the period 1982 to 1983."

"Archaeologists? Construction workers?"

"Anyone at all. Any information will be treated in confidence." He gave the Bath number.

"There you have it, then," Jeremy Paxman said to camera. "Don't call us, call the Bath Police. We'll display the number at the end."

In Make-Up, they wiped away the powder and told him he deserved a medal.

"What for?"

"You gave as good as you got. No one's ever called him a monster."

"I expect he thrives on it," said Diamond. "They'll edit that bit out."

"No, they won't. It was good television."

Wearily, he returned to his car and cruised around the city's infuriating one-way system looking for the route to Bath. He always got it wrong. At one stage, trying to read the directions, he drove through a red light. It was a pedestrian crossing and nobody was in the way, but with a sense of inevitability he saw in his mirror the pulsing blue beacon of a police car. They overtook him and forced him to stop.

"This is all I need," he told the young officer whose head appeared at the window.

"Superintendent Diamond?"

"You know me?"

"We were under orders to find you, sir. You're asked to make contact with Bath CID."

"That's why you stopped me?"

The young man grinned. "Well, it wasn't to ask the way."

Revived, he got out and ambled across to the patrol car to use their radio. Keith Halliwell answered the call.

"What's this—overtime?" Diamond asked, chirpy again.

"I've been trying to reach you, sir. You were supposed to get a message at the TV studio. We had a call from the lab at Chepstow earlier. They found something."

"What's that?"

"In the bits of concrete that came with the hand bones, they chipped out a piece of metal shaped into a skull."

"Full size?"

"No. Really small. Like a badge. This was curved, so they assume it was attached to a ring originally. You can see where it broke at the back."

"A ring? What are we talking about here? The kind of thing kids wear?"

"Yes. Cheap metal."

"In the shape of a skull, you said?"

"An animal skull, like a bull, but with large teeth sticking up, as far as the eyes."

"Motorhead."

"I'm sorry?" said Halliwell.

"You should be," Diamond chided him. "Don't you remember Heavy Metal?"

"Would you say that again, sir? I'm getting some static."

Diamond rolled his eyes at the young officer beside him. "He's getting some static. Rock music in the seventies, Keith. The animal skull with the teeth was the Motorhead emblem. Your musical education is sadly lacking. Where were you—at the ballet?"

"I was just a baby."

"Oh, yes?"

"The point is, sir, the ring could have broken when the body was dismembered. It may have belonged to the victim."

"Where's the rest of it, then? Shouldn't it be with the bones?"

"The killer could have removed it from the victim's hand, thinking it would help identify the corpse."

"Equally, it could have belonged to the killer and snapped off when he was doing his grisly work."

"His what, sir?"

"Never mind, Keith. You can knock off now."

He said goodnight to the patrol team, ambled across to his own car and drove home thinking it had not been such a bad day's work. Starting off with no more than a few bones to investigate, he was ending up with a mental picture of someone: probably young, in leathers and jeans, long-haired, a rocker. Rightly or wrongly, victim or killer, this had to be progress.

Then he remembered the ACC's 'At Home'. He would never make it there by eight. Steph would be sitting at home, dressed and ready to go. He'd better get to a phone.

NOT LONG after Joe left Noble and Nude, Ellis Somerset returned with the vanload of antiques from Si Minchendon's house in Camden Crescent.

Peg helped unload. To be precise, she unloaded the two pictures. The rest she left for Ellis to move.

She had been on tenterhooks to inspect those pictures. There could be no question that they were watercolours in William Blake's style, with the strange, archaic look his drawing had acquired from making hundreds of studies of medieval tombs during his apprenticeship as an engraver. They were essentially graphic illustrations in quill and ink, using the colour mainly as tint, rather than to indicate form. But the subjects of the pictures, if Peg's interpretation was correct, were not recorded anywhere. On her way back from Camden Place she had called at Bath Library and looked at the major biographies of Blake by Peter Ackroyd and David Erdman;

neither made any mention that he had illustrated Mary Shelley's *Frankenstein*.

She was sure in her mind that they could represent nothing else. The first had to be the frozen valley of Chamonix, with Mont Blanc "in awful majesty" as a backdrop for the meeting between Frankenstein and the creature he had brought to life. The figures facing each other differed markedly in physique, the one a mere man, puny beside the abhorred monster, who was unlike the Hollywood version, but faithful to Mary Shelley's concept: yellow skin thinly covering the muscles and arteries, lustrous black hair, pearly white teeth, black lips and watery, dun-white eyes.

In the second picture, the same grotesque face was staring through the window of the inn where Frankenstein's bride Elizabeth lay strangled on her wedding night. The gloating, grinning monster was mocking Frankenstein. What other interpretation could anyone make?

Peg had worked long enough in the antiques trade to know that synchronicity occurs from time to time in a quite eerie fashion. So she was not troubled that Mary Shelley had cropped up in another context the same day. It was not mere coincidence, nor entirely the mysterious working of fate. With the idea of Frankenstein already planted in her mind, she would have been alert to anything in Simon Minchendon's house that made connection with the story.

Were the pictures genuine? Blake had been so prolific, despite failing health towards the end, that no one could be certain how many unrecorded works had survived. *Frankenstein* was published in 1818. Blake would certainly have known of the book; he was illustrating and engraving to the end of his life in 1827. The theme of the novel would have found a resonance with his hatred of perverted science.

Peg decided there was only one way to find out. Using a penknife, she cut into the already disintegrating brown paper backing one of the frames. Methodically she prised out the rusty pins and removed the board that held the picture against the glass. The age of the mount and frame was of no importance, but did the drawing paper pass the test? Was it almost two hundred years old?

With extreme care, she lifted out the painting and studied it. Certainly the paper smelt old. There was foxing at the edges, which were rough and fraying. She was not an expert on the age of paper, but her knowledge of antiques of all sorts gave her a pretty reliable sense of what was genuinely old. This, she decided without wishful thinking, could safely be placed in the first two decades of the nineteenth century.

Nothing was written on the reverse. A faker will often try too hard and add some embellishment to bring extra conviction.

She performed a similar dissection of the second frame and mount. No further clues were revealed.

"I'm all fired up, Ellis. You know whose work this is, don't you?"

"They're not signed," he pointed out.

"That's no guide, ducky. Blake often left his work unsigned. These look to me like studies for engravings. He did thousands." She smiled. "Well, it would have been nice in a way if there was a signature, but then I would never have got them so cheap."

"Are you sure they're kosher?"

"What's your opinion?" Holding it delicately by the edge to avoid marking it with her dusty fingers, she handed him the exterior scene.

"You think this is Frankenstein and the monster?"

"It's the core of the book, their meeting in the shadow of Mont Blanc. The monster has strangled Frankenstein's young brother, the child William, and the servant Justine has been hanged for the crime."

"It's a long time since I read the story," Somerset admitted.

"I've seen plenty of films, of course, but we all know the liberties they take."

"Take it from me, this is straight out of the book. No liberties at all."

He held the picture at arm's length. "Blake and Mary Shelley? I've never linked them in my mind before."

Peg said, "I did some checking this afternoon. He collaborated with Mary Wollstonecraft, Mary Shelley's mother. She wrote some rather indifferent stories for children and dear old Blake illustrated them. So there is a link, in a way."

"What will you do with them? Is there a space on the wall anywhere?"

She shook her head. "People come here looking for bargains, and these are something else. I've got an arrangement under way."

"A dealer?"

"Get away." With a mysterious smile, she held out her hands to take back the precious painting.

"You know someone?"

"Someone who will want these."

"Who's that? A collector?"

"Big game, darling. The rare beast we all pursue, a party who really must buy. The entire trade depends on people like them."

"Aren't you going to tell me?"

She gave him a skittish look. "I may—after I've had my bit of fun."

"You're being mean to me, Peg."

"This is the jungle, ducky."

"Local?"

"Oh, yes," she said, "I've been on the phone. I'm expecting an offer tonight, if that doesn't sound indelicate."

Ellis looked away, pink-faced. A vein was throbbing in his neck.

* * *

DONNA HAD not, after all, booked for a meal. She was old-fashioned enough to believe restaurant reservations ought to be made by men. She wouldn't enjoy her dinner if the waiters knew she had made the phone call.

Joe came in and, typical Joe, gushed apologies like a man who had just walked into a ladies' changing-room. He went on to claim confidently that when she heard the reason why he had neglected her for so long, she would not only understand, she would throw her arms around him and give him the biggest kiss ever. Donna doubted that.

Worse, he suggested they had room service. He would order champagne and caviar as well, he offered.

"Why?" said Donna, keeping herself under control with difficulty. "Why don't we go out?"

"It's getting late, honey. We don't want to walk the streets looking for a place with a free table. I can't wait to tell you what happened. Shall I call room service?"

They walked the streets looking for a place with a free table. To be exact, they walked as far as Brock Street, a mere three minutes from the hotel, and found a table straight away in a quiet restaurant.

Joe launched into his account of the trail that led to Mary Shelley's writing box.

"How do you know it's hers?" Donna said, as yet feeling no urge to throw her arms around Joe.

"It's got to be. I've got a feeling about this."

"I've got a feeling this woman saw you coming. She's running rings around you, Joe Dougan. You show her the book and she sees a chance to unload an old box on you. If it was Mary Shelley's, where's the sense in using it as a stand for a heavy vase?"

He opened his palms to emphasise the simple logic. "She didn't know it was Mary Shelley's. This is the whole point,

Donna. And there's a very good chance that I'll get the proof when the box is opened. There could be other things inside."

"Like Mary Shelley's credit cards?"

"Oh, come on."

"You said she claims to have found the book inside the box."

"That's right. And a sketchbook that she sold. That's more evidence."

"It's not if she doesn't have it any more."

"No, listen. While Mary Shelley was staying in five, Abbey Churchyard, she was having drawing lessons from a a teacher called West. That's on record. She wrote in a letter to Leigh Hunt about finishing a picture she regarded as tedious and ugly. Oh, boy, I'd love to find that sketchbook."

"Joe."

"Honey?"

"I've had it up to here with Mary Shelley."

"Sure," he soothed her. "I can understand why. Listen, tomorrow let's do something totally unconnected with *Frankenstein*."

"Such as?"

Conveniently for Joe, someone had pinned some tourist leaflets to the wall behind Donna, and over her shoulder Joe could just read the large print. "I thought we might take a bus-trip somewhere. They do excursions to all kinds of places. How would you like to see Wilton House, where the Earl of Pembroke lives?"

"Is it open to the public?"

"Sure. I wouldn't mention it if not."

Donna melted a little. "I'll think it over."

"After tonight," said Joe rashly, "we'll draw a line under Mary Shelley."

"Thank God."

He looked at his watch. "There's only one more thing I need to do this evening, and that's go back to Noble and Nude and see if she found the key to the box."

Donna was lost for words.

*   *   *

IT WAS after eight when Diamond got back from the TV studios at Bristol. He'd phoned Stephanie, knowing she was sure to be uneasy about turning up late to the 'At Home'. She hated being late for things.

"You can afford to make an entrance in that terrific dress," he said with conviction. He'd had time to prepare a rallying speech on the drive back from Bristol. And it *was* a classy dress, a floral print in some silky material, worn with a shiny black belt. "In fact, it demands to be noticed. I like it. By God, I don't know where you found it, but it's a smashing little number."

Without a trace of acrimony in her voice Steph informed him that she'd found it in her wardrobe. If it demanded to be noticed, he should have noticed it last Christmas Day, when her sister came, and last April at the charity do at the Theatre Royal. Then she returned to her main concern. "Your boss could be waiting to serve the food."

"I don't think it's that kind of do," he told her airily. "It'll be cheap Bulgarian wine and peanuts in little silver dishes." He said he would freshen up and change into some party gear.

"Snap it up, then, Peter. It's going to be close to nine by the time we arrive."

"Georgina will have to make allowances. I was on police business."

They managed to get to the house in Bennett Street within the half-hour.

"Good. You're here," said their hostess. Out of uniform and in a blue cashmere dress she looked more approachable, but hadn't discarded the parade ground manner. "I was just about to serve the supper." She shook Stephanie's hand and said she was fascinated to meet the wife of Peter Diamond.

The wife of Peter Diamond was made to feel more like an exhibit than a person, though probably no slight was intended.

Steph managed a sociable smile while Diamond explained the reason for their delay. He wasn't sure how to address the ACC in this setting, so he started with "Ma'am".

"*Newsnight?* Who interviewed you?" Unexpectedly the ACC's voice piped in excitement, "Don't tell me you met Jeremy himself, my all-time favourite television presenter? You did. I can see it in your eyes. I can't possibly miss that! What time do they show it—ten-thirty? We'll switch on and let everyone have a goggle."

"Ma'am—"

She flapped her hand. "You don't have to be formal . . . Peter. It's Georgina tonight."

"Understood," said Diamond. "About *Newsnight*, Georgina. I don't know if that's such a good idea."

The advice wasn't heard. Georgina had rushed away to serve the supper.

With Diamond blanching at the prospect of people being ordered to watch that mortifying interview, he and Stephanie started the process of meeting other guests. Rarely had so many local bigwigs been gathered in one small space. Directly ahead, the Chief Crown Prosecutor was in serious conversation with the two other ACCs. "Not that way," Diamond murmured to Steph. "Go right."

"Straight for the blonde in the corner?" said Stephanie. "The story of your life."

"At least it's someone I don't have to say 'sir' to."

"Don't be so sure. Wait till Blondie turns round."

But it *was* a woman. Ingeborg Smith gave a wide smile of recognition and said, "Hi, you're late." She was in a black sparkly outfit that left one shoulder and a good deal of leg exposed.

Diamond had the feeling this was one of those nights that would sear his soul for ever. He stumbled through the introductions, stressing—without actually nudging Steph—that Ingeborg was a freelance reporter. Ingeborg laughed and said she wasn't on duty now.

"I'm forgetting," he said. "You know our hostess through the choir." To Stephanie he explained that Ingeborg sang with the Bath Camerata. "I'll get you ladies a drink," he offered.

"I'm being looked after," Ingeborg said at once. "A gorgeous man called John Sturr is fetching me a refill from the other room. I think I've struck gold. He's on the Police Authority."

Diamond winced. "Councillor Sturr?"

"Councillor? I don't think anyone stands on ceremony here."

He turned to Stephanie, "Ingeborg won't want us around when her friend comes back. Let's head towards the drinks ourselves."

"Go for it, guys," Ingeborg cheerfully urged them. "You've got some catching up to do. It's bubbly—the real thing. I don't know how many I've put away."

The food was served soon after from a huge table in the dining room.

Georgina had lashed out on an amazing array of exotic dishes and was helpfully explaining to the more wary guests how to tell a spicy Chicken Tikka from a milder Kashmiri concoction. Steph, knowing Diamond's tendency to panic in the presence of foreign food, took his arm and steered him firmly past the multicoloured sauces to a tray of dishes topped with mashed potato, with steamed vegetables nearby.

"So much for my forecast," Diamond murmured.

"I did wonder where the peanuts were," Steph murmured back.

Besides helping people to food, Georgina was waving them outside to the patio, where they could sit at garden tables. The warmth of the day was lingering nicely. The Diamonds found places with a couple they didn't know who introduced themselves as Danny and Karen. "Better than a barbecue, this," Diamond said, to start a conversation. "Burnt things on skewers taste all the same to me."

"I know just what you mean about barbecues," said Danny. "This is recognisable food."

"Marks and Spencer."

"Peter, you've *got* to be a detective," said Karen. "How do you know that?"

"Can you prove it?" said Danny.

"We could check the kitchen for empty packets."

"Oh, Pete!" said Steph. She explained, "If he doesn't get his M & S shepherd's pie at least once a week, he isn't safe to be with."

"I'm still impressed," said Karen.

"Don't take my word for it," said Diamond. "You ought to check."

"No need," said Karen. "I believe you absolutely. Nothing gets past our lads in CID."

Diamond was beginning to like Karen. "I'll let you into a secret," he said, with exaggerated glances right and left before leaning confidentially forward and dropping his voice. "Outside the nick in Manvers Street we've got some tubs of flowers. Have you ever noticed them?"

Karen nodded.

Diamond nodded, too. "We lads in CID pass them hundreds of times a week. Not one of us spotted some extra foliage among the pansies. It took a member of the public to tell us we had a fine crop of cannabis growing in front of the central police station. Some joker had scattered cannabis seeds in there. That's how smart our lads in CID are."

"Is that true?" said Danny.

"Gospel truth." Diamond tapped the side of his nose. "Keep it to yourselves. We don't want our new boss to find out."

They talked on for a while before he asked Danny how long he had known Georgina.

"Only since I took over as Chair of the Police Authority," said Danny.

The food didn't taste so good after that. The Diamonds made

an excuse and went back inside the house. "God, I'd like to escape," he told Steph. "What time is it?"

"Twenty to ten. We can't," she said. "We've got to wait for the TV programme."

"That!"

"Did something go wrong?"

"Only that I called Georgina's pin-up a monster."

"Oh, Pete!"

"It was said in jest."

"Sometimes when you say things in jest they sound horribly serious."

"That's what bothers me."

The next fifty minutes went slowly. It was the kind of party when people said, "Isn't this fun?" whilst glancing furtively at their watches. Georgina flitted from group to group promising a surprise item at ten-thirty.

Across the room, Ingeborg's voice was showing the effects of the champagne. She seemed to be the only one enjoying herself, except John Sturr, her escort, who had his hand draped around her shoulder. They looked like gatecrashers from another party, Sturr with his lounge lizard looks and Ingeborg all legs and glitter.

Eventually Georgina began suggesting people move into the room where the TV was set up. "What are we in for?" one of the Assistant Chief Constables asked Diamond. "A blue movie?"

"Just blokes, I think."

"Really? What a bore."

Diamond drifted out of the room while the interview was transmitted and helped himself to a large scotch. By ten-forty, his bit of the show was over. Immediately after, people started making excuses and leaving. It was not really a response to the interview, more an opportunity made by the change in the pattern of the party.

Among the first through the front door were Sturr and Ingeborg, but not before the councillor asked Diamond sarcastically if it was safe on the streets of Bath tonight.

"Why—do you want a police escort?" Diamond asked.

Ingeborg giggled, clinging to Sturr's arm. "Thanks for the offer, darling, but I'm a simple lass. Two's company."

Sturr told her, "Anyway, Mr Diamond should be back at Manvers Street taking all the phone calls from his television audience."

"That's what lower ranks are for," said Diamond. "I'm off to my bed."

"I'VE SEEN worse things on the box," Stephanie assured him when they got home.

"I get brassed off with all the *Frankenstein* nonsense."

"That was obvious from your face. Television is very revealing."

"The young woman in Make-Up said I deserved a medal, but she was biased."

"Oh?"

"She thought me rather sexy."

Steph threw an oven glove at him. "Are you getting anywhere at all with this case?"

He held up his hand and showed a tiny space between his thumb and forefinger. "To be honest, I was hoping to put it on the back burner. It happened so long ago. But now it's in the headlines I'm not allowed to ignore it."

"What have you got so far, apart from the hands in the vault?"

"The very latest is that forensic have found an interesting relic in the bits of concrete from the vault: a Motorhead emblem that seems to have been part of a ring."

"You're talking about that rock group?"

"Heavy Metal. Remember?"

"When we married, you still had most of their LPs. You were nuts about them. And Black Sabbath."

"Black Sabbath . . . Lord help us," he reminisced. "Iron

Maiden. God, I was going about in a black bomber jacket when I was past thirty."

"I should have spotted a case of retarded development."

He let that pass. "Motorhead. It's easy to talk about fifteen or twenty years ago, but it takes a find like this to give you a sense of how long ago it was."

"So was your victim a Heavy Metal freak?"

"It's got to be considered. The victim or the perpetrator, or both."

"A gang killing?"

"I doubt it. Rockers had a tough reputation, but it didn't often run to murder."

"Especially not in Bath."

He gave a tired smile. "I picture this as a dust-up between two labourers on the site. We're trying to trace people who worked there at the time."

"You made that very clear on television."

"Well, I hope it jogs someone's memory. We don't have many names so far."

"It's all very bizarre," said Steph.

"What is?"

"The link with Mary Shelley and *Frankenstein*. How did the press get onto it?"

"The first I heard was some reporter from the *News of the World*."

"But who tipped them off?"

"Does it matter?" He was uninterested, or appeared so. Then he shifted his head abruptly, like a thrush detecting a movement under the ground. "Maybe it does."

AT TEN past two in the morning, long after the calls from the *Nationwide* audience had dwindled to nothing, a 999 call was routed to Bath Central Police Station. It was put through to the senior officer on duty that night, Inspector George Flynn. The caller had an American accent, and was clearly agitated.

"I need your help. I'm a guest at the Royal Crescent Hotel. My wife is missing."

"Your name, sir?" Flynn asked.

"Dougan. Professor Joseph Dougan. I'm on vacation here with my wife Donna. I've been waiting for her since before midnight. She ought to be here. I've been right through the hotel, all the public rooms, I mean. I've had the staff make a search. She isn't here."

"When did you last see her, sir?"

"Middle of the evening. Eight-thirty, nine, something like that. We had dinner out. I walked her back to the hotel, saw her right up to our suite, then I had to go out. I was back by eleven-thirty. No sign of Donna. I went downstairs and across to the Dower House to see if she was in the bar, or something. No one remembered seeing her. So I went back to our room to wait. Nothing. This isn't like her. This is the middle of the night and my wife is missing. I want you to find her, please."

"Right, sir, two of our officers will be with you shortly. Are you speaking from your hotel room?"

"The John Wood suite."

"Stay where you are and they'll meet you there."

"Listen, I want you to get on the job, find Donna. There's no sense in wasting time talking to me."

"Professor, we need a description."

"Okay, okay. Just be quick. I have a bad feeling about this."

After the line went dead, Flynn spoke to the switchboard operator. "Did we get that on tape?"

"Yes, sir."

"Keep it. And send a car up to the Royal Crescent to get the full story. Professor Joseph Dougan. He said he has a bad feeling about this. So do I."

fourteen

THE MORNING PAPERS HAD gone bananas about human remains found in a cellar they called Frankenstein's vault. Here, in Bath.

He read every word with grim fascination. The press cynically mixed fact and fiction, severed hands, decapitation and Frankenstein. There was stuff about the miles of vaults under the city. No one with a cellar would sleep easy until the killer was arrested, his paper said—as if Mary Shelley's monster was alive and out for blood, living the life of a rat and coming up to kill at nights.

They had no conception.

fifteen

AS USUAL, FROM EARLY on Friday, people were staring over the parapet on Grand Parade, watching the water flow over the weir—a flight of broad, shallow steps in an elegant inverted horseshoe tapered at the ends. Even when the current is slow, as it was this day in August after a week without much rain, the patterns created in the foam are worth a few minutes of anyone's time.

The watchers will notice anything floating towards the weir. After heavy rain, there can be quite an accumulation of broken foliage and driftwood caught on the rim, waiting to tip over. In these conditions, however, all was sublimely clear until twenty to eleven, when an object more like a bundle of fabric than driftwood glided slowly down the Avon from the Walcot stretch. For a time it lodged unnoticed against one of the piers under the bridge. Then a small fluctuation in the current allowed it to ease free and float sedately towards the first of the descending steps.

Of all the people watching—and there must have been thirty or more ranged along Grand Parade—none noticed that the bundle was human in origin until it reached the lip of the weir. There, its form appeared to divide. A narrow portion flopped over the edge and hung, still attached, causing foam to fan out on the level below. The overhanging part was a sleeve and it was not an empty sleeve. At the end was a white hand.

The sightseers were more horrified than alarmed. It was obvious that the body was lifeless. Somebody went to look for a police officer, and found a traffic warden, who called the police. The crowd along the parapet increased.

Soon they saw two policemen in waders walk out along the edge of the weir to investigate. One of them stooped and grasped the body. For a second, the head was lifted clear of the water, a lily-white face with gaping mouth.

One of the crowd said, "It's a woman, poor soul."

The face was lowered again.

The police seemed uncertain what to do. Normally they would leave a body in the place where it was found for the scene of crime team and the forensic pathologist to inspect. In this situation there was a clear risk of its tipping over the weir and being carried downstream.

The two officers returned to the side for instructions. More senior policemen had arrived. A consultation followed, dominated by a man in plain clothes with a large moustache. After what seemed an age, a decision was taken, for the two in waders stepped out to the centre again and took a firm hold on the body and lifted it. One was unbalanced by the weight and lost his footing. He sank to his knees. His companion, trying to help, let go of his burden, stretched forward, stumbled over the corpse and fell face down into the water. The spectacle had its black humour that certain of the onlookers found amusing. The majority watched in silence.

In this undignified way, with several more stumbles, the body was dragged and carried around the arc of the weir to dry land, where it was placed on a stretcher, covered with a sheet of black plastic and loaded into a van.

The two officers in wet clothes got into a police car and were driven away. The van containing the corpse remained. Nothing more happened for twenty minutes. The watchers began to lose interest. A number of them left.

Down beside the undertaker's van, the CID officer with the moustache, John Wigfull, was assessing the situation. He hated dealing with anything that departed from routine procedures.

Already those two buffoons sent to retrieve the body had made the police into a laughing-stock. His preference was to get away from here as soon as possible, but it took him some time to reach the decision. He had to satisfy himself that this was not the sort of incident requiring a search for evidence at the place where the body was found. The water would have carried any traces well downstream by now. The body had been seen floating towards the weir, so it must have entered the water higher up the river. To call a pathologist to the weir would surely be a waste of time.

Just to be sure he had missed nothing, he climbed into the van for a final look at the body, forced into closer proximity than he really wanted. So far as he could judge when he lifted the plastic covering, the victim had not been in the water for more than a few hours. She was small, even girlish in stature, with dark, bobbed hair. She appeared middle-aged, maybe in her forties, allowing that no one looks in the bloom of youth after drowning. Plain white blouse, black skirt and dark tights. No shoes. No evidence of violence other than superficial marks consistent with being in the river. Remembering that many suicides are drugs-related, he examined her arms for injection scars and found none.

Outside, he told the driver to take the body to the mortuary. Then he mopped his forehead, got into his own car and drove away.

DIAMOND DEVOTED the morning to Hands, as he had now dubbed the owner of the bones found in the vault. The case couldn't be soft-pedalled any longer. Two of the tabloids had splashed the story across their front pages that morning and even the most solemn broadsheet papers had covered it some-where. He'd been forced to run the gauntlet of mikes when he'd arrived for work.

At least there was something promising to work on: the

Motorhead emblem. It was a fair assumption that either the victim or his killer had worn it.

"Talk to every one of the builders you traced, Keith," he told Halliwell. "See if they remember a Heavy Metal freak who worked on the Roman Baths extension. It may be a name they supplied already, or someone they remember now, or just a face they can't put a name to."

His appeal for information on *Newsnight* had brought in over fifty calls, and he had a small team sorting the wheat from the chaff. The ratio of useful information was about one to twenty, if that, but they all had to be taken seriously. After a first sifting, he followed up on anything even faintly promising.

And something did emerge. Towards mid-day, he found himself talking to a retired plasterer in Winchester who had worked on the site for about five weeks in 1982. Retired, yes, but encouragingly all there. He reeled off a string of names, several that tallied with the list Halliwell had compiled.

Diamond wrote them all down, and found himself slipping into precisely the sort of shorthand he had mocked Halliwell for: *Barham, talkative, ex-Korean War; Sims, short, snooker; Page, fancy rats; Andy, , , ? nervous dyspepsia; Marshall, white Anglia* . . . More than a dozen altogether.

"Is that the lot?"

"It's all I can think of now. I was only there a few weeks, chum."

"Was there anyone interested in rock music?"

"You want a lot for your money."

"Heavy Metal."

"Most of the young blokes, I reckon."

"So was there anyone who wore a Motorhead ring?"

"Motorhead?"

"Their trademark was the skull of a bull, with two big canine teeth."

After a pause came the statement that would transform the

case. "There *was* someone with a ring like that. He didn't last long."

"What do you mean? He left?"

"Didn't turn up for work one day. They was casual labour, a lot of them blokes. They got a better offer and jacked in the job."

"You didn't see him again?"

"That's right."

Diamond's hand tightened on the phone. "Do you remember his name?"

He barely took time to think. "No. That's gone."

"Would you try, please?"

"Give me a break, guvnor. It was getting on for twenty years ago."

"Even so."

"Can't help. Sorry."

"Anything about him? What was his trade?"

"Trade? I told you he wasn't a tradesman. General labourer, most like. An overgrown kid. Scruffy hair. You know, rats' tails. Didn't wash it much, or didn't appear to. Brown leather jacket. The reason I remember the ring is he was real proud of it. Any time we had a tea break, he'd be sitting admiring it, turning it round on his finger, tapping his heel at the same time, like he could hear the music in his head. He didn't talk much. These days he'd have one of them Walkman things, wouldn't he?"

"This is someone young?"

"Twenty. Not much over."

"And he left suddenly?"

"He wasn't the only one. Other kids gave up. There were all sorts, and some of them wasn't suited to the work. Students, school-leavers."

"Was he a student?"

"I doubt it. No, he wasn't no brain."

"A loner?"

"I wouldn't say that. Now wait a bit. He had an oppo." The

voice grew more animated. "This is coming back now. We used to call them Banger and Mash."

"Any reason?"

"Banger. Head-banger, I suppose. Kids who go in for that rock music, right?"

"What about Mash?"

"Well, Banger and Mash. Geddit?"

Diamond would forgive this man anything. "Was there any other reason for calling him Mash?"

"Not that I can think of. Except a Masher is a kind of ladies' man, isn't he?"

"Was he?"

"Search me."

"Can you describe him, this Mash?"

"It's so long ago. I've got a feeling he kept himself cleaner than Banger, fancied his looks a bit. No, I'm probably guessing now. You'd better forget what I just told you."

Nothing would be forgotten from this productive conversation. "After Banger stopped coming, did Mash carry on working?"

"Couldn't tell you. I was on a short contract myself. I left soon after."

"Did you come across either of them again, on other jobs?"

"No. Never saw 'em again."

"You said they were oppos. Did they spend time together outside work?"

"I've no idea, mate."

"If they had these nicknames," Diamond persisted, "it suggests they were thought of as a pair."

"They could have been stuck on a job together, couldn't they?" the old plasterer said. "Sometimes you get put to work with some bloke you never met, and before you know it, everyone's treating you like a double act."

"You think that's more likely?"

"I saw them shovelling wet cement out of a barrow. They must have been teamed up for that."

Diamond gripped the phone and leaned forward as if he was face to face with his informant. "They actually worked with cement?"

"I keep telling you they was general labourers. They had no trade. They was put to carting the cement across to the brickies, I reckon."

No more of any use emerged, though Diamond continued to try. Finally, he thanked the plasterer, and asked him to get in touch if anything else surfaced in his memory.

Progress. A Motorhead fan *and* his workmate. The cement squad.

He told Halliwell the salient bits. "I won't say we're closing in, Keith, but we're on the move now."

"How do we keep on moving?"

"By cross-checking. We go back to your contractors and all the others you traced and see if any of them have memories of Banger and Mash. More important, can they put a name to them?" He stood up and pushed his chair under the desk.

"You said 'we'?"

"And I meant you." He put a hand on Halliwell's shoulder. "My oppo."

DOWNSTAIRS IN an interview room, John Wigfull was face to face with the American professor whose wife had disappeared. It was apparent that Joe Dougan had not yet heard that the woman's body had been taken from the Avon. Either that, or he was giving the impression he knew nothing of it. Wigfull was doing his best to keep an open mind, but keeping an open mind didn't alter a fact well known to criminologists: that most murders are committed within the family.

"I don't understand it," said Joe with some conviction. "I

reported this at two in the morning. You've been on the case twelve hours. Where is she?" To do him credit, he looked and sounded like a man in anguish. He had bluish bags under his red-lidded eyes and his face had sprouted overnight stubble.

Wigfull handled him calmly. No one was better at taking the heat out of a stressful situation. "I can assure you, professor, we put out a missing person report directly. I checked that. Can I just go over the description with you?"

"We did that in the night."

"Yes, sir, but you were in a state of shock. You may have missed something out." Wigfull picked up a copy of the description that had been circulated. "Looking at this, you did miss something. You didn't say what she was wearing, apart from a cream-coloured Burberry raincoat."

"I can't tell you what else she had on," said Joe.

"You must have seen what she was wearing earlier that evening. You had a meal out with her."

"I honestly don't remember. I don't look at her clothes. I can tell you what she said, how she was looking, what she had to eat."

Wigfull found himself insensitively thinking that what she had to eat might be of some use to the pathologist. "Didn't they go through the wardrobe with you?"

"Sure, but I couldn't help them. Call me an airhead if you like, but I don't know what she brought with her."

Wigfull sighed. It is a sad fact that a majority of men, if caught unprepared, cannot tell you what their wives are wearing. "Does she have any distinguishing marks?"

Joe Dougan frowned. "Birthmarks, you mean?"

"Tattoos."

"Donna?"

"Operation scars, vaccinations?"

"Why do you need this? She's not going to show anyone her appendix scar."

"So she has one?"

"I think so, but I don't see . . ." He turned paler. Panic threatened. "You mean she could be lying somewhere?"

Wigfull was not ready to tell all. "It's got to be considered when someone is missing this long. Has she ever done anything like this before?"

"No, sir, she has not."

It was wise to move on swiftly. "I'd like to go over your movements last evening, professor. After eating out, you returned to the Royal Crescent Hotel with your wife between eight-thirty and nine, and then you left her. You went out again."

"So I left her at the hotel. She's a grown-up. She's able to be on her own for an hour," Joe pointed out.

"Where did you go?"

"To an antiques store on Walcot Street. Noble and Nude. I was there earlier. I promised to come back."

"The shop was open as late as that?"

"The lady was taking in furniture. She told me she'd be there until midnight."

"You're speaking of the owner?"

"Her name is Miss Redbird."

"She can vouch for you, then?"

"Hey, what is this?" said Joe, his red eyes widening. "Am I under suspicion, or what? Would I call you people in the middle of the night if I'd done something wrong?"

Wigfull skipped that question. "Was your wife in any way upset that you went out so late without her?"

"I wasn't going after girls, for God's sake."

"But was she upset?"

Joe gave a slight, grudging nod. "Donna didn't see why it was important to me to go back to the store. I tried explaining, but she wasn't in a mood to be reasonable."

"You had a row?"

"A difference of opinion."

"Enough for her to walk out?"

"In a strange town in the night? I don't think so. Not Donna."

"She took her raincoat," Wigfull pointed out. "We established that. Do you have any friends she could have gone to?"

"In Bath? No."

"Nearby, then?"

"No, sir. We're tourists. The only people we spent time with here are other tourists."

"Does she have money?"

"A couple of hundred pounds, I guess. Sometimes she goes shopping without me. She also has credit cards. Her bag isn't in the room."

"Did you give details of the credit cards to the officers who saw you in the night?"

"Sure, as much as I knew."

"Was there any place your wife mentioned that she planned to visit while she is here?"

"We're finishing up in London, if that's what you mean. Tomorrow—I mean today—we were going to visit Wilton House. She loves big houses."

"Was that what brought you to Bath?"

Joe gave a nervous, angry sigh. "Look don't get me wrong, but talking about our vacation isn't helping to find my wife. I told you we're tourists."

Wigfull pressed on regardless. "All right. Would you mind telling me what you were doing visiting an antique shop as late as nine-thirty in the evening?"

Joe thought before he spoke, as if deciding how much to say. "There was something I was interested in buying, an antique writing box about two hundred years old. I found it in the afternoon, rummaging around, only it was locked and the key was missing. The lady had hundreds of keys in her office. We looked for one that fitted, but couldn't find one. I had to get back to the hotel to take Donna out to dinner. I promised to go back after and see if the lady had found the right key. That's all."

"You explained this to your wife?"

"Of course I did."

"And . . . ?"

"She thought it was stupid. Couldn't it wait until next day? You know how they go on."

"You argued."

"I promised her the trip to Wilton House."

"But she had a point. Couldn't it have waited?"

"If you know anything about antiques," Joe said as if to a child, "you see something you want, you'd better buy it. If you go back later you can bet your life it won't be there. It might have been sitting in the store collecting dust for ten years, but some wiseguy will have moved in and beaten you to it. That's the first law of antique-buying."

"Did you get it, then?"

Joe shook his head. "No, sir. It's still down at the store. The lady won't part with it until she finds the damned key. So it was a wasted evening, and you can imagine how I feel about the whole fiasco."

Wigfull weighed the explanation, studying the little man's face: creased with the ordeal, vulnerable and nervous.

What else was he hiding?

"You were there until what time?"

"Eleven, or soon after."

"Trying keys?"

"Sure. By then, I figured Donna would be getting anxious about me, or apeshit, to be honest, so I beat it back to the hotel."

"Walked?"

"Yes, sir. No taxis in sight. I carried a map. I was back by eleven-thirty, easy. And Donna wasn't in the room. I told myself there must be some rational explanation and she would soon come back. I got more and more worried and asked the hotel staff to make a search. They couldn't have been more helpful, but we didn't find her. At two in the morning, I called the emergency number."

"We have it logged at two-ten."

"I'm being approximate here."

"Understood," said Wigfull. "I was just confirming your statement." Aware that he could not much longer delay telling Joe about the corpse in the river, he leaned back in his chair and pressed his thumb and forefinger against his big moustache, tracing the shape, as if to make sure it was still there, hiding his own insecurity. He had never been good at breaking bad news to people. "I, em, was down at the river an hour ago. It's probably someone else, but we have to check in a case like this."

Abruptly, Joe opened his eyes wide. "What are you saying exactly?"

"A woman was found."

"You mean in the river?"

"By the weir." Wigfull tried to soften the remark by adding, "Do you know Pulteney Weir?" Even as the words left his mouth, he realised how crass they sounded, like some conversation-piece at a cocktail party.

Joe gripped the arms of his chair. "She's dead?"

"It may not be your wife. This woman wasn't wearing a raincoat."

The detail made no impression on Joe. He covered his face and cried out, "Oh, Jesus, I can't believe this."

Wigfull looked down at the table and wondered what to say next.

Joe said, more to himself than Wigfull, "What have I done? So help me, what have I done?" When he opened his eyes they were streaming tears.

Wigfull was in turmoil himself. He didn't know how to react, whether to say something reassuring or lean harder on the man in the expectation that he was about to confess to murder. Finally he blurted, "I'll get you a coffee," got up and quit the room.

sixteen

"WHAT'LL IT BE, Mr D?"

What else *could* it be after the morning's breakthrough?
"Bangers and mash."

Pandora, the catering assistant known as Pan to everyone
who used the police canteen, gave Diamond a beguiling smile
and picked up the largest, gleaming sausage with her tongs.
"Does this one look like yours?"

"How did you guess?"

"Inside information, Mr D. Another one?"

He held up three fingers.

She heaped sausages and mash onto his plate, winked and
said, "One thing I always say about a big man. He's no use if he
can't keep it up."

"Talking from experience, Pan?"

"His strength, I mean. Isn't that a fact? Next."

He took the tray to a table. Nobody would be joining him.
His spiky personality was enough to ruin anyone's digestion. So
he sat alone, making short work of the meal and wondering if,
after all, the mystery of the hand in the vault was capable of
solution. It would please him immensely to crack it.

He went back for jam roly-poly—setting Pan off on a whole
new flight of innuendo—and shortly afterwards, needing to dispose of some calories, stepped outside and took a walk along
Manvers Street. Still the heat-wave persisted. He was over-

dressed in his suit and soon had the jacket slung over one shoulder.

He had not gone far when he was conscious of a blonde head bobbing at his side. Ingeborg, the newshound, songbird and partygoer, was dressed more sensibly than he, in what he old-fashionedly thought of as running-kit and gym-shoes.

"Any progress, Superintendent?"

"You haven't given up, then?"

"Why, have you?"

He caught some extra inflexion in the words that made him turn to look at her. "Should I?"

"Just that it was obvious yesterday you didn't share in all the excitement about the vault. It made me wonder if you're going to switch to another case."

"It doesn't work like that, unfortunately."

"I meant in view of the body found this morning."

His face was flushed already from the heat. Now it caught fire. "What did you say?"

"The body. Haven't they told you? Some poor woman dragged out of the river at Pulteney Weir. Your Chief Inspector Wigfull seems to be handling it."

"Oh, *that* body," Diamond extemporised, completely in the dark.

"Do you happen to know if she's the missing American?"

Instead of giving her the satisfaction of asking which missing American, he said, "I've been flat out on other things."

Ingeborg laughed. "Don't tell me you got lucky at the party."

It was a cheap joke and he ignored it.

She said, "I wouldn't have mentioned it, but as the woman in the water seems to have been the wife of that professor who talked his way into the vault the other day, I thought there might be some overlap."

"Not necessarily," he managed to say quite smoothly, "but we follow everything up, as you know."

They had stopped at the top of Pierrepont Street. Diamond had stopped, anyway. Manvers Street was exerting a powerful pull now he knew what was going on there. *Your Chief Inspector Wigfull seems to be handling it.* Indeed.

"Any time you need the woman's angle, you only have to ask," Ingeborg told him. "You're missing Julie Hargreaves by now, I'll bet."

"No one is irreplaceable."

"I couldn't agree more, Mr Diamond. I wouldn't be any great loss to journalism if I joined the police."

"Still on about that, are you?" he said mechanically, his mind more on Pulteney Weir than Ingeborg's next career move.

"I picked up some forms yesterday." She hesitated. "You wouldn't give me a reference, would you?"

"Mm?" Her request penetrated slowly. "I don't know enough about you."

"We could remedy that." She must have realised as she spoke that it sounded like a come-on that she didn't intend. She gave a laugh that—unusually for her—betrayed some nervousness.

He shook his head. "Get someone else. What about your friend the councillor?"

"John?" She frowned. "I slept . . . I can't ask him for a *reference*."

"He's on the Police Authority."

"Oh, God. He is, isn't he?" She turned pink. "I could end up being interviewed by him."

He was anxious to be off, but it was obvious that she really did have this ambition. He was not too old to remember being passionate himself about joining the police. If she was willing to sacrifice the high fees she earned from journalism and face a couple of years in uniform, she ought to be encouraged. In this warm-hearted spirit, his mind took a devious route. "This choir you belong to."

"The Camerata?"

"Yes. How long have you been singing with them?"

"A couple of years, maybe three."

"The choirmaster. Does he know you reasonably well?"

"Reasonably." She frowned. "Do you think he would do as a reference? If I couldn't get you, I was going to ask my bank manager or a solicitor, or someone like that."

"Go for the choirmaster. I can't think of anyone better placed to swing it for you."

Her eyes shone as she realised what he was driving at. The Assistant Chief Constable—Georgina—would turn somersaults to become a permanent member of the Camerata. She could hardly ignore a reference written by the choirmaster. "Thanks!"

He nodded, turned and marched briskly back to the nick.

WIGFULL HAD just left for the mortuary with the American professor, so Diamond got the story of the body in the river from Sergeant Leaman, his deputy, who had sat in on the interview. Leaman was a keen young detective, unlikely to have missed any of the salient facts.

When he had heard it all, Diamond asked, "What does your boss think?"

"About what, sir?"

"The dead woman."

"He's keeping an open mind."

"I should have saved my breath, shouldn't I? John Wigfull's mind is so open you can see daylight through it. How is the husband bearing up?"

"Professor Dougan? It's difficult to tell, sir. He's obviously in a state of shock, but you've got to remember he's missing a night's sleep."

"Did he have any explanation?"

"For his wife's death? Not really, sir. Seems to blame himself for leaving her alone in the hotel last night. Says he had no idea she would take it so badly."

"Was she neurotic? Depressed?"

"Mr Wigfull didn't ask."

"There must be more to it than the husband going out for a couple of hours."

"I expect you're right, sir."

"If that was cause for suicide, the river would be teeming with dead wives."

"Perhaps it was the last straw."

"Perhaps." Diamond didn't sound convinced. "How is she supposed to have done it? Walked out of the hotel, found her way to the river somewhere above the weir, a fifteen-minute walk, easy, taken off her coat and jumped in? I don't see it, sergeant."

"I'm only reporting what I heard, sir."

Diamond gave a nod. Why take out his frustration on young Leaman? He would have it out with Wigfull later. "Keep me informed."

He returned upstairs to see if Halliwell had made any more progress. He had not. The two builders he'd managed to reach on the phone had no memory of a pair of casual labourers known as Banger and Mash. It was evident in Halliwell's voice that he felt this was leading nowhere. The quest wasn't helped by the ludicrous names, like an outdated music hall turn.

"Keep trying," he told Halliwell, and added as encouragement, "I was impressed by that plasterer from Winchester. It's the best lead we're likely to get."

"It's all we've got," said Halliwell. "We've followed up all the calls that came in after your spot on *Newsnight*. The rest were dross. It gives some people a sense of importance, helping the police. 'I had tea in the Pump Room in 1963 and I remember seeing a man with staring eyes.' That's the quality of information we got from most of them."

"It was the bill for the cream tea, I expect."

"What's that, sir?"

"The reason for the staring eyes."

His wit had not infected Halliwell, who had spent far too long on the phone.

"Have you eaten?" Diamond asked him.

"Not yet."

"Better get down there, hadn't you? It's gone two."

"You just told me to keep trying, sir."

"Within limits, Keith. I'm not a slave-driver."

Halliwell refrained from comment. He was on his feet and heading for the canteen when Sergeant Leaman appeared in the doorway.

"Hold on a minute, Keith," said Diamond. "What is it, sergeant?"

Leaman looked right and left, as if he was about to impart something confidential. "I'm not sure what to do, sir. I just heard from the hospital. The mortuary. They wanted to speak to Mr Wigfull. I said he was on his way there with Professor Dougan."

Diamond glanced at the clock. "Ought to be there by now. What did they want?"

"It was about the body—the woman found at the weir. They said the police surgeon called in to look at her. It seems he found something nobody noticed down by the weir. She had injuries to the back of the head. Really nasty injuries, hidden by her hair. The skull is impacted in a couple of places. It *could* have happened when she fell into the water, or after she was in it, but—"

"Someone could have beaten her over the head and dropped her in?"

Leaman smoothed his hands nervously down his sides. "That's it, sir. Mr Wigfull ought to be told before they go in to view the body, but not while the professor is with him. It's possible—"

"You're damned right, it is," said Diamond, galvanized. "Keith, get on the phone. Get the mortuary-keeper, or whoever is in there, to keep them waiting outside. He's to tell them nothing about the injuries. Make out that the body isn't ready to be seen. If Wigfull wants to know why, tell him I'm on my way and I'll explain all."

HE WAS at the Royal United Hospital inside ten minutes, thanks to a good young driver and a siren that would carry on ringing in his ears twenty minutes after it was switched off. He found Wigfull and Professor Dougan waiting in a sideroom. Wigfull was pacing the room, the professor hunched on a chair. This was Diamond's first sight of Joe Dougan, a short, tanned, middle-aged man with anxiety deeply etched across his features.

The first duty was to take Wigfull outside and tell him what the police surgeon had found.

Predictably, Wigfull's reaction was to exonerate himself. "How could I have noticed injuries to the back of the head? When I looked at her, she was lying face up in the undertaker's van."

"It doesn't matter, John. What matters is the way we handle the professor."

"*We?*"

"This could be murder."

"But it's my case. I was down at the weir directing the operation."

"She was just a floater then." He waited for Wigfull to grasp the altered situation.

He was defiant. "So she could be a murder victim. I can handle it myself."

"I think we should work together at this stage," Diamond said firmly. If he had to pull rank, he would. He had prior responsibility for murder cases.

"I thought you were fully stretched on the other inquiry—the body parts in the vault—what with all the media interest."

"You've put your finger on it, John. The professor may be involved. He conned his way into the vault the day before yesterday. The lads stupidly took him for a pathologist."

"I heard about that. It was just a mistake."

"He lost his way. Oh, yeah."

"What's it got to do with his wife being found dead?"

"We'll find out presently. Before we show him the body, I want a preview, a look at these injuries, if you don't object."

"I'll come with you," Wigfull said quickly.

Inside, a mortuary attendant had the body ready on a trolley. He lifted the sheet from the bloated face of a small-featured, middle-aged woman with dark hair.

Neither detective spoke. A few hours' immersion in water has dramatic effects on the appearance of a body. Not only does the face swell. After removal from the water the pigmentation darkens.

"The back of the head, if you don't mind," Diamond said.

The attendant put his hands under the shoulders and raised the torso towards him, untroubled by the strange embrace. Diamond lifted some matted strands of hair and the injuries underneath were obvious. The surface was concave in one place. It must have taken a terrific impact.

"A cosh?"

Wigfull shrugged.

Diamond thanked the attendant and went to a sink to wash his hands.

Joe Dougan stood up when they returned to the waiting room. His eyes were bloodshot and deep ridges of tension had appeared at the edge of his mouth. "Can we get this over now?"

"I didn't introduce myself," said Diamond. "Detective Superintendent Peter Diamond. Murder squad."

"Joe Dougan." Then he reacted, blinked and swayed. "Did I hear you right?"

"I head the murder squad," Diamond said genially. "I don't

think we've met. I missed you the other day when you visited one of our crime scenes, the vault under the Pump Room."

"That seems a long time ago now," said Joe. "You did say murder?"

"That's my job. Someone has to do it. What was your interest in the vault?"

"What did you say?" Joe was ashen-faced.

"The vault. What were you doing there?"

"Do I have to explain at this point in time? If you don't mind, I'd like to get this ordeal over with and get out of this place."

"Understood, sir," said Diamond, unusually considerate. "We'll talk about it after."

They went back to the main post mortem room, a tiled, white place. The corpse had been covered again for this formality. The attendant stood ready.

Wigfull explained, "It's just a matter of letting us know if you recognise her. I'd better warn you that her face has puffed up and darkened a bit. The water does that."

He nodded to the attendant. The dead features were revealed again.

Only a faint sibilance, a slight indrawing of breath, came from Joe.

Diamond put the necessary question to him.

The little man was silent some time before saying in a low, but steady voice, "Yes, I recognise her."

Unable to deal impassively with the stress of the moment, Wigfull swept suspicion aside and said, "You have my sympathy, professor."

Joe turned to him and said with raised eyebrows, "All I said is I recognise her. This isn't Donna. It's a lady who runs an antique store I visited. Miss Redbird."

seventeen

"WHERE ARE WE GOING?" Joe Dougan asked Diamond.

"Bath Central Police Station."

"You taking me in, or what?"

"Depends what you mean. We just want to ask you some questions."

"Can't it be done here?"

"In the hospital grounds? We'd rather do it at the nick."

"And if I refuse?"

Diamond was being unusually considerate. "Is there somewhere else you would rather go?"

"My hotel."

"Fine. We'll go there."

"I'm thinking my wife may have come back."

"Let's find out, then."

From the car, they radioed headquarters that the body taken from the river was that of Peg Redbird and gave instructions for her shop to be sealed as a possible crime scene.

THE ROYAL Crescent Hotel is at the centre of the great terrace from which its name is taken. At the sedate pace of a horse-drawn carriage, they were driven over the cobbles in front. A top-hatted concierge in blue livery automatically started towards the car, saw that it was a police vehicle and hesitated.

Joe swung open the door and hailed him by name. "Any news of my wife yet?"

"I haven't heard anything, professor."

"Darn."

The Dougans' suite was on the second floor. The two trim members of the party moved towards the elegant main staircase. Diamond stopped to press the lift button. They looked round for him and came back.

He said with an air of dignity, "If there's such a place as Heaven, and I get the nod from St Peter, he'd better not expect me to use the stairs."

Wigfull passed no comment.

This went over Joe's head. He was still talking about his wife. "She may have come back when the concierge was off duty."

"It's possible."

But when they entered the John Wood suite, nobody was there.

"Hell," said Joe, and he couldn't have been talking about the accommodation. The lounge area in a toning scheme of brown, orange and cream, was bigger than the dining room of some hotels. Padded settee and armchairs, fireplace and huge pelmeted and draped windows with front views across the lawns to the city. Up a couple of steps a white balustrade like a communion rail separated the bedroom from the rest.

It definitely had the edge over an interview room at the nick.

"I'm not paying for this," Joe thought fit to explain, as if affluence would damn him in the eyes of the law. "We ordered a simple bedroom at one-sixty a night, but as this suite wasn't in use they upgraded us for no extra charge."

"Lucky for you."

"My luck ran out last night. So what are you going to do about Donna?"

"A missing person alert has gone out to all our patrols. We can't do more," Diamond explained, "unless there's something else you want to tell us."

Joe's voice shrilled in outrage. "What do you mean? I told you all I know."

"Then you've got to be patient, sir."

"I'm doing my best." He sighed, and made an effort to unwind. "Anyone want a drink?"

The room had its own cocktail cabinet. The guardians of the law shook their heads.

"Well, I'm having a scotch," Joe declared.

"How did you know the woman in the mortuary is Miss Redbird?" Diamond asked him when he had poured the drink.

"Didn't I say? I met her yesterday."

"In her shop?"

"In her shop, right."

"Pure chance, or what?"

"No, I was directed there. You want to know how it happened?" He went to the chest of drawers and took out his precious book, the edition of Milton's poems, and showed them the inscription on the cover and explained why he believed this was Mary Shelley's personal copy. In a dogged account that revealed the persistence of his character, he took them through the various steps of his quest to trace the previous owners: Hay-on-Wye; the Abbey Churchyard; O. Heath, the retired bookseller; Uncle Evan at the Brains Surgery; and Peg Redbird at Noble and Nude.

Diamond was a brooding, restless listener to all this. "You make it all sound reasonable," he responded finally. "The part I don't understand is where you thought this trail was leading. Surely you weren't expecting to trace the book all the way back to Mary Shelley?"

"You never can tell." A faint smile followed, edged with self-congratulation.

"We're listening," said Diamond, becoming intrigued.

So they heard the remarkable story Peg Redbird had given Joe, of the writing box that had once contained the book.

At this John Wigfull cut into the narrative. "This is the box you told me about this morning, the one that was locked, and you went back for?"

"Correct."

"You didn't tell me it belonged to Mary Shelley. You said it was an antique."

"That's the truth."

"No, professor, that's evasion."

Joe Dougan shrugged and spread his hands. "I can't say for certain it belonged to her."

Wigfull was furious. "You went back to the shop at the end of the evening because you believed it was hers. You didn't say a damned thing about Mary Shelley this morning."

"What's your problem?" said Joe. "Donna is gone. That's all that matters to me. Can't you appreciate that?"

Diamond broke up the exchange before Wigfull burst a blood vessel. "Let's move on. Would you mind telling me what happened when you went back to Noble and Nude?"

"Nothing happened. Miss Redbird wasn't there."

"The shop was closed, you mean?"

"No, it was open."

"But unattended?"

He nodded.

Wigfull blurted out accusingly, "You didn't tell me any of this."

"You didn't ask."

"You implied she was there. You said you spent some time trying to unlock the box."

Joe remarked as if to a child, "You got it. I sat down in her office to wait for her. The writing box was still on her desk and so were the tins of keys, so I tried some more. But the lady didn't show up at all. In the end I thought about Donna alone here and I gave up."

Diamond said with more control than Wigfull, "Are you telling us the whole story this time, professor?"

Joe seemed to shrink a little into the thick upholstery. "I'm doing the best I can."

"When you found the shop unattended, did you make any effort to find Miss Redbird?"

"I called her name. There was no answer."

"A golden opportunity to try more keys on the precious box. Did you get it open?"

Joe looked away, out of the window, as if he wanted to be anywhere else but here.

"Did you hear my question?" Diamond pressed him.

"I don't know what she did with the damned key."

"You must have been tempted to force the lock."

"It crossed my mind a couple of times, but I didn't do it."

"The box is still intact, then?"

"Should be. That's how I left it."

"On Miss Redbird's desk?"

"Yep."

"And you say she didn't show up at all?"

"That's the truth of it."

"How long were you there?"

"Hour and a quarter, hour and a half."

"Did anyone see you?"

"No one I noticed."

Diamond continued to probe. If Peg Redbird *had* been bludgeoned to death that evening and dropped in the river, that hour and a half was crucial.

"When you found the shop open and let yourself in, did you notice any sign of a disturbance?"

"No, sir, I did not."

"Any damage would be obvious in an antique shop, I imagine."

Joe gave him an abstracted look. "What did you say?"

"Things get knocked over if people fight in a place like that."

"You're losing me."

"Everything was as you'd seen it before?"

"I guess so."

"We can assume, then, that she left the shop before you arrived, and nobody forced her to go."

Joe Dougan was a tired, troubled man, and he had reached the limit of his patience. "All you guys want to talk about is this dead woman. She's gone. No one can help her now. You should be finding out what happened to my wife, for God's sake. Don't you have any priorities?"

They left soon after.

"WHAT DID you make of that?" Diamond asked in the car.

Wigfull sniffed. "He spins a good yarn."

"Do you think it's all an act—his concern about the wife?"

"I caught him out over Peg Redbird, didn't I? He changed his story."

"He was pretty uncomfortable about it."

"The man's a killer," said Wigfull. "We should have taken him in."

"I don't know what you base that on."

"He was at the scene, wasn't he? He went to the shop the evening she was killed. He admits that now. He coveted that box. It was an obsession with him. You've got to understand the mentality of these people who buy antiques. They spot a bargain and nothing will put them off. But Peg Redbird was a canny dealer. She guessed the value of the box from the way he conducted himself. I expect she made the fatal mistake of trying to withdraw it from sale. He saw the prize being snatched away and he lashed out. If that isn't motive enough, I don't know what is."

"He comes across as a mild character."

"So did Crippen."

They drove directly to Noble and Nude. Walcot, where the shop stood, was one of Diamond's favourite areas of Bath. With its craft workshops, secondhand goods and a market style of shopkeeping, it preserved a link with the medieval traders who had once done business here. The down-at-heel, but chipper character of the place was staunchly defended against the city developers. There was even a guild of sorts that had organized a Walcot Street Independence Day the previous summer.

A uniformed PC stood on duty outside.

"Before we go in," Diamond said, "I'll check how close we are to the river."

"It's only a stone's throw. It runs parallel to the street."

That wasn't enough for the head of the murder squad. "I'll take a look."

Professional competence was at stake here. Not wanting to miss a thing, Wigfull tagged along. There were a couple of passageways through private premises that had gates in front. These, Diamond reasoned, were almost certainly locked at night. He found the nearest open access to the river some sixty yards up the street, through Chatham Row, a cul-de-sac lined with gentrified eighteenth century terraced housing. In silence, the two detectives paced the short distance past the houses to a set of railings overlooking the Avon. A gate gave access to a flight of twenty-two stone steps down to a section of river bank.

"Could she have bashed her head falling down the steps?" Diamond mused aloud.

"You mean by accident?" Going by the tone of Wigfull's voice, it was as likely as abduction by aliens.

"If she did," Diamond went on, "I don't know how she got in the water. She would have ended up on the grassy bit down there."

"He killed her in the shop and dumped the body in the water."

"That little man we saw in the Royal Crescent?"

"Who else?" said the man who usually kept an open mind. No comment from Diamond.

For a few moments they watched the river's placid progress towards Pulteney Bridge. Any current was barely discernible here, along one of the wider stretches. Further on, the course narrowed a little, but not enough to propel a floating corpse against an obstruction with enough force to cause head injuries. Even at the weir, the flow would be minimal in present conditions.

Diamond was working on logistics. "If you're right, he must have brought the body here somehow. He doesn't have a car. He's not a big man. It was a short walk for us, but a fair old distance to carry a corpse."

"She was a small woman."

"Another thing," said Diamond. "He's a stranger to Bath. How did he know the river was so close? You can't see it from Walcot Street."

"He carried a map."

"Do you know that for certain?"

"He told me," said Wigfull with an air of triumph.

Diamond continued to stare at the river.

Wigfull added, "He said he used a map to find a quick way through the side-streets to the hotel."

In a moment Diamond said, "Seen enough?"

Wigfull nodded.

They returned to Noble and Nude.

"Do you collect antiques?" he asked Wigfull before they went in.

"On my salary?"

He gave Wigfull a speculative glance. "You can pick up some useful things quite cheaply. The Victorians made special mugs for people with large moustaches. There was a trough across the top to keep the whiskers from getting soggy. Worth looking out for."

Wigfull's brown eyes above the great friz were a study in hostility.

No trace of amusement crossed Diamond's features. He contained it all.

Inside the shop, the sheer spectacle of bric-a-brac at every level was an immediate distraction. The two detectives stood for a time, taking it in. To Diamond's right was a stuffed grizzly bear, forever up on its haunches with a tray resting across its forepaws piled with what looked like junk mail. Opposite was a Victorian Bath-chair with its black hood.

"You wanted to know how he shifted the body," said Wigfull, pointing to it.

Diamond gave a grudging nod. "It's possible."

They edged past a ship's figurehead, a huge, bare-breasted wooden torso threatening to crush anyone who brushed against it. Suspended over them, by wires to the ceiling, was a model of a Tiger Moth aircraft not much smaller than the real thing. Beyond was an area staked out by grandfather clocks lined up like guardsmen. It was dominated by a leather-topped desk of the sort owned by newspaper barons—except that the leather was torn in places and the wood was crying out for some polish. At one end were three biscuit tins without lids.

"The key collection," said Diamond after glancing into one. "Where's Mary Shelley's writing box, then? The professor said it was here when he left."

Wigfull eased his way carefully around the desk and looked behind. Peg had a bentwood chair in the peacock design, with velvet cushions. Ranged beside it he found a paraffin stove, a safe, a wastebin and a stack of magazines and reference books.

No writing box.

"Dougan was definitely lying," Wigfull said.

"Stupid, if he was. We were sure to check."

"Stupid he is not."

"So he wasn't lying."

Wigfull glared back, defeated by the logic, or what passed for logic.

"No signs of a fight," Diamond commented. "He was right about that."

"He could have tidied up."

They made a slow inspection of the shop. Necessarily slow. It was difficult in such a warren to retain a sense of where they were. Not only were the rooms small and connected by confusing flights of stairs; the way through was serpentine, dictated by the arrangement of furniture.

The wax woman on the swing gave them a moment's unease, and in another room they found a broken fragment of pottery, presumably from the urn Joe claimed to have smashed, but otherwise the tour was uneventful. On the way out, Diamond scooped the heap of junk mail from the grizzly bear's tray and handed it to Wigfull. "Something to pass the time."

"Thanks," Wigfull said ironically.

"Check it before you chuck it, won't you?"

They returned outside and stood by the car. Twenty minutes of wandering through the shop had brought on symptoms of claustrophobia in the case of Wigfull, and, on Diamond's side, hunger.

"I wonder if there's a chippie round here."

"It looks dead to me."

"I wouldn't mind trying the kebab takeaway in Kingsmead Square."

Resignedly, Wigfull drove them there. It was a no parking zone, but they sat outside in the car. He leafed through Peg Redbird's junk mail whilst Diamond started on a kebab that must have represented everything the shop stocked.

"What size was this writing box?"

Wigfull gave a shrug.

"It can't have been all that large," Diamond developed his theme.

Wigfull continued to look at pamphlets about double-glazing and insurance. There was nothing personal in all this rubbish.

"If it was owned by a woman, it had to be light enough to carry about."

"You're thinking the professor walked out of the shop with it?"

"I'm thinking whoever walked out with it wouldn't have had any trouble tucking it under an arm."

"The professor?" Wigfull repeated, determined to nail the man who had strung him along.

"Who else knew it was worth taking?"

"Because it once belonged to Mary Shelley?" Wigfull was

becoming interested. He slung the junk mail onto the back seat and turned towards Diamond. "No one else. Only the professor. He was on to the find of a lifetime, so he wouldn't have shared the secret with anyone else. He *must* have nicked it."

"He had the opportunity," Diamond continued to think aloud, "and the temptation." He was silent for a moment, testing his own hypothesis. "But if he stole the box, why did he tell us the place was unattended when he went back? We're bound to suspect him. He ought to have insisted Peg was there."

"He did originally," said Wigfull. "At any rate, he gave the impression. That's why I got so stroppy when he denied it."

"Did he say she was there?"

"Not exactly. He let me assume she was. You know why he changed tack, don't you?"

"Go on."

"When I spoke to him first, he didn't know the body was found. He thought he'd disposed of her. Plenty of people—intelligent people—don't know that a dead body thrown into water still has air in the lungs and may not stay under. After she was found he had to think again. He came out with this load of codswallop that the shop was empty."

"You're saying Peg Redbird was actually here when he came back the second time?"

"I am. And I'm saying he wanted that writing box so badly that he killed her for it. It stands out a mile. She refused to sell, or asked some exorbitant price, and got her head beaten in."

"If that's true," said Diamond, "where did the killing take place? Not in the shop."

Wigfull was unstoppable. "Here. Outside. He grabbed the box and walked out with it. She followed, he cracked her over the head with it and killed her."

"In the struggle, you mean?"

"Then he had to dispose of the body. Either he carried her to the river, or he used that invalid chair."

"Without being seen?"

"The place was in darkness. There's damn all going on at that end of Walcot Street after ten at night. When it was done, the body dropped in the river, he came back to the shop, collected the precious writing box and legged it back to the Royal Crescent."

Diamond pondered the theory.

"There's no one else," insisted Wigfull.

"If you're right, how does his wife's disappearance fit into this?"

For a moment it seemed Wigfull was thrown by the question, but then his eyes widened again. "I know. She was in the hotel room when he got back. She saw the state he was in and realised something dreadful had happened. She got the truth out of him. He'd just killed a woman. She was so appalled that she couldn't stay in the same room with him. She left."

"To wander the streets?"

"Booked into somewhere else, I expect. We should check all the hotels and boarding houses."

Diamond thought about it coolly, tapping the end of his chin with the empty kebab stick. "There's a big hole in all this, isn't there, John?"

"What's that?"

"Dougan's behaviour since he got back to the hotel. He calls us at two in the morning to report his wife missing. He gets on the phone and sets in train an inquiry that is sure to put him in the frame for Peg Redbird's death. If he'd kept quiet, you and I wouldn't have heard of Professor Joe Dougan."

Wigfull listened to the objection and dealt with it adroitly. "Someone else saw him at Noble and Nude."

"Who was that?"

"Doesn't matter who. Anyone. Another customer. Dougan expected to be fingered, so he did the smart thing and told us he was there."

"Not many killers behave as artfully as that, John."

"This one is a professor."

"It doesn't explain why he called us when he did. You say he went to the trouble of dumping her in the river. If so, he hoped to get away with it. His best plan was to wait and see if the body was found and identified."

Wigfull would not give up. "All right. Try this for size. His wife didn't walk out. He killed her."

"Two in one evening?" The line of Diamond's mouth arched sceptically.

"She threatened to turn him in, so he did for her as well. He made the emergency call after he'd disposed of her."

"Disposed of her where?"

"I don't know yet. I just thought of this."

"Difficult, getting rid of a corpse in the Royal Crescent Hotel, even in the small hours of the morning."

"Not all the rooms are in use this week."

"How do you know that?"

Wigfull had that special glint in his eye that meant he was ahead of Diamond. "Dougan told us he was upgraded."

"True."

"Her body could be lying in an empty room."

"Waiting for some unfortunate chambermaid to walk in?" Diamond said as if this grim hypothesis had worn him down at last. "If you're right, we should be hearing soon." He left a judicious pause. "But I won't hold my breath."

eighteen

PEG REDBIRD HAD LIVED over the shop.

"I don't believe this," said Wigfull when they forced open the door to her flat and looked in.

"It's not a bad principle," Diamond commented.

"What's that?"

"Never take your work home."

There was not an antique in sight. The sitting room furniture was modern in style, in light ash, with pale upholstery and scatter cushions in strong colours. She had sunken lighting, roller-blinds, steel-framed Hockney prints of his Californian swimming-pool phase, cork-tiled floors with plain, pastel-coloured rugs, and a total absence of clutter.

Finding this hard to reconcile with the glorified scrapyard that was Noble and Nude, the two detectives opened the doors to the bedroom and kitchen. Those, also, were straight out of a Sunday colour supplement.

"Obviously a split personality," said Wigfull the Open University degree man, in that self-regarding tone that Diamond found so irritating. "Jekyll and Hyde."

"That's putting it strongly considering she was the victim."

"You should have been on the Bramshill course in criminology that I did last year. Victims often provoke their attackers."

"With their choice of interior decoration? Come off it, John."

"People's rooms reveal more than they realise about their inner selves."

"I'll stick with the outer self, thanks. Let's get to work. You do this room. I'll take the bedroom."

"Shouldn't we call in the SOCOs first?"

Diamond eyed him with searing scorn. "Does this look like a scene of crime to you? Do you really believe she was bludgeoned in here and dragged all the way downstairs through the shop and off to the river?"

After a lengthy pause, Wigfull admitted, "It doesn't appear so."

"Well, then."

"What are we looking for?"

"I don't know until we find it, do I? Anything that links her to the rest of humanity. Answerphone messages, letters, address-books, diaries. You've done this before, man."

He stepped into the bedroom. This should not take long. Seeing it, he began to have second thoughts about Wigfull's Jekyll and Hyde theory. Peg, it seemed, had been slavishly tidy at home. The duvet was squared on the bed, the pillow plumped and all the clothes put away. The bedside drawers contained no item more interesting than a bottle of herbal sedative pills.

From the sitting room, Wigfull called out, "No answer phone, but there's an address-book here."

Diamond confirmed that nothing of interest was secreted in the dressing-table drawers and was on his way through when the phone rang.

Wigfull put out a hand for it, then hesitated.

Diamond gave him the go-ahead with a nod.

The right way to deal with an incoming call at a possible crime scene was to listen and say nothing. If you spoke and the caller heard an unfamiliar voice, you could be sure they would slam down the phone if they had anything to hide.

Wigfull knew the procedure. He had the phone to his ear.

After listening briefly, he rolled his eyes and said, "I'll put him on." He handed the phone to Diamond. "Keith Halliwell."

Disappointing.

"What is it now?"

"Something new has come up, sir," Halliwell told him.

"Another stiff?"

"Not entirely."

"What do you mean—not entirely?"

"Not an entire body. We're talking parts. Some leg bones, a rib cage and a piece of an arm."

Bones. With an effort he made a mental switch to the case Halliwell was working on. "Not in the vault? We dug every inch of the vault."

"No. The River Wylye, near Warminster."

"That's *Wiltshire*."

"It's only a half-hour drive."

"It's not our patch."

"With respect, sir, killers don't work to county borders like us."

"What do you mean—'with respect'?" he rasped into the mouthpiece. "I'm not questioning whether the bones are worth checking out. I'm trying to work out how we got onto them. Are they still available for inspection?"

"At Chippenham. I've just been speaking to CID there."

"When you said a piece of an arm . . ."

"The radius."

"Come again."

"Radius. The long bone in the forearm. In my opinion . . . em, I wonder if you think it's worth comparing it with the hand we have, see if they join up at the wrist."

"It's a long shot, considering our bones were in the cellar nearly twenty years."

"These haven't just been found, sir. They were picked up in 1986 by some boys fishing."

"And this is the first we've heard of it?"

"It didn't get much attention at the time."

"It's going to get plenty now. When the press get to work on it, they'll tell us Frankenstein's monster is roaming the country ripping people apart. Get it organised, then," Diamond said mechanically, more interested in the way this came to light. "Was this your idea, Keith, checking old files?"

"I can't take the credit, sir."

"Don't depress me. You got it off a flaming computer."

"No. It's one-up to the human race. Someone had the bright idea of checking newspapers. They found this report in the files of the *Wiltshire Times*."

"Nice work. One of our rising stars in CID?"

"Actually it was a tip-off."

"Oh, yes? From a member of the public?"

"Not exactly." Halliwell's stonewalling was ominous.

A chill note of reserve crept into Diamond's voice. "Anyone I know?"

"You do know her actually. Ingeborg Smith."

Diamond sighed in a way that confirmed the inevitable. "Something else to put in the job application."

"She'd like to tell you about it herself. I told her if she looked in here again about five-thirty . . ."

"Thanks a bunch, Keith."

Muttering, he put down the phone and shifted his thoughts back to the immaculate home life of Peg Redbird. The address book Wigfull had found was helpful only in the sense that it contained about three hundred entries. Peg had not been short of contacts.

"We'd do just as well knocking on doors," he said. "What we want first is an itinerary of the last hours she was alive—the last day, in fact. The only information we have so far comes from Joe Dougan."

"And I wouldn't put any reliance on that," Wigfull sourly added.

"But do you agree with me?"

"About what?"

Some subtle power-play was in progress here. Diamond wanted more than a consultative role. He was willing to cede the nuts-and-bolts work to Wigfull and his team whilst reserving the crucial decisions for himself. "Knocking on doors."

"Of course I agree."

"Then will you get a door-stepping team on the job, or shall I?"

"Leave it to me," said Wigfull, thinking this was the opening he needed. "You've got enough on your plate."

"Enough on my plate? You know me, John. No table manners at all. If I see something tasty on another fellow's plate, I help myself, whether mine is full or not."

BY USING the back door of the nick, he avoided being waylaid by Ingeborg. She would be out front somewhere, wanting her pound of flesh for providing the breakthrough in the case. He wasn't ready to admit such a thing. Ingeborg had given him one false lead already—Violet "Tricks" Turner—and the bones from the River Wylye might prove to be another.

So he gave Ingeborg the slip—and that was how he met the Assistant Chief Constable coming out to the car park with Councillor Sturr. A polite exchange of words was inescapable.

The councillor said with a smile as slick as his three-piece pinstripe, "Fancy meeting you, superintendent. Only just now I was reminded of your comforting remarks at the PCCG meeting. The Assistant Chief Constable tells me you have another violent death to investigate. Ironic, isn't it? Rather bears out my point that Bath is a dangerous place to live these days."

"One swallow doesn't make a summer," was the best Diamond could think to say in reply.

"Quite a high-flying swallow, Peg Redbird. The antiques trade is not going to like this. They're a close-knit group, as I'm sure you're finding out, and they'll expect some rapid action from you."

"People always do," said Diamond. "Rapid can mean hasty, and hasty can mean faulty, so I don't let it get to me."

"Well, if I can be of service . . ."

"I don't suppose you can, sir, unless you were in the area of Walcot Street last evening."

"I'm not offering myself as a witness. I meant in my official capacity, backing your efforts."

"Much appreciated, sir."

"I was on the other side of town," Sturr volunteered, in case there was any doubt, "at a rather enjoyable 'At Home'." He smiled at Georgina Dallymore.

"Of course you were," said Diamond.

"If you want to know who I was with . . ." Sturr was milking this for more than it was worth.

"I saw you leaving together."

"So it seems I can't help you after all."

"Shame. I'll have to widen the net."

For this ill-considered quip, Diamond received a cold stare.

Sturr shook hands with Georgina and strolled across to his car.

Diamond, too, started to move on, but the ACC asked him to wait.

"That last remark was uncalled for," she rebuked him.

"I'm sure he's heard worse than that, ma'am. He's a politician."

"But we're not in the business of baiting people, least of all the people who make decisions about resources." She raised her hand in salute as the councillor drove past them in his silver Mercedes, out of the car park.

"He was having a swipe at me, going on about the murdered woman. Right, I was out of order," he said quickly, noting the muscles tighten at the edge of Georgina's mouth. "Pressure of work, I expect."

"I'm glad you mentioned that," she said. "I was going to raise it with you anyway. This is too much, the murder of the antiques dealer, coming on top of all the brouhaha about the hand in the vault. It's obvious that you can't run two inquiries yourself. You must delegate."

The word was not in Diamond's vocabulary. "I've got Chief Inspector Wigfull on the antiques case," he said at once.

"In theory, yes, but you're breathing down his neck. I understand you've been with him almost all day, at the Royal Crescent, at Walcot Street."

"It's my job," he pointed out. "I'm the murder man here."

"Yes, and Mr Wigfull ran the show when you were otherwise employed." Georgina was revealing a grasp of events that happened long before her arrival in Bath. "This new case is well within his capacity. Let him run it his way. Keep an overview, by all means. But concentrate your efforts on the *Frankenstein* business. That's the number one investigation. Do you understand?"

"Has Wigfull complained?"

She said, "Just do it, Mr Diamond. You're too easily provoked for a man of your rank. You won't go any higher in the police until you learn about priorities."

AT ABOUT six the same evening in the Royal Crescent Hotel, someone was at the door of Joe Dougan's suite, disturbing his deep, delayed sleep. Joe's tired brain registered dimly that the knocking had been going on for some time. Groaning, he rolled off the bed and groped his way forward, practically falling over the little white balustrade that acted as a room divider. Still dressed only in boxer shorts, he opened the door to find one of the detectives who had called earlier, the one with the large moustache. This time Chief Inspector Wigfull was accompanied by two younger men in plain clothes.

"Have you found her?" Joe asked, eyes dilating like oil slicks.

"Not yet," said Wigfull. "With your permission, we'd like to search these rooms, sir."

He kept a firm hold on the door. "What for?"

Mary Shelley's writing box was the true answer to that one, but Wigfull didn't give it. He answered obliquely, "You want us to spare no efforts in finding your wife?"

"For the love of Mike, she isn't here," said Joe, still barring the way. There was no mistaking this detective's hostility.

"We know that."

"You already made a search."

"The officers who were here before weren't trained in CID work."

"What's that in plain English?"

"Criminal investigation." The stress Wigfull put on the first word made it into a personal slur. "There may be other clues to her disappearance, and you wouldn't want to get in the way of the search, would you?"

Joe couldn't argue with that. He took a half-step backwards. "Do what you want."

CID-trained the officers may have been, but the search did not take long. The possible hiding places for an object as large as the writing box were few. Once they had looked behind furniture and curtains, above and beneath the four-poster bed and in the bathroom, the job was virtually done. With no success.

"Where are your suitcases?" Wigfull asked.

Joe's eyes bulged. "You don't think she's in a *suitcase?*"

"I don't see them here, sir."

"The hotel people put them in storage for us, to give us more room."

"We'd like to see them."

"They're empty."

"The keys?"

Joe picked his trousers off the back of a chair, took out the keys and handed them across.

Wigfull tossed them to one of his men, who left the room.

"You said you left Noble and Nude when?"

"Around eleven."

"Without the writing box?"

"I left that on the desk."

"Well, it isn't there any more."

"You're wrong," said Joe. "It's there."

"I promise you it isn't."

The little American passed a hand distractedly through his dark hair. "It's got to be," he said as if beginning to doubt himself.

"Who—besides you—knew that the box may have belonged to Mary Shelley?"

"No one."

"Except Peg Redbird herself?"

Joe shook his head emphatically. "She's the last person I would have told. I wanted to buy at a fair price."

"Fair?"

"Used goods are worth as much as people are willing to pay, no more."

"She seemed reluctant to part with it if you had to go back a second time."

"I thought about that," said Joe. "I guess she could see I badly wanted that box. She thought there was something inside, a hidden drawer maybe, and she wasn't going to sell until she'd seen inside."

"So Peg Redbird didn't know what she was selling. Did you tell anyone else? Those other people you mentioned? The old bookseller? The Welshman, Uncle Evan?"

"Wise up, will you? How could I have told them? I didn't know the writing box existed when I spoke to them. I only found out when I got to the shop."

"Your wife?"

Joe drew in a quick, shallow breath.

Wigfull said with an air of triumph, "Over dinner you told your wife you had found Mary Shelley's writing box?"

"Yep, I told her," Joe admitted. "She's the woman I share my life with, for God's sake. She was entitled to know why I kept her waiting so long."

"In a public restaurant."

"Give me a break. It was quiet there. Nobody was listening."

"How do you know?" said Wigfull.

"We had a seat in the window. No one else was near."

"Except the waiter."

"Get away!" said Joe, becoming annoyed. "What are you trying to prove?"

"See it from the waiter's point of view. A couple come into the restaurant," said Wigfull, and as he laid out his scenario he found it increasingly persuasive. "The man is obviously excited. He starts to speak to his wife about something sensational that happened to him. The waiter is intrigued. He overhears a phrase or two that get repeated several times. 'Noble and Nude' and 'Mary Shelley' and 'writing box'. That's enough. This waiter sees a chance to get rich quick. At the end of the evening, when the restaurant closes, he decides to take a look at Noble and Nude. He makes his way down to Walcot Street, by car, motorbike—I don't know. This is after midnight. He finds Noble and Nude and it's open and nobody is about. He can't believe his luck. The writing box is on the desk in the office. He picks it up and walks out with it."

"Is that it?" said Joe. "Have you finished?"

"It was either your wife or the waiter. Who else knew the box was worth taking?"

"Now you think Donna took it?" Joe fairly squeaked in disbelief.

"That might explain why she went missing."

"I'm going to let you in on something," said Joe. "Donna wouldn't go out on the streets after dark in a strange city if you paid her a million bucks. And the waiter was a young girl about fifteen years old. I think she was Greek. She didn't understand English. We had to point to the items on the menu. That little girl wouldn't know Mary Shelley from appleseed."

It may have been Joe's imagination, but he thought the big moustache sagged a little. Certainly the mouth below it sagged. Wigfull had suffered a serious reverse.

The officer who had gone to look at the suitcases returned. He shook his head. Joe got his keys back.

He hitched his thumbs assertively in the waistband of his boxer shorts. "Any other business, gentlemen? Or can I go back to sleep?"

nineteen

DIAMOND USUALLY TRIED TO keep Saturdays free for shopping and sport, or—more accurately—looking at shopping and sport. This morning there was no chance he would be standing in some dress shop while Steph tried on the latest creation. Or relaxing in front of the television. Dr Frankenstein had put paid to that.

Without much confidence of progress, he drove up to Chippenham to look at those bones. They were brought out in a cardboard evidence box tagged with the details of when and where they had been found. It was hard to believe they might have belonged to Hands. Stained yellowish brown, they were quite unlike the chalk-white bones from the vault. But he told himself these had spent time in the river and over ten years in this box.

He handled them with respect, as if the act of touching would give some clue to their origin. Dry bones, chipped and broken, difficult to think of as once having supported living tissue. A small, curved section of a rib-cage; a complete femur; a fibula; and the one that interested him most, the radius, or main bone of a forearm. This one was broken close to where the wrist would have been, and it was obvious that the bone had been shattered, not sawn through. He fingered the splintered end thoughtfully.

"Nothing's ever simple, is it?" he said to soften up the evidence sergeant who acted as curator of the macabre little collection. The man had already made it clear that he was a stickler for protocol and inclined to be pompous, a Jeeves in police uniform. "The bones I want to compare them with" (Diamond said) "are in another country."

"That is inexpedient, sir."

"But not a catastrophe. The country is Wales."

"A pity. The Welsh are peculiarly possessive about bones, sir."

"But these are in the forensic laboratory at Chepstow."

"That's more promising."

"Just across the water, but it might as well be Zanzibar," said Diamond. "They're a stubborn lot over there, as you were saying. They have a skeleton hand broken off at the wrist. I sent it to them myself. I'd like to see if it fits this arm bone, but do you know they won't let the hand out of the building?"

"They wouldn't be permitted to take such a liberty, sir. I'm under the same obligation myself."

"Are you telling me these old bones aren't allowed out?"

"That is the rule."

"It isn't as if I want them all. I'm only interested in this arm bone and it's broken already."

"That's immaterial, sir. It's all about continuity of evidence."

A fact well known to Diamond.

The sergeant coughed politely. "One could make a sketch."

"If you saw my sketching . . ."

"A photo?"

Diamond shook his head and introduced a hint of conspiracy. "Be easier if you turned your back."

"I'm not permitted to do that, sir."

"One pesky bone that nobody has looked at in years?"

"Much as I would like to assist, sir, turning my back is not an option."

"You'd get the thing back."

The sergeant sensed the heavy pressure he was under. "If I may tender a suggestion, I could make you a cast."

"A cast?"

"A plaster cast."

"How long will that take?"

"With quick-drying plaster of Paris? Less time than it would take to subvert me, sir."

Clearly the sergeant also resembled Jeeves in resourcefulness. He went to a shelf and took down the wax for the mould and the packet of plaster.

CHEPSTOW IS an easy run from Chippenham, up the M4 motorway and across the old Severn Road Bridge. Diamond could have sent someone of lower rank, but after handling the bones himself, he had a boyish curiosity to see if the jigsaw fitted.

He was never going to be the flavour of the month at the Forensic Science Unit, having blasted the men in white coats for years, but by good fortune he was seen by a young officer called Amelia who had never heard of him. He had to brandish his ID to get in. Once admitted, he refrained from mentioning that the place was not exactly a hive of industry. They all stayed in bed on Saturday mornings, he supposed. And how many times had they told him they were working round the clock to get results?

Amelia had some difficulty in finding Hands, but eventually they tracked the bones to a lab bench upstairs. They had been cleaned of most of the cement.

"They must be working on them now," said Amelia.

"Oh, yes?" Diamond said evenly. It was obvious that nobody had been in the lab all morning.

Humming "Dry Bones" as he worked, he took the cast from his pocket and tried fitting it to the stump of bone, watched by the young woman.

It didn't match.

"Too bad," he said, resisting the impulse to swear, and chucking the cast into the nearest bin. "Thanks for your help, love. It was worth a try."

Amelia gave a sympathetic murmur.

He asked if it was coffee time.

Amelia said tentatively, "Do you mind if I have a go? You were a bit quick making up your mind."

"It's a lost cause."

She retrieved the cast and began trying it with more sensitivity than Diamond, rotating it minutely each time. He watched with a bored expression, thinking of that coffee. His clumsiness was renowned, but he was not expecting to be shown up.

She said as she worked, "The thickness is about the same. Looking at the jagged end, I'd say it's quite likely that there was some splintering, in which case you're not going to get a perfect join." She held the cast steady. "Ah. Now look at the points where it's touching. They're coming together. Clearly there's a biggish piece missing, but if the bone shattered, that's to be expected."

Diamond screwed up his eyes in the attempt to see.

Amelia said, "I think it's worth looking at under a magnifier."

In another ten minutes she had convinced him that the bones at Chippenham belonged to Hands.

HE FORGOT to wind up the window as he approached the nick, so half a dozen microphones were thrust in his face when he turned off Manvers Street. If anything, there were more hacks about than yesterday. They wanted something juicy for the Sunday papers.

No, he told them blandly, he had nothing new to say and he did not expect to make any kind of statement that day.

Inside the building, he was more forthcoming, treating Keith Halliwell to an overcoloured account of the morning's discovery. In this version, he took all the credit for the plaster cast and he surprised the scientists at Chepstow with his deft work matching the cast to the bone.

Halliwell, who knew Diamond's limitations with technology as well as anyone at Manvers Street, listened to this with patience and then summed it up. "So Ingeborg was right."

"What?"

"She said the bones were worth comparing. She came up trumps."

"This time, yes," Diamond grudgingly conceded.

"Are you going to tell her?"

The thought had not occurred to him. "Why should I?"

"Give her the exclusive. She's earned it."

"If I do, the jackals out there will tear me to bits tomorrow." He gave a rueful smile as he thought it through. "And if I don't, she'll talk to her friend the ACC and I'll be serving on that cruddy committee for the rest of my days."

He rummaged among the papers on his desk for Ingeborg Smith's business card.

Halliwell tactfully found something else to do.

ALL THE ballyhoo about the vault meant that hardly any media attention was being given to Peg Redbird's death. Out at Walcot Street, house-to-house enquiries were being conducted without any interference from reporters.

Before lunch, Diamond decided to take what the ACC termed as an overview. He went looking for Wigfull and found him downstairs in what had swiftly been set up as an incident room, with phones, computers and a board covered in maps and photographs.

"How goes it?"

"As well as I can expect at this stage," Wigfull answered guardedly.

"Is the professor still in the frame?"

"Naturally."

"You had another go at him, I heard."

"I searched his hotel suite yesterday evening, yes."

"For Mary Shelley's writing box? No joy?"

"It was a long shot anyway, but it had to be tried."

"If he nicked it from the shop, he'd be a fool to keep it in the hotel. He isn't that."

Wigfull shrugged.

"No news of the wife, I suppose?" Diamond continued to press for information. "Do you take her disappearance seriously?"

"Is that meant to be sarcastic?" said Wigfull. "Of course I take it seriously."

"I mean when do you step up the search?"

"I'll run this in my own way, if you don't object."

"Just enquiring, John. That's my job. Has anything come out of the house-to-house?"

Wigfull gave a nod so slight he might have been watching a money spider crawl down Diamond's shirt front.

Diamond pricked up his eyebrows. "A witness?"

"Good Lord, no. Nothing so helpful as that. Just a name."

"Who's this, then?"

"Oh, a fellow by the name of Somerset helps out in the shop. He was seen there on the day of the murder."

"Acting suspiciously?"

"No, no. We've got nothing on him. By all accounts he was a big support to Peg. They got on well. I'll be talking to him later. He may give me something on the professor."

"So Joe Dougan is still your main suspect?"

"Definitely. Motive, opportunity."

"Means?"

"She was cracked over the head with something. It could have been that precious writing box he was so desperate to own."

"Which has disappeared."

"For the time being, yes."

"The box has disappeared. The wife has disappeared. How will you stop Joe from disappearing with them?"

"I've covered that. The hotel people will call me the minute he tries to check out. But I don't think he will. He's too smart."

"You could ask for his passport."

Wigfull sighed.

"All right," said Diamond. "Do it your way."

"This is a battle of wits," said Wigfull. "I know he killed her, and he knows I know. He'll put a foot wrong some time, and I'm going to keep going back to him until he does."

"Like Columbo."

"Who?"

"Detective Columbo on the telly."

"I don't follow you."

"That's his style," said Diamond. "The battle of wits. He knows who did it before the first commercial break. He always gets his man in the end." But he couldn't help thinking that Columbo was light years ahead of Wigfull in wheedling out the truth.

IN THE spirit of Saturday, he took Halliwell across the street for a beer and a bite of lunch at the Bloomsbury, that unique watering-hole that combined Virginia Woolf, fried scampi and a pool table. Under a "Duncan Grant" mural, they talked football and the prospects for the coming season. They were into their second beer before Halliwell looked out of the window and remarked that the press people seemed to have quit the front of the nick.

"It's Saturday, isn't it?" said Diamond. "They file their stories early for the Sundays. I was giving them nothing, so they shut up shop. They'll be back tomorrow."

"Did you speak to Ingeborg?"

"I did."

"She was pleased, no doubt."

"More 'I told you so' than pleased, but you were right, Keith. She earned her scoop."

"She wants a job on the force."

"Don't I know it!"

"She's bright."

He eyed Halliwell amusedly. "Has she recruited you as her agent?"

"She'd fit in all right, that's all I'm saying."

"Squeezed into your corner of the office?"

"No problem."

Diamond's mood had improved. Regardless of whether Ingeborg claimed credit for the morning's work, it had given a boost to the inquiry. "We've moved on, haven't we?" he said. "We're looking for someone who dismembered his victim and disposed of the parts in more than one place. Someone with transport, probably in the building trade. A van, maybe. Someone who thought he'd got away with it until the news broke a couple of days ago. That will have come as a shock. He'll be even more shaken if he reads Ingeborg's report in the paper tomorrow."

"A bloke?"

"Almost certainly. Dismembering is hard work. The way the bones shattered, my guess is that he used an axe or something like it, heavy as well sharp."

"We're still looking at these two brickies, then? Banger and Mash."

"One of them. Or bits of him, or bits of his victim." He looked expectantly at Halliwell. "Any progress?"

He wouldn't yet be shouting for drinks all round, if Halliwell's sigh was anything to go by. "I called everyone—well, everyone we traced—and there isn't much to report. I think they were only in the job a few weeks. Apart from that plasterer who put us onto this, just one other man had any memory of them."

"And . . . ?"

"Similar descriptions. Banger's long, messy hair and leather."

"Did he notice the Motorhead ring?"

"No. But he gave us a better description. Banger was lanky. Well over six feet tall and thin as a streak of chewing gum, as he put it."

"That may help. What about Mash?"

"He was more like average height. Went in for jeans and tee-shirts."

"No clue as to their real names?"

Halliwell shook his head. "One thing he does remember is that the vault was used for storing bags of cement."

"That's good. We know their job was wheeling the cement to the brickies working on the extension. Did you ask how these two got along?"

"Were they buddies, do you mean? He seemed to think so. They took some verbal from the older men, being inexperienced, and they got treated as a pair and stood up to it together."

They finished their drinks and crossed the street again. John Wigfull drove out of the police station as they approached and didn't even give them a nod.

"He's on the case," said Diamond.

"Which one?"

"Peg Redbird."

"Has he taken it over?"

"To all intents and purposes. I'm nominally in charge, but I've been told to keep at arm's length."

"I thought he looked pleased with himself."

"He thinks he's the dog's bollocks."

Unable to resist stoking up the old rivalry, Halliwell commented, "He's worked it well if he can get away as early as this."

"Not that bugger," Diamond said. "He's a workaholic. He's off to have another go at Joe Dougan if I'm any judge."

"The American professor?"

"Yes. He'll keep wearing him down."

"If I was the professor, I'd check out of that hotel and get back to wherever I came from," said Halliwell.

"Ah, but his wife is missing. If he hops it, he'll be revealed as callous and uncaring, which is what Wigfull wants."

"So it's cat and mouse," said Halliwell.

Diamond rolled his eyes.

Back in the office, he put through a call to his friend the evidence sergeant at Chippenham. "Thought you'd like to know we scored a hit. That plaster cast fitted the hand at Chepstow."

"Congratulations, sir. I dare say Chepstow will want to see the bones, then?"

"No doubt—in due time and through official channels and without violating the rules of evidence. Tell me, sergeant, when they first came in, those bones, I expect you got a forensic report on them. They weren't just put in the box and filed away."

"There's a report for sure, sir."

"I knew you'd say that, sergeant. The minute I saw you, I thought here's a man who misses nothing. You probably know what I'm going to ask next."

"You want to know if forensic were able to tell us anything about the deceased, sir."

"Right on."

"I'll check the report and call you back directly."

"Directly" was an under-estimate. The call came back a good forty minutes later, but it was worth waiting for. The deceased, according to the expert who had measured the bones, was likely to have been over six feet in height and below the age of twenty-five.

"So it was Banger who bought it."

"I beg your pardon, sir."

"No need, sergeant. I was talking to myself. How do they tell the age?"

"It's to do with the growth centres at the lower ends of the limb-bones, sir. If you remember this set of bones, they included a complete femur. The ends are soft—well, relatively soft—during the growing period. They harden as you get older, and by the time you're twenty-five they form solid bone and fuse with the rest of the skeleton."

Before the end of the afternoon, Diamond decided to go public on Bangcr and Mash. He would harness the media interest and appeal for information on the two young men who had worked in the vault in the spring of 1983.

"And that," he said to Keith Halliwell, "can wait till Monday. You and I are taking tomorrow off. I've been a lifelong supporter of the Lord's Day Observance Society."

JOHN WIGFULL, too, was using his Saturday afternoon profitably. Among the junk mail Diamond had handed him at Noble and Nude had been a flyer about a major antiques fair in the Assembly Rooms at the weekend. It was still on the back seat of his car. A real bonus. These fairs were big business in the antiques world. This one was sure to attract the local dealers and collectors—a marvellous chance for him to stroll about unnoticed doing surveillance, listening to unguarded gossip and perhaps getting information that would lead to an early arrest. It mattered to him more than anyone else could guess to get one over Diamond and make a favourable impression on the new Assistant Chief Constable. So he was playing this close to his chest. He hadn't even entered it in the diary. If it led to nothing, he lost nothing. He looked up last night's *Bath Chronicle* and, as he hoped, found an article describing some of the pieces on sale. He could pose as a genuine visitor.

He paid his entrance fee and went in, and spent some time in frustration, overhearing nothing at all of use. Eventually he identified Peg Redbird's helper, Ellis Somerset, a flamboyant character who didn't mind talking, and gave some useful information about what had happened in Noble and Nude on Friday. Nothing dramatic, but helpful. Somerset would make a good witness, he decided, intelligent, articulate and observant. The only cause for regret was that nothing he said conflicted with Professor Joe Dougan's statements.

The antiques fair had disappointed. Fortunately, John Wigfull had a back-up plan.

From there, he drove the short distance to Victoria Park. Earlier, whilst checking the *Bath Chronicle*, he had spotted a notice for a "Grand Day Out" for charity organized by the Bath Rotarians and featuring a traditional merry-go-round, dog obedience competition, pony rides and—the main attraction for Wigfull— Uncle Evan's Puppet Theatre. His sharp eye had spotted the words as if they were printed in red. Uncle Evan definitely existed, then. Joe Dougan had not invented the name.

Unlikely as it seemed, the Chief Inspector was now sitting on the grass with about thirty small children and a few parents in front of a wooden structure with an eight-foot-high proscenium arch and curtains, erected against the open back of a white van. The puppeteer could reach inside for extra puppets and scenery without interrupting the show. Helpfully for Wigfull, Uncle Evan was in view working the strings, a man probably past forty, of the sort you see in large numbers at folk festivals, with dark hair to his shoulders, beads around his neck and metal-framed glasses. Generally they are with thin women in long dresses and sandals.

The stage had a section cut out to allow Uncle Evan to step forward and make full use of the space. The children were not troubled by seeing how the puppets were controlled; they were wholly engrossed in the story, an action-filled plot borrowed from fairy tales, pantomime and television. There was even a Frankenstein's monster looking like Boris Karloff, a large cloth puppet that fitted onto Evan's arm and drew delighted screams from the small audience.

You would have to be totally insensitive to interrupt the show. Wigfull was only ninety per cent insensitive.

"The Monster, the Monster!" chorused the audience, as Uncle Evan made the Frankenstein figure sneak up on the little boy marionette who was the link for the story. Wigfull gave the drama only scant attention. He was thinking what he would ask Uncle Evan after the show. This, after all, was the man Joe Dougan claimed had pointed him in the direction of Noble and Nude. It was a heaven-sent chance to check out Dougan's story.

twenty

THE DAY OF REST started restfully enough. Peter Diamond remained horizontal until about nine, when Raffles the cat started hunting in the bed, the quarry being human toes and the toes at serious risk of getting clawed in the process. The Diamonds had invented the game when Raffles was a kitten. They had got some good entertainment simply by wriggling their toes. Raffles was fully grown now, still more than willing to play kitten games with a set of claws that would not have disgraced a leopard. This cat, and perhaps all cats who ever chanced upon a set of bare toes, treated them as separate entities unconnected with the owner. Under a winter duvet there had been some protection, but this was heat-wave weather and the Diamonds slept with a cotton sheet loosely over them. An uncovered foot was irresistible to Raffles.

The man who held Manvers Street in thrall moaned in submission, rolled out of bed, put on his moccasins, padded downstairs and opened a tin of Whiskas.

In twenty minutes, he was showered, dressed and off to the paper shop. Sunday might be a day off, but he was curious to see whether Ingeborg's story had made the front page.

It was there in a banner headline with the word "Exclusive" printed over it in red:

FRANKENSTEIN FRESH BONES HORROR

He scanned it rapidly, not expecting much correspondence with the facts. "Fresh" was hardly the word for those dusty bits of skeleton that had been lying in a box in Chippenham nick since 1986. Broadly, however, the paper had got the story right, dressed up as it was with horror movie trappings and sensational writing. He was styled as "Bath's burly Murder Supremo". He could live with that. Was it Ingeborg's phrase, he wondered, or dreamed up by a sub-editor?

Strolling home in the sunshine, he planned his day. Nothing strenuous in this weather. The garden would benefit from some water after so many days of sun—if he could summon up the energy to unroll the hose. First, he would cook a good breakfast and tempt Steph downstairs with the world's most potent appetizer, the whiff of fried bacon.

But when he turned the corner she was standing at the front gate in her dressing gown, extraordinary behaviour for Steph. Her strained, anxious expression was alarming enough, and she was also signalling to him to hurry. A series of potential disasters raced through his mind: someone in the family had died; the kitchen was on fire; the tank had burst and flooded the house. He ran the last yards.

"What's up, love?"

"They called from Manvers Street. John Wigfull has been attacked."

"Attacked? What? How come?"

"A head injury, they said. Someone found him in a field this morning."

"What—dead?"

"He was alive when they called, but it sounds bad. He's unconscious, in intensive care in the RUH. They need you, Pete."

"They'll get me."

Driving in from Weston, still dressed in his Sunday casuals, he was at a loss to understand, seesawing between anger and guilt. What in the name of sanity had Wigfull been doing, to get attacked in a field? The last he had seen of him was driving out of the nick on Saturday, the cue for some unkind comments that had to be regretted now. "He thinks he's the dog's bollocks." What a tribute to a wounded colleague. What an epitaph, if it came to that.

Because the Royal United Hospital was on his side of town, he drove straight into the Accident and Emergency reserved parking. Inside A & E, they sent him to another section. He stepped out along the corridor, breathing in the sick-sweet air that you only ever find in hospitals. There was a Sunday morning indolence about the place. No sign of a doctor. Smokers in dressing gowns and slippers stood in the small courtyards between the wards. Then a set of swing doors ahead burst open and a patient on a trolley was wheeled towards Diamond, with nurses walking at speed to keep up, holding containers connected by tubes.

He moved aside, his back to the wall, and caught a glimpse of a dead-white face, half-bandaged, the comical, overgrown moustache caked with blood. It was Wigfull. They rushed him by.

Diamond had not fully believed until this moment. The shock gripped him. He stood rigidly long after the trolley had been hurrried through another set of doors. Someone in a white coat passing the other way asked if he needed help. He shook his head and left the building.

AT MANVERS Street, the desk sergeant told him the Assistant Chief Constable wanted him in her office.

"What for?" he snapped, targeting his troubled emotions on the first hapless person within range. "I know sod all of what's going on."

Georgina, grim-faced, was on the phone when Diamond arrived upstairs. She beckoned him in. He strode across to the window and stared out, knowing he ought to compose himself before saying anything.

From this end of the conversation, he gathered she was getting the latest from the hospital. The back of Wigfull's skull was impacted and more X-rays were being taken. He was still unconscious. The ACC asked what his chances were. Her reaction to the answer was more than Diamond wanted to know.

She put down the receiver. This was a hard emotional test for her as well. She let out a long breath, closed her eyes for some few seconds, then said in a low voice, "We're not to expect anything except bad news."

He had to say something, and it sounded trite to the point of callousness. "He's survived a few hours, anyway."

She added, "There's a grace period, if I've got the term right. The shock to the nervous system puts everything on hold. The real crisis comes after."

Still Diamond found himself taking refuge in platitudes. "In all my time here, we've never had an officer killed."

"Was he investigating the woman found in the river?"

"Peg Redbird, yes."

"Wasn't she beaten about the head?"

"That's right."

"Do you know who John Wigfull was seeing yesterday?"

"No, ma'am." He was going to add, "Your orders," but wisely held back the words.

"We must find out from his team. I suppose he got too close to the truth and panicked the killer."

Diamond said nothing about that. If she wanted to speculate, fine. He would wait a bit.

Georgina was making a huge effort to sound rational, in control. "I don't attach any blame to you, Peter. It was my decision to put him in the front line, though I didn't expect this." She sighed and looked away. Then she turned and prepared to speak to him, folding her arms decisively.

Diamond had a fair idea what was coming.

"I'm going to ask you—instruct you—to drop whatever you were doing and take this on."

"Find the scum who clobbered him?"

"Yes. For God's sake, don't take any risks. There's real danger out there. Don't do anything without back-up. John Wigfull must have been alone when he was attacked."

"Where was he found exactly?"

"In a cornfield near Stowford. Do you know it?"

He knew Stowford, but he did not understand. So far as he could remember, the place was out in the country, a picture postcard setting beside the River Frome, a few ancient farm buildings converted to holiday houses and craft workshops. One Sunday afternoon a couple of summers ago he had driven there with Steph and sat in a rickety chair in the farmhouse garden and put away an unforgettable cream tea. But what could have taken Wigfull out there? Cream teas were not his scene at all. "It's on the A366, near Farleigh Hungerford."

"I couldn't even find it on the map," Georgina admitted.

"There isn't much there. He was in a field, you said?"

"A woman walking her dog across a footpath found him, or the dog did. This was early this morning, 6.30. His warrant card was in his pocket. Trowbridge Police notified us."

"So the scene is secured?"

"Yes, and being searched."

Diamond skimmed through the possibilities. "He had Joe Dougan in the frame for Peg Redbird's murder."

"The American?" This ACC was right up with events. "You've met this man, haven't you? Did he strike you as dangerous?"

"You can't tell. He's under stress. His wife is missing."

"No reason to attack a police officer."

"Unless John Wigfull is right and he really has something to hide."

"You'd better check his movements yesterday."

He cast his thoughts back. "And there was someone else Wigfull planned to see, someone he didn't rate as a suspect because he was supposedly friendly with Peg. He told me the name. Peg Redbird's assistant. Ellison? No, Ellis. Ellis was the first name. Ellis Somerset. He meant to talk to Ellis Somerset."

"You'll check him, too?"

"Of course."

"The other business, the bones in the vault, had better be given to someone else."

"Keith Halliwell is on it already."

"Can he handle all the hassle from the media?"

"He handles me, ma'am."

He left the room to go down and talk to Wigfull's team, his emotions still churned up. Years of despising the man could not be shrugged off because of the attack. Everyone in Manvers Street knew of the bitterness between them. Yet when a colleague is seriously injured, the entire police force stands together, outraged, committed to finding the attacker. He cared about Wigfull as a brother officer, and there was something more that he would not have admitted until now. For all the feuding, there had evolved a recognition of each other's way of working amounting—on the better days—to something like respect, though sugared by amusement. The image of his old antagonist, bleeding and unconscious, being wheeled past in the hospital, was not amusing. It would stay in his mind.

He found Sergeant Leaman at Wigfull's desk, going through the diary. They wasted no words on the sense of shock they both felt. Diamond said simply that he had been asked to inquire into the incident. "What I need from you is Mr Wigfull's itinerary."

"That's what I was trying to find, sir. There's no entry for yesterday afternoon or evening."

"That's unlike him."

"Yes, he took a lot of care about procedures. I mean he *takes* a lot of . . ." The sergeant's words trailed away in embarrassment.

"Didn't he tell you his plans? I saw him drive out of here some time pretty close to two o'clock. He wasn't going home."

"How do you know, sir?"

Diamond backed off a little. He wasn't going to talk about a gut feeling. "We both know he's a workaholic, don't we?"

Leaman gave a faint smile. No one in Wigfull's team ever spent much time in the canteen.

Diamond thought of another angle. "His car. Have the Trowbridge Police found his car?"

"Not to my knowledge, sir. I don't suppose they know what he drives."

His measured calm hit an obstruction. "It's our bloody business to tell them. What is it? I ought to know. I was in it the other day."

"A red Toyota Corolla, sir."

"Send out an alert, then. Have them check the farm at Stowford. That won't take five minutes. The damned car can't be far from the field unless he was driven there by his attacker. Get someone onto it."

While Leaman organized that, Diamond picked up the diary and leafed through it, sifting possibilities at near computer speed.

He said to Leaman when he returned, "This murder case was the biggest thing to come his way this year. He'd have cancelled his weekend. Yours, too, I reckon. How was he using you?"

Leaman said he had been collating witness statements, to get a picture of Peg Redbird's final hours. It had been an absorbing task. Not much had passed between Wigfull and him all morning.

"Didn't he say anything at all before he left?"

"About where he was going? No, sir."

"About anything?"

Leaman frowned, trying to remember. "He looked over my shoulder at the screen and asked if any new names had come up."

"People Peg Redbird met?"

"Yes. I said there was nothing he didn't know already. He asked me to leave a print-out on his desk."

"So he was coming back later in the day?"

"I thought so at the time."

"And you did as instructed?"

"Yes, sir. The print-out is still here."

"So we have this almighty gap between two p.m. Saturday and six thirty this morning when he was found in the cornfield. Let's assume he went to interview a witness, someone who visited Peg the day she died. The names are here, are they?" He picked the print-out off the desk.

"It's chronological," Leaman explained. "Starting Thursday morning. She was seen leaving the shop at ten a.m. by Miss Barclay, a neighbour. At ten oh five, she buys a pint of milk from a shop in Walcot Street."

"Cut to the chase," Diamond said. "Who came into Noble and Nude?"

"The first caller we know about is Ellis Somerset, who helps in the shop."

Diamond was all attentiveness. "Go on."

"He turned up about one thirty, after lunch."

"That's still lunch in my book."

Leaman looked for a hint of a smile and wasn't treated to one. Diamond's humour was difficult to read under any circumstances.

"Do you have a statement from Mr Somerset?"

"Yes, sir. He looked after the shop while Peg went up to Camden Crescent for a valuation. He was there for much of the afternoon. He's our main source."

"Who took the statement?"

"DC Paul."

"Did anyone follow it up?"

"Not yet, unless . . ."

Diamond gave an approving nod. Leaman didn't need to say it. Wigfull may well have decided on a personal meeting with Ellis Somerset. Perhaps he wanted it off the record, which would explain why it wasn't in the diary. "I'll catch up with Somerset shortly. And what about this valuation? Who was that for?"

"A Mr Pennycook, the nephew of Simon Minchendon, who died recently. It was in the local paper."

"Has anyone spoken to Pennycook?"

"He lives in Brighton."

"Yes, but has anyone—"

"The Brighton police took a statement, sir. It's on the computer if you want to read it."

"Have you?" Sitting in front of the screen was not Diamond's idea of police work.

"Yes, sir."

"Anything startling in it?"

Sergeant Leaman shook his head. "Except that Brighton have him down as a druggie."

"Crack?"

"H."

Diamond vibrated his lips. A drugs-related motive always had to be taken seriously.

He studied the print-out again. "Some time between three and four Professor Dougan arrives in the shop. This is while Somerset is in charge, right?"

"Yes, sir. He spends some time looking around. He's still there when Peg returns from Camden Crescent about four-thirty in the afternoon."

"So you now have three people helping you with your inquiries into the murder, so to speak: Somerset, Pennycook and Dougan. Any others?"

"No, sir. Other customers came into the shop, but we don't have their names."

"We're stuck with the ones on the list, then. Pennycook lives a hundred miles away. Dougan has been put through the grinder several times already. Putting myself in John Wigfull's shoes yesterday afternoon, I'd have Ellis Somerset top of my visiting-list."

THE ANTIQUES Fair was into its third day at the Assembly Rooms. Diamond and Leaman arrived there thanks to a tip-off from a neighbour of Somerset's in Brock Street. "Ellis is something to do with the committee," they were told. "He'll be there all day, parading up and down. Look for the chappie in the bow-tie and brothel-creepers and a hideous coloured suit."

True, Ellis Somerset stood out, even among the colourful crowd who tour the country with the antiques fairs. His carroty hair would have made you look twice, regardless of the mustard yellow three-piece.

He said in a carrying voice that half the room must have heard, "This is over-egging the cake, isn't it? Two visits from the Bill in two days."

Just what Diamond wanted to know.

"You saw another officer yesterday?"

"He didn't precisely *say* he was from the police, but you can tell. The fellow stood out like a camel in a horse race. Large moustache—"

Diamond cut him short. "Was this in the afternoon?"

"Shortly after lunch."

"In here?"

"We went for a cup of tea."

"What a good idea."

"But I'm supposed to be on hand to answer questions," Somerset mildly protested after being escorted to the tea-room.

"Which you are," said Diamond. "First question: do you take sugar? Second: did you smash the policeman's head in?"

Somerset rocked back in his chair, giving the table a kick that spilt tea across it. Any interrogator knows the trick of going straight for the jugular. It gets a reaction. The difficult part is to pick out the signs of guilt.

He was losing most of the colour from his cheeks and the effect did not sit well with the mustard suit. "What the blazes do you think I am—a psychopath?"

"Would you answer me?"

"No, I do not attack policemen and I protest in the strongest terms at being asked such a question." A little of the colour seeped back as he went on the offensive.

"Drink some of that tea, sir," Diamond suggested. "Did Chief Inspector Wigfull ask you about your employer, Miss Redbird?"

"My 'employer'?" He spoke the word as if it was distasteful. "Peg was a friend, a very dear friend, as it happens. I helped out in the shop from time to time on a voluntary basis. I explained all this yesterday afternoon." He spread his hands, looking to Sergeant Leaman for a more sympathetic hearing, but Leaman was poker-faced.

"I'm sure you did, sir," Diamond answered. "My difficulty is that John Wigfull is lying in the Royal United with his head stoved in. We don't know what you told him because he can't speak to us."

Ripples appeared on Somerset's smooth facade. "The man who was here yesterday?"

"He came to talk to you about a murder and now he's critically wounded himself."

"Surely you can't believe I . . . ?" His voice trailed off as the seriousness of his position sank in.

"Where did you spend the rest of yesterday? What time did you leave the Antiques Fair?"

Somerset clawed at his red hair distractedly. "When it closed, at six."

"And then?"

"I had a drink in Shades Wine Bar with a couple of friends for twenty minutes and then I walked home."

"How did you spend the evening?"

"Reading a book."

"You didn't go out again? Saturday night and you stayed in?"

"Officer, if you'd spent most of the day on your feet at an antiques fair, you'd be glad of a quiet evening." Then a thought struck him and he became more animated. "There was a man he was asking about, an American who came into the shop while I was looking after it. That's who your inspector friend was interested in."

Diamond heard this without surprise. "What were you able to tell him?"

Seizing the chance to deflect attention from himself, Somerset answered, "That the American was with us a long time on Thursday afternoon. An hour and a half to my certain knowledge, and probably longer. Some of the time he was waiting for Peg to come back. He insisted on seeing her personally and would not be put off when I told her she was out doing a valuation. He went off upstairs, rooting around the shop. To tell you the truth, I'd clean forgotten about him by the time Peg finally came back. Rather embarrassing actually. I introduced them and then went out myself to organize some transport. She'd bought a few things up at Camden Crescent and wanted them collected."

Diamond glanced towards Leaman. "I wish I had friends like that."

"I wouldn't do it for everyone," said Somerset. "Peg was special."

"More than just a friend, you said?"

All his colour returned now, and more. "That is not what I

said. I referred to her as a very dear friend. We respected each other."

His face was making a stronger statement. He had been smitten. Diamond would put money on it. The friendship may not have amounted to an affair, but not through want of passion on Somerset's side.

"So what did you do? Hire a van and collect these antiques from Camden Crescent?"

"Exactly that. Some small bits of furniture and a few pots and pictures."

"Valuable?"

"Peg seemed well satisfied."

"That's ducking my question. You're an antiques man yourself, Mr Somerset. Were these items going to make her a tidy profit?"

"Listen, officer, profit is a taboo word in the antiques trade. We talk about everything else under the sun, but we don't mention our mark-up."

"Was it quality stuff?"

"Peg wouldn't have bought rubbish. The pots were all right. Furniture so-so. She was more excited about the paintings. She insisted on unloading them from the van herself. A couple of watercolours. Not my field at all. You have to specialise. She thought she'd found a pair of Blakes."

"Sextons?"

"I beg your pardon."

"Sexton Blakes. Fakes. Rhyming slang. That fellow who became a celebrity on the strength of his forgeries. He called them his Sextons. What was his name?"

"Tom Keating," said Somerset. "I'm with you now. No, the Blake I referred to was genuine enough. The mystic, poet and engraver, William Blake."

Diamond dredged deep into his memory and brought up a fragment from an English class in his grammar school one sunny afternoon when he would rather have been out on the school field. He could hear Mr Yarrow speaking the words: " '*Tyger! tyger! burning bright*'?"

"The same," said Somerset with a sniff.

"And was it good to find a pair of Blakes?"

"Spectacularly good, if that's what they were, and I can't believe we were wrong. Blake's style was so individual that one couldn't confuse it with anyone else."

"You seem knowledgable."

"A specialist wouldn't think so."

With that satisfying sense of things slotting into place, Diamond remembered meeting a specialist only a day or two before. Councillor Sturr had boasted of owning one of the best collections of English watercolours. Hadn't a Blake been the main attraction of those insipid daubs on the wall of the Victoria Gallery?

He returned to the main business. "You told all this to John Wigfull yesterday, right?"

"I believe I did, yes."

"Was there anything he asked in particular? Anything we haven't covered?"

"He kept on and on about the American professor. By the time we finished I was wrung dry."

"Did you tell him anything useful?"

"I haven't the faintest idea."

"Fair enough. Dumb question. Have you told me everything you told him?"

"Just about."

"When you got back from Camden Crescent on Thursday evening, was Professor Dougan still there?"

"No, he'd left by then."

"What time was this?"

"About eight, I suppose. Peg was expecting him back, though. There was this early nineteenth century writing box on her desk that he was extremely keen to buy. I don't know why. It had been gathering dust in the shop for donkey's years. The key was missing—or so Peg claimed." A thin smile fleetingly surfaced.

Alerted, Diamond leaned forward. "What are you saying—that she had the key all the time?"

"You can't blame her. She wanted to get the best price she could for the goods."

"Are you telling me she unlocked the box after Dougan left?"

"It was open when I first got back. I expect she wanted to see what was inside. A private look, while the professor was away. If he was so keen, there could have been something valuable inside, couldn't there? She'd have been daft to part with it without checking."

"And was there anything in it?"

"Nothing she was telling me about."

Diamond digested this. If Joe Dougan could be believed, the box had been locked when he returned to the shop after having dinner with his wife. In Peg's absence, he had spent more time fruitlessly trying keys. *If he could be believed.* This part of his story could so easily be a cover-up.

Suppose, instead, Dougan had returned to Noble and Nude and found Peg there, with the box open, its secrets revealed. Here was a scenario for violence: Peg setting an impossibly high price, or even refusing to sell. Dougan, crazed by the prize being snatched away, striking out.

"Did you tell Chief Inspector Wigfull what you just told us, about the box being open?"

"Yes, that came up in the questions."

"You said the box was open when you *first* got back. Did it get locked again?"

"It was still open when I left."

"What time was that? Before Dougan returned?"

"Oh, yes," said Somerset. "I finished unloading the van by nine and then I was off."

"Off where?"

He frowned, not liking the shift in the questioning. "To Brock Street, where I live."

"In the van?"

"Yes. It was due for return by eight the next morning."

"So you parked it overnight. Where?"

"In Brock Street. There are spaces by that time."

"Did you speak to anyone? Is there a neighbour or someone who can vouch for you being home at that time?"

"Did you make any phone calls?" Leaman sensibly asked.

Now Somerset gave a nervous, angry sigh. "No, I don't have an alibi. You'll just have to take my word for it. I was Peg's devoted friend. I wouldn't have harmed her in a million years." Just to confirm it, a tear rolled down his cheek and made a dark spot on the yellow suit. "I'm sorry. This is all too much."

Diamond would be the judge of that. He was not finished yet. "You left by nine, you say. She was still in the shop, is that right?"

"Yes."

"Expecting a second visit from Professor Dougan?"

"Not only him. She had other business to attend to."

"Other business?" Diamond repeated the words in a more animated tone. Somerset had spoken them like a dirge.

"She already had a buyer for those watercolours I mentioned. She'd been on the phone and expected an offer the same evening."

"Who from?"

"She wouldn't say. She was being mysterious about it. To tell you the truth, I was more than a little upset. She made it sound like an assignation."

"A what?"

He hesitated, needing to swallow before the words would come. "As if she was meeting a . . . lover. She was being mischievous, trying to make me jealous. Her exact words—I remember them clearly—were 'I'm expecting an offer tonight, if that doesn't sound indelicate.' "

"How did you react?"

"I was too hurt to speak. I know she was only playing with words, but they were meant to wound, and I didn't care for that one bit."

"You don't have any idea who she meant?"

"You're not expecting me to point the finger at someone?"

"Come on, Mr Somerset," Diamond said, his patience snapping. "This isn't junior school. Your friend was murdered and dumped in the river."

He was still reluctant to speak. He swallowed deeply and took a look around the room. "I could be mistaken. The only serious collector of English watercolours I know in Bath is John Sturr. But he's a well respected figure in the city. He's on the Council."

Diamond heard this without surprise. He had got there five minutes before, from personal knowledge. But it was still an intriguing link-up. "Would you cast your mind back and tell me exactly what Peg said about this deal she was setting up?"

"I just did."

"You repeated one sentence that you found hurtful. I want to know what else she said, about the paintings and the client."

"That's not easy."

"Try."

"Well, she talked about the subject matter, how it seemed to be straight out of *Frankenstein*."

"You're serious?" This added an extra dimension. Diamond was beginning to feel plagued by the wretched monster.

"Peg was convinced of it and she convinced me. She knew the book, and she'd brought back a copy from the library. One of the pictures was the meeting of Frankenstein and the monster in a Swiss valley and the other was Frankenstein discovering his bride had been killed, with the monster staring through the window. Incidents straight out of the book."

Diamond said, "I remember seeing a film—"

"Forget it," Somerset cut him short. "The cinema versions of

Frankenstein are a travesty. They make the monster out to be brain-damaged, an unmitigated villain. I've been reading the book again. It's Frankenstein, the creator, who is the true villain. The monster isn't inherently evil. He is driven to cruelty by Frankenstein's neglect and bad treatment. He's deprived of a soul, a friend, a love. It's a very modern story in that sense. A terrible upbringing warps the poor creature's development."

"He needed a social worker to straighten him out," said Diamond, too flippantly, but Somerset did not react.

"They even get the make-up wrong. He's said to be grotesque, yes, but not like the Boris Karloff version. Mary Shelley's creature has lustrous black hair that flows, and fine, white teeth. Instead of those dark pitted eye sockets you see in all the films, his were white. True, the lips are said to be black and the skin yellowy, but I'm sure the author wouldn't have recognised most of the screen versions you see."

"You think she would have recognised the monster in the paintings?"

"I'm certain of it."

"Blake and *Frankenstein*," Diamond mused. "It's a connection I hadn't made."

Somerset took this as a literary observation. "I was rather caught off-guard myself when Peg showed me the pictures. Think about it, though. The book was published in his lifetime. Writers, poets and people tended to know each other, didn't they, Shelley, Coleridge, all that crowd, or at least take an interest in what was being written? Peg told me that Blake knew Mary Shelley's mother, the Wollstonecraft woman. He illustrated some of her children's stories."

"And he decided to illustrate *Frankenstein*?"

"It seems so, yes, unless these are brilliant fakes. We looked pretty closely at them. Took them apart, in fact. The paper is usually the giveaway. A clever forger can make a fair stab at an artist's style, but he can't fake the paint and the paper."

"Was it old enough, the paper?"

"We were convinced of it. In this trade you acquire a sense of how old things are. It's more a matter of experience than science. I reckon that paper could be dated to somewhere between 1800 and 1825."

"Is it usual, for an artist to illustrate a book?"

"In the case of Blake, yes. He was an engraver, so it was very much his line of work. Perhaps you're familiar with his series on Milton and Dante?"

Diamond didn't rise to that. "You were saying you studied these pictures together and she decided she knew of a buyer."

"She said she had a quick sale in mind, not to a dealer, but someone who would pay—to use one of her expressions—top dollar."

"And she wouldn't tell you who it was."

Somerset's lip quivered a little. "She seemed to be relishing the prospect, talked about having her bit of fun. She said this was a rare beast, someone who had no choice except to buy."

"Those were her actual words?"

"As near as I can recall."

Diamond glanced at Leaman. "Did you get them?"

The sergeant looked up from his notebook and nodded.

Diamond turned back to Somerset. "Did any of this come up in yesterday's interview with John Wigfull?"

"It did."

"And did you give him Mr Sturr's name?"

Somerset swung to Leaman, appealing for the sympathy he had failed to get from Diamond. "Look here, I don't want this to get back to Councillor Sturr—that I put you onto him. He's a powerful man in Bath. He could make life very difficult for me."

"That makes two of us," said Diamond.

twenty-one

"HOW CLOSE TO STOWFORD?" Diamond asked over the intercom.

"Less than a mile across the fields, sir."

"The field where he was found?"

"Yes."

John Wigfull's car had been located in the Wiltshire village of Westwood.

On the drive out there, the big man treated Sergeant Leaman to his thoughts on the case. "Two people struck on the head."

After that, as if no more needed saying, he stared out at the thickly wooded slopes of the Limpley Stoke Valley.

Leaman didn't know Diamond well enough to pass a comment. As a statement it was not in the Sherlock Holmes class.

Eventually Diamond added, "One of them dead."

It was beginning to sound like verse. Leaman couldn't believe that the head of the murder squad was composing rhymes about a vicious assault on a colleague. He knew of the rivalry between his boss and Diamond, and he knew Diamond had a reputation for speaking out, but to hear the tragic events rendered into verse was too awful to contemplate. Something needed to be said.

"Are they connected, sir, Peg Redbird's death and the attack on Mr Wigfull?"

"Let's assume it," said Diamond at once, and Leaman was willing to believe the rhyming had been coincidence. "John

Wigfull got too close to Peg Redbird's killer and provoked an attack. So who is it? Professor Dougan was his prime suspect and he has to be ours as well. But there are others in the frame. You saw what Somerset is like. He was devoted to Peg Redbird, and she was taunting him that night, talking of a secret meeting with someone else."

"The picture collector?"

"Right. Somerset has no alibi. The question is whether he was made jealous enough to kill."

"And then thrown into a panic when Mr Wigfull got onto him?"

Diamond gave a nod. "Then there's Pennycook, the guy on the fiddle with the antiques. He could have got panicky, too. It's easy to assume he was in Brighton yesterday, but was he?"

"We can check," said Leaman.

"We will. We've got to see him. And we have another dark horse, Councillor Sturr, who happens to collect early English watercolours."

"Why would he take a swipe at Mr Wigfull?"

"That isn't the question," said Diamond, making it sound as if taking a swipe at Wigfull was standard behaviour. "The question is: why would John Sturr have killed Peg Redbird? And how could he have killed her, considering he was at the ACC's party that night and spent the rest of it with Ingeborg Smith?"

"That's what I call a good alibi."

"But if he *did* kill her, and CID in the shape of John Wigfull got on his tail, then it's no surprise he went for him with a blunt instrument."

"In a field out in the country?"

"That's a mystery we face with each of them. How does an American Professor find his way to a remote spot like Stowford? What's Ellis Somerset doing in a cornfield when he said he was at home with a good book? How does a junkie like Pennycook happen to be there? Let's see if we can find a clue."

Wigfull's car, now festooned in crime scene tape, stood among twenty or thirty others in the shadow of a tall stone wall that marked the boundary of Westwood Manor, a National Trust property. The iron gate to the church was on the same side of the lane.

"Plenty of cars," Leaman commented.

"Visiting the Manor House," Diamond aired his knowledge, having just caught sight of the board that welcomed people inside. "They open Sundays. I'm more interested to know if there were cars here yesterday."

The constable from the Wiltshire Police guarding Wigfull's car had the answer. "Scarcely anyone was about, sir. The house wasn't open."

Diamond thanked him and asked if he was just as well informed about the interior of the car.

"Personally, I haven't looked inside, sir, but I understand nothing of any use was found."

"I'll decide that for myself. What was in there?"

"Just what you see, sir. The local paper on the back seat, Friday's edition. There's also a leaflet advertising the Antiques Fair. And a parking ticket on the dash, dated Saturday."

"That'll be when he called at the Assembly Rooms." Diamond looked at the ticket though the windscreen. It was the kind you buy from a machine, the standard ticket issued by Bath Council, whichever car park you used. Wigfull had paid £1.40 for two hours, and the time would have elapsed at 4.21 p.m. But there was no way of telling the actual time he had left. "I'll look inside."

"It's sealed, sir."

"Unseal it, then."

The constable eyed him in amazement. "Forensic haven't finished yet."

"Their look-out, constable, not mine. Don't wet yourself. I'll take responsibility."

He lifted the police tapes enough to open the rear door and remove the newspaper and leaflet. The *Bath Chronicle* was folded open at a page covering the weekend's entertainments and attractions. The Antiques Fair had both a display advert and an article about some of the items on offer. But Wigfull had gone rooting for information, not bronze cherubs. The fair was an opportunity, and he had kept it to himself. Out for personal glory, Diamond decided.

No clue as to why he had gone from the Assembly Rooms to a field in Stowford.

The paper was tossed back onto the car seat. "Forensic are welcome to this. Let's look at the scene."

The constable pointed across the fields. The two detectives climbed over a stile and started to take the footpath across a chest-high crop of maize. "Keep your eyes peeled," he told Sergeant Leaman. "They must have come this way, John Wigfull and his attacker."

"Together?" said Leaman.

"Not exactly arm in arm. My picture of it is that Wigfull is in pursuit. He follows someone in the car from Bath. That part is simple. Then the suspect drives into Westwood, parks, jumps out and heads across the field. Out here you can't follow a man without being noticed. Just look ahead of you. In this stuff you'd spot another man half a mile away, easy. So he knows Wigfull is on the trail. He ducks down somewhere, ambushes him and clocks him one. Then he legs it back to his car and drives off."

They reached the wall at the far side and climbed over another stile into a small uncultivated area of grass and a few trees. Ahead, under a sycamore's shade, was a lone figure in police uniform having a smoke. Galvanized, the constable dropped the cigarette, slammed his cap on and picked up a clipboard.

"Are we as obvious as that?" Diamond muttered to Leaman. "It must be the way you walk."

A large area around the spot where Wigfull had been found was marked with metal stakes and checkered tape.

"So what did they pick up in the fingertip search this morning?" Diamond asked when the introductions were over.

"Not a lot, sir," the constable answered. "A horse-shoe, some plastic bottles, a few cigarette butts, all of them looking as if they'd been here for years."

No mention was made of the fresh butts around his feet.

They went over to the plastic tent protecting the spot where Wigfull had been found. Soil samples had been taken, but the scene looked unlikely to yield much information. There were no indications of a struggle. The theory of an ambush was the most plausible.

"What size was the horse-shoe?"

"Average." The constable made the shape with forefingers and thumbs.

"Not large enough for a weapon, then?"

"Don't know, sir."

"I mean a weapon heavy enough to brain a man. If he had any sense, this bozo, he'll have got rid of the weapon in that cornfield we walked through." The fact that the crop was maize didn't undermine the point; you could have driven a motorbike into the field and lost it among the tall stocks.

He pursued this question of the weapon. "If, as we were saying, he was running from Wigfull, he's unlikely to have been carrying the thing he used. It's more likely he picked something up, any damned thing that came to hand."

"A piece of timber?" suggested Leaman.

"That's the way my thoughts were heading." He looked around for a convenient pile of chopped firewood. Nothing so obvious was in sight. "What's behind us, over there?"

"A pond, sir."

He went to see for himself. The pond was outside the staked area, supposedly of limited interest to the scene-of-crime team.

Large enough to have floated a rowing boat in it, but you wouldn't have needed oars.

Sergeant Leaman, at his side, said unwisely, "Are you thinking he might have chucked the piece of timber in here, sir?"

"Timber would have floated, wouldn't it?"

Leaman reddened.

Diamond was examining the ground at the margin of the water. He scraped at the soil with his foot, then crouched and rubbed some on his finger and sniffed. "Bonfire. There's just the possibility that he *found* something here that he used as the weapon. It's the sort of spot teenagers pick for whatever they get up to over a few drinks. See the ring-pulls? Fag-ends? The cheapest drink is cider. That's the one most kids start with, and cider comes in bottles, thick, heavy bottles. It's speculation, but I'm wondering if our villain picked up an empty and bashed John Wigfull with it."

"And chucked it in the pond?" said Leaman.

Diamond gave him a look that said don't push me.

twenty-two

" . . . ONE THOUGHT, ONE CONCEPTION, *one pur-
pose. So much has been done, exclaimed the soul of Frankenstein—
more, far more, will I achieve, treading in the steps already marked, I
will pioneer a new way, explore unknown powers, and unfold to the
world the deepest mysteries of creation.*"

Like Frankenstein, he was treading in steps already marked,
but only to reach new territory. The way was dangerous, better
travelled in darkness. More than ever now, he needed to cover
his tracks. He was a hunted man.

twenty-three

JOE DOUGAN APPEARED MORE calm than he had at any point up to now. "Nice timing, superintendent," he said, rising from a chair in the garden of the Royal Crescent Hotel. "Why don't you gentlemen join me? I just ordered afternoon tea."

Tea in the Royal Crescent was something special and a waiter was approaching the table, but Diamond waved him away. This was not a twenty-year-old murder he was investigating now. The time of leisurely tea-breaks was well past. He sat opposite Dougan and sent Sergeant Leaman for another chair. "I'd better say at once we have no news of your wife," he told the professor.

"No problem," said Joe with a serene smile.

Diamond widened his eyes.

Joe said, "Donna is fine."

Fine? Diamond had to play the statement over in his mind before fully taking it in.

Joe added, "She called me at lunchtime. She's in Paris, France."

"*Paris?*"

"It surprised me, too. She just needed time out, she said. Things got a little heavy for her, my fling with Mary Shelley, as she calls it. Yeah, that's the way Donna saw it. She felt neglected. When I went back to the antiques store on Thursday evening, Donna went looking for sympathy. She knocked on the door of some people we met here, a Swiss couple, the Hacksteiners. They had the best suite in the hotel and they took pity.

They let Donna spend the night in a spare bed in their suite. The next day she picked her moment to leave the place without being seen and travelled to France with them."

"Without luggage?"

"It's only a train ride."

"Passport?"

"She has it with her. And credit cards." He gave the long-suffering smile one man shares with another when talking about the ways of women. "She wants one more day in Paris. Not many shops are open Sundays over there."

"Why didn't she get in touch before this?"

Joe shrugged. "To pay me out, I guess. I'm so happy to know she's alive and well that I didn't ask her."

"You're positive it was your wife?"

"Are you kidding? I know that voice. In twenty-four years I've heard plenty of it."

Heart-warming news, apparently. Diamond was not convinced. He would not believe until he had seen Donna himself. It was all so convenient just when the heat was on Joe. He couldn't produce her because she was in another country.

"So when is she coming back to Bath?"

"She won't. I'll travel out there tomorrow."

Like hell you will, Diamond thought. Suspicion of Joe was driving him now, just as it had driven Wigfull. "Let's talk about yesterday. How did you spend the afternoon and evening?"

Joe's manner changed abruptly. He drew back in the chair, gripping the arms. "Hey, what is this? More dumb questions? I've taken more than my share from you guys in the past two days. I'm going to get onto my embassy if you don't let up. Police intimidation. We don't take that stuff."

"It's not intimidation, professor."

"And what if I refuse to answer?"

"Why should you?"

"Because I'm sick of your questions, that's why. You had cooperation from me all the way, you and that other cop with the mustache. You tell *me* something: who identified the woman who was found in the river? I did. I'm supposed to be on vacation, not looking at dead bodies. The other evening your people searched my room, treating me like a goddam criminal. I'm standing in my boxer shorts, the Dodge Professor of English, watching two cops go through my possessions."

"Who was that—Chief Inspector Wigfull?"

"With the mustache."

"This was when—Friday?"

Joe nodded. "They didn't find a thing."

"Do you know what they were looking for?"

"You'd better ask the mustache."

"I can't," said Diamond. "John Wigfull is lying unconscious in hospital. Somebody caved his head in."

Joe was silent for a time. "And you're thinking I'm the somebody?"

"It will help us to know your movements yesterday, sir."

Joe flushed. "I'm not a violent man. I'm an academic, for God's sake." His outraged innocence was worth an Oscar nomination if he was acting.

"Yesterday afternoon?" Diamond pressed him, while Leaman waited with notebook open.

With a sigh, Joe capitulated. "What was yesterday . . . Saturday? I went around the hotels, asking about Donna. It was a long shot, but I wanted to satisfy myself that she wasn't still in Bath. I carry a picture of her and I showed it to the reception people, concierges, bellmen, anyone I could."

"Which hotels?"

"You name it. The Hilton, the Francis, the Bath Spa. You can check. They'll remember me."

"That was in the afternoon?"

"All day, from eleven on."

"Until . . . ?"

"Until my feet cried out for mercy. Do you have any idea how many hotels there are? I got back around five, I guess. Sat in the bath tub for a long time. Had a meal on room service. Watched television until I was falling asleep in the chair."

"Make any phone calls?"

He shook his head.

"Did you see Chief Inspector Wigfull at any stage yesterday?"

"You don't give up, do you? No, I did not."

"And now you're proposing to leave Bath and join your wife in Paris?"

"Tomorrow. You don't have to sound so grudging. I'm a free agent."

"Where is she staying?"

"The Ritz. Donna doesn't do things by halves."

"Have you made your travel arrangements?"

"Sure. I'm catching the 10.28 to London tomorrow morning. I booked a seat on the Eurostar train."

"Without Mary Shelley's writing box?"

He rolled his eyes upwards. "Don't break my heart. I wish I knew what happened to that."

Before leaving the hotel, Diamond checked on room service to the John Wood suite. An evening meal of asparagus soup, sole *meuniere* and fresh strawberries and cream had been logged at 6.20 p.m. Saturday. "It still leaves him out of the hotel for long enough to attack John Wigfull and get back," he commented to Leaman.

"He'd need transport, sir."

"There and back. Don't say it—the logistics are difficult. If we knew for sure when the attack took place, it would help. My feeling is that it happened in daylight. Wigfull would know there isn't much point in chasing a wanted man across fields after dark."

"Maybe the house-to-house will turn something up," Leaman said.

"Maybe." Diamond hadn't much confidence.

Wiltshire Police were at present knocking on doors to find a witness who had seen someone on the footpath over the fields, or noticed the cars outside the Manor House. There was also a large search-party combing the fields for the weapon used on Wigfull. They had to try.

They returned to Manvers Street, where the police station was like a prison before an execution. The only news of John Wigfull was that he was still unconscious, his condition critical.

AT THE time Avon and Somerset Police acquired their heli-copter, Diamond was heard to say it was an expensive toy that he would never use. Like many of his stands against technology, this one was fated to be undermined. Strapped into the seat, staring fixedly ahead, he was being flown over the great expanse of Salisbury Plain towards the South Coast. Privileged views of the ancient sites of Stonehenge and Avebury passed unnoticed. He did not enjoy the sensation of flying.

They touched down on the lawn in front of Montpelier Cres-cent, Brighton, the address of Ralph Pennycook, the young man who had sold antiques to Peg Redbird on the day of her murder. The journey was done in under an hour. When Diamond looked about him, after stepping down and battling with the draught created by the rotor blades, he had the strange sensation that he had never left Bath. The neo-classical facade of the crescent was, if anything, grander in scale. Each large house with its own pillars and pediment might have been the front of a theatre.

Helicopter travel is convenient, certainly, but not discreet. People had opened their doors to watch and children were run-ning across the grass towards the chopper. "After this puppet-show, let's hope he's at home," Diamond muttered to Sergeant Leaman.

He was—already at the front door—and their mode of travel

had impressed him markedly. His hand was at his throat, pinching at a fold of loose skin, and his eyes behind the plastic lenses had the staring roundness of a nocturnal creature.

There was no need to explain who they were. The chopper had *Avon and Somerset Police* in large letters on the outside. Pennycook ushered them in fast—as if the entire Crescent had not noticed the police making a call on him. Diamond's quick assessment was that he had the look of a young man out of step with his generation. His casuals on a warm Sunday afternoon amounted to a thick yellow cardigan over a black T-shirt, with blue corduroy trousers and brown leather slippers. The cardigan had the label showing; it was inside out.

The room they were shown into was nicely-proportioned, and that was all that could be said for it. Beer stains disfigured the wallpaper. The furniture amounted to a chipped and rusting fridge and some wood and canvas folding chairs that belonged to Brighton Corporation. He must have nicked them from around the bandstand in one of the public parks. And this was the heir to Si Minchendon's fortune. He could certainly use some money.

Diamond lowered himself cautiously onto one of the chairs; he had a history of bursting through canvas. It creaked, groaned and just held his weight. He considered how to begin. With a helicopter standing on the lawn outside, he was in no position to say what he would normally have said, that this was just a routine enquiry. "You were in Bath a couple of days ago, sir?"

"Yup."

"Would you mind telling us what brought you there?"

"My uncle's funeral." The voice was toneless and barely audible.

"That would be the late Mr Minchendon?"

Pennycook nodded. His fingers were twitchy. He plucked at the sleeves of the cardigan, tugging the cuffs over the backs of his hands.

"Of Camden Crescent?" Diamond said, more to encourage a response than glean information.

Another nod.

"Nice address."

"If you say so." He ran the tip of his tongue around the edge of his mouth.

"When was the funeral—one day last week?"

"Yeah."

This was like chiselling marble. "Which day was the funeral, Mr Pennycook?"

"Dunno."

"Speak up."

Leaman said, "It was Tuesday."

"Tuesday," said Diamond. "And you were there, and you don't remember?"

"I've had a lot going on."

"So you stayed longer."

"Things to see to."

"What things?"

"Papers to sign, and stuff."

"Your legacy?"

"Yeah."

"I understand your uncle left you everything."

"Right."

"Does that make you the owner of the house in Camden Crescent?"

"More or less."

"What does that mean?"

"I have to wait for probate, don't I?"

"So you're not the legal owner yet?"

The pallid face registered pain, as if Diamond had struck him. He blurted out a few inarticulate words that sounded very like a confession. "I don't want no aggro. Needed cash in hand, right?

Cash in hand. The stuff was coming to me anyway. Ask them, if you like. If you lay off, I'll square it with the bank."

"You did a deal with Peg Redbird, the owner of Noble and Nude?"

"Is that her name?"

Diamond reacted angrily. "Don't play the innocent. You don't do dodgy deals with people without finding out who they are. You went to some trouble to pick a dealer likely to connive at this fraud. Had you met Peg Redbird before?"

"No, and that's the truth."

The phrase slipped easily from his tongue and added to Diamond's impatience. He leaned forward menacingly. "Young man, every word you say to me had better be the truth. Understand?"

Pennycook understood, and showed it. Beads of sweat were rolling down the side of his face.

"So who put you onto her?"

Now he gathered himself and launched into a stumbling explanation. "I had some time after the funeral, didn't I? Sniffed around like. Antiques markets and stuff. Got talking to the stall-holders."

Hard to imagine you talking to anyone, Diamond thought.

"They gave me the buzz on the trade in Bath. Not the la-de-dahs up Bartlett Street. The other end of it. No questions asked."

"Nod and a wink?"

"Right. Her name kept coming up. Peg Redbird does the business, I was told. She had this shop in Walcot Street full of junk."

This was rich, coming from a man who furnished his room with chairs from the local park. "Didn't you want to use the furniture yourself?"

"Don't go in for fancy gear."

"I can see that."

Pennycook saw fit to add, "In case you're wondering, this here was my gran's place."

Diamond nodded. "Another inheritance? You're a lucky man."

"I took it over at a peppercorn rent, didn't I? I pay peanuts for this."

"But you still have a cash-flow problem."

He glared resentment. "Had to update my computer system, didn't I? Mega expenses."

Diamond rolled his eyes. This was obviously bullshit. Some of Pennycook's initial nervousness had gone. He was beginning to behave as if he felt he had sidestepped the crisis.

Time to turn the screw.

"What are you on?" Diamond asked.

The face drained of what little colour had been there. He drew his arms defensively across his chest. "What do you mean?"

"Come on. Look at the sweat on you. People don't wear cardigans in a heat wave. Show us your arms."

"No way."

"It's back to front, that cardigan. You only put it on when you saw us coming."

"That's no crime."

"Tell you what," said Diamond. "If you're shy about your arms, you can show us something else. Where do you keep this super new computer?"

Pennycook was starting to shake. He remained seated, staring.

"It doesn't exist, does it? We know a smackhead when we see one, Sergeant Leaman and I. Keep your needle marks covered, if you want, but the other signs are pretty obvious. Pinhead pupils, the sweats, your body wasting away. I mean, we've only got to look at the state you live in. I guess this place was furnished when you took it over. Are you a registered addict?"

Pennycook nodded. He looked wretched now.

"How much are you paying to kill yourself? A hundred a day? Two hundred? Listen, my friend, we're not here to dump on you because you're on the needle. We're not even after the blood-suckers who supply you, though someone had better be. We want the truth about your trip to Bath. How did you travel?"

He said in a low voice, "Bummed a lift from a mate of mine, didn't I?"

"You don't have wheels of your own?"

"Does it look like I would?"

"This mate. Was he staying with you in Bath?"

"No chance. He was on his way to Bristol."

Diamond locked eyes briefly with Leaman. Here was another suspect without his own transport.

"How long were you there?"

"Went for the funeral and stayed till the weekend."

"Stayed where?"

"My uncle's gaff."

"The will hasn't been proved yet and they let you stay in his house?" Diamond said in surprise.

Pennycook looked away, out of the window, towards the heli-copter on the lawn. "It weren't a case of letting me."

"Meaning what?"

"I fixed it, didn't I?" Now he gave Diamond his full attention, taking obvious pride in the guile he had used. "The bank are the executors, right? They got the front door key. They know he left the whole bloody lot to me. I told them it was Uncle's wish for some of his old mates to go back to the house for a jar or two after the funeral." He chuckled. "They couldn't argue with that. About eight guys came back, said they were his mates. I don't know who they were. He had no family apart from me. Anyway, I found some wine downstairs and handed out cheese biscuits. At the end I was supposed to lock up and return the key to the bank. They sent a geezer in a suit to make sure I did. I give them back their key and kept the key of the basement. So I could let myself in later and save some money putting up in Bath."

It rang true. The ingenuity of the heroin addict is well
known. "Then what?"

"I already told you."

"You scouted around for an antiques dealer, and Peg was the
obvious choice."

"Went to look at her place first. Took a walk around and give
it the once-over. Then I give her a bell from Camden Terrace
asking for a valuation. I knew she'd come."

"You let her pick out some plums."

"She got what she wanted. She could have had more, but she
was playing it cool."

"How much cash changed hands?"

"Grand and a half."

"She carried that much?"

"No. She told me to call for it later."

"Later the same day?"

"Yeah."

Diamond's eyes widened. "Thursday evening? Did she now?"
This was a detail neither he nor Leaman had included in their
picture of events the evening Peg Redbird was murdered. "You
went, of course?"

He shrugged. "What do you think?"

"What time was that?"

"Don't know. Don't keep track of time."

"After dark?"

"Yeah."

"That would have been later than eight-thirty, then. Was she
alone?"

Pennycook seemed to sense that he was walking into quicksand. "She was bumped, wasn't she?"

"Let's talk about your actions that evening."

"I didn't touch her. I collected my dosh and cleared off back
to Camden Crescent."

"Fifteen hundred pounds?"

"Like I said. That was the deal." His thin body was starting to shake. "Look, if you think I'm the one who stiffed her, you're bloody mistaken. She was all right when I left."

"Did you see anyone else?"

"In the shop? No."

"Outside? Anywhere near the place?"

The temptation to steer suspicion to someone else must have been strong. "Don't remember."

Diamond was as energised as if he had taken a jab from one of Pennycook's syringes. This was crucial evidence: someone who had visited Peg shortly before she was murdered. "You came to the shop some time after dark, but before ten, correct?"

Pennycook gave a perfunctory nod.

"Shape up. I'm trying to help you." Encouragement, followed immediately by warning words. "You're under strong suspicion of murder. What you're about to say could convince us you're not the killer."

There was some doubt whether Pennycook was about to say anything.

"Tell us all you can remember about that meeting you had with Peg Redbird."

"There's sod all to tell."

Not in Diamond's estimation. "You arrive at Noble and Nude to collect your money. You walked, I suppose?"

"Yeah."

"Try and remember Walcot Street. Was it quiet?"

"I told you I didn't see no one. Just cars."

"Cars going by, or parked outside?"

"Going by. Nothing was parked there."

"A van? You didn't notice a van?"

"You're not listening."

"So you got to the shop. Was it open?"

"Course it was, or how would I have got in?"

"She could have let you in. What was happening when you entered?"

"She was in there, facing me, behind a big desk with boxes on it. I said—"

"Hold on," Diamond stopped him. "The boxes. Tell us about them."

"There's nothing to tell. Boxes, I said."

"What were they made of?"

"One was wood, I think, polished wood, dark. She closed it when I come through the door. Locked it up."

Mary Shelley's writing box. "You're sure of that?"

"Sure of what?"

"That the box had been open?"

"I wouldn't say it if I didn't remember, would I?"

Diamond nodded mechanically, thinking that this squared with Ellis Somerset's statement. It meant that Pennycook visited Peg after Somerset had left. The hired van was no longer outside and the box was still open. "What size was it? The size of a box file? You know what a box file is?"

"Yeah. Thicker than that. Like two of them, one on top of the other."

"And you mentioned other boxes."

"Rusty old tins without lids. Two or three, up at one end of the desk."

"You don't recall seeing anything else on the desk?"

"Nothing on the desk."

There was just the suggestion of more to come. Diamond coaxed it out. "But some other thing caught your interest?"

"Yeah?"

"Something else you happened to notice."

"Oh, yeah. On top of the safe I saw some of the stuff I sold her. Two old pictures off the wall. Scenes."

This clinched it. He had come after Ellis Somerset had delivered the goods to Noble and Nude.

"Scenes?" repeated Diamond, testing him. "What kind of scenes?"

"I don't know. Old-fashioned stuff. Not my taste at all."

"You couldn't tell me the artist?"

"I know sod all about art. I was telling you what happened," Pennycook said in a tone suggesting he finally understood the importance of giving an account. "I tell her I've come for my money and she says yes, it's ready. She opens a drawer in her desk, takes out a key and opens the safe. She has the money ready in a brown envelope. Fifteen hundred, mostly in twenties. She asks me to count it, and I do. I say something about doing more business with her, how I'd give her a second chance when I got the probate. She doesn't say much. I reckon she wanted to get rid of me and close the shop."

"What made you think that?"

"Don't know really. She wasn't so talkative this time. But I got what I came for, so it didn't bother me. I cleared off back to Camden Crescent."

"And the street outside—was that the same? Nothing waiting?"

"If it was, I didn't see it."

Diamond looked towards Leaman. "Anything I missed?"

The sergeant shook his head.

"Right," said Diamond, turning back to Pennycook. "That was Thursday night. What happened to you since?"

"Since?" He frowned. "Is that important?"

A look from Diamond told him that it was.

"I stayed in Bath. Friday I had to visit the bank to sign some papers. I hung about the streets until late to see if I could buy some H for less than they charge here in Brighton. No chance. The bastards fix the price all over, the same as cigarettes, or bloody cornflakes."

"And then half of it is filler, talc or some such," Diamond commented. "So you spent Friday evening there. How about Saturday?"

"I came back here, didn't I?"

"What time?"

"I keep telling you, I got no sense of time."

Well, Diamond thought wryly, railway timetables were supposed to be the detective's salvation. "How did you travel? On the train?"

"You're joking. Thumbed it, didn't I?"

The budget of the drug addict didn't run to train fares.

Pennycook claimed he had hitchhiked to Southampton on a juggernaut lorry bound for the docks and from there along the coast roads to Brighton with a couple of students. He had got back some time in the early hours of Sunday and slept until the afternoon.

No alibi for Peg's murder or the attack on John Wigfull.

"During your time in Bath, did any other police officer question you about Thursday?"

Pennycook shook his head.

"*Can* you drive?"

"What?"

"You heard me. Have you ever had a licence?"

"Yeah, some time. What are you trying to pin on me now?"

"Filling in the gaps in your statement, that's all. Maybe you went for a drive in the country yesterday afternoon."

"What with, for Christ's sake? I got no wheels."

"I reckon you have, amigo. Somewhere in a garage round the back of Camden Crescent, there's a nice, shiny motor that old Si used to drive about in. I'd put money on it. In fact, we can check on our computer."

"It ain't mine yet, even if there is one," he pointed out.

"The house isn't yours, and that didn't stop you."

"Bog off, will you?"

Which, presently, they did.

Outside on the lawn, interested residents still stood around the helicopter. Diamond looked about him as if for an escape route. "Where's the nearest pub, do you reckon?"

Leaman looked surprised. "Do you need a drink after that, sir?"

"Anything but. I didn't fancy using his toilet."

They headed across the grass to the roundabout at the north end and spotted a pub sign a stone's throw away on Dyke Road. And they did have a quick beer.

"What did you make of him?" Diamond asked, on the way back to the helicopter. Any conversation had to be got through before they boarded.

"Typical junkie," said Leaman. "They'll do anything to get the stuff. Sell their own mothers. Anything. We don't have to dig deep for a motive. He needed cash. She had it stacked away in the safe, didn't she? We don't know how much. All there was when we opened it was a few antiques, letters and things."

"If he did kill her, he didn't help himself much talking to us," Diamond commented. "Admitting he was at the shop that night and going on about how desperate he was for cash in hand."

"He's not very bright, is he?" Leaman said. "His brain's gone soft."

"I don't agree. It's easy to confuse poor speech with low intelligence, but there are plenty of big achievers, artists, musicians, inventors, who prove that wrong. I've known druggies smarter than anyone I've met in the police. Brilliant people. They channel all their intelligence in one direction, that's the tragedy."

"So you don't rate him as a suspect?"

"Didn't say that, did I? I just said he's smarter than you think, and probably smarter than both of us. He's putting one over everyone—the bank, the taxman, his landlord, Brighton Deckchair Services. Why shouldn't he put one over us as well?" As they stooped to enter the wind funnel under the rotor blades, he shouted to Leaman, "You wouldn't catch a bright lad like Pennycook risking his life in one of these."

twenty-four

BACK IN BATH THAT Sunday evening, there was no better news of John Wigfull. He had not recovered consciousness. His closest relative, a brother, had travelled down from Sheffield and was at the bedside; the hospital were making arrangements for him to spend the night there.

The search of the fields around the scene of the attack had produced a number of lumps of wood that could conceivably have been used as clubs. They were being tested for bloodstains, but no one was optimistic that the weapon had been found. And the door-to-door enquiries had proved negative for witnesses, except a couple of people who remembered seeing a red car—Wigfull's, presumably—outside Westwood Manor late Saturday evening.

"How late?" Diamond asked the DI who was on the phone from Trowbridge.

"Ten-thirty was the first sighting, but it's a little-used lane, sir. The car could have been there some hours without being noticed."

Trying to be positive after he came off the phone, Diamond pointed out to Sergeant Leaman that this narrowed the time-span. He still firmly believed that the attack took place on Saturday in daylight, the direct result of Wigfull's questioning of suspects. The way to discover Wigfull's assailant was to go for broke and find the killer of Peg Redbird.

"Did John Wigfull do anything about her phone?" he asked Leaman.

"Her phone, sir?"

"The calls she made on the day of her death. If they can do it for my phone bill, they can do it for us, pronto. It's all routinely logged. The date, the time, the duration and, worst of all, the charge."

"I'll see to it."

A little later, Leaman reported that British Telecom would supply a list by the morning. This young sergeant's support was a real asset. Together, they went down to the canteen for supper.

The ever-cheerful, ever-saucy Pandora greeted them with an offer of roast lamb at half the price listed on the board.

"What's the catch?" Leaman asked.

"The catch," said Diamond, "is that it was cooked this morning. It's as dry as Deuteronomy."

Pandora dipped a formidable ladle into a pot. "Not when I pour some of this delicious gravy over it. See, you're slavering at the mouth already, Mr D, or is it me you're drooling over?"

"That's a leading question."

"Lead me anywhere you like, darling. My shift ends at ten."

He was too wary of double meanings to say anything about Pandora's shift. "Thanks. I'll see if I survive the roast lamb."

They spotted Keith Halliwell sitting alone, staring ahead with a look that could have stripped paint. It was quickly apparent that Frankenstein jokes were not the cure. Canteen humour palls after a long, unproductive day.

He said, "If we can talk shop for a moment, sir, I'd like to put out that appeal tomorrow—for information on the two labourers known as Banger and Mash. I prepared a press release. Would you mind giving it the OK?"

In the last hours the mystery of the bones in the vault had gone as tepid as the half-price lamb, but Diamond somehow conjured up some interest. "No more progress, then?"

"I don't expect any until someone's memory is jogged."

"Right you are. I'll run an eye over it before I leave tonight. How are the press treating you?"

"It isn't so crazy as yesterday. They realize there isn't any mileage in this story now we've finished in the vault."

"There's an unexplained death."

"Yes, but a nineteen-eighties unexplained death. The *Frankenstein* connection doesn't hold up."

Diamond's thoughts swung back to the other case. "It's mighty odd that we have links with the killing of Peg Redbird."

"The writing box?"

"Yes. Apparently Mary Shelley's copy of Milton came out of it, so there's some chance the box actually belonged to her. Joe Dougan seems convinced."

"What happened to it?"

"The box? Don't know. It was gone from Peg's desk by the time we arrived on the scene. Joe could have nicked it and hidden it, with the idea of taking it back to America. Or someone else may have understood its value and carted it away."

Leaman reminded him, "It was still on the desk when Pennycook came for his money."

"It was still there when Joe decided to quit at eleven."

"According to Joe."

"According to Joe, yes."

Doubts of Joe's testimony hung in the air.

"Was the box worth killing for?" asked Leaman.

Diamond put down his knife and fork. The lamb had the texture of car tyres. "To you or me, probably not. To someone who has set his heart on owning it, yes. You had a unique object there. Remember the last Commandment."

Leaman and Halliwell exchanged an uneasy look. They didn't know which was the last Commandment and they wouldn't have expected Diamond to know, either. This was the second reference to the Old Testament in a few minutes from a man not noted for his piety.

" 'Thou shalt not covet.' They weren't thought up on the spur of the moment, those Commandments."

Sergeant Leaman was puzzled by the reference. "Isn't coveting when you get a craving for someone else's property? I thought the writing box was up for sale."

"Well, yes." Diamond retreated slightly. "In theory it was, but she wasn't willing to part with it. And Joe was extremely keen to own it. I call that coveting."

"I see," said Leaman in a tone that was not quite convinced. "It's not the Commandment I would have thought of."

" 'Thou shalt not kill'?" said Halliwell.

"We could all have thought of that," said Diamond.

"So is Joe a murderer?" said Leaman.

Diamond answered opaquely, "I can't at the moment think of anyone with a stronger interest in possessing the writing box. And tomorrow morning, he's off to Paris," he added in a fatalistic tone.

Halliwell became animated. "Can't we catch him with it?"

"He'll have arranged for it to be shipped, if he *is* our man. Unless . . ." The words trailed away for a moment while a better hypothesis fell into place. ". . . unless his wife took it with her. Suppose she didn't walk out on him that night. Suppose they planned it together over that meal they had in Brock Street. She would go ahead with the writing box. He would create a smokescreen by pretending she was missing. Days later, he'd announce that she had turned up in Paris and he was joining her."

"Big thing for a woman to lug about," said Leaman.

Diamond shook his head. "It wasn't that heavy. It was a woman's writing case, remember. It was designed to be portable. And she had no other luggage."

"Sir, are you saying his wife was in on the murder?" Leaman

asked in a tone that showed he was not persuaded. He was so new to Diamond's inner circle that he didn't realise the risks he was taking.

"I don't know what passed between them. He could have told her anything."

"So Mr Wigfull was right to be suspicious of Joe Dougan."

That was tactless in the extreme. In view of Wigfull's condition, Diamond chose to ignore it. "Is the ACC about?"

"She was in most of the day," said Halliwell. "Wants to be part of the action, by the look of it."

"I'd better see if she's there."

He got up, leaving Leaman and Halliwell bemused. For Peter Diamond actually to go looking for the Assistant Chief Constable was about as likely as rocking-horse manure.

SHE WAS dictating letters into a tape-recorder in her office. "Peter, come in. How's it going?"

The use of his first name still grated. She was so new in the job.

He summarised the day's work: the questioning of Ellis Somerset at the Antiques Fair; the finding of Wigfull's car; the visit to the scene of the attack; the interview with Joe; the news that Donna Dougan was alive and shopping in Paris; and the helicopter trip to Brighton to establish that Ralph Pennycook had visited Peg Redbird on the evening she was killed.

Georgina complimented him, "You've quartered the ground pretty thoroughly by the sound of it."

She got up, and for a moment he thought she was about to make a move towards the whisky cupboard, but she only went to the window and closed it.

"Draughty. The days are hot, but have you noticed how temperatures are starting to drop in the evenings now?"

"Yes." And something to warm our insides wouldn't come amiss, he thought.

"So you've interviewed all the people who spent time with Miss Redbird on the evening she was killed?"

"There was another, I believe."

"Oh?"

"Peg had an appointment with someone else that evening. 'Other business', Ellis Somerset called it when he told me. She was trying for a quick sale of the Blakes she bought from Camden Crescent. She upset Somerset the way she put it, teasing him about expecting an offer that night."

She gave a prim tug at her ear lobe. "An offer of a sexual character?"

"That was the implication."

"Did Somerset have a relationship with her, then?"

"He says not. He was keen, he admits, but she kept him at arm's length. So he was jealous when she spoke of this other meeting late in the evening."

"Are you sure he wasn't making this up?"

"Why should he?"

"It's one of the oldest tricks of all, inventing an extra suspect to deflect suspicion."

There was a glint in Diamond's eye. Georgina had made a telling point. "You're assuming Somerset killed her?"

"He was the last to see her alive, wasn't he?"

"True."

"Then he's got to be in the frame."

"Yes, but what's his motive? Anger at being jilted?"

Georgina smiled. "I do believe you're a romantic, Peter. No, I don't think he'd kill her for that. The motive is theft. That writing box had been revealed as valuable, and so had the watercolours from Camden Crescent. He was in on the secret, but he wasn't getting a share of the loot."

He let Georgina's theory shake down with his own.

"Have you got a piece of paper, ma'am?"

"Paper? What for?"

"I'd like to show you something."

"Will this do?" She handed him the pad she kept by the phone.

"This is my shopping-list," he explained, while he was writing.

He slid the pad back across the big desk. "Her visitors that evening."

She studied what he had written:

Somerset	Arrives about 8 p.m.	Leaves before 9.
Pennycook	Arrives "after dark".	Leaves quickly.
X	??	??
Dougan	Arrives about 9.30.	Leaves about 11.

The ACC examined the list for some time. "This 'X' is the mysterious art fancier, if we believe in his existence?"

"Yes."

"And you believe Pennycook visited her after Somerset?"

"Can I tell you why? He's hopeless about times, but I did establish that it was dark when he called at the shop for his money. That's after 8.30 this time of year. She was alone, then, so Somerset had left. The watercolours were stacked on the safe, so we know he'd already delivered them."

"That makes sense," she admitted.

"By the time Dougan arrived at 9.30, Peg was no longer there, if he's speaking the truth. She could have been dead."

"You're telling me now that Pennycook was the last to see Miss Redbird alive?"

"Pennycook, or X. Pennycook didn't stay long. She handed him the money, he counted it and left. He said she wasn't talkative. She seemed to want to get rid of him."

"When exactly did Pennycook leave?"

He spread his hands.

"But he'd gone by 9.30, when Dougan arrived?"

"That's my reading of it."

"He'd left, and so had Miss Redbird, apparently. Yet you have X, the mystery man, slotted in between Pennycook and Dougan. That's impossible, isn't it? The time is too short."

"No, ma'am, I don't think it is. The way I see it, she finished with Pennycook as quickly as she could and went for her meeting with X. She wasn't seen again."

"She went out?"

"Taking the pictures she intended to sell."

The ACC scrutinised the list again. "Why would she have gone out when she knew Dougan was coming back?"

"She didn't know how soon. She may have thought she was safe for a couple of hours."

She put her hand nervously to her tight-curled silver hair as if to check that it was still there. "Do you have a theory who X might be?"

"Yes, I do, ma'am. Someone with a special interest in early English watercolours. Councillor Sturr."

Sharply, she said, "What do you know about John Sturr's interests?"

The remark hit him hard. In Georgina's eyes, he was a yob who knew sod all about art. She wasn't far wrong, but he didn't like it taken for granted. "He showed me some of his pictures at the Victoria Gallery last week."

"Showed you? Personally?"

Nonchalantly he said, "A private view. Not the most exciting stuff I've seen. He claims to have one of the best private collections in the country, as I'm sure you know. If I were selling a couple of Blakes locally, that's who I'd approach."

The muscles at the side of her face tightened. "This is not a good way to go, Peter."

"I know." He left unsaid his determination to go on, regardless. She could see it in his look.

She said, "You're not seriously suggesting a member of the Police Authority is implicated in these events?"

"I'd like to know if Mr Sturr was in communication with Peg Redbird last Thursday."

"But he spent last Thursday evening at my house. The dinner party I gave. You know that."

"Would you mind telling me precisely when he arrived, ma'am?"

"But you know."

"I turned up late, if you remember."

White-faced, she said, "This is absurd. I invited everyone at seven-thirty for eight, and he was there. It must have been after ten-thirty when he left with Ingeborg Smith. Yes, I'm sure of it. After we looked at your interview on *Newsnight*."

"He didn't leave the party at any point and return later?"

"Don't be ridiculous, superintendent. Let it rest, will you?"

Staunchly, Diamond said, "I still need to speak to him, ma'am."

"John Sturr's integrity is not in doubt. He has an alibi supplied by me. That's enough."

He let a few seconds pass, inviting her to modify the last statement. She did not.

"Ma'am, if there is someone else in Bath well known as a collector of early nineteenth century watercolours, I'll be glad to have the name. I'll see them first thing tomorrow."

She clutched at that. She was as uncomfortable as Diamond. "I'm sure there are several serious collectors in a city like ours."

Diamond nodded. "I don't know who they are. The only name I have is John Sturr. That's who Ellis Somerset thought of. He didn't name anyone else." He let that take root, then said, "Councillor Sturr and I have an understanding. I can handle him civilly."

"No."

"Would you prefer to question him yourself, ma'am?"

She didn't dignify that with an answer.

He said in a measured, unemotional voice, "Ma'am, this

morning when we got the news of John Wigfull you asked me to take over, to give it top priority."

"Finding his attacker, yes. If you think John Sturr is the kind of man who bludgeons police inspectors . . ."

"This is the way I'm working. If I can't proceed—"

She blurted out, "I've vouched for him personally. Isn't that enough for you?"

"You vouched for his presence at your dinner party. You don't know what went on before and after it."

"God, you don't give up."

He waited.

She got up and walked to the window, twisting a handkerchief into a thin cord and wrapping it tightly around her fingers. "When do you propose to see him?"

"Now."

She winced, but she had given up the struggle. "The questions relate to the possible sale of the pictures from Camden Crescent?"

"Yes, ma'am, and his movements."

She reached for the phone. "Then I'll call him and soften the blow—if I can."

twenty-five

THE WORRY LINES FADED from Georgina's face. Her friend the Councillor was not at home, or not answering his phone. Diamond quit her office, promising nothing.

Mindful of his blood pressure, he left the building and took a steady walk along Manvers Street towards the Abbey. The street lights were on and not many people were about.

The great West window of the Abbey was illuminated from inside, and the sound of Evensong drifted across the paved yard. With difficulty in the fading light, Diamond looked for the carved figures of angels ascending the twin ladders on either side of the window. He was not a church-goer and was not sure about God's existence, let alone the angels', but these were less than perfect angels anyway, old friends he returned to in times of stress. Weatherbeaten after five hundred years, some with stumps for limbs, they still had a restorative effect on a less than perfect policeman. They always made him smile. They were not, as many supposed, climbing Jacob's ladder, but the ladder seen in a dream by the builder of the Abbey, Bishop Oliver King. A nice triumph of human vanity over piety, Diamond always thought, for the Bishop to insist that his own dream was on the front of the Abbey, and sucks to Jacob.

Across the yard by the railings in front of the Roman Baths was a human shape Diamond took for one of the dossers. He went over to see who it was. He knew most of them. Unusually, the man wished him good evening and called him "sir". The voice was Keith Halliwell's.

"What are you doing here, leaning on the railings?"

"It's all right, sir. I'm sober. Just taking stock, that's all."

"Me, too."

"To be truthful, I came up here hoping for some inspiration."

"From the Abbey?"

"The vault. It's below us."

"Right. So it is. The bloody vault."

"Locked up now. This is the closest I can get."

"You think the answer is down there?"

"I don't know, sir. I don't know if we'll ever get an answer."

"We will, Keith. It's coming together. It's the key to everything, what happened down there."

"But I'm getting nowhere with it."

"Don't say that." Diamond put a hand on Halliwell's shoulder. "I looked at your press release. Fine."

"Thanks."

They started walking back towards the police station. The experience between them, two old colleagues united at the end of the day, encouraged confidences. Halliwell asked what would happen about Joe Dougan.

Diamond said simply, "He'll leave for Paris in the morning."

"Is he in the clear?"

"That's another question. I'd pull him in if I knew we had something that would stick. You know the rules as well as I do."

"Do you believe his wife is alive and well in Paris? Can't we get the French police to check?"

"I checked already. There's a Mrs Donna Dougan registered at the Ritz."

"She's OK, then? He was speaking the truth."

"It doesn't mean we have to believe every damned thing he said."

They walked on, and although no more was said about the

investigation, it got through to Halliwell—he was seized with the conviction—that Diamond knew everything now. He had worked out precisely what had happened. It was only a matter of nailing his man.

The old tyrant could be a pain to work with, but no detective on the Force had such clarity of mind.

As if he was a mind-reader too, Diamond said with compassion, "You should go home now. You've done enough today."

Halliwell agreed.

OF THE Murder Squad, only Sergeant Leaman remained. Diamond asked him to bring in copies of Joe Dougan's statements.

Predictably, John Wigfull's paperwork was immaculate. He had painstakingly recorded things from the interviews at the Royal Crescent that Diamond would have disregarded. There was the whole chain of contacts that had led the dogged American professor to Noble and Nude.

He asked Leaman, "Did John Wigfull follow up any of this stuff Joe Dougan told him—the bookshop at Hay-on-Wye and so on?"

Leaman shook his head. "Have you ever been to Hay, sir?"

"Never."

"I was there once. I do a bit of cooking and I wanted a book by Fanny Craddock that had been out of print for thirty years. It's incredible, the number of bookshops in a small country town. A whole cinema stuffed with old books. A castle. There's no way you could trace a particular sale."

Diamond studied the notes. "How about these Bath people, Oliver Heath and Uncle Evan?"

"They certainly exist. They're known locally, sir. Mr Heath owned a bookshop in Union Passage for many years and Uncle Evan has a puppet theatre."

"Did anybody go to see them?"

"To check on Dougan's story? It wasn't thought necessary, sir, seeing that he didn't invent the names."

"You didn't bother."

Harsh words that pained Leaman. "Those people were stepping-stones, so to speak. Things only began to happen after he found his way to the antiques shop."

"We need to see them."

"Tomorrow morning?"

"Too late."

Leaman had rashly hoped there was still time for a quiet Sunday evening drink with his girlfriend.

THE RETIRED bookseller Oliver Heath greeted them at the door of his Queen Square apartment, dapper for an elderly man in shirt and cravat, grey slacks and tan-coloured brogues. "I was only listening to the radio," he said, making clear that he didn't at all object to having his Sunday evening disturbed. "Sometimes you get some interesting talks on Long Wave with the Open University, but tonight is not my cup of tea exactly: Feminism in the Third World."

Diamond explained their visit.

"Oh, yes," the old man confirmed. "The professor was here, just as he said, and showed me a copy of Milton that once passed through my hands. I say passed through them; actually it was on my shelves for years. I never regarded it as anything special. It wasn't a first edition or anything. Some of the fly-leaves were missing, I recall."

"The blank sheets at the front?"

"And the back. You often find this with old books. Paper was far more expensive in former times than now. People used the sheets as notepaper. Can't blame them, but it does ruin a nicely bound book. What I failed to notice—or appreciate the significance of—was the inscription on the cover."

"Mary Shelley's initials?"

"And of course the Abbey Churchyard address." Oliver Heath managed an ungrudging smile. "Good spotting on Professor Dougan's part—and good luck to him."

"Was it genuine?"

"The writing on the cover? I've no reason to think it wasn't. But you see I was ignorant of Mary Shelley's connection with Bath. Well, I knew the Shelleys had stayed here at some point, but I didn't know *Frankenstein* was written here. I've checked since, and he was right. Five, Abbey Churchyard. It's a salutary thought that the world's most famous horror story was penned within a few yards of our great Abbey Church."

"A first edition of *Frankenstein* would be worth a bit, I imagine?" said Diamond, seeing that Heath was so generous with his information.

"My word, yes. A set in good condition would fetch a huge sum. I think the 1818 edition amounted to only five hundred copies. It was in three volumes, to appeal to the circulating libraries. They liked books published that way because one book could be loaned to three different readers at the same time. But library copies are not of much interest to collectors."

"It wasn't an immediate bestseller, then?"

"Far from it. Out of print for years. They produced a new edition in 1831 with some changes to the text, but it didn't really take off until the 1880s, long after the author was dead."

"You're well up on all this."

The old man smiled. "I took the trouble to gen up after having my ignorance shown up the other day. The story is more popular now than it has ever been. I must say, I can't fathom how it has become a set text in university English courses, but apparently it has, here and in America. An article in *The Times* stated that Mary Shelley is more studied than Coleridge, Byron, Keats and Shelley."

"Is that surprising? If I was given a choice of *Frankenstein* or poetry, I know which would get my vote," said Diamond.

"You might be disappointed. It isn't exactly Stephen King."

Diamond put the conversation back on track. "Did Professor Dougan tell you what he was up to?"

"He wanted to find out where the Milton came from, who was the previous owner, and so forth. The provenance, we call it."

"And you helped?"

"I had to dig very deep in my memory. I recalled buying it quite cheaply from a local man who calls himself Uncle Evan. He must have a more formal name, but that's the one he is known by. Have you heard of him? He runs a puppet theatre and I'm told it's very good entertainment. Does everything himself, makes the puppets, the scenery and writes the scripts. A multi-talented young man. He built a stage of some sort that he carts about in the back of a van."

"You sent the professor to see him?"

"I told him where Evan might be found, and that was the Brains Surgery."

"The pub in Larkhall?"

Oliver Heath smiled at the recollection. "My American visitor was somewhat thrown by the name. I have to confess that I didn't immediately say it was a pub. I'm sure he had visions of something like Dr Frankenstein's laboratory."

"Is the Brains Surgery Uncle Evan's local?"

"It's the one you visit if you want to book his puppet show. I couldn't tell you where he lives."

"MORE USEFUL than I could have hoped for," Diamond commented as Leaman drove them out to Larkhall.

"Did we learn anything new, sir?"

"Sergeant, you're beginning to talk as if it's been a long day.

Of course we learned something new. We learned that *Franken-stein* was published in 1818 with only five hundred copies. Did you know that?"

"No, sir."

"Well, then. Ponder the significance."

At the Brains Surgery, they were told by the barman that Uncle Evan had not been in for a couple of days. The looks from deep-set eyes around the bar seeming to regard that as a betrayal left Diamond in no doubt that further questions about the puppeteer would not lead to much. Nobody had an address or phone number. Nobody knew his real name.

"If he *does* come in . . ." said Diamond, but he knew he was wasting his breath.

THE DRIVE back to Manvers Street was mostly in silence. At one point Diamond muttered something cynical about the great British public, but later he said more philosophically, "Why should everyone be there when we want them? We drew blanks with Councillor Sturr and Uncle Evan, but we saw a lot of others today."

To Leaman it sounded encouragingly like a line being drawn at the end of a long day. And that was what Diamond intended—until they took the turn into Bridge Street and he spotted a parked van and someone carrying things from the lighted interior of the Victoria Gallery.

"What's going on there at this time of night? Drive right round and we'll have another look."

Leaman, to his credit, did not even sigh. He took the car rapidly round the circuit formed by Grand Parade, Orange Grove and the High Street and entered Bridge Street for the second time.

"Pull up here."

They went to look.

It could conceivably have been a heist in progress. Large objects cocooned in bubblewrap were being carried from the gallery and loaded in the van. But nobody took flight.

"Police," Diamond announced. "What's going on exactly?"

A figure he recognized as the gallery caretaker stepped out of the shadows. "No problem, officer. Everything's in order. They've just dismantled the exhibition and now they're loading it onto the van."

"From the main gallery?"

"The annexe."

Diamond became more interested. "The watercolours?"

"Right."

"Councillor Sturr's collection?"

"Yes."

"Now where do they go—back to the owner?"

"You'd better speak to the driver."

A young bearded man said from inside the van, where he was loading with a young lad as assistant, "Back to Mr Sturr's house, yes."

"Is he home, then? We tried to get hold of him earlier and he wasn't there."

"He went out for a meal. That's why it's a late job. We're unloading at ten at his house."

"We'll follow you, then," said Diamond cheerfully. "Wouldn't want to miss him, would we, sergeant?"

"No, sir," said Leaman in a hollow tone.

They waited while the remaining pictures were put aboard and roped to the floor. The van with its police escort in trail moved off at 9.50 p.m.

"I'll be interested to find out why this operation had to wait till now."

Leaman didn't answer. His level of interest was waning by the minute.

Sturr's residence was a Victorian villa the size of a town hall at the lower end of Lansdown Road. Security lights flashed on as they entered the gravel drive. A white sports car was parked under some tall trees.

The driver of the van tried the doorbell and got no answer.

"Where's his Holiness?" said Diamond.

"It isn't ten yet," said Leaman.

Three minutes later, Diamond said, "It is now."

A further seventeen minutes passed before the silver Mercedes swung sedately onto the drive and pulled up next to the van. The tall figure of Councillor Sturr got out and walked around the front of the car as if the removal men and the police did not exist, and opened the door for his passenger. There was a gleam of thighs caught in the glare of the security lamp and out stepped Ingeborg Smith.

twenty-six

"REMEMBER, I AM NOT *recording the vision of a madman.*"

There used to be a phrase applied to certain murderers that they were "guilty, but insane". The gentler version was that they killed "while the balance of their mind was disturbed". A comforting phrase in the days when the alternative was a date with the hangman. If you were temporarily unbalanced, you were not responsible for your actions. Instead you were sent to a prison for the criminally insane.

He was not mad.

He was not unbalanced.

He was responsible for his actions. Proud of most of them.

twenty-seven

COUNCILLOR STURR USHERED INGEBORG through his front door and then turned to face Diamond, and his expression was not welcoming. "It's inconvenient."

"It's necessary, sir."

"You can see I've got pictures to unload."

"Isn't that the removers' job?"

"Don't you tell me how to unload pictures. I must check every one for possible damage, the glass, the frames."

"How many? That won't take long, sir. We've been waiting hours to see you."

"You made no appointment."

"We don't," said Diamond. "We just drop in."

For a time, Sturr ignored them to supervise the unloading of his pictures. Each had to be unwrapped in the hall and inspected before being taken into a front room. The removal team got on with the job while Diamond and Leaman stood by the front porch like two immovable Jehovah's Witnesses.

Diamond said confidentially to Leaman, "Did you recognise the woman?"

"I've seen her hanging about the nick."

"Ingeborg Smith is a hotshot reporter. Wants to join the police."

"Must be out of her mind. Is that her car, the white Peugeot?"

"Presumably."

"Did you know she was a close friend of Mr Sturr's?"

"She's upwardly mobile, is Ingeborg."

"I already noticed that."

The unloading of the pictures was completed with no damage discovered. Sturr took out his wallet and tipped the removal team. They returned to the van, closed the rear doors and drove off.

Diamond stepped up to Sturr before he could retreat inside the house. "Can we get this over, sir?"

"I told you it's not convenient."

"It's not convenient for us, but we're here."

"Look, it's ten-thirty on Sunday evening, damned near my bed—" He broke off, cleared his throat, and rephrased the statement. "You can see I have a visitor."

"You have three visitors, and two of them are from the police."

"Anyway, what is this about?"

"The death of Miss Redbird and the attack on our fellow-officer, John Wigfull."

As a member of the Police Authority, Sturr could not avoid making sounds of concern. "That was shocking. How is he?"

"Still out, I think. I've been too busy to ask." Diamond stepped closer. He'd had enough. "Either we talk here, Councillor, or down the nick. It's up to you."

Sturr braced, as if for a fight. He thrust his face towards Diamond. Then, quite suddenly, he submitted like an ageing stag faced by the herd leader, turned and walked into his hall, leaving the door open for the two detectives to follow.

The pictures had been carried into a sitting room and propped against the wall. There, as a centre piece, in competition with the artistry of Cotman, Cox and Blake, Ingeborg was seated in her short summer dress, all leg and cleavage, looking faintly amused. Sturr told her, "This is extremely tiresome, my dear, but would you mind waiting in another room?"

She said with spirit, "That's all right. Mr Diamond and I are old chums."

Sturr moved right up to her and muttered something in her ear. The smile vanished. Colour blazed in her cheeks. Here she was, perfectly placed for an exclusive, and they wanted her out.

Sturr said something else, earnest and forceful. Ingeborg still looked in two minds. She shamed him with her large, intelligent eyes.

"If I step out," she said in a voice everyone was meant to hear, "it's out of your life, John. I'm not your plaything, to be brought out when you feel like it."

"That's unfair," protested Sturr.

"It's business before pleasure with you, isn't it?" she continued bitterly. "If you're not on the phone to America, or checking your precious pictures, you're in conference with the police. Meanwhile I'm supposed to sit around waiting, and if the other night's anything to go by, I could wait for ever."

"For God's sake, Inge!"

"I'm off. You can stuff your vintage Mumm up your vintage bum."

With that, she got up and walked out of the building. She refrained from slamming the front door behind her, but certainly closed it with firmness. From the window, they watched her walk to her car in the glow of the security light, and start up.

Diamond saw no reason to apologise. He had not asked her to leave.

Sturr's way of dealing with the incident was to ignore it. He said tersely, "You'd better tell me what you want."

"Miss Redbird," said Diamond. "Did you know her personally?"

"I knew *of* her. She wasn't a friend, if that's what you mean."

"Did you ever do business with her?"

"Buying stuff from her shop? No, no, I don't go in for antiques."

"Pictures."

"I buy from specialists. Dealers." He gestured towards the line of paintings ranged along the wall. "If you think these were found in junk shops like hers, you're mistaken."

"Have you visited her shop in the last year?"

"Certainly not. What is this about?"

"Ever?"

"I must have looked in at some point, but it would have been a long time ago."

"Have you been in touch with her recently, on the phone, or by letter?"

"No."

Liars will often give themselves away by nuances of timing and tone. Nothing in John Sturr's responses suggested anything but the truth.

"She hasn't contacted you?"

"She has not, and I can't think why she should."

"We'll come to that presently, sir. Last Thursday evening, you were a guest at the Assistant Chief Constable's house. What time did you arrive?"

"Around eight. And you know when I left, because you were there."

"Driving?"

He said with impatience, "It's a bit late to fit me up with that one."

Diamond, calm as a ministering priest, explained evenly, "I'm not interested in the state you were in. I want to know how you travelled."

"Yes, I drove."

"Straight home?"

"Yes."

"And Ingeborg Smith was with you?"

"Since when was that a crime?" said Sturr. "I can't believe you have the neck to ask me things like this."

"What time did you get in, sir?"

A sigh. "I don't know. It must have been about ten to eleven."

"And you didn't go out again?"

"At that hour?" Sturr cast his eyes upwards. "Hasn't it struck you that I'm a little old for the night club scene?"

"Miss Smith stayed the night?"

"Yes. Are you satisfied now?"

This sort of counter-punching from an aggrieved suspect was nothing new in Diamond's experience, the only extra element being Sturr's position of influence on the Police Authority. Without apology, the questioning moved on to his movements on Saturday, the afternoon of the attack on John Wigfull.

"I was visiting friends in Castle Cary."

Twenty miles or more from Westwood and Stowford.

"I was there for lunch and stayed until late. I suppose you'll want to go harrassing them. God knows what they'll make of it."

The martyred air was becoming increasingly irksome to Diamond. If he nailed this man for anything at all, it would bring immense satisfaction.

"How late is late, sir?"

"I don't know. After tea. Six, I reckon. Then I drove back to Bath and went to a choral recital at the Forum in the evening. Elgar's *Dream of Gerontius*."

"Did you have a ticket for that?"

"I expect I still have the stub somewhere. Hold on, I was wearing this suit." He started trying pockets.

"You were alone?"

"At the concert? Yes. And here it is." Triumphantly he produced a piece of torn card from an inner pocket and handed it over.

Diamond gave it a glance and handed it back. "The seats weren't numbered, then?"

Sturr frowned.

"This proves only that you bought a ticket."

"But it's torn in half. That shows I was there."

Diamond didn't deign to comment.

"Did you meet anyone you knew? You're a well-known man in Bath."

"During the interval, I spoke to several people, among them the Bishop." He paused and asked sardonically, "Will he do?"

Technically, this meant only that Sturr had been at the Forum for the interval, presumably around eight-thirty to nine. But it was increasingly hard to picture him out in the country mounting a vicious assault on John Wigfull, and then hurrying back to Bath to listen to Elgar.

"You've met Chief Inspector Wigfull, of course?"

"Frequently."

"Oh?"

"At the PCCG."

"The what? Oh, yes." Thrown again.

"I keep a finger on the pulse," Sturr bragged. "I was one of the first to know what happened."

Diamond, in the right frame of mind for black humour, was tempted to say, "Surely not just *one* of the first?" Wisely, he bit back the comment. "You haven't spoken to him lately, I suppose?"

"Why should I?"

"Your finger on the pulse. He was handling a murder case."

"I'm sorry to disappoint you. The last time I spoke to Mr Wigfull was at the PCCG."

Much of the ground had now been covered, yet there was still one avenue to explore. Diamond shifted his attention to the line of pictures ranged along the skirting-board. "That evening at the meeting, you were good enough to show me these. One, you said, was thought to be by William Blake, the poet." He pointed to the icy landscape with the tall figure striding purposefully across.

"Poet, painter, visionary, call him what you will." Sturr was more ready to talk about art than his own recent doings. "What do you want to know about him?"

"The subject might be mythological, you told me."

"That's my best guess, yes, knowing Blake's absorption in such things, but I couldn't tell you if the figure represents one of the characters from classic mythology, or something from his own strange inner world."

"It's Frankenstein's monster."

Silence dropped like a guillotine.

For an interval there was a real danger that Sturr would erupt. He contained himself, frowned, bent and picked up the picture and held it at arm's length. "What makes you say that?"

"I haven't read the book, but isn't there a chapter when the monster goes wandering through the mountains?"

"You believe this is how the monster looked?"

"Not Boris Karloff. The original monster."

"If you haven't read the book, how the devil . . ."

"Someone gave me a description."

"It's a long time since I read it," said Sturr. If he had heard this theory before, he was doing a remarkable job of making it appear unexpected.

"Long, black, glossy hair." As if describing a wanted man, Diamond listed the details he had got from Ellis Somerset. "Yellow complexion, pale eyes, good, white teeth, black lips. Wouldn't you say this matches the figure in your painting?"

Sturr remained cautious. He continued to study the painting for some seconds longer. "Blake's figures tended to look otherworldly. The hair is invariably long. I can show you engravings of characters from *Paradise Lost* and the Bible just like this."

"And what if I told you two other paintings by Blake had been discovered, one showing this character or creature, whatever it may be, in a mountain landscape meeting a man about two feet shorter, and the other of it staring through a window at a murder scene? A woman lies strangled on a bed and the man—

the same man from the other picture—is wide-eyed in horror. Scenes straight out of *Frankenstein*. What would you say to that?"

Sturr's face lit up. "You really mean this? I'd be fascinated to see them. Are they signed?"

"I couldn't tell you."

"Where can I see them?" His eagerness had transformed him. All the truculence had fallen away.

"Miss Redbird acquired them in a private deal. They disappeared from the shop at the time of her death."

"What?" Now Sturr looked seriously alarmed. "I don't follow you."

"They've gone, sir. They were in her office and they've gone. She bought them with some other goods from a house in Camden Crescent."

"When?"

"On the day she died. She had them collected. She was excited, believing them to be Blakes and worth a tidy sum."

"They would be if they were genuine. I'm not surprised she was excited."

"She had a buyer in mind. She spoke of this to her assistant."

"I would buy them," Sturr said, regardless of the quicksand he was stepping into. "I'd buy them like a shot. Why didn't she come to me?"

"That was our reaction," said Diamond. "You're the obvious person, with your collection."

"With this." He was still holding the Blake and he brandished it like the captain of a winning team with the trophy. "They could be part of a series that no Blake scholar is aware of. If he illustrated *Frankenstein*, it's sensational news. The art world is going to be amazed. I wonder if Blake knew Mary Shelley."

"He knew her mother, anyway."

"What—Mary Wollstonecraft? You're right! He illustrated one of her books. I haven't seen them, but I remember them in a catalogue. I even remember the title: *Original Stories from Real Life*. Well, isn't this amazing? I've owned this painting all this time without suspecting any connection with *Frankenstein*."

"Where did you get it?"

"I bought it at auction in Bristol in 1989. It was a single lot, 'attributed to Blake', which means it's of his style, but can't be proved as one of his works. So I got it for a few hundred, and I consider I got a bargain. The chance of anyone else producing something like this in Blake's style is remote. He's out on his own as a painter. Very difficult to imitate."

"Do you know who put the picture into the auction?"

"Good point. I could look it up."

"Were any others up for sale?"

"Blakes, you mean? I'm certain they were not. I would have bid for them, you see."

Sturr replaced the picture in the line-up along the wall and offered to go off and look up the details of the sale. Each of his pictures had its own file, he said, and it should be easy to find out. He could not have been more obliging now he was on the trail of the unknown Blakes. It was a re-run of the enthusiasm he had shown the evening he had dragged Diamond around his collection.

Left in the room with Leaman, Diamond picked up the picture that had caused so much excitement and examined the flaking brown paper on the reverse. Nothing was written there. "I'd like to show this to Ellis Somerset, see if he thinks it looks anything like the other two."

"Will he let you borrow it?"

"I can ask nicely."

"Where's this leading us, sir?"

"To a plausible motive for murder. You've just seen the grip it can get on a man, this passion for collecting. They hear about something and they have to possess it. It's an addiction."

"Is he the killer? If he is, he would have known about the other two Blakes. He's a bloody good actor if he did."

"Let's not jump to conclusions . . . yet."

"Nobody else around here collects Blakes, do they?"

Diamond didn't answer. Sturr's tread was sounding across the hall. When he came in, he was carrying a dark red pocket file. "I'm afraid I can't tell you the previous owner of my Blake," he told them, still fired up. "The catalogue lists vendors for some of the other lots, but not this one."

"A secret seller?"

"Anonymous. It's not unusual for a vendor to want his name kept off the catalogue, and you'll find that all auctioneers guard people's privacy if requested. You said these others were owned by someone from Camden Crescent."

"Simon Minchendon."

"Who died last week? Good Lord, I knew him. Visited his house. I had no idea he was interested in Blake."

"Maybe these were not on view."

"I would certainly have noticed them if they had been. It was a fine house, filled with interesting things. This is so tantalising. You say they were stolen from Noble and Nude?"

"No, I said they disappeared on the day the owner was murdered. She could have sold them. We're trying to get a picture of her last hours."

"That's why you came to me?" The Councillor's features creased into a smile. "I wish you'd mentioned it first. Do you know, I was beginning to think you suspected me of murder?"

twenty-eight

DIAMOND LET HIMSELF IN, not expecting to find Steph still up. They had an understanding that if ever he got home late, she would be in bed. So he took off his shoes by the front door and padded through to the kitchen to see if she had left anything in the oven. Some hours had gone by since his visit to the canteen, though the half-price lamb was not forgotten. Bad meals have ways of lingering on the palate that good meals do not.

Under his arm he had Councillor Sturr's Blake, cocooned in bubblewrap. Easing the picture from its owner had been a triumph of persuasion. The lure: the chance to have it examined by forensic scientists specialising in art works, who, using the latest technology, would surely confirm it as genuine—or so Diamond had suggested. Sturr could then announce to the art world that he possessed an accredited Blake, and moreover that it was one of a previously unknown series illustrating *Frankenstein*.

No one excelled the big detective at exploiting a suspect's vanity.

He switched on the light, put the picture in a place of safety on top of the fridge and looked for Steph's note about supper. It wouldn't be like her to go to bed without leaving a note.

No note this time, but there was a chicken dinner on the table covered in clingfilm. Steph had not let him down. Roast potatoes, runner beans, peas and carrots. It was still slightly warm. He would give it a whirl in the microwave and shortly expunge the memory of the lamb.

An ice-cold lager would go down nicely with the chicken. He reached for the fridge door and was surprised by a sudden movement at the edge of his vision that made him lean sharply to the left and put up a protective arm. Something dark leapt up from the floor. Warm fur brushed the back of his hand, Raffles, expecting to be fed.

A cat will judge the minimum effort required to make a leap, and will always succeed unless the unexpected happens. Nudged in mid-air by Diamond's flailing hand, Raffles lost some momentum, got the front paws up, but not the rest. Two sets of claws caught in the bubblewrap covering Councillor Sturr's Blake. The hind paws scraped frantically against the side of the fridge, trying for a purchase that was not there. The package was dragged inexorably to the edge and tipped over. Cat and picture crashed to the tiled floor. There was the sickening sound of glass breaking.

Diamond shouted, "Bloody hell, I'll skin you."

Raffles bolted out of the kitchen and upstairs, all prospect of a late supper gone.

So unfair. Diamond was notorious for being clumsy, but this time he'd taken special care. You'd think the top of a fridge would be a safe place.

He picked the package off the floor. It chinked. He placed it on the kitchen table and untied the string.

"What was that?"

He jerked again. His nerves were bad. Steph had come in, as silent as the cat.

He explained the accident, while she watched him ease aside the bubblewrap. The splintered glass was mostly still in place, but a few pieces had fallen out of the frame. Steph warned him not to touch. They upended the picture and let the loose fragments fall onto the wrapping.

"The worst thing is it doesn't belong to me."

"Thank God for that," Steph commented.

"Why do you say that?"

"It's not the sort of thing I'd want on the wall, that's why. It's a Blake print, isn't it?"

"It's an original."

"Oh, Pete!"

"Well, I can't see that it's damaged." He let out the tension with a long breath. "Where did you come from? I thought you'd gone up."

"I was dozing in my armchair in the back room. You gave me a proper shock."

"The cat did."

"It wasn't the cat that shouted. All right," she said, lifting a hand to pacify him. "You've had one hell of a Sunday. Did you find who attacked John Wigfull?"

"Not yet."

"They say there's a slight improvement. He's drifting in and out of consciousness. I phoned a friend at the hospital two hours ago."

One of Steph's network. Nothing happened anywhere without her hearing about it.

"They won't let us near him," he said. "They never do."

"He won't remember anything," she said.

"You're probably right."

She put the dinner in the microwave and pressed the reheat pad. "It isn't obvious, then?"

"What isn't?"

"The person you're after."

"Not obvious, no." Steph had a remarkable gift for unlocking mysteries, so he summarised his day, the interviews with Somerset, Dougan, Pennycook, Heath and Sturr. "I can't see any of them bludgeoning a police officer. Well, old Heath isn't in the frame, anyway. He's too old and too frail."

"Why did you bother with him, then?"

"Checking back on Joe Dougan—who was the man most likely to be chased across a field by Wigfull. There's no question Wigfull had him top of the list. But everything the little rogue has told us is true."

"Sounds as if you like him."

"That means nothing, but, yes, I do. In spite of everything, he's chirpy."

"And the others?"

"Not so lovable." He returned to the fridge for that lager. "But I haven't caught them seriously lying. Somerset is the bloke in a bow-tie you don't see out of doors, let alone wielding a bludgeon in a Wiltshire field. Pennycook is a junkie without a car. And Sturr doesn't have any reason to bash Wigfull. He wasn't even seen by Wigfull. What's more, he has an alibi."

"There's no one else?"

"No one I would call a suspect. I tried to see a character known as Uncle Evan who Wigfull may conceivably have gone to interview, but he's proving elusive."

"Where does he fit in?"

"He was one of the people Joe Dougan visited the day Peg Redbird was killed. At one time he owned the book that started Joe on this trail—Mary Shelley's copy of Milton."

"Uncle Evan?" The microwave pinged and she opened it and peeled the clingfilm off the plate. "I'm sure I've heard of him."

"Puppet shows. He tours the fetes and fairs all summer."

"That's it, then. I've seen his advert in the paper. Do you want to eat here?"

"Fine."

"Brown sauce?"

"Please."

"Better take the picture off the table, then. You know what happened last time you shook the bottle."

She moved it to the safety of the front room. While Diamond

ate, Steph gave some thought to the problem of Wigfull's attacker. "This all happened out Stowford way, didn't it?"

"A field between Westwood and Stowford."

"Where did they start—Westwood?"

"Must have. We found his car there."

"John Wigfull's?"

"Yes."

"Presumably he was following someone—or someone followed him. Have you worked out where he was going?" She doggedly thought through the logic of events, as she liked to do, but this time she appeared to have come full circle.

"Stowford, like I said."

"Why Stowford?" Steph persisted. "Not for a cream tea, surely?"

He thought about that, frowning. Then he smiled.

twenty-nine

"THE MURDEROUS MARK OF *the fiend's grasp was on her neck, and the breath had ceased to issue from her lips.*"

Strangulation was the monster's method. How inconvenient that his victims didn't shed blood.

thirty

MONDAY MORNING, AND WHATEVER happened to the weekend? Feeling blue, Diamond drove into his space at Manvers Street nick, switched off the ignition, sighed, felt for the door handle, heaved himself out and slammed the door. Then he heard a shout of, "Hi," from the far side of the car park. He stared across the car tops. She was blonde, a blonde to make Monday morning feel like Friday afternoon. What was even better, she waved and started running towards him.

He no longer felt blue. There was a definite tinge of rose.

"Mr D," she called out, and he recognized the voice as Ingeborg Smith's. The rose turned purple. It was time he had his eyes tested.

She stopped in front of him, breathless. "I won't keep you a moment."

"That's for sure."

"I just wanted to ask how John Sturr took it last night."

"You mean your dramatic exit? He didn't say much at all. Stunned, I expect."

"He didn't mention anything about my chances?"

"Your chances?"

"Of joining the police."

"Forget it, Ingeborg. He's a big wheel. He's not bothered with recruiting. You're pushing at an open door. You've done enough to get noticed."

Her face relaxed into a confident smile. "You've heard then."

"Heard what? Don't ask me, I only work here."

"Didn't they tell you? My recruitment interview." She let that sink in, and then said, "I got my application in just in time. They phoned me specially. They're seeing some applicants today and could I come in at short notice? Could I, man, oh man!"

"I'll cross my fingers."

"For me?"

"For Bath Police—if you get taken on."

She laughed and said, "Fat chance really. All bets are off after last night. John Sturr can pull the plug on me even if they like me."

"Did you tell him about the interview?"

"Yes. I thought it would help me. Didn't know I was going to blow a fuse and foul up everything."

"You spoke for all of us. But I thought you two were friends."

"Just because he took me to Georgina's party?"

"I saw you leave with him. You did stay the night?"

She said, level-eyed, "I did."

"You don't mind me asking? Did you go straight from the party to his house?"

"Yes."

"And then . . . ?"

She laughed. "Oh, come on."

He wanted to know. "You spent the entire night with him?"

"You know I did."

"You'd had a few drinks by that time. Maybe your memory—"

She said with scorn, "I may have looked pie-eyed, but I know exactly what happened . . . or didn't."

"Didn't?"

Now she clicked her tongue and looked away across the car park. "Forget it. This is too personal."

"Yesterday you made some remark about business calls to America."

She nodded. "You don't miss much, do you? When we got in, there were messages on his answerphone. He said he needed to phone New York. Over there it was still business hours. He opened a bottle of bubbly, poured me one and took me into another room and put on some rock and roll video while he went off to make his call. I was too loaded to the gills to make an issue of it. When he finally got off the phone, a good forty minutes later, he was all apologies." She looked away again. "The story of the night."

"Yet you made another date for Sunday."

"Right. I met him by chance at the Forum Saturday night."

"The Elgar concert?" he said with interest. This could be crucial.

"Yes. I was sitting two rows behind him. He suggested this meal on Sunday. By then I knew about this interview. I'm not stupid."

John Sturr's movements on the afternoon and evening Wigfull was beaten unconscious had become central to the investigation. "Tell me, was he there from the beginning of the concert?"

"That's when we spoke—before it started, I mean."

He nodded, but wistfully. This piece of information clinched Sturr's alibi for that afternoon. He was at Castle Cary until six. It was impossible for him to have attacked Wigfull and made the start of the concert.

"What time are the interviews?"

"Seven o'clock?"

"You're about ten hours too early."

She laughed again. "Right now I'm wearing my other hat. Inspector Halliwell's press conference."

"Busy day for both of us, then." He took a step away, but Ingeborg still wanted to say something.

"I wasn't going to stay another night at John Sturr's. You don't think I'm that desperate?"

"Ingeborg, at the moment I just want to get to work."

"Why were *you* there?" she asked, becoming the journalist again. "What was it about? Is he up to naughties?"

"I reckon he thought he was," said Diamond, "even if you didn't."

"That isn't what I meant."

Buoyed up just a little, Diamond ambled into work.

INSIDE, HE asked Keith Halliwell how the press briefing had gone.

Some of the crime reporters, it seemed, had been touchy about Ingeborg's exclusive on the bones found in the River Wylye until they heard it confirmed by Halliwell that it really had been her digging in back numbers of the *Wiltshire Times* that had made the breakthrough. But there was real satisfaction over the appeal for information about the two men known as Banger and Mash. Papers can make something of names like that.

"We're back in the news," Halliwell claimed, not without pride. He'd handled a large press conference smoothly.

"Were we ever out of it?" Diamond commented.

"I've done a load of interviews for TV and radio."

"You'll have your own chat show next."

He strolled into the incident room where the information on Peg Redbird's murder was being co-ordinated. The man he wished to speak to was busy on the phone, so he stood by the board where photos of the crime scene were displayed, a custom that had never, in all his years as a murder man, been of any practical use. There were shots of Peg's office in Noble and Nude, of her body lodged against Pulteney Weir and of the stretch of river bank closest to the shop where, presumably, the body had been tipped into the Avon.

Leaman, still with the phone to his ear, snatched up a sheet of paper and waved it. Diamond went over.

The paper had the BT heading familiar from countless phone bills. They had supplied a longish list of numbers, the calls Peg Redbird had made on the day she was killed. Someone had scribbled notes in pencil beside some of them. *British Museum, Tate, Courtauld, Fitzwilliam*. It seemed Peg had devoted the first part of that afternoon to calling art galleries and museums. Later she had spoken to someone at Sotheby's, the auctioneers. Then there were two local calls, as yet unidentified.

"Helpful, sir?" Leaman said, now off the phone.

"Could be. Are these your notes?"

"Sally Myers, sir."

One of the younger members of the squad looked up fleetingly from her keyboard.

Leaman said, "It's clear Peg was pretty active that afternoon, trying to check on something. It has to be the Blakes, doesn't it?"

Diamond had worked that out and moved on. "What about these Bath numbers? Why haven't we got names beside them?"

"Sally's working on it. I thought we'd trace the long distance calls first."

Diamond made a sound deep in his throat that registered disagreement. The local calls were of more interest. "What's the news of John Wigfull?"

"Slightly better. He's semi-conscious some of the time, but in no condition to talk."

"Wigfull can't help us. Even if he sits up and asks for meat and two veg, he won't remember a damned thing. People don't after serious concussion."

"We checked Councillor Sturr's statement, sir—the people in Castle Cary he went to see Saturday afternoon. It stands up well. He was with them until ten to six."

"And by seven-thirty he was at the Elgar concert in Bath," said Diamond. "He met Ingeborg there. She just told me."

Barely disguising his disappointment, Leaman said, "He's squeaky-clean, then. Shall I rub his name off the board?"

"Christ—who put it up there? If Georgina sees it she'll go ape. Give me the damned duster." He grabbed it and erased the name himself. "Don't you have anything new to report?"

Leaman shrugged. There was no pleasing some people.

"I'm off to Stowford for a bit," Diamond announced.

Nobody applauded, but they must have cheered inwardly, and he knew it. He was no fun to have around this Monday morning.

STOWFORD SCARCELY merits a name at all. You wouldn't call it a village; a hamlet would be an exaggeration. It is a farm and a cluster of buildings presenting their backs to the A366 between Radstock and Trowbridge. Only the cream teas board at the side of the the road would persuade a passing driver that there was anything to stop for. The place is a relic of the wool trade that flourished for four centuries, now just an ancient, crumbling farmhouse, some farm buildings and a mill.

"*Why Stowford?*" Steph had asked.

Diamond left the road and took the track that curved left towards the farmyard. He parked against a barn. Nobody seemed to be about, just a black cat sunning itself against the barn wall. On seeing the visitor it rolled on its back and looked at him upside down, suggesting it would not object to some admiration, but no cat stood a chance with Diamond so soon after last night's incident in the kitchen.

He walked around the side of the barn and looked through a window. The interior was fitted out as a furniture-maker's workshop. Nice pieces, too. A table and chairs he would have been happy to own. These buildings, he remembered from his previous visit, barns, cowsheds or whatever, had been put to use as craft workshops. Next door was a stonemason's studio and beyond that a metalwork shop.

"*Why Stowford?*"

Why not?

He continued the slow inspection of the buildings and the cat came with him, intermittently pressing its side against his legs. Not one of the workshops was in use. Well, it was only Monday morning. How nice to be self-employed, he thought.

Through the farmyard he went, across to the gabled farmhouse where he and Steph had gone for the cream tea. Fifteenth century, this building was said to be, and, candidly, looked its age. Moss was growing in profusion on the tiled roof.

He rang the handbell provided on a table by the door. The sound seemed excessive.

No one came. Although the small front lawns at either side of the path were filled with tables and chairs, the people didn't do morning coffee, it seemed. Just the cream teas.

He tried the front door and found it open. He recalled coming in here to pay for the tea. If you didn't notice the low lintel you paid with a bruised head as well.

Ahead was a narrow hallway with a kitchen off to the left. The cat trotted confidently in there.

"Anyone about?"

He was beginning to get that *Marie Celeste* feeling. The large room to the right was obviously the living room, with a generous fireplace, a piano and a box of children's toys. A table big enough to seat ten stood at the centre and other tables filled the window spaces, with pews instead of chairs. When the weather was unkind, the cream tea clients came in here.

He called out again.

The silence was not helping his Monday gloom.

Rather than venturing into the private rooms beyond, he returned outside and explored around the back, thinking possibly he had heard some sounds from that direction.

The source was revealed. He looked over a low wall at a large sow. It eyed him and seemed almost to smile.

Then a voice behind him said, "Lift me up, please."

A small girl had come from nowhere, perhaps six years old, with fair hair in a fringe and dressed in a pink T-shirt and black Lycra shorts. As small girls go, she was not the most prepossessing. Pale, snub-nosed and gap-toothed. And barefoot.

He asked, "Who are you?"

"Winnie."

"Do you live here, Winnie?"

She shook her head.

"Just visiting?"

A nod. "I want to see the pig."

"It's here."

"I can't see over the wall."

He knew better than to lift up a child he didn't know, natural as it may have seemed. "I can fix that," he said, spotting a blue plastic milk crate. "You can stand on that."

"I'll fetch it."

She was back with the crate very quickly and placed it in position herself and stepped up. "I can see now."

"Good."

"I call her Mrs Piggy."

"That's not a bad name," he said. Talking seriously to a child was a rare treat.

"She can't be Miss Piggy," Winnie said in a way that begged a question, and he wondered if he was about to be told something intimate, with the candour you must expect from small children.

"Why is that?"

"Get real. Miss Piggy is a Muppet."

"So she is. And where's your Mummy this morning?"

"Shopping, I 'spect. Look at all her titties. Why's she got so many?"

He should have been expecting something like this. "Those are for all the piglets. When she has a litter—that's baby pigs—they come in big numbers. Each one needs a place to suck."

"Miss Piggy doesn't have all those titties."

"Get real," he said. "Miss Piggy is a Muppet."

She almost fell off the crate laughing.

If she were ours, he thought, mine and Steph's, we wouldn't leave her and go shopping. Some people didn't deserve children. "Are you staying in the farmhouse?"

She shook her head, still watching the sow.

"Where, then?"

"Van."

He'd seen a tractor and some farm machinery where he'd parked the car. No van.

"Over there," said Winnie, gesturing in the general direction of the fields, but without taking her eyes off the sow.

He remembered seeing a caravan with a tent attachment on the far side of the field as he drove in.

She turned and jumped off the crate. She'd seen enough of the sow. "What shall we do next?"

Such confidence. He said, "I was about to leave. Aren't there any grown-ups about?"

"Don't know. Do you want to see the Muppets?"

"Watch TV, you mean? I'd really like to, but I don't have time today."

"Not telly Muppets, stupid. Real ones," said Winnie. She gave him one of those challenging looks children have for adults, daring him to disbelieve.

"Some of your toys?" This was not a good idea.

"No, silly. I'll show you." She walked a few steps and looked round to see if he was following.

He took a last look at the scene. The whole yard was still deserted. Even the cat had gone. He let Winnie lead him away from the farm. Not, he discovered with some relief, in the direction of the caravan, but towards a spinney, following the mill stream.

The child ran ahead, obviously familiar with the path. Diamond had to step out briskly. Butterflies swooped and soared and a startled pheasant scuttled out of the cover and crossed his path.

The water mill came into view, just. It was well camouflaged by creepers, a building long since fallen into disuse. Once it would have been used as a fulling mill, making the local cloth stronger and more compact. Winnie ignored it and ran on.

She stopped finally at another ivy-clad structure that must have been associated once with the production of wool and cloth. The miller's cottage maybe. This building was better hidden than the mill, but Winnie was familiar with it from the way she ran confidently to a window and stood on tiptoe to look in.

"See?"

He caught up with her. Surprisingly, the window was intact. In fact, it must have been cleaned recently. The interior was dark, and he screwed up his eyes to make out anything at all. Then he felt a gathering of tension as he saw what so excited the little girl. The place was fitted out like a coat check, with stands and hangers, except that instead of coats suspended from the hangers, there were weird and mis-shapen figures with heads hanging grotesquely and limp, shrunken bodies.

His first impulse was to drag the child away from the ghoulish spectacle. But she was clearly exhilarated by it, and he saw that she had been right, for these were puppets with the faces of people, animals and fantasy creatures. Some were lifesize, some quite small. Further in, were wood puppets on strings.

Winnie was singing the theme music from the Muppet Show, swaying rhythmically.

"Who does this belong to?" Diamond asked, knowing the answer.

To the same tune, she sang, "Don't know . . . Don't know. Don't know."

"Have you seen the man who comes here?"

She didn't answer.

He walked around the building, trying to see in, but the other

268   P e t e r   L o v e s e y

windows were boarded, the door fastened with a padlock. "Well, you've solved a mystery, Winnie," he said when he came back to her. "I didn't need a grown-up after all."

"Do you want to go in?" she asked, looking up at him with her steady brown eyes.

"In here?"

"He keeps the key under that thing."

A boot scraper made of bristles mounted in wood. He looked underneath and found she was right.

The key fitted the padlock.

Winnie pushed past him when he drew the door open. "Hold on," he warned. "We don't know what's in there."

But Winnie knew. She was already inspecting the puppets, skipping up and down the racks, lifting faces and pulling strings, humming her tune again.

It was a kids' treasure-house. Along the walls were tea-chests crammed to overflowing with the materials the puppets were made from, rolls of latex, sponge rubber, bright-coloured, glittery fabrics, gauze, coils of wire, balsawood, spray-cans, marker pens, wigs, beards and moustaches. At the far end was an old metal filing cabinet with a basket of golden eggs on top.

Diamond tried the top drawer, hopeful of finding some correspondence. Surely an enterprise like this had to have some organisation. But the drawer had no files. It was filled with cans of paint. And the lower drawers contained only string, newspapers and pots of glue.

"Careful with that, Winnie." She was swinging on the tentacles of an octopus, stretching them alarmingly. "I think we'd better leave now."

"Don't want to."

"We've had our fun now."

"Haven't."

He started walking towards the door. "I'm going, anyway, and I'll have to shut you in if you're not coming."

"Don't care."

By the door, hanging from a nail in the wall, he found something helpful at last. An office-style appointments calendar. Someone had scribbled in the names of places and organizations, with times. He checked to see if there was an entry for Saturday. *Bath Rotarians, 11-5, Victoria Park.* The day Wigfull had been attacked.

Thursday, the day of Peg Redbird's murder. Blank.

Today, then. Monday. *Little Terrors, 11 a.m.* What on earth was he to make of that? From Bath Rotarians to Little Terrors in one weekend. Quite a comedown.

"What does it say?"

Winnie was at his side, not choosing after all to be left alone with the puppets.

"I don't know," he said.

"Can't you read?" she asked.

"I mean I don't know what it is. It says Little Terrors."

"Don't you know?" said Winnie with a superior air. "It's a play place in Frome. I been there hundreds of times."

thirty-one

LITTLE TERRORS.

The old market town of Frome was a mere eight miles south of Stowford. Diamond knew it well—or so he thought. He hadn't heard of Little Terrors.

Neither had Leaman when he called him on the phone. "What is it, sir—a toyshop?"

"A play place."

"Like a park, you mean?"

"Don't you know what a play place is?"

"With swings and things?"

It had been easier discussing this with Winnie. "You're a detective. Find out."

They arranged to meet on the Frome town bridge. Leaman was to come with clear directions to Little Terrors, whatever it turned out to be.

After this fresh tweak to the investigation, Diamond drove down the A36 with the Muppet tune refusing to go out of his head and his thoughts jigging to it. Who would have expected the violence done to Wigfull to link up with puppets and a play place?

There was a strong temptation to make the connection with Uncle Evan, the puppeteer Joe Dougan had spoken about. But what connection could that be? Uncle Evan was not really in the frame for Peg Redbird's murder or the attack on Wigfull. He was simply one of the people who had once owned Mary Shelley's copy of Milton.

Who was Uncle Evan anyway? His real name had not emerged so far. From Joe's account, he was a fortyish hippie with John Lennon glasses and a pony-tail hairstyle who got his bookings through the Brains Surgery at Larkhall. He'd bought the book at Noble and Nude some years ago and sold it on to Oliver Heath, the old gent with the shop in Union Passage. Heath had called him a multi-talented young man—"young", presumably, from the perspective of eighty years or more.

If it *was* Uncle Evan's puppet workshop at Stowford, who was it who had crossed the fields towards it some time Saturday afternoon or evening? Wigfull, for sure. But who else? Evan himself, returning from the show for the Bath Rotarians? Why would he approach it on foot across the fields rather than driving straight there as Diamond himself had just done? The footpath route made no sense. He'd have a vanload of equipment with him.

The heat was back on Joe Dougan. It always came back to Joe. Joe had met Evan. Of the other remaining suspects, Somerset and Pennycook, neither had any known link with the puppet man. Joe had sought him out on the day Peg Redbird was murdered.

So where had Joe been on the Saturday? He'd spent the whole of the afternoon doing the rounds of the Bath hotels looking for Donna, or so he claimed. What if—as well as checking hotels—he'd called at the Brains Surgery to find out more about Uncle Evan? The people in the pub could have told him Evan had a workshop out at Stowford. And Joe, being a stranger to the district, could easily have found himself in Westwood instead of Stowford and then spotted the sign for the footpath across the fields.

Why would Joe still be interested in Uncle Evan? Diamond's best answer was this: Evan had learned from Joe that the copy of Milton's poems he had bought and sold cheaply was worth much more. A prize had slipped through his hands. Years before, when he acquired the book from Peg, she may have told him she had found it in an antique writing box. Last week he would surely have reached the same conclusion as Joe: that if the book had belonged to Mary Shelley, so had the box.

Evan would know Mary Shelley's writing box would be worth a bit.

And the box disappeared from Noble and Nude on the night Peg was murdered. If Joe was the killer, it was easy to assume he'd stolen the box. The fanatical desire to own the thing was the reason he'd done it, his motive. There had been a struggle and Peg had been cracked over the head. But what if Evan came to Walcot Street the same night with plans to nick the box? His chance would have come while Joe was dumping the body in the river. Joe would have been appalled to find it gone when he returned. But he was intelligent. With time to reflect, he must have worked out the identity of the one other person who knew the value of the box. Determined to have it for himself, he returned to the Brains Surgery and picked up the trail of Uncle Evan. It was worth risking a trip to Stowford to see what was there.

It was looking as if Wigfull had been right all along about Joe. For Peter Diamond, that was humbling, if not galling. Joe was on a train to London by now. He'd be in Paris before the day was out.

At Frome, he called Manvers Street and said he wanted Joe Dougan stopped at Waterloo and brought back for questioning. A call to the Railway Police should do it.

LEAMAN WAS waiting on the town bridge. He had got the address of Little Terrors, he said. It was up the hill at the top, opposite the church.

"So what is it?" Diamond asked.

"An old factory, or warehouse, so far as I can make out."

"I mean what is it now?"

"A play place."

"OK. Be like that."

Leaman drove ahead in his car, through the town, and most of the way out of it. The church came up on the left and they turned right along a narrow street that presently opened out. And there was the name, bizarre in bold lettering over an innocent-seeming door.

Small children with their mothers were going inside.

Leaman cleared his throat in a way that signalled a problem.

"Yes?"

"Sir, has it crossed your mind that we're going to stand out a mile? Surrounded by little kids, with a few young mums."

"So?"

"This Uncle Evan is going to spot us the minute we walk in."

"We could be dads." After a pause, he added, "All right, grandad in my case."

"Thought I'd mention it, that's all."

"I'm going to mention something, too," said Diamond. "Once upon a time, I went into a house to make an arrest. I pushed a kid out of the way and he hit a radiator and cracked his head. I lost my job over it. We're going in to ask Uncle Evan to step outside and give us some help, right? That's all. Gently, gently. If anything goes wrong in there and kids are hurt . . ."

Inside, the Little Terrors were not so fastidious, ripping off their shoes and slinging them on racks, a rule of the house, it seemed. The noise was deafening. They could have called it Bedlam.

But at the point of entry some order was imposed. When the kids were in their socks they paid—or were paid for—and passed through a small turnstile.

"Yes?" said the chewing teenager with cropped hair dyed green who collected the money.

"We're police."

She was silent, stunned, it seemed. Until she grinned and said. "Is it, like, a bust?"

Diamond returned the grin. "They start young in Frome, do they?"

"So what's the problem?" she asked. "The council know about us. We're licensed."

"No problem," said Diamond. "Community relations." A useful phrase.

She had to shout to be heard. "You picked the wrong day. We got something special, a treat for the end of the summer holiday. Puppet show. You won't be able to move in there. I've never seen so many."

"We'll manage," Leaman bawled back. "We'll enjoy the show."

"It takes all sorts. Just watch where you put them big feet."

They passed through the turnstile into what would normally have been a place where the parents sat and drank coffee while the kids exhausted themselves playing. Today the serving counter was in use as the upper tier of the auditorium, with Little Terrors perched along its length banging their heels against the woodwork. Diamond and Leaman side-stepped around the mass bunched together seated on the floor. The idea was to reach the back, where the adults were. The show was already under way, the stage set up at the far end. Two skeletons on strings were being put through a dance and some of the young audience were enthralled. Plenty continued to fidget and talk as if nothing was going on.

A woman whose view was blocked said, "D'you mind?"

"Sorry." In trying to reach a space behind, Diamond made matters worse by nudging her chest with his arm. There just wasn't room for two men their size, so they had to progress right round the other side to where a sort of infants' assault course, clearly the centrepiece of the building, was set up. It was the only observation point left to them.

"House rules," said another woman, pointing to their feet. Obediently they took off their shoes and carried them in.

Some children, bored with the puppets, were playing on the apparatus. The space extended a long way back into the building and was equipped with rope ladders, balance beams, trampolines, tubes to climb through, shutes and rings. Plunging their feet into a sunken area filled with thousands of plastic balls, the murder squad waded kneedeep to their vantage position. Two resourceful mums and their kids were already sitting in there watching the show through the mesh that kept the balls from spilling out.

They joined them, and it felt more comfortable than it looked.

After all the trouble it was some relief to catch a line of dialogue that went, "I work for Uncle Evan. Who do you work for?"

On the stage, the skeletons had been supplanted by a caterpillar and a butterfly on a stick. The man working them was visible, in fact prominent, standing up in an inset in the stage; his presence didn't seem to affect the illusion. The kids had their eyes fixed on the puppets; and, just as fixedly, the policemen had theirs on the puppeteer.

Diamond would have put him at younger than forty, Joe Dougan's estimate, but these things are always subjective. Hippy? Well, the hair was longish, blond, untidy. Hardly enough for a ponytail, he would have thought. No beard, not even a coating of stubble. Black T-shirt and jeans. The real surprise was that a young woman was assisting, getting the next set of puppets ready to hand to him. She was clearly visible from this side angle, her brownish-red hair tied Indian-fashion with a pink scarf.

The story-line quickly became clear. A boy puppet called Daniel was looking for his long-lost sister and meeting some strange, comical and whimsical characters in the process. They were borrowed freely from film, fairy tale and cartoon, and each had a few moments' interaction with the Daniel puppet. Half the fun for the kids was bawling out the names of characters they recognized: Donald Duck, Kermit, Popeye, Paddington, Barney, the Teletubbies. The copyright infringements were legion. And when a monster figure lumbered in, to spooky music, there were knowledgable shouts of "Frankenstein!"

After ten minutes Diamond said in an aside to Leaman, "Is there much more of this, do you think?"

"They must be running out of puppets."

"They could easily bring them on again."

The puppets themselves were superbly crafted, no question. It was a pity the script—if you could call it that—was so abysmal. Even a half-intelligent four-year-old must have found it repetitive.

The performance reached its finale—or ran out of puppets—mercifully soon, with the slaying of a giant and the release of Daniel's little sister from a spell that had put her to sleep.

There were cheers from the kids and the grown-ups clapped.

"That's the end of the show, boys and girls," announced the female puppeteer in her natural voice. "Don't all move at once, will you? And, whatever you do, please don't touch the puppets."

Just about everyone stampeded towards the activity area. A few tried to go against the tide in search of their mums. Some gave up, some cried and others used their elbows. Three remained helpless on the serving counter, sucking their thumbs. At the front, the puppeteers were totally occupied in preventing their stage being pulled apart.

Scattering plastic balls, the murder squad stumbled out of their vantage point, getting puzzled looks from some of the small children coming the other way.

In a short time, the area where the audience had been was almost clear. The hidden interior of the building must have been large to absorb so many.

The puppeteers started dismantling the stage. Diamond went over, tapped the man on the shoulder and said, quietly, "Police."

He turned, startled. "What's up?"

The woman was more controlled. "Is it the van? Did we park in the wrong spot?"

"Nothing to do with the van. Would you mind telling me your name, your real name?"

The man frowned and ran his fingers nervously through his blond hair. "Paul Anderson. What am I supposed to have done?"

"Where do you live, Mr Anderson?"

"Larkhall."

"Up near the Brains Surgery?"

"That direction, anyway."

"Where you're a regular?"

"I wouldn't call myself that."

"You met a man there a few days ago—Thursday of last week—Professor Joe Dougan, from Columbus, Ohio."

"Did I?"

Diamond was beginning to be annoyed, but he persevered. "American, middle-aged, on the short side."

"Doesn't mean a thing to me." He added, gathering confidence, "Listen, mate, I think you may have got your wires crossed. I visit the pub, yes, but I'm not Uncle Evan."

"That's the truth," said the woman.

"Annie and me, we're filling in for him. Couldn't you tell from the crap show we just did?"

This, more than anything, made Diamond hesitate. It *had* been a godawful show, even though the puppets were beautifully constructed and painted. He would have expected something more classy.

"We had to wing it," said Annie. "We haven't seen Evan's show. There wasn't time."

The man who called himself Paul Anderson said, "He only asked us yesterday. We used to have our own show, right? We got fed up. Everyone wants you to do it for peanuts."

"It's not worth it. It's bloody expensive, setting up the gigs," Annie said in support.

"So Evan asked you to fill in. What's he up to?"

"God knows. Well, he did say something about a family crisis," said Paul Anderson. "I've never heard him talk about his family before. Didn't know he had one. We don't know him all that well. It's just that with all our experience . . ."

"When somebody's in a spot, you help them out, don't you?" said Annie.

They had convinced Diamond. He was disappointed and elated at the same time. Uncle Evan's behaviour was deeply suspicious and his "family crisis" looked like a flimsy excuse to avoid being traced and questioned. He was behaving like a guilty man. Diamond continued to question the couple, but they said nothing more of substance. They claimed not to know Evan's real name, or where he lived. He had handed them the keys of the van containing everything they needed for the show and they had driven it away from the pub the previous afternoon. He didn't want it back for a week.

"That's handy," said Diamond, "because we're going to take it over."

LEAVING LEAMAN to arrange for forensic to pick up the van, he set off to keep an appointment in Mells, a few miles west of Frome. He sang a little in the car, something he only ever did when alone, and feeling upbeat. The Queen number, *Another One Bites the Dust*. The words were right, even if he had to strain to get the notes.

He didn't know Mells. Driving through the village looking for a particular cottage, he quickly understood how an expert on English art fitted in there. The ambience was orderly, understated, timeless and redolent of decent living. Personally, he would not have lasted there a week. Many of the gardens were surrounded by high walls, but what you could see through the gates was as clean as a cat's behind, and a pedigree cat at that.

Stuart Eastland was one of the team of specialists who advised Avon and Somerset Police on stolen property. Diamond had met him only a couple of times before, and then briefly; others dealt with thefts of art and antiques. "This isn't the usual problem," he explained, setting the bubble-wrapped parcel on a round oak table in Eastland's thatched cottage. "I have it on loan from the owner. I'd like an opinion."

"On what, precisely?" Eastland had a pair of half-glasses lodged at the top of his forehead. He flicked them downwards with his little finger on the bridge. All his movements were elegant.

"I'll show you." Diamond grappled ineptly with the first knot in the string.

"May I?" Eastland had it open almost at once, smoothing the bubble-wrap to reveal Councillor Sturr's watercolour. "What happened here, then?"

"The glass? My fault. An accident in the kitchen." Diamond didn't mention the cat. His admission that a work of art had been taken into a kitchen was shocking enough.

"A Blake," said Eastland, more to himself than Diamond. "What sort of Blake? William—or Sexton?"

Diamond waited.

"Am I permitted to touch?"

"No problem."

He picked up the picture and turned it over, and a chip of glass fell on the table.

"Sorry," said Diamond. "Thought I'd got it all out."

"Since it will have to be repaired," said Eastland, "presumably it won't matter if we remove the painting?"

"I don't see why not."

After some deft work with a knife and pliers, Eastland eased the paper from the frame and held it close to an anglepoise lamp. "The thing about Blake is that his style is so mannered. In one sense, he's a gift to a forger. I mean, the Blake hallmarks are well known and very persuasive, the pen and wash technique, the detailed musculature, the statuesque effect, the rather ineptly drawn background. He took immense trouble over the figures and then got bored with his backgrounds. You get some laughable trees." He put a jeweller's magnifier over his right eye and bent close to the painting. "This is all very suggestive of Blake. On the other hand, he's devilishly difficult to copy. Well known forgers like Tom Keating and Eric Hebborn left him well alone. It's one thing to mock up a Samuel Palmer, quite another to tangle with Blake."

"So is this genuine?"

"I'm not sure yet. If it's a fake, it's an exceptionally skillful one, I'll tell you that for nothing."

Diamond chose not to say at this point that he would be telling him everything for nothing. The murder squad was well over budget this year. Good thing Eastland was so obviously enjoying this.

"Dear old Blake was one of the most prolific of all artists. He never stopped. The list of works runs into thousands. As an engraver by training, he worked in series, you see. He would take a subject like the poems of Thomas Gray or the Book of Job and produce scores of pictures. This one, I can't place. The solitary figure in what looks like a frozen landscape with mountains." He turned the sheet over and held it at an angle, studying the grain. "Very old paper. A Whatman, I would think. No watermark, unfortunately."

"Old enough to be by Blake?"

"Oh, yes. The paper can so often be the giveaway when a work is not authentic. The poor old faker has a double problem. First he has to find a sheet of paper of the right age and quality. That's difficult, but not impossible. A favourite trick is to remove the fly leaves from the fronts of old books. And occasionally scrapbooks, sketchbooks, even stacks of unused paper turn up in attics. But old paper deteriorates. This would have been given a coat of size, or glue, when it was first manufactured, to provide a surface. Without it, you'd get an effect like writing on toilet paper. The paper is absorbent. You can't produce a fine line. So they apply this coating of size. In time, as I was saying, the size breaks down and the paper loses its surface. Result: the faker or restorer has to apply a fresh coat of size, preferably several thin coats, before the damned paper is workable."

"More trouble than it's worth, I should think," said Diamond.

"Not at all. The rewards are considerable if you get away with it. There are old recipes for these glues, just as there are recipes for the ink they used. It can be done."

Now he took a larger magnifying glass from a drawer and studied the edges of the paper. "This has not been cut recently. The size of the work is about right for Blake, but you would expect nothing else in a piece of this quality." He held the picture at arm's length again. "What are you expecting me to say—that it's not authentic?"

Diamond hoped to God he would. His entire case rested on it. "You said you didn't recognise the subject?"

"Correct."

"You also said he did his work in series."

"I did."

"Have you ever heard of a series based on Mary Shelley's *Frankenstein?*"

Eastland shook his head at once.

"There are two other watercolours of scenes from the book," Diamond went on. "Two, at least. I can't show them to you, but they exist. The tall, long-haired figure in this picture appears in the other two."

Eastland glanced down at the painting again. "This is Frankenstein's monster?"

"The original monster, yes, not the Hollywood version."

"Can you describe these other works?"

"One is a meeting in the mountains between this figure and a man of normal size who must be Frankenstein. The other is a death scene. A woman lies strangled on a bed. The Frankenstein character is beside her in despair while the monster leers through a window."

"It's a long time since I read the book, but I remember that scene vividly enough."

"The story was published in 1818, when Blake was sixty-one, still active as a painter," said Diamond, sounding like an expert himself.

"Indeed, he was painting on his deathbed, nine years later," Eastland topped it, "but I've never heard of a *Frankenstein* series."

"You sound doubtful."

"It doesn't chime in too well with the rest. Mostly he illustrated religious subjects, or the classics, or his own mythology." He put the picture down. "On the other hand, the theme is a moral one that might well have appealed to Blake. As I recall it, Mary Shelley told a story distinctly different from the versions the cinema has given us. The monster is not inherently evil, not the result of spare parts surgery gone wrong. The mistakes come after he is created, when Frankenstein abandons him and treats him badly when they meet again. It's about rejection. The monster is sensitive, intelligent and innocent—innocent in the way Blake used the word. He becomes violent as a response to the way he is treated. Blake would have approved of the theme."

"Enough to illustrate it?"

"That's the nub of it. 1818, you said?"

"There's another thing," said Diamond. "I discovered that only five hundred copies of *Frankenstein* were printed and most of them went into libraries. It wasn't exactly a bestseller. You have to wonder if Blake had heard of the book."

"Perhaps it was reprinted soon after."

Diamond shook his head. "After Blake was dead."

Locked in thoughts of his own, Eastland bent over the picture again with his eye-glass. For some time he didn't speak. Finally he told Diamond, "I'd like to believe this is genuine. The draughtsmanship is exceptionally fine. Unknown Blakes have been known to turn up."

"But . . ."

"But the ink has not behaved as I would expect it to after a hundred and eighty years or so. Under magnification you can usually spot some disintegration, not so obvious as the cracks in old paint, but discernible. These lines are still surface marks. Nowhere has the ink amalgamated with the paper. I wish we could compare it with an undisputed Blake. I think we would notice a difference." He looked up. "I presume you'll send this for scientific tests."

"Yes, but I was hoping for a quick opinion."

He peered through the glass at another section. "I wouldn't testify to this in court, not without scientific backing, but I'm increasingly confident that I've detected the flaw. It's beautiful work, exquisite, only the artist hasn't aged the ink."

"It's a modern ink?"

"No, no. It's old—or made with genuine old ingredients such as oak galls. That's only half the battle. The marks have to be given the effect of ageing."

"How would he do that?"

"They distress it with a combination of heat, moisture and mild corrosives. There's a terrifying risk of overdoing it and messing up many hours of painstaking work. Probably he thought he'd done enough to get by."

"It *is* a fake?"

"It still needs to be analysed," Eastland hedged.

"But . . . ?"

"I now believe it is."

"Brilliant."

"Brilliant is the word. Do you know who did it?"

Echoing the statement, Diamond answered, "I now believe I do." In his head he added, "And another one bites the dust."

thirty-two

JOE DOUGAN WAS ABOUT as livid as a mild Midwestern professor can get at being brought back to Bath. "This is the end," he complained to Diamond. "I should be halfway under the Channel by now. What am I doing here?"

"Helping the police with their inquiries."

"Is that sarcasm?"

"It's only a form of words we use."

"Oh, yeah? Coded words for the third degree?"

Diamond put on a pained expression. "Haven't you been treated with courtesy?"

"By the cops who brought me back? No complaints. My quarrel is with you, sir. You fixed this."

"Did they let you phone your wife?"

Joe gave a nod. "To Donna, it's another day's shopping."

"Don't bill us," said Diamond, trying to defuse the bitterness a little. He preferred dealing with Joe in his good tempered mode. "Coffee?"

"How long do you figure this will take?"

"I wish I knew. I have things to do, the same as you. Would you mind opening your suitcases?" Two vast cases had been brought back with Joe from Waterloo and now lay on a table against the end wall.

This triggered Joe into another protest. "What do you think is in there? For crying out loud, you don't think I have Mary Shelley's writing box in my baggage?"

"The keys, professor."

Muttering, Joe felt in his pocket and handed over a small leather key-case that Diamond passed to the constable brought in to conduct the search.

Joe said he would have a black coffee.

A pink nightie lay folded on top of the other things in the first suitcase, surrounded by glittery shoes padded out with panties. Joe had done a reasonable job of packing Donna's things. Methodically the constable lifted layer after layer of women's clothing and made a stack on the table. Then he started on the second case: more skirts and blouses, the overspill from Donna's shopping and, some way underneath, Joe's things. None of it brought Diamond from his chair.

"Now your hand luggage."

This was a shoulderbag with an array of zips and pouches. "Careful," Joe warned as he lifted it off the back of his chair and onto the desk. "Some of the stuff in here is fragile."

"Empty it yourself, if you like."

Joe co-operated. One of the first things out was the edition of Milton's poems.

Diamond reached for it, but Joe's hand curled over it first. "You know what this is?"

"That's why I want to examine it. The last time I was given a sight of it, you held onto it."

"You bet I did. Would you mind using both hands? The spine is weak." He handed the book across.

After the accident with Councillor Sturr's picture, Diamond was only too willing to take extra care. He glanced at the finely inscribed M.W.G., 5, Abbey Churchyard, Bath on the cover. Tentatively opening the book, he looked for the place at the front where the fly leaves were missing. The job had been neatly done. He would not have noticed unless it had been pointed out. The remnants of three sheets, tucked between the board cover and the title page. The cut was straight, sharp and as close to the hinge as you could get.

"I know all about that," said Joe. "The book is mutilated. If I were looking for an investment, I'd be worried, but the missing endpapers don't bother me. To me the value of this little property is who it belonged to, not the state it's in."

"I appreciate that," said Diamond, transferring the book to his other hand to look inside the back cover. "I see they've been cut from here as well. I was speaking to someone only this morning, an art historian. He was telling me forgers do this. They buy old books and cut out the blank sheets to get paper of the right age."

Joe's eyebrows twitched. "You think a forger damaged the book?"

"I wouldn't bet against it."

"In recent times, you mean?"

"I'd need a microscope to answer that."

Joe's interest in his book was sufficient to ride over all the day's frustrations. "I'm not sure if I buy this theory of yours. When I talked to the bookseller, Mr Heath, he told me something I should have appreciated, but didn't, about the scarcity of paper a couple of hundred years back. It was a valuable commodity. People would use those blank pages as notepaper. So it's quite possible Mary Shelley cut them from the book herself."

The possibility didn't much appeal to Diamond. His theory of the forger held more promise right now. "Maybe."

"She could have used them for sketching," Joe continued to speculate as he removed more things from the shoulderbag. "We know she sketched."

"We do?"

"She was having lessons from an artist while she was in Bath."

"Is that so?" Diamond said with the preoccupied air of someone working to a more significant brief.

"As a matter of fact, Miss Redbird told me a sketchbook was found in the writing box, along with the book and an ink bottle."

Abruptly Diamond's attention was focused again. "You didn't tell me that before."

"You didn't ask. You wanted to know about this book and I told you everything I know. The rest is only something I was told."

"This could be crucial information."

"You think I don't know? Dear God, I'd like to get my hands on Mary Shelley's sketchbook. No chance."

"What happened to it?"

"Sold—a long while back, she said."

"Did she say who bought it?"

"No, sir. You see, at the time she had no idea who it belonged to so it had no special interest," Joe continued implacably. "I'm trying to remember the name of Mary Shelley's art teacher. It began with a 'W'. Wood? No, West. Mr West. She mentions him in letters. She found the drawing tedious. I guess it would have been, the way it was taught at the time. Her imagination ran to more exotic things than still life and perspective."

"This sketchbook couldn't have been all that big," Diamond said. "To have fitted in the writing box, I mean."

Joe indicated some modest limits with his hands. "It wasn't so small. If she wanted to work small she could have used those sheets from the book to practise on." The sheets cut from the book had ceased to hold any interest for Diamond. The existence of the sketchbook had set him off on a more promising track.

"You can put the stuff back in the bag now." His brain worked through the possibilities while Joe began the task, sighing like a grounded balloon. Then Diamond said, "On Thursday evening when you returned to Noble and Nude, no one was there. That's what you told me?"

"That's the truth."

"But the place wasn't locked. Did that surprise you?"

Joe weighed the question before replying. "Not at first. It's such a warren, that shop, I took it that the owner was in another room somewhere. Called her name a couple of times and she didn't answer, so I started trying keys in the box. You know how it is. When you concentrate, really put your mind to a job, the time flies by."

"Did you have any suspicion someone else was present in the building?"

"What do you mean?"

"Isn't it clear? If I was in your situation that night, walking into an empty shop, my senses would be primed for someone to come in. If a floorboard creaked, I'd hear it."

"I heard nothing."

"And you estimated you were there from around nine-thirty to when? Almost eleven?"

"That's what I said."

"The writing box was still there when you left?"

"On her desk in the office, where I found it." Joe leaned forward, stressing the next remark with his open hand. "Listen, whatever else you think of me, I'm not stupid. If I'd walked out with the writing box, she would have known right off who took it."

"She was murdered," Diamond pointed out.

Joe, wrong-footed, blinked and frowned. "I didn't know that at the time. How could I have known that?"

Diamond left the question hanging.

Joe stared at him woodenly for a moment, then said, "And another thing. Her colleague, the guy in the bow-tie, knew all about my interest in the box."

"Ellis Somerset."

"He would have blown the whistle on me if I took it."

Diamond nodded. "Now I'll tell you something, professor. You have a way of making everything sound reasonable. Strange things happen to you through no fault of your own. You go down into a vault at the Roman Baths and you're mistaken for a forensic pathologist. Your wife disappears and turns up in Paris. You're trying to do deals with a woman on the night she is murdered. You can explain it all. There's one thing I wish you would explain because I can't see a way round it myself."

"Try me."

"The problem is this: someone stole the writing box on the night Peg Redbird was murdered and I haven't heard of anyone else but you with an interest in it. Only you. You worked out that it once belonged to Mary Shelley. No one else knew that."

Joe frowned. He had no easy solution.

Diamond twisted the knife. "Do you know of anyone else? Anyone?"

"I told my wife, but she wouldn't . . ."

"And you wouldn't have let Peg Redbird in on the secret because she would have raised the price."

Joe partially closed his eyes, straining for an explanation. This was desperation point. "At the time I half wondered if the lady figured it out."

"Peg?"

"Right. I was never any use as a poker player. I may not have said anything—no, let's be clear, I *didn't* say anything—but I couldn't disguise my interest in the writing box. I wanted it badly. She was good at her job. She saw the initials on the cover of that book and she saw the address. Yeah, I reckon she figured it out."

"Letting you off the hook?"

"She could have talked to someone after she saw me."

"I get the drift," said Diamond with a wry smile. "They killed her for it?"

"Listen, I'm trying to help you with your inquiries. Literally. And I have one great advantage over you."

"What's that?" said Diamond, all interest.

"I know I'm an innocent man."

Diamond couldn't help grinning.

Joe was nodding solemnly. "Some other guy must have done these things."

"In the furtherance of theft, you think? Was it really worth killing for? Just an antique somebody famous once owned?"

"People have killed for less. It depends what price they put on a human life."

Sergeant Leaman looked around the door and Diamond beckoned to him to come over. He had brought Joe Dougan's coffee. He said in confidence to Diamond, "Those phone numbers, sir—the local calls Peg Redbird made on the day she died. We've traced them now. The first was to a pub in Larkhall."

"The Brains Surgery?"

"Right. And the second was a private number, a Mr E. Tanner-Jones. It has to be Uncle Evan, doesn't it?"

"Got the address?"

"One Tree Cottage, Charlcombe Lane."

"Any previous?"

"Nothing known."

"What time is it now?"

"Ten to three."

"We'll pick him up pronto."

Leaman asked after a pause, "Do you mean you want to come, sir?"

"Try and keep me away." He stood up.

Joe Dougan let out a breath that seemed to come from the depth of his soul.

Diamond glared.

Joe said, "I was blowing on the coffee." After some hesitation he asked, "Have you finished with me?"

"For the present," said Diamond. "I'm going to ask one of our people to book you into a hotel for the night. It won't be the Royal Crescent, but it should be comfortable."

*   *   *

ON THE drive, he told Leaman about Mary Shelley's sketch-book. "What a gift for a forger—sheets and sheets of paper dating from the first years of the nineteenth century."

"Is that what happened to it?"

"How would I know? I'm speculating. If they're working in ink or watercolour they need genuine old paper, sheets of the stuff. It was made differently in those days, with rag, or something. No good using modern paper. It has to pass all the dating tests. Larger sheets would be hard to come by. So you can imagine the use a forger could make of an entire sketchbook."

"Peg Redbird?"

"As the forger? No, she simply found the sketchbook in the writing box and put it on sale."

"Someone else bought it for the paper, to fake pictures on?"

"That's the way I'm thinking. Some clever forgeries have been unloaded on the art market in Bath."

"The Blakes?"

"Or what passed for Blakes. Councillor Sturr owns one and Minchendon had two. There may well be others on the walls of smart houses in the area. I'm hoping to get a sight of an art forger's studio."

"At this cottage?"

"It has to be somewhere. That afternoon when Peg got her hands on the pictures from Si Minchendon's, she spent a lot of time on the phone to galleries and museums and I can only think she was trying to find out if Blake ever painted a *Frankenstein* series. He didn't. At the end, she phones two local numbers, the Brains Surgery, where Uncle Evan hangs out, and One Tree Cottage. Why? We'll find out presently, I hope."

*   *   *

IT TURNED up unexpectedly in another half-mile—unexpectedly because the building was no cottage in the ordinary sense of the word. Set back at the end of a gravel drive in an isolated stretch of Charlcombe Lane, it was a modern two-storey house in the Georgian style, built the expensive way in the local stone, not the reconstituted sort. Gables, sash windows, portico, coach-lamps, conifers in white tubs.

They saw it through closed wrought-iron gates equipped with an entry-phone. Leaman drew up alongside the grille and put down the car window.

"Do we say who we are?"

"Let's see who we get."

A woman's voice announced, "Mr Tanner-Jones isn't at home."

Diamond muttered an obscenity, then leaned across Leaman and said genially, "That's all right, my dear. We're the police. We'll talk to you."

"I'm only the cleaner."

"But you know how to press the button that opens the gates."

It got them through the gate. She had the front door open before they were out of the car, a nervous-looking young woman wiping her hands on a red overall. "I can't help you."

"You can," said Diamond. "You're just the right person. What's your name?"

"Linda."

"We won't keep you long, Linda. Shall we do this inside?"

The Tanner-Jones residence was as fine inside as out. They were standing on an Afghan carpet in a hall with an antique grandfather clock and a huge celadon-ware vase containing pampas grass.

"Out for the day, is he?" Diamond asked.

"He often is when I come in to do the house," she said. "I'm not supposed to let anyone in."

"But you wouldn't obstruct the police in the course of their duty, would you? That's against the law. Where's the art room?"

"The what?"

"Art room, studio, whatever he calls it. As the cleaner, you should know."

Linda shook her head. "There's nothing like that."

Too easy, Diamond decided. He would have to think in terms of hidden rooms, something in the attic, or outside in the garden. "How does he relax, then? I thought he was a painter."

"I don't know anything about that."

"What's his job?"

"I don't know if he has one."

"How does he live so well if he doesn't work?"

"I couldn't say. He must have been left some money, or won the lottery, or something."

"You don't mind if we look around?" He didn't wait for her answer, but opened a door and stepped into a large sitting room with a tan-coloured leather suite. The pictures on the wall were modern abstracts; nothing remotely resembled a Blake. "What does he look like, your boss?" he asked Linda. "Is there a picture of him anywhere?"

"I've never seen one. He's tall and thin. Mostly he dresses in casual clothes, jeans and things. He has long hair, really long for a bloke, I mean, in a pony-tail, and glasses."

It was Joe's description of Uncle Evan, near enough.

"He hasn't gone missing, has he?" Linda asked anxiously.

"I hope not."

Diamond strolled into another room, a dining-room with walnut chairs and oval table. The taste in art still favoured the twentieth century. The end wall had a huge Frink charcoal drawing of horses. "Does he entertain much?"

"I only come in two afternoons a week," said Linda.

She didn't seem aware of the ambiguity, and he didn't make anything of it. She was too soft a target. "We'll look upstairs."

"I haven't done the upstairs yet," Linda said.

She tagged along while they looked into five bedrooms, each

with its *en suite* bathroom. The most lived-in still told them
nothing except that Tanner-Jones owned about twenty pairs of
designer jeans and read John Updike and *GQ*. Halfway along
the landing was a hatch to the space under the roof. "Is there a
room up there?"

"I've no idea."

"You've never been up to clean it?"

"No. It's not on my list."

Diamond nodded to Leaman, who reached up, released the
catch and pulled down the hatch door. A light came on automatically. A folding ladder was attached to the hidden side of
the door. With the sense of occasion of an astronaut bound for a
new planet, Diamond climbed upwards.

He found himself standing among cardboard boxes, rolls of
wallpaper and lampshades. He came down like the manager of
the national football team after it has lost six-nil to San Marino.

They went into the garden, opened the sheds and found only
tools, deckchairs and grass-seed.

"I've seen all I want of this sodding place."

They returned to the car. "Where to, sir?" Leaman asked as
they got in.

"Just get us out of here," said Diamond. "No. Hold it." He
stared along the gravel drive. The automatic gates had opened
and a black sports car was entering. It braked. There was a
moment's hiatus. Obviously the driver had spotted their car in
front of the house. Then he reversed with a screech of tyres and
headed back along the road.

Leaman didn't need to be told what to do next.

thirty-three

"FEAR NOT THAT I *shall be the instrument of future mischief. My work is nearly complete.*"

But he approached the end with reluctance.

thirty-four

"I KNEW IT. I bloody knew it!"

The gates were closing and there was no chance of getting through in time. The black sports car powered off in the direction of Larkhall, gears forced through a series of rising notes.

Diamond flung open the door of their car and ran back to the house to tell Linda the cleaner to press the gate control. She was slow in responding.

He got back in and slammed the door. The other car would be out of sight by this time. "It doesn't happen like this in the movies."

"Yes it does, sir. The baddies always get a head start. We catch up."

The gates moved apart and Leaman put his foot down.

"Christ, you don't have to kill us both. That isn't in the script." He hated being driven at speed and this was only a CID car without light and siren. There had to be a more intelligent way. "What make was it?"

"Couldn't tell you, sir. I only caught the front view."

"Did you get the number?"

"Too far off."

So it was no use radioing for assistance. If orders were issued to stop every black sports car on the roads of Bath, there would be chaos.

Diamond was running out of ideas. "You're overdoing it," he complained again. "I can't think at this speed."

"The A4's up ahead, sir," Leaman informed him.

"What's that in English?"

"The London Road. Shall we go up the new by-pass? If he went that way, we might get a sight of him."

The big man sat on his hands pressing his fingers into his fleshy thighs. "Might as well, then," he said with an air of doom.

Presently they were in the outside lane overtaking everything.

"It says fifty."

Leaman smiled. He thought Diamond was joking.

They passed a black Porsche being driven sedately by an elderly man in a turban.

Diamond said, "We don't know for sure if the guy coming through the gates was Uncle Evan."

"He used a remote control to open them," Leaman pointed out.

"True. Ease off a bit. We can get through to Sally-in-the-Woods up here."

"The 363?"

"One thing you should know about me, sergeant, is that I don't think in numbers."

"Except speed limits, sir?"

Diamond lifted an eyebrow. After a promising start, this sergeant was beginning to give some lip.

"Sally-in-the-Woods, then. Have you got a plan, sir?"

"I'm full of plans. That's something else you should know."

This winding road through trees along the eastern scarp of the Avon valley would take them past Bathford in the direction of Bradford on Avon and Trowbridge.

Diamond made yet another appeal for moderation. "You can cut the speed now. We're not chasing any more."

"Have we given up, sir?"

"We're using our brains."

Not much was said in the next twenty minutes. Whether this was because brains were in use was open to question. At Bradford, he told Leaman to drive through the town centre and along the Frome Road.

"To Little Terrors, sir?"

"No. In about a mile you'll come to a set of traffic lights. Take a right there."

"Stowford—where he stores his puppets?"

"That's my best shot."

Leaman put his foot down just a little more. They left the road at Stowford Farm and swung left onto the dirt track. And Diamond's best shot seemed to have scored. A low black Mercedes sports car with dark windows was standing on the space behind the workshops. They drew up beside it.

No one was inside, but the engine was still warm. Leaman tried the doors. Locked.

"Want me to radio for help, sir?"

"We can handle him."

Diamond was on his way, striding around the farm buildings towards the copse at the edge of the mill stream. High in the branches above them, a colony of rooks had been noisily disputing the best roosting places. At the sight of Diamond in motion they took to the air.

Beyond the derelict water mill stood the cottage where the puppets were stored. Diamond pulled up, breathing hard, and put out his hand to stop Leaman. "The padlock is still on the door. He can't be inside."

"Is there a back way?"

"Boarded up, if I remember. We can check."

They skirted the building without going close enough to be obvious to anyone inside. The rear door had planks nailed across it. The only possible way in was from the front.

"Crafty bugger," said Diamond. "Where's he hiding? One of the workshops?"

"We're going to need extra men, sir."

"We'll try the mill." He wasn't waiting for reinforcements. He was energised.

The ancient mill clothed in ivy and Old Man's Beard stood at the side of the sluice from the River Frome. The water wheel had long since been dismantled; only the old hub-ring was visible among the weeds.

Diamond tramped through the long grass. He hadn't the patience or skill to look for signs of someone going before. The only sign he noticed was the one screwed to the wall warning that the building was dangerous. He put his hand against the door and felt a slight *frisson* at how easily it opened.

"Hold on, sir." Sergeant Leaman pressed a cigarette lighter into his hand.

As a source of light in the dark interior it was better than nothing. It showed them an iron face-wheel about five feet in diameter that must once have transmitted the power from the waterwheel to the machinery. The main vertical shaft rose like the mast of a ship to the floor above. It looked reasonably stable up there; down here, the damp had got to the foundations. The floor sagged and the boards were rotten in places. Some living thing, probably a rat, scuttled across the floor and disappeared into a gap. Diamond held the lighter higher and saw the outline of a figure lurking to his left. He jerked into a defensive posture before finding he was fooled by the weird shapes of fungi growing up the walls. Recovering his dignity, he gave Leaman a look that did not invite comment, and moved on. He was interested in a vertical ladder to an upper level by way of an open trapdoor. He tried his weight on the first rung. It was iron and supported him well.

Leaman offered to go up first. Diamond shook his head and told him to hold the lighter.

Considering what had happened to John Wigfull, this was a rash move. Anyone up there could take a swipe at him the minute his head showed through the trap. He had this thought too late to make a difference. He was already above the level of the floor straining to see.

He asked for the lighter again and Leaman passed it up. The flame was now burning tall and yellowish. He wasn't sure if this meant that the fuel was running out; he was just grateful for the extra light, treating him to a sight he had not dared to expect in this place.

This storey had been renovated and furnished. There were two modern office desks, a plan-chest, stools and a table. He climbed the last rungs and stepped onto a carpet made of sisal squares. He could now see more equipment, a viewer for looking at slides, a magnifying lamp and a photocopier. On the larger of the desks under an angle-poise lamp was a draughtsman's drawing-board with a sheet of paper fixed to it with masking tape. Ranged along the side were numerous tubes of paint and several jam-jars, some holding brushes, some filled with water. The other desk was covered in books, many of them open. No question: he had found the forger's studio.

He said aloud, "Where the hell does he get his electricity?"

Leaman called up, "What's that, sir?"

"Come up and see."

Then the lights came on, dazzling Diamond, and a voice said, "Got my own generator, see?"

He swung around. The speaker was behind him, half hidden by the hatch of the trap-door: the thin, long-haired man in glasses he was so curious to meet. Evan Tanner-Jones, alias Uncle Evan, stood with his palms facing forward as if to make clear that he wasn't holding a weapon.

Leaman heard the voice and was up that ladder like a fireman.

Diamond gestured to him with a downward movement of the hand that no threat was being made.

"The rozzers?" said Evan—an expression Diamond had not heard in years.

He lifted his shoulders a fraction in a way that was meant to reassure as well as confirm.

Evan said, "I thought I'd lost you back in Bath."

"You did," Diamond admitted. "I had to think where you would hide up. This is where you turn them out, then?"

Evan didn't care for the choice of phrase. "It's my studio, if that's what you mean."

"Is it safe to move around?"

"Worried about the floor, are you? There's no damp up here. You want to see the size of the timbers."

"It's your work I want to see." He walked over to the drawing board. The painting taped to it was in the early stages, outlined, with only a few sections lightly tinted. Unschooled in art as Diamond was, he could still tell it was superbly draughted. The subject was melodramatic: a wild-eyed, long-haired figure loomed over a corpse lying in an open coffin. "*Frankenstein* again?"

The eyes behind the glasses opened a little wider.

"I've seen one before," Diamond explained without a hint of censure. "You're good at this."

"This is out of the final chapter. Do you know the book?" Evan responded, his voice becoming animated as he realised he was free to talk about the painting. Years of secrecy must have been hard to endure. "We're on board the ship here looking at the scene from Captain Walton's point of view. That's Frankenstein lying dead in the coffin. And that's the monster, desolated." He began to quote from memory, " '*I entered the cabin where lay the remains of my ill-fated and admirable friend. Over him hung a form which I cannot find words to describe—gigantic in stature, yet uncouth and distorted in its proportions.*' Have I done it justice, do you think? Soon he'll leap off the ship onto the raft and be '*borne away by the waves and lost in darkness and distance*', and that will be my final painting. God knows when I'll get the chance to do it."

"You've been working some time on these?"

"Five or six years. A long-term project. '*The energy of my purpose alone sustained me*'. Thirty-six paintings, and I'm a slow worker."

"Unlike William Blake."

He swung round, reacting sharply. "Who's talking about Blake? I didn't say a word about Blake."

So that's your get-out, thought Diamond as he changed emphasis. This was not the moment to pursue the link with Blake. "You've sold some of them already."

"Yes."

"Trying to make it cost-effective?"

Evan gave a nervous smile and brushed some hair from his face.

"But you're not short of a few pence, going by your car and your house."

"Is that a crime? My grandfather was a colliery owner in Merthyr before the war and my Dad inherited half a million and invested wisely. It all got left to me when he died. I don't need to work, but I don't like being idle either."

"You're not compelled to sell the paintings."

"Not compelled, no."

"Perhaps you wanted to test the market, see what collectors would make of them?"

"That's no crime either."

"Since you keep mentioning crime," said Diamond with a smooth transition, "what about assault on a police officer?"

Evan wrapped his arms across his chest and lowered his head, eyes closed.

Diamond waited.

The man was groping for the right words. "I'm, I'm . . .

ashamed of what happened Saturday. I got in a panic, you see. He was following me, that cop."

"You knew he was a cop?"

"He had to be. He came to watch my show in Victoria Park— you know I have this puppet theatre—and I could see him sitting alone in the audience."

Wigfull at a puppet show? It was so bizarre that it had to be believed. Rapidly Diamond constructed a scenario. There had been a copy of the local paper in Wigfull's car. He must have seen an advert for the fair in the park, spotted Uncle Evan's name there and decided it was a heaven-sent opportunity to take stock of one of the key witnesses.

"He had no kids with him," Evan was saying. "Just this man in a suit with the big moustache taking no interest in the show. All he did was watch me. I thought, Evan boyo, he's got your number. You've had a wonderful run, but it's coming to an end. He had this look like a tiger after its prey. I can't describe it."

No need to try, Diamond found himself thinking. 'Tyger! tyger! burning bright.' I know Wigfull's predatory stare.

Uncle Evan had not paused. "And after the show ended and I packed everything away, he was still there watching. It was giving me the creeps, I tell you. I got in the van and drove off, meaning to come back here to Stowford. Somewhere along the road I looked in my rearview and he was following. The same bloody great moustache. What could I do? I didn't want to lead him straight here. He'd find this place for sure and put me in deep trouble. My best bet was to abandon the van and take the footpath across the fields. I hoped he might give up."

"Not Mr Wigfull," Leaman commented with undisguised admiration for his boss. "Mr Wigfull wouldn't give up."

Evan heard that and pressed on. His face was mobile, sensitive to the events he was recalling. "I managed to put a bit of distance between us, enough for me to get out at Westwood and leg it into the field, where I couldn't be seen if I ducked down with my head below the crop. Like you say, he didn't give up. Stopped his car and came after me. Terrible. I happened to put my head up just as he was facing my direction. There was no question he'd seen me and was coming after me. I bolted like a bloody rabbit, right across that field and over the gate." He took a couple of shallow breaths, remembering. "There was a bit of open ground ahead near a pond. You know where I mean. You must have been there. I panicked. I got on my hands and knees and tried to hide in some bushes. My last hope was that he would go by and lose me. I was scrambling out of view of the footpath and my hand happened to touch something solid."

"An empty bottle?" asked Diamond, with touching faith in his own theory.

"A piece of metal tube. You know what I'm going to say, don't you? He came looking for me in the bushes. I guess it was obvious where I was. When he got level, I sprang up and struck out with the tube. It was an automatic action really. I can't tell you what it's like being hunted down. I cracked him on the head a couple of times and he went down. In all my life I've never done anything violent before. He was out cold. I chucked the tube in the pond and ran back to the van and drove off." Evan paused, and his breathing was as agitated as a dog's. "I'm really sorry now."

The last words may have been sincerely meant, but they were too much for Sergeant Leaman, who suddenly turned vengeful. "Sorry? That's easy to say now. We don't take crap from bastards who lay into unarmed coppers. John Wigfull was my guvnor. 'Never done anything violent before'! Bloody liar." He caught Evan by the arm and swung him against the wall.

"Leave it out," Diamond snapped.

"He's all wind and piss, sir."

"I said leave it. Are you deaf?"

Leaman put his face close to Evan's and said, "Scumbag." Then he took a step back.

The outburst was understandable but unexpected from the man who had given the impression nothing would make him lose his rag. Later, they would talk it through. Diamond was far from blameless in the treatment of suspects, but even as a youngster he wouldn't have cut loose with a suspect who was singing like an Eisteddfod winner.

Now Evan was cowering against the wall, terrified. It was a real setback.

Diamond tried again, and felt the scorn of Leaman as he said almost apologetically, "You've been frank about John Wigfull. Now I want you to tell us about Peg Redbird."

Evan seemed not to have heard.

"Miss Redbird, the owner of Noble and Nude," Diamond had to repeat.

"What about her?"

"What about you, the evening she was killed."

"That wasn't me," he answered, his voice shrilling, close to hysteria. "You can't pin that on me, for pity's sake."

"We know she phoned you at seven forty-three and had a six minute conversation with you."

"You know that?"

"She tried the Brains Surgery first. It was about the paintings she'd just acquired, wasn't it, two watercolours in the style of William Blake?"

"If you know it all, why are you asking me?"

"It's up to you, my friend," said Diamond. "You can tell it to me now and I'll listen. You're the one with a lot to explain. Or you can go back to the nick with Sergeant Leaman and see what he can do."

Evan found that unappealing. The words began to flow again. "Peg and I knew each other pretty well. I won't say I was a regular in the shop, but I looked in from time to time. You could find useful things there. Once I bought a Victorian paintbox from her in beautiful condition. Five pounds. Treasure for me. Well,

Peg phoned me Thursday evening, as you know. She'd put two and two together, of course—my interest in art materials. Remembered selling me a certain sketchbook years ago, an old one, almost unused. I can't tell you exactly when it was. Ten years? Fifteen? I don't know. I bet she knew exactly. Peg was nobody's fool. And she sold me an old book about the same time, the poems of John Milton. I wanted it for the blank sheets inside. Proper paper made from rags. Lovely for the style of painting I do. Got rid of it after. I only mention the book because someone came into the Brains Surgery with that book a few days ago."

"An American?"

"Tourist, wanting to know who owned it before him and willing to buy drinks to find out. You see how this all ties up? He asked me where I got the bloody book and I told him about Noble and Nude. He must have jogged Peg's memory. Well, on the phone to me she wasn't on about Milton. She wanted to know about the sketchbook, if I still had it. She was mighty keen to get it back, whatever the state of it."

This made sense to Diamond, who was adding a subtext of his own. That Thursday evening when she made the call to Evan, Peg had just discovered she had Mary Shelley's writing box in her shop. Little wonder she was desperate to recover the sketchbook it had once contained. Those drawings would create massive interest in the literary world, regardless of their competence. Marketed right, with maximum publicity, they would bring in a small fortune.

"I wasn't keen," Evan said. "Actually, I'd cut out all the blank sheets already, getting on for fifty, I reckon. When they're as old as that they need sizing before you can paint on them, and you don't mess about with single sheets. You do a batch of them together. So the sketchbook was in tatters really. The only sheets left were four or five used ones drawn on by the original owner, pencil sketches, rather dull still-life studies." He paused and something new crept in, a catch in the voice that promised bigger revelations. "Except one. This was right at the back, the last sheet in the book, as if the artist kept it for something special, unconnected with the boring old still life. An amazing page. I don't know what you'd call it. An elaborate doodle, I suppose, the paper totally covered in thumbnail sketches of mountains, snow scenes, little houses, forests, sailing ships, all interspersed with a strange mix of faces, men and women, some of them normal enough, others horrific, corpselike. The drawing was not good in a technical sense, but the effect of the whole thing was striking. It appealed to my imagination, anyway. I kept returning to it and finding new things. Actually it was inspirational. I really think it turned me onto fantasy, the great gothic horror themes of the nineteenth century, and led me to embark on this *Frankenstein* series."

"You know who the artist was?"

"Artist?" Evan smiled. "Artist isn't the word I would use. I haven't the faintest idea."

Diamond chose not to enlighten him at this point. "You wanted to keep the sketchbook because of this one drawing?"

"Exactly. I told Peg the truth, that the paper in the book was all used up now, and that was a mistake, because it was pretty clear I'd used it myself. She was getting very excited. You know how voices on the phone give away more than they realise. She was eager to know if I'd kept the old drawings, the ones already in the sketchbook. I said I thought I still had them somewhere. She wanted to come and see them. That night. I tried to put her off, but she wasn't having it." He looked down, his face still strained, as if he needed to gather himself before going on. "And then she shook me rigid. She told me about these two pictures she'd bought that afternoon. They were in the style of Blake. Clever fakes, she called them. She said she was planning to blow the whistle on them, get an expert to expose them. She asked me if I'd heard of the fraud squad. I was pissing in my pants. She didn't say so, but it was obvious she knew it was my work. She offered them to me in exchange for the remains of the sketchbook, with a promise that the deal would be confidential. Neither of us would speak of it again." Evan groaned at the memory. "She'd got me over a barrel. She could expose me as, em . . ."

"A forger."

He didn't like the word. "I've sweated blood over these paintings, getting them right. I study the text, immerse myself in the words. I'm not ripping people off."

"You're turning out fakes."

"They're originals. I haven't copied anything."

"Come off it," said Diamond. "You go to all the trouble of finding antique paper and covering it with size and backing them with paper that crumbles in your hands. You're passing them off as something they're not."

"I've never claimed they're Blakes. If people want to make that assumption, so be it. Look, I'm a painter. For years I did better things than these in my own style, miles better, and got no bloody recognition for them."

"But these are in demand. That's how you get your revenge, is it? When some expert thinks he's found an unknown William Blake?"

"That's out of my control."

Diamond found the reasoning specious, but he wanted to hear the rest of what happened, so he didn't pursue it. "Peg threatened to blow the whistle on you and you agreed to meet her?"

"What else could I do?"

"That evening?"

"Yes."

"What time?"

"We agreed on nine-thirty. First I had to drive out here and collect the sketchbook. I kept it in the plan-chest, see?"

"Where did you meet?"

"She didn't want me coming to the shop. You know the old

horse trough in Walcot Street, the one built into the wall? It's just a short walk from the shop. I drove down there and she got in the car. She had no transport of her own. She was carrying the pictures."

It chimed in neatly with Ellis Somerset's version, the conversation that had so upset him, about the meeting that sounded like a heavy date. *"I'm expecting an offer tonight, if that doesn't sound indelicate."*

"Did you make the exchange?"

"I tried. I had the remains of the sketchbook with me. I'd removed one drawing."

"The one you just described to us, with all the detail?"

Evan nodded. "I didn't think Peg Redbird knew it was in there, but she did. By God, she did. I told you she was smart, didn't I? When she first had the sketchbook in her hands she must have flicked through and found it at the back, same as me, and she *remembered*. She asked if I still had that crowded page from the back. Believe it or not, I find it difficult to lie. I said yes, but I wasn't willing to part with it. She could take the other drawings."

"She wouldn't agree?"

"No way. She called me a cheat. Said she knew enough to put me away for years. That drawing was part of the deal, she said. If I didn't produce it, she would have me exposed as a forger." He shook his head miserably. "What could I do? She wouldn't leave the car until I drove her out here, to Stowford, and collected it."

"Is that what you did?"

"Yes. I wasn't happy, I can tell you. It was blackmail, wasn't it? But I had no remedy."

At this, Leaman said with heavy sarcasm, "Oh, no?"

The muscles tightened at the side of Evan's face. "I drove her back to Bath and set her down where I met her."

"What time?" demanded Diamond.

He gave it some thought. "It was by eleven, I tell you that. She had to be back by eleven, she said. I didn't do bad, getting her there on time, allowing for all the wrangling, and the drive out here and back."

"Was it much before eleven? Did you look at the clock in the car?"

"I was too bloody angry to look at the time."

"You set her down in Bath and that was the last you saw of her?"

"Correct."

"Was anyone around, anyone who might have seen you?"

"Not that I noticed."

"What did you do after?"

"Drove home and went to bed. I was shocked when I heard what happened to her."

"You didn't come forward as a witness."

"Would you, in the circumstances? I was bloody terrified."

"Can you produce these paintings she exchanged with you?"

He went to a drawer of the plan-chest and took them out, still loosely covered in bubblewrap. At Diamond's suggestion, Evan himself uncovered them and lay them on the desk for inspection. The ham-fisted detective wasn't risking another accident.

They were the scenes from *Frankenstein* just as they had been described by Ellis Somerset, dramatic images, skilfully drawn and painted. Peg Redbird must have been a shrewd judge to have spotted them as fakes.

Evan was talking aloud, but to himself, quoting Mary Shelley. " ' . . . *the figure of a man, at some distance, advancing towards me with superhuman speed. He bounded over the crevices in the ice, among which I had walked with caution; his stature, also as he approached, seemed to exceed that of a man.*' "

Diamond said, "They're remarkable."

Evan turned to him. "Everything I told you is the truth. I hit out at the copper in a panic, and I'm sorry. I swear to God I didn't touch Peg Redbird. I'm not a killer."

"Don't count on it," said Diamond. "John Wigfull is still on the danger list."

thirty-five

AFTER SO MANY YEARS in the police, Peter Diamond was not surprised by much, but he was rendered speechless when he walked into the Manvers Street control room and recognized an elegant young woman in a dove grey suit chatting to one of the sergeants.

She turned and smiled.

He eventually said, "Well, who would have thought it?"

DI Julie Hargeaves, his much-missed deputy, said, "It hasn't been all *that* long."

She was supposed to be on attachment to Headquarters.

"What brings . . . ?"

"Interviewing duty," she explained. "They're taking on new recruits, some women among them. I had an evening off, or so I thought. I haven't now."

He was disappointed. "I thought for a moment . . ."

"No," said Julie firmly.

"Are you doing the interviews alone?"

She shook her head. "Someone has to represent Joe Public. Regulations. I'm teamed up with Councillor Sturr. Have you met him?"

"Him? God help us if the rest of the public is anything like him."

"He's on the Police Authority," said Julie. "A sledge-hammer to crack a nut, if you ask me, but I gather he insisted."

"Typical," said Diamond, thinking of the shock Ingeborg was going to get.

Julie shrugged and said, "How's it going here? I heard about John Wigfull, poor old lad."

"He's getting over it."

Her lips shaped into the beginning of a smile. "Shouldn't I waste my sympathy?" She well knew of Diamond's feud with the injured chief inspector.

He made an effort to sound upbeat. "I just got the latest from the hospital. They're saying there's been a big improvement in the last hour. He's fully conscious. All the signs are that he'll make a full recovery."

"That's wonderful. And you phoned up to ask how he was doing?"

He gave the honest explanation. "I needed to know in case he was dead. We just nicked someone for the assault."

"Reliable?"

"Cast iron. He confessed. Runs a puppet show. Calls himself Uncle Evan."

"Did he also murder the antiques lady?" Julie, as he would have expected, was well up on the case.

"He had the motive. He had the opportunity."

"Going by the tone of your voice, you don't think he did."

At this point, the Assistant Chief Constable steamed in like the royal yacht, straight towards Julie. "Inspector Hargreaves?"

"Ma'am."

They shook hands and Georgina—who didn't go in for small talk—started explaining how the interviews were arranged. Diamond, sidelined by all this, left them to it. He'd missed his chance to put in a good word for Ingeborg. He just hoped Julie would remember her from press conferences as a bright young prospect ready to take on the world. With Sturr on the panel, Ingeborg's chances had taken a nosedive.

Annoyed with himself, he went over to talk to Halliwell. The hapless inspector had been beavering away on the bones in the vault case for days. Now he had a new stack of paper on his desk, the first telephoned responses to the appeal for help in identifying Banger and Mash.

"What's the story, Keith?"

"What you'd expect, really. Any number of people thinking they must have known the dead man. Parents whose sons left home and haven't been heard of since. Women who got ditched by blokes and would like to think it wasn't their fault. All a bit sad really. The only thing I can say for sure is that Motorhead must have had a big following in the nineteen-eighties."

"Most of these are on about the victim?"

"That's right."

"What have we got on the other one, Mash?"

"Bugger all, sir. We couldn't give them much of a description. What do we know—that he kept himself clean and fancied his looks a bit? You can't put that in a press release."

Diamond picked up the sheaf of papers, jottings taken by the civilian women who answered the phones. The handwriting reflected the speed at which the notes had been taken.

"There's one possible girlfriend of Banger who might be worth following up," said Halliwell. "Near the top, marked with the highlighter. A Mrs Warmerdam, living in Byron Road."

Diamond found it and started to read: "*11.20 a.m. Mrs Celia Warmerdam, Holt House, Byron Road. "Going steady" 1982 with rock fan Jock Tarrant—casual labourer Roman Baths extension. Description fits. Remembers Motorhead ring. Still has her diary. JT failed to turn up for date on 10/9/82. Never heard from again.*"

Halliwell said, "I thought I'd go and see her in the morning."

Diamond was still charged up from collaring Uncle Evan. He wasn't in tune with the slower tempo of the Banger and Mash case. "Byron Road isn't far. It's one of those streets on Beechen Cliff named after poets."

"I know," said Halliwell impassively. "I live there."

"What—Byron Road?"

"Longfellow, actually."

"We can go now. You've had a day of it. I'll drive you home after."

CELIA WARMERDAM would have been worth visiting whatever she had to say, as unlikely an ex-rocker as you could hope to meet, a plump sugar-plum fairy in her late thirties. Her silver-highlighted hair stood out like a seeded dandelion. She brought them tea in bone-china cups in a pink front room with a baby grand piano and lace curtains gathered in great, dramatic scallops. "It's all so laughable now," she said, making the "so" last as long as the rest of the words together. "My Heavy Metal phase. I knew nothing whatsoever about the bands or the things they performed, but I dressed the part, in my thigh-length boots and faded denims and motorbike jacket. I just had this enormous pash for Jock Tarrant, my bit of rough. And was he rough! Kissing him was worse than rubbing your face against a pineapple. He had the most revolting, smelly hair down to his shoulders, incredibly evil clothes, all studs and leather and engine-oil, and of course I adored the brute." She giggled. "I've had two husbands and a partner since, and they were all nicely groomed. They shaved and showered every day, and didn't dream I once slept with an apeman—well, more than once." She smiled wistfully. "More times and more ways than I'd care to describe. It was hearing you on Radio Bristol this morning that got me thinking about Jock, because he had one of those rings with the animal's skull or whatever it was and he was easily the size you said, six foot two or three. I only came up to his elbows."

"And he went missing?" Halliwell prompted her.

"Yes. When did I say? I looked it up in my diary and told the young lady on the phone."

"September 10th, 1982."

"I know I was devastated at the time. Heartbroken. Jock was going to take me to one of the best hotels in Edinburgh for the weekend. God knows what they would have thought of us. He'd had a bit of luck, he said. Some money was coming his way. Bread, he called it."

Diamond latched onto that at once. "Did he say where from?"

"Something to do with work, I think. He was a casual at the Roman Baths, on the extension. I thought it sounded an interesting job, but he said it was boring. My best guess is that he dug up something Roman, a piece of jewellery or some coins, and smuggled it out to sell somewhere. He didn't say and I didn't ask."

This was more useful than they had dared to hope. A possible motive for violence in the vault.

"So you arranged to go away for the weekend?"

She laughed at her youthful folly. "I stood on Bath Station with my overnight bag for hours. It was a Friday, and really cold for September. Jock didn't turn up. I caught a chill and spent the rest of the weekend in bed shivering and crying. I never saw him again."

"Did you ask around at the places where you met? Clubs? Pubs?"

The hair quivered. "I had my pride. Friends asked me about him. Nobody seemed to have seen him anywhere. I just assumed he'd gone off with his money to start up in some other town. I cried buckets, but you get over it eventually, don't you?"

Diamond caught a significant glance from Halliwell. The crucial question still had to be asked.

He prolonged the moment, sipping his tea. Then: "Did he ever talk about the people he worked with?"

"Only that they were brain dead, or words to that effect."

"Yes, but did he speak of them by name?"

"If he did, I don't remember. Between ourselves, Jock wasn't much of a communicator."

"I'm thinking of one man in particular," Diamond tried again, "one he was teamed with, mixing cement for the bricklayers."

Briefly, it seemed she hadn't taken in the suggestion, for she said, "Shall I take that cup and saucer now? You look as if you aren't used to it." And after rescuing her china, she surprised them both with, "Would he have been a college boy called John?"

"I'm asking you, ma'am."

"Jock called him a college boy anyway. I suppose he was a student on vacation work. They skived off for a smoke sometimes. That's about all I remember."

It was all they were destined to find out from Celia Warmerdam. They tried, and she tried too, for a surname, or the name of the college, or some physical description. If she had ever known such details, they had sunk into oblivion with her thigh-length boots and faded denims.

Outside in the car, Diamond asked Halliwell which year it was that sexual intercourse began.

Halliwell stared at him.

"Some time early in the nineteen-sixties. Dates are not my strong point. I thought you might know it," Diamond tried to explain. " It's something I heard a few days ago, in a poem by Philip Larkin. Hold on, the words are coming back to me:

'Sexual intercourse began
 In Nineteen Sixty-Three
(which was rather late for me)—
Between the end of the Chatterley Ban
And the Beatles' first LP.'

That's all I wanted to know. Sixty-three."

"Right," said Halliwell, still mystified.

"A man born in sixty-three would have been—what, nineteen?—in 1982, when Banger disappeared? That's about right for a college boy called John."

The Diamond system of mental arithmetic was too occult for Halliwell to follow.

"Check the graduation lists for 1983, 84 and 85. Start at Bath. Then try Bristol. Then the polytechnics. It's a chemistry degree."

"You want me to do this now, sir?"

Diamond had forgotten that Halliwell was supposed to be on his way home. "Soon as we get back to the nick. Get on the phone to the universities."

"John who, sir?"

"Sturr."

"Councillor Sturr?"

"Of the Bath and North East Somerset Police Authority. And may the Lord have mercy on our souls."

JOHN STURR had been awarded a B.Sc. in chemistry at the University of Bath in 1984, the registrar's office confirmed. Triumphant at finding gold at his first strike, Halliwell informed Diamond.

"Right," came the response, so low key that it sounded to Halliwell like a putdown. "Now we need to know if they keep records on their students. Well, of course they must. Try the chemistry department. See if there's anything in Sturr's file about vacation work."

Unfortunately there was not.

"Let's think a bit," said Diamond. "There's another way to find out if he worked on the Roman Baths. There must be."

"We've been through this before, sir," Halliwell reminded him. "We tried the Trust, the building firms. No joy at all."

Diamond stared ahead.

Halliwell waited, consoled only by the knowledge that in this sort of impasse, his obstinate, boorish boss was capable of brilliance.

"Okay," the big man said after some time. "Get on to the chemistry department again. Ask about references."

"I already did," said Halliwell, disappointed. "The professor did write a couple for him when he applied for jobs, but there's no mention of holiday work."

"That isn't the point, Keith. Who were the references for?"

Halliwell frowned.

"If we find out who he worked for," Diamond went on, "they may have his job application on file. A student applying for his first job had damn all to put down except exam results. Work experience would help pad out the form."

Halliwell grinned, liking it. "I'll try them again."

And Diamond's persistence paid off. In August, 1984, the chemistry department had supplied a reference on John Sturr for a stone-cleaning firm called Transform. The records showed that he had got the job and stayed with them for three years. Better still, Transform were still in business. They had kept Sturr's records, and his original application listed various vacation jobs, among them construction work at the Roman Baths in July and August, 1982.

"Got him!" said Halliwell, flinging up his arms like a golfer at the eighteenth.

Diamond shook his head. "Not yet, Keith."

thirty-six

PROMPTLY AT FIVE TO seven John Sturr arrived at Manvers Street spry and smiling for the recruitment interviews. He was welcomed by the Assistant Chief Constable and introduced to Julie Hargreaves. "This should be straightforward, shouldn't it?" he said. "How many are there?"

Julie said she thought there were eight candidates. It was agreed that about ten minutes would be sufficient for each interview. Before going in, Sturr asked Georgina if what he had heard was true: that a man had just been brought in for questioning about recent serious crimes.

"I'm happy to confirm it," Georgina said, "and we've charged him."

"So soon?"

"He confessed."

"To everything?"

"To assaulting DCI Wigfull. It's enough for us to hold him. There's a lot more to come out."

"Did you discover why . . . ?"

"He's an art forger. It all stems from that."

"Forgery," said Sturr, flushing at the word and then recovering his composure with several nods of the head, as if to confirm a melancholy truth. "Now I understand. I was able to provide some crucial evidence from my own collection."

"We appreciate your help, John."

"Little enough. Be sure to pass on my congratulations to your man Diamond."

"Diamond? I don't know where he is at this minute," said Georgina. "Probably down in the cells with the suspect."

But he was not. Unknown to Georgina or anyone else except Keith Halliwell, who was with him, Peter Diamond was on his way to Sturr's house in Lansdown Road.

THE CANDIDATES were assembled in a waiting area at the end of a corridor, five men and three women, among them Ingeborg Smith. A uniformed sergeant was with the group, doing his best to allay last-minute jitters. This was just a preliminary interview, he explained. The selection would be based on a series of assessments including practical exercises overseen by serving constables. No single element in the process was a "pass" or "fail". This evening's interview was meant to be a two-way process, a chance for them to have their questions about the police answered. They should feel relaxed about it.

Nobody believed him.

"Who are they—the interviewers?" one twitchy young man asked.

"A detective inspector—female—DI Hargeaves, from Headquarters, and a lay person, Mr Sturr, who serves on the Police Authority."

Nothing else was said about Sturr, but as soon as the sergeant had gone, Ingeborg hurried away to the ladies' room.

DIAMOND TRIED the side gate and found it bolted. "Over you go, Keith."

Halliwell was halfway over when Diamond added, "Watch out for the Rottweiler."

Halliwell froze.

"Joke. Just jump down, open up and let me in."

Sturr's garden was large, with mature fruit trees and a well-tended lawn, too well-tended to be of any interest to Diamond. "The vegetable patch at the end looks promising," he said, striding across the lawn.

"Promising what, sir?"

"Evidence, Keith. Everything up to now is circumstantial." He started up a paved path between rows of runner beans and onions, heading for the garden shed at the end. "Right. Spades and a sieve."

"Has he buried it?"

"If he has, it will take more than you and me to find it. No, I picture this as more of a cremation than a burial. We're looking for ashes."

They found a heap reduced to whitish powder under a wire mesh incinerator behind the rhubarb in a corner of the vegetable garden. Halliwell stooped and felt the texture of some of the ash between finger and thumb. "This won't tell us much."

"Get some on your spade and put it through the sieve."

He obeyed.

Diamond gently shook the sieve and picked at the few fragments remaining. They disintegrated in his hand and fine ash wafted up and settled on his suit.

Halliwell was resigned to a wasted trip. "Do you want me to go on?"

"That's why we're here."

"Isn't this a job for forensic?"

"In the first place, I can't ask forensic to climb over Councillor Sturr's gate. In the second, there isn't time. I want a result now."

"I meant we don't have the facilities."

"You don't need facilities to find bits of metal in a heap of ash."

There was no response from Halliwell. The mental leap was more than he could make.

"The lock, the hinges."

"Ah. Wouldn't he have destroyed them?"

"Like as not, but he must have missed something. Maybe as small as a screw. Try another spadeful, Keith."

THE ORDER was alphabetical and Ingeborg was the last candidate to go in. The wait had been stressful. She seriously considered not going in at all, in spite of reassurances from the others, who came out saying it had been a doddle. She was no coward, but she felt certain John Sturr had got himself onto the panel to give her a hard time. The sadistic bastard had put himself up for this at the last minute as an act of revenge for the things she had said on Sunday night.

Hers was no pushover.

The two interviewers were in chairs over by the window, clipboards in hand. Julie Hargreaves had the kindness to smile—and she represented the police, Ingeborg reminded herself as she sat down.

It was Sturr who began, staring at her as if she were a stranger. "Miss, em, Smith." He made her name sound like a cheap joke. "You're a freelance journalist according to your application, successful, earning a good living. What on earth are you doing here, sitting in front of us?"

She resisted a sharp answer. She was not going to let him goad her into a verbal fencing match that she would win, but at the cost of appearing too bolshie for the job. "I think I'm suited to police work," she answered evenly. "I've seen it at close hand as a reporter, and it's a worthy occupation and a challenging one, more worthy and more of a challenge than my present job."

"In other words you're fed up to the back teeth with journalism?"

"I'm looking for something closer to the action, if that's what you mean, rather than reporting it."

Julie Hargreaves said, "That's good, but I have to say that there's a lot of report-writing in police work and some of it is extremely dull."

"I understand," said Ingeborg. "I can handle that."

Below them, in the car park at the back of the police station, some large vehicle was manoeuvring, sending a heavy throbbing noise through the open windows.

Sturr said something that was drowned by the sound.

"I'm sorry," said Ingeborg. "I didn't catch the question."

He spoke it again, practically shouting. "How do you feel about taking orders?"

A joke about waitressing popped into her head, and she popped it out again. "There's discipline involved in every job, certainly in freelance journalism. I'm very willing to learn."

Julie jotted something on her pad, something positive, Ingeborg hoped. Sturr, obviously unimpressed, was increasingly distracted by the engine sound from below. He leaned back in his chair and tried to look out.

Raising her voice, Julie suggested, "Why don't we shut the windows?"

Sturr didn't reply. He continued to stare out.

Julie gave Ingeborg a sympathetic look. "Sorry about this."

In a move so sudden that it startled both women, Sturr stood up and said stridently, "What's going on? God, that's my Mercedes they're moving. There's a towaway truck being hitched to my car." He pulled the window open wide and shouted, "What the bloody hell do you think you're doing? That's my car."

Julie Hargreaves got up to look out.

Ingeborg remained seated, conducting herself as well as she could in the strangest interview she had experienced.

"I'm going to sort this out," Sturr said. White-faced, he turned with such force that he knocked over his chair and sent it sliding across the floor.

Ingeborg was aware of another movement on the far side of

the room. She had not heard the door open and Peter Diamond come in.

The head of the murder squad said, "My orders, Councillor. I want the car examined."

Sturr's voice climbed at least an octave. "You what?"

"For traces of blood, hair, DNA, whatever."

Ripples of tension ran over Sturr's cheeks. Then he blustered. "You . . . you have no right."

"Probably not," Diamond agreed.

"You can't just take possession of someone's car."

"I couldn't agree more, but I'm sure we can rely on you to co-operate and let us have the keys. I don't think you'll be using the car for some time, sir. You've got questions to answer."

"What about?"

"The deaths of two people—Jock Tarrant, in September, 1982, and Peg Redbird, on Thursday of last week."

"This is totally out of order."

"Yes," said Diamond. "I'm sorry to interrupt the interview, but I'm sure DI Hargreaves can make the right decision on her own."

Sturr said loftily, "I shall bring this to the attention of the Assistant Chief Constable."

"I've just spoken to her," Diamond said, "and got her backing. I showed her these." He held up a transparent bag. "A couple of tiny screws that we found among the ashes in your garden."

"You've been in my garden?"

"Just left it. I'm no antiques expert, but these screws are not modern, I'm sure of that. They're all that is left of Mary Shelley's writing box. You got rid of all the other metal fitments. Destroyed all traces, except for these."

Sturr shook his head. "Why should I—?"

"It was the box that linked you to the killing of the young man Tarrant in the vaults of the Roman Baths."

Sturr switched from taking offence to refuting the charges. "Two rusty screws from a garden don't prove anything."

"You're right," said Diamond. "That's why I want your car examined for evidence that you moved Peg Redbird's body from the place where you killed her."

"I didn't—" He stopped.

"You didn't use the car to move the body," said Diamond. "Right?"

Sturr was silent.

"Either you had some other means of moving it or you attacked her close enough to the river to drag her there and throw her in."

"You're talking through your fat arse," Sturr snapped back at him. "You know I wasn't with the woman the night she was killed. I was at the same party as you, man. You saw what time I left."

"Around a quarter to eleven."

"And she"—he flapped his hand towards Ingeborg—"was with me. We drove back to my house, and she was with me all that night."

Diamond exchanged a brief look with Ingeborg, still seated impassively in the candidates' chair. "Yes, Miss Smith and I have spoken about this alibi of yours. You get in, and there's a message on the answerphone requiring you to call New York for the next forty minutes, while your guest is left listening to pop music and drinking champagne. Your house on Lansdown Road can't be more than five minutes from Noble and Nude. Forty minutes is more than enough for you to meet your victim, hit her over the head and dump her in the Avon."

Sturr said tautly, "She told you this?"

Diamond nodded, "And I'm not surprised you couldn't get your end up after that."

"Bitch!" Sturr took a stride towards Ingeborg, grabbed her shoulder and swung his fist at her face. The blow would have

split her mouth and knocked out some of her teeth had not Diamond reacted fast. He grabbed the raised arm and twisted it
sharply behind Sturr's back.

The councillor cried out with pain. Diamond steered him
back to his chair, thrust him into it and stood over him.

When his breathing allowed, Sturr said, "That lying bitch
wants to frame me."

"You made no calls to New York that evening," Diamond
said. "I had your line checked. The only call was a short one at
six ten to Peg Redbird. No prize for guessing what that was
about."

"Oh?"

"You were setting up the meeting that was to be her execution. The reason Peg had to die is that she was the only person
who could link you to the killing of Jock Tarrant all those years
before. She remembered who sold her the writing box."

At the mention of Tarrant, Sturr went silent, his eyes lowered. He was not the sort to roll over and tell all. He would
protest his innocence all the way through the legal process,
admitting nothing, insisting on having a solicitor beside him
when they questioned him formally, but the fight had gone out
of him. He knew he would go down.

Diamond spared him the ignominy of handcuffs as he
escorted him down to the cells. But there were amazed looks
from the row of candidates seated outside watching the man
who had interviewed them being led away.

IN THE incident room, the murder squad gathered to drink to
the successful conclusion of two inquiries. Halliwell took it all
calmly, as an old-stager; young Leaman was more animated; and
Julie, her interviewing duties over, was a welcome visitor. At
Diamond's suggestion, Ingeborg was invited in as well, pink with
excitement at having convinced Julie she had a future in the

police. And, just inside the door, uninvited, but impossible to turn away, stood Georgina.

Nobody insisted Diamond explain the logic of the case, but once he started telling it to a small group, the entire room closed in to listen. Individuals knew their own bits, and now for the first time, they learned how it came together. "Back in 1982, John Sturr was a chemistry student at the University here. He was a local lad and got a vacation job as a general labourer on the Roman Baths extension. There, he was teamed with another youngster, Jock Tarrant, down from Scotland. Jock wasn't a student. He was a drifter, into rock music, Heavy Metal, and the site-workers nicknamed him Banger. Naturally enough, Sturr was given the name of Mash. Their main job was mixing cement in an underground vault and wheeling it out to the bricklayers. The vault had not been used for many years. It was outside the area of the Roman remains, of no interest to the archeologists.

"One day the two lads made a discovery. Whilst shifting sacks of cement into some obscure corner of the vault they found an antique writing box. They weren't antiques experts, but once they'd dusted it off they could see it was worth a few weeks' wages at least. Maybe more than that. Especially when they got it open and found it contained an early edition of Milton, a sketchbook and a cut-glass ink-bottle.

"Each of those two young blokes felt he had a claim. As often happens with easy pickings, they argued, and it turned to violence. I don't suppose we'll ever know precisely what happened, except that they fought with the spades they used and Tarrant was killed. Manslaughter, I would guess, rather than murder. Sturr, to his horror, found himself down in that vault with a dead body. In one way he was fortunate. Nobody else had reason to go in there, so he had time and opportunity to dismember the corpse, removing the head and the hands. He buried the hands in cement in the vault and drove the torso some miles off and buried it in the soft earth beside the River Wylye. Where the head ended up, only Sturr knows.

"He waited some years before cashing in on the writing box. Sold it—with contents—to Peg Redbird without realising who it had once belonged to. Neither did she. Sturr's secret seemed to be safe. Nobody had raised alarm bells about Jock Tarrant. Casual workers come and go in the building trade. Tarrant had come and he'd gone." By way of illustration, Diamond took a long drag of lager, crushed the can and dropped it into a wastebin.

"Fast forward to last week. The security guard finds the hand bones in the vault and brings them to us. After a hiccup or two, we know we're dealing with bones from about twenty years back. Someone tips off the press that Mary Shelley once lived in the house above the vault and suddenly we're in the news. And this is when John Sturr has a double shock, because he hadn't the faintest idea until then that the vault where he'd buried the hands was part of the house where *Frankenstein* was written. You see the problem? He sold the writing box and its contents to Peg Redbird. On the pretext of keeping up with developments—" Diamond avoided eye contact with Georgina "—he learns from a high-ranking source that the book he sold to Peg has turned up again, and it once belonged to Mary Shelley. An American professor is touting it around Bath and asking questions. Sturr does his proverbial nut. He's certain Peg Redbird will remember him selling her the box and its contents and work out where they came from. TV and radio are already putting out bulletins about the mystery bones in the Frankenstein vault. A police inquiry is under way.

"He looks for a way out of this. He believes Peg is the only person alive who can finger him. He's a pillar of society now, a city councillor, on any number of committees, not least the Police Authority. He reckons if he can dispose of Peg, his problem disappears. So he makes a plan. He's been invited to a party at the ACC's. Could you think of a better cover than that?"

Over by the door, Georgina flushed to the tips of her ears and said nothing. To her credit, she stayed to hear Diamond out.

Diplomatically, he shifted the attention elsewhere. "At the party he makes a pitch to a blonde charmer. Where's Ingeborg?"

A hand was raised coyly to shoulder level.

"It happens that this blonde charmer is looking for a chance to get into the police, and this interest from a member of the Police Authority is not the kind you turn down. It's a mutually helpful arrangement. He keeps her tanked up all evening. She won't mind me saying she's well bevvied by the time they leave together. He takes her home, opens another bottle of champagne, puts on some music and then makes some excuse about a phone call to New York.

"The only call he made that evening was to Peg Redbird at ten past six, arranging to meet her later. He used a false name on the phone, of course, and—this is only my theory, I have to say—offered to give her a prior look at some mouth-watering antique on offer at the antiques fair starting next day in the Assembly Rooms. Unknown to Sturr, Peg had a prior engagement. She was putting the screws on a forger called Uncle Evan. That's a story for another time. All that matters here is that Evan told me Peg was most particular about getting back to the shop by eleven.

"So, at eleven or soon after, he calls at Noble and Nude, where the first thing he sees is the writing box sitting on Peg's desk. She's surprised to find that her mystery caller is John Sturr, but not alarmed. He says he has something of exceptional interest outside in the car. Ever alert to a bargain, but not her own safety, Peg thinks he must be about to offer her another of Mary Shelley's possessions. She goes with him round the back of the shop to the car. He bashes her over the head, killing her, and moves the body the short distance to the river and drops her in, confident it will look like an accident, the injury caused by the fall. Then he goes back into Noble and Nude, picks up the writing desk and drives home. It's not much after eleven-thirty and Ingeborg is still where he left her, listening to the same CD. Is that fair, Police Cadet Smith?"

Ingeborg spoke up clearly. "It may not be fair, sir, but it's true."

"What happened after?"

She looked up in surprise. "Do you really want to know?"

"You were there," said Diamond. "You can tell it better than me."

"All right. It was like that famous quote from Sherlock Holmes about the curious incident of the dog in the night-time. Watson said, 'But the dog did nothing in the night-time' and Holmes said, 'That was the curious incident.' "

"You mean . . . ?"

"My date did nothing in the night-time. I should have known something was up—because he wasn't."

There was laughter. Police Cadet Smith was a definite addition to the strength at Manvers Street.

JOE DOUGAN and the luggage finally arrived at the Paris Ritz the next afternoon. He was tired. The Bath police had kindly driven him to the train station early that morning, but the last forty-eight hours had been stressful. Relieved to have the bell-captain take charge of those enormous suitcases, he stepped over to the check-in.

The young woman on duty asked him his name and he gave it, adding, "My wife arrived at the end of last week."

"Yes, sir," she said in the delightful way Parisiennes have of speaking English, "I 'ope Madame Dougan enjoyed her days shopping."

"I'm sure she has. Now, if you tell me the number of our suite . . ."

"One minute, if you please, professor." She picked a note from the rack behind her. "A little note for you."

Sighing, Joe opened the envelope and took out a short letter in Donna's handwriting:

Joe, Baby,

I finished shopping here. The bell captain has charge of the two suitcases I bought here, cosmetic case and hatboxes. Would you be an angel and pick them up for me? I figured you were sure to want to make the trip to Switzerland to look up the place where *Frankenstein* was first thought of, so I booked us in at the Intercontinental in Geneva. I'm told the Swiss jewelry shops are something special.

See you as soon as you can fix a flight. Don't forget the baggage, will you?

Your ever loving,

Donna
X X X